Books by John Patrick

Non-Fiction
A Charmed Life: Vince Cobretti
Lowe Down: Tim Lowe
The Best of the Superstars 1990
The Best of the Superstars 1991
The Best of the Superstars 1992
The Best of the Superstars 1993
The Best of the Superstars 1994
The Best of the Superstars 1995
The Best of the Superstars 1996
The Best of the Superstars 1997
The Best of the Superstars 1998
The Best of the Superstars 1999
The Best of the Superstars 2000
The Best of the Superstars 2001
The Best of the Superstars 2002
What Went Wrong?
When Boys Are Bad
& Sex Goes Wrong
Legends: The World's Sexiest
Men, Vols. 1 & 2
Legends (Third Edition)
Tarnished Angels (Ed.)

Fiction
Billy & David: A Deadly Minuet
The Bigger They Are...
The Younger They Are...
The Harder They Are...
Angel: The Complete Trilogy
Angel II: Stacy's Story
Angel: The Complete Quintet
A Natural Beauty (Editor)
The Kid (with Joe Leslie)
HUGE (Editor)
Strip: He Danced Alone
The Boys of Spring
Big Boys/Little Lies (Editor)
Boy Toy
Seduced (Editor)
Insatiable/Unforgettable (Editor)

Heartthrobs
Runaways/Kid Stuff (Editor)
Dangerous Boys/Rent Boys (Editor)
Barely Legal (Editor)
Country Boys/City Boys (Editor)
My Three Boys (Editor)
Mad About the Boys (Editor)
Lover Boys (Editor)
In the BOY ZONE (Editor)
Boys of the Night (Editor)
Secret Passions (Editor)
Beautiful Boys (Editor)
Juniors (Editor)
Come Again (Editor)
Smooth 'N' Sassy (Editor)
Intimate Strangers (Editor)
Naughty By Nature (Editor)
Dreamboys (Editor)
Raw Recruits (Editor)
Play Hard, Score Big (Editor)
Sweet Temptations (Editor)
Pleasures of the Flesh (Editor)
Juniors 2 (Editor)
Fresh 'N' Frisky (Editor)
Taboo! (Editor)
Heatwave (Editor)
Boys on the Prowl (Editor)
Huge 2 (Editor)
Fever! (Editor)
Any Boy Can (Editor)
Virgins No More (Editor)
Seduced 2 (Co-Editor)
Wild 'N' Willing (Co-Editor)

Worldwide Praise for the Erotica of John Patrick and STARbooks!

"John Patrick is a modern master of the genre! ...This writing is what being brave is all about. It brings up the kinds of things that are usually kept so private that you think you're the only one who experiences them."
– Gay Times, London

"Barely Legal' is a great potpourri ... and the cover boy is gorgeous!"
– Ian Young, Torso magazine

"Collections of stories have become increasingly popular in the past couple of years: leading the way is the prolific and consistently entertaining John Patrick who, under the STARbooks imprint, has edited fifteen or more collections of erotica written another dozen books himself and published several handfuls more by other authors. ... Burly (500-plus pages) anthologies of erotic writing, the perfect bedside companions..."
– Richard Labonte, Q Magazine

"A huge collection of highly erotic, short and steamy one-handed tales. Perfect bedtime reading, though you probably won't get much sleep! Prepare to be shocked! Highly recommended!"
– Vulcan magazine

"Tantalizing tales of porn stars, hustlers, and other lost boys....John Patrick set the pace with 'Angel!"
– The Weekly News, Miami

"...Some readers may find some of the scenes too explicit; others will enjoy the sudden, graphic sensations each page brings. Each of these romans clef is written with sustained intensity. 'Angel' offers a strange, often poetic vision of sexual obsession. I recommend it to you."
– Nouveau Midwest

"Angel' is mouthwatering and enticing..."
– Rouge Magazine, London

"Superstars' is a fast read...if you'd like a nice round of fireworks before the Fourth, read this aloud at your next church picnic..."
– Welcomat, Philadelphia

"Yes, it's another of those bumper collections of steamy tales from STARbooks. The rate at which John Patrick turns out these compilations you'd be forgiven for thinking it's not exactly quality prose. Wrong. These stories are well-crafted, but not over-written, and have a profound effect in the pants department."
– Vulcan magazine, London

ISBN No. 978-1-61303-073-8

Many thanks to graphic artist John Nail for the cover design. Mr. Nail may be reached at: tojonail@bellsouth.net.

Herndon, VA

ANY BOY CAN

EDITED BY JOHN PATRICK

Herndon, VA

Editor's Note Most of the stories appearing in this book take place prior to the years of The Plague; the editor and each of the authors represented herein advocate the practice of safe sex at all times. And, because these stories trespass the boundaries of fiction and non-fiction, to respect the privacy of those involved, we've changed all of the names and other identifying details.

CONTENTS

INTRODUCTION:
JUST TICKLING MY FANCY?
John Patrick

Richard Patrick, wild, waif-like lead singer of the rock group Filter, sets the tone for this collection. A couple of years ago, he found himself in a real publicity pickle after an interview in Ray Gun wherein he told about his flirty past with Nine Inch Nails' Trent Reznor: "Me and Trent had a sexual tension all the time. He won't admit it, but we used to make out for fun at clubs and stuff." One night Patrick says he got a boner, and Trent got a boner and, Patrick insists, "he didn't know what to do, and he ran away." Patrick himself doesn't claim one particular sexual preference. "I don't know whether I'm a pervert or gay or hetero," he says. "Anything sexual is exciting to me." Now that is the way to be, if you ask me!

Many of us have fantasized about having sex with supposedly straight guys, but, just so you know, straight guys' penises are, according to the latest scientific research, a bit smaller than ours on average. Simon Sheppard, columnist and co-editor of Rough Stuff: Tales of Gay Men, Sex, and Power, says. "Their fashion sense is stolen – okay, 'borrowed' – from ours. Many of them can't dance. And, if straight women are to be believed, a number of heterosexual men could use coaching on sexual technique. Even so, there are plenty of queer guys who fantasize about having sex with 'em. Fetishize it. Work at it. Now, why is that?

"There's no denying that, for a number of gay men, the idea of doing it with a straight guy is hot. My friend Will thinks the whole thing goes back to high school. Remember all those het boys in the locker room you lusted after but knew you'd never have? Well, now that you're all grown up, you actually have a chance to get in their pants. Those unfulfilled desires provide an extra tweak of lust.

"There's the power of seduction, getting straight guys to do stuff they're not supposed to gives us a certain power of them. ...But at the heart of things there's the concept of 'masculinity... And since we're attracted to men, the thinking goes, why not chase after men who are real men? One guy I met on-line told me, 'There's just something raw about straight guys ... the idea that they're not meticulous ... sometimes gay guys are too neat, too clean.'

"Curiously, gay men who want straight tricks usually want to stick them. Not to get fucked by them, not to top them in any significant way, but to get down on their gay knees and give pleasure to some straight stud. It's interesting on several levels, because though the one who sucks 'services' the straight suckee, he also takes temporary control of the dick being sucked, and walks away with something of the straight guy's load. So who's using whom? Also, getting sucked is pretty damn gender-neutral. With his eyes closed, can a man really tell if it's a man or a woman doing it? Like I said, interesting."

One guy who frequently gives oral service to straights told Simon, "They're always horny as hell and you don't have to care for them when they are sick. And they don't stay for breakfast. And I'll never have to wash their underwear."

Many a gay man has discovered that one way to a man's cock is through his feet.

"The foot is a major erogenous zone, as many of us know, er, first-hand," Sheppard, explains. "Rich in pleasure-producing nerves, the soles and toes are, as Dr. Alfred Kinsey pointed out, 'areas which may be erotically sensitive under tactile stimulation.' But, more than that, the foot is also a well-known phallic symbol, a stand-in for the penis. No wonder that foot play – as foreplay or as the Main Event – is sexy for so many guys. There's stroking, there's tickling, there's even foot bondage. But, just like fellatio, the most popular form of foot play involves the meeting of the erotic object and the hungry mouth. Lots of guys, if truth be told, really get off on kissing, licking, and sucking on another man's foot. And those of us who've been on the receiving end know just how pleasurable having one's toes sucked can be.

"Because of the lowly position of the foot in the day-to-day world, servicing it can be seen as a form of submission, and many a bondage-and-discipline scene incorporates foot worship. But as in most matters sexual, the opposite can also be the case. Stripping off the shoe and sock, getting one's hands on the five-toed fella, playing with the pretty thing... it can easily be a power trip.

"There's also the powerful meeting of foot and penis. While rubbing your feet all over a partner's body can be fun for all concerned, jacking him off with your sole can be truly special. And there's toe-in-the-hole sex, too.

"As in most matters sexual, foot play has its own specialists, organizations, and porn. And yes, there are foot-size queens. But others go for the aesthetic – preferring beautiful over big. And, because the combination of foot sweat and bacteria can produce some mighty potent odors, some guys really get off on the smells – from mild to truly ripe. The more fastidious among us prefer their feet newly washed and gleaming. As with any fetish, foot worship can seem just plain foolish to those not into it. But no less an authority than Leonardo DaVinci called the human foot 'a work of art.' Perhaps the Mona Lisa's fractured smile was induced by someone sucking on her toes."

In this collection we feature Peter Gilbert's "Florida Flames" in which the esteemed author creates a scene with a foot massage that will really get you going.

Regular readers of our collections know that one of the leading proponents of foot massage as a prelude to heavy sex with straights is Thom Nickels, a frequent contributor and renowned Philadelphia columnist. Thom got started early seducing straight boys, long before he discovered the power of the foot. Thom recalls when he and his friend Andy, both five, took turns lying on top of each other: "We called our romp 'The Ice Cream Sandwich' because it was two bodies lying on top of one another. Being smart kids, we knew to close the bedroom door whenever we indulged. I don't know whose idea it was to begin experimenting, Andy's or mine, I only know that whenever my neighbor Mrs. Elizabeth came to visit my mom with Andy, Andy and I would head to my bedroom and do the ICS.

"Our little romps lasted five or ten minutes but that slice of time was among the most delectable of my childhood. Yet sometimes when we got together and were smack in the middle of an ICS, Mrs. Elizabeth would start calling Andy's name. It was as if Mrs. Elizabeth had some sort of radar and could tell when something different was 'up' with Andy. Mrs. Elizabeth's uncanny knack for yelling for Andy whenever we were smack in the middle of an ICS amazed me even as a preschooler.

"Were other kids doing the ICS? You bet.

"When my family moved out of Andy's neighborhood, Andy and I continued to play ICS whenever his family came to visit. The routine was always the same: wait till kids our own age cleared out of my bedroom or until the adults were otherwise occupied with their cocktails and chatter. Then we could lock the door and proceed. We did the ICS until we were both 17. At that point nature was beginning to steer Andy in a different direction: during one ICS romp I remember how Andy produced a photograph of a girl and held it up as he worked the ICS to a final climax. I never felt guilty about doing the ICS with Andy or with a few other kids, and I certainly would have never thought about telling my mom about it. It was none of her business, after all. Kids have a private secret life. It's always been that way, and it will never change.

"After Andy came Cookie and Betsy, both robust heterosexual girls. Cookie and Betsy were sixteen-year-old babysitters who peroxide their hair and wore high heels on the weekends. Betsy was a respectable cheerleader. Cookie lived next door in our Bucks County neighborhood. She often babysat for my brother, sister and I (three more kids would come later) and then she'd tuck my brother and me into bed. I was 13, my brother 10 or 11. Cookie liked to play games with us. She'd ask us to lower our pajama bottoms so she could flick her finger against our ding-a-lings. These encounters were giggly affairs with Cookie saying, 'Make it wiggle' or 'Make it go sideways!' I remember being shy with her (as well as refusing to lower my pajama bottoms – but only because she was a girl). These play sessions never progressed beyond small finger flicks and Cookie's stream of giggles.

"Though I vaguely remember sitting at the breakfast table one morning and thinking if I should tell my mother. I decided in the end that spilling the beans on Cookie would cause more trouble than it was worth.

"With Andy I never felt any guilt or shame. Indeed, in our first neighborhood in Drexel Hill a group of us, both boys and girls, were constantly playing doctor, with toy stethoscopes and pretend bottom thermometers that only glazed the surface of our small downy slopes. Doctor was only a piece of a larger puzzle that included games like

King and Queen, Davy Crockett, and others like catching tadpoles to see how they turned into frogs

"Post-ICS experiences included experimenting with boys other than Andy. Some were two years younger and one several years older. The older one was a lifeguard (a Mark Spitz lookalike) at our country club pool. He was a boy I'd fantasized about for ages and, finally, early one summer day in the low end of the pool, I felt his hand on my swimsuit. It was an ICS explosion! Not to mention the beginning of a three-summer teen romance, my first torrid, closeted affair, and we did it everywhere we could.

"Today Andy is happily married and living in California and the lifeguard has a lover and owns a florist shop. Go figure." Thom says that the nice thing about having a brother just a couple years younger than he was that his brother often asked his friends Robert or Ben to spend the night: "For me this was a time to plot. I became adept at sneaking into my brother's room when he and his friend were fast asleep. I knew when and where to poke, probe, and press, but I also knew when to draw back (my thing was to initiate and then ask for permission to proceed). Usually I'd begin by hovering in a corner of the room, listening to their breathing patterns and wondering when to descend like Bram Stoker's 'Dracula.' "But with Robert, I scored big. Our 'meeting' over art books was the first of many mini-and-prolonged sessions in woodsheds, bedrooms, deserted back lots, and assorted garages. When he'd sleep over with Paul he'd wait till Paul was asleep and then come up to my bedroom. Ben was more difficult. When I showed interest (hovering over his bed – like a night watchman) he thought I was joking: 'You're just waiting to see if I'll say yes, and then a bunch of your friends are going to come rushing in and call me a faggot!' A little convincing did the trick, even though Ben couldn't keep a secret. "'Don't tell anyone about this, okay? Keep this between us.' "'All right,' he promised.

"But the next morning he blew it when I heard him tell Paul 'Did you know you're brother's a queer!'

"Robert was better at keeping secrets no doubt because he enjoyed what we did. One time he followed me to a neighbor's house where I was babysitting, a copy of Playboy magazine in his hand.

"'How did you know where to find me?' I asked him then.

5

"'Paul told me where you were. '

"It now occurred to me that my brother might be helping me get sex!

"Robert and I continued having sex on the sly until I turned twenty-one. Then things just ended. I remember our last session. I was in my bedroom reading. Robert was in my brother's downstairs room. I was surprised to hear a knock at my door considering what happened a couple years before.

"Robert, you see, was moody and sex always had to be on his terms. During one overnight visit I'd stayed up late waiting for the inevitable knock on my door. When that didn't happen I decided to sneak into my brother's room to see what was wrong.

"I tiptoed over to Robert's bed (lying on his back, the snoring Adonis was clad in just a pair of briefs). Given that I'd already convinced myself that because Robert loved war movies he wanted a surprise attack, a sort of fun re-enactment of a WWII style torpedo ramming, I interjected my hand in several places. I no sooner began the probe than he jumped up like I'd injected him with tetanus horse serum. 'What the fuck! What are you doing?' he screamed, punching the air.

"What he was doing, of course, was saving face in that small room with my brother. As for me, well, I just wanted unbroken continuity. Sweet, long lost luv."

In this same vein, another man recalls when a straight friend came to live with him temporarily one summer: "He was 19, very hot looking and a real ladies' man. He enjoyed hanging out wearing only his briefs. I avoided acting on my impulses until the very last night in town. He worked all day and came in around eleven. I was already in bed, and he came in to talk to me. He lay down in the floor on his stomach. I ask him if he was tired. He said he was sore all over from work. So I got down on the floor beside him and began to rub his back. He had told me he did not like to get his back rubbed but he did not mind right then.

"After about thirty minutes of this, and the point that I could not take it anymore, I started rubbing the back of his legs. They are very hairy and I was having a hell of a time. I rubbed them a good while then I started rubbing almost to his butthole. After about thirty minutes of leg rubbing he said he had to take a bath and go to bed. He went in to

6

get his shower and I watched him dry off through the key hole in my bathroom door. I had been doing this all summer anyway, so I had to that night. He has a beautiful dick. It is not really great big but it is just so fucking pretty the whole picture of it and his balls and all that damn hair. He came out and went and laid down on the couch and pulled a sheet over him.

"I went in and sat on the end of the couch and he pulled his legs up to his balls almost to give me room to sit. I started rubbing his calf, just slowly up and down it like I was jacking it off. As I was doing this, I realized the back of my hand was ever so lightly touching his brief-covered balls. So I thought what the hell it's his last night here anyway. I just made sure that my hand started hitting them a little more.

"Then I started rubbing up and down the thigh of his other leg, which was stuck up in the air with his foot right at his butt, if you can get this position in your minds. After a long time of this, I started rubbing the very inside of his leg right against his briefs. He adjusted himself, it seemed, for me to have better access. I did this a little then I just put my hand on his balls and dick all together through his briefs and started rubbing that thing for him. He was as nervous as I was because he was shaking and so was I. He just started talking faster about whatever it was he was saying, I could not hear him by now anyway. I slipped one finger into his briefs and ran it all the way to the head of his dick.

"I played around like that for a good while and he got up quickly to go piss, he said. He went to the restroom and then went into his room and put on a pair of shorts. He came back and sat down on the couch in an upright position this time. He was shaking like a leaf when I sat down beside him. I told him he must be cold and to put the sheet back on.

"After I put it back around him, I just moved right back into his shorts and briefs. I started just very lightly jacking him off. I had to undo the button on his shorts to have more room. I had already been playing with him for three hours by now. He could not take it much longer I knew. I was fixing to ask him if I could get his clothes out of the way as I still just slowly jacked on that beautiful dick. I did not get the chance to ask before he reached down and grabbed the head of his dick. He held it a little bit and turned loose, but he still shot his load all

7

over himself and the sheet. I had to rub it around some since it was there. I also went to the restroom with him and cleaned him up. I thought he would probably hate me for it, but he does still come to see me and I told him I was sorry for doing it. That is all that has ever been said about it. I really wonder if I should do something else or just let everything go. He had not had a girlfriend for a while before that and I knew he was hard up for something anyway. He is the type guy that is used to fucking every single day. He still tells me about all his dealings with girls and what they do to him. He loves to have his dick sucked, probably better then fucking. I know I could do a damn good job of that too, but I am scared to try anything else really. He is a very sexual person; he just loves sex in general."

"As a kid," another man recalls, "when I was called on in class, I remember kind of leaning forward with both hands on my desk to prevent an obvious pants tent from showing. Fortunately, most of the teachers I had were men and they probably knew what we were doing. I had heard that female teachers would yell at some of the guys 'stand up straight.' A bigger problem was riding on the school bus. The lurching and jiggling invariably would set me off! I learned to stand up early and keep my book bag or briefcase in front, applying some downward pressure before moving to the door."

"In college," recalls a former student, "I took a lot of art classes in college. The male models were always the hottest campus jocks and they were always eager to pose nude. They started out posing in a jockstrap but when the jockstrap was removed, most of the time they would get a full boner within five minutes. This was a real sight when they did the standing poses with eight inches or more pointing to the class! There was a separate women's college so the 20 or 25 students in the class were all male. The instructors had been seeing this for years and were careful to make nothing of it., just puffed nervously on cigarettes the way artists used to do. The jock models definitely enjoyed it. I enjoyed it especially if the guy was uncut. The uncut cock telescoped out and unfolded and the students would get nervous and I would get really turned on."

"Many years ago," a professional man recalls, "I worked for the Kidney Foundation and I went around to various high schools lecturing. At one school, from the moment I began speaking I noticed this great looking teenager in the front row. He had a broken foot so he was just wearing light gray baggy sweat pants. I noticed he kept fidgeting in his seat and I finally noticed why. He had a raging hard-on. I tried hard not to look at it, but he kept getting my attention by trying to adjust it. He realized that wearing baggy sweats was a dumb thing especially when it was obvious he hadn't put on any underwear. He finally subtly reached into his pants and adjusted it to point up and lay against his belly, so it wasn't so obvious. Then he looked at me at one point realizing I knew what was going on, and I was the only one. He rolled his eyes, as if to say, 'What am I to do?' So he just stayed that way for the rest of the lecture. After the class, the teacher came to speak with me and while we talked, I noticed this kid was the last one to leave. When he stood up, junior was still 'stretching the skin. ' The kid just got on his crutches and tried to hang his book bag in front and hobbled out of the room."

And speaking of taking turns, Boyd McDonald, editor of Lewd and Raunch and other classic anthologies, once confessed that a man never seems more masculine to him than when he is fucking a woman. Of all the ways of having sex, three-way sex with a man and a woman is near the top of his list: "I have had some wonderful and some not so wonderful, encounters of that kind. The first was a kind of 'Ménage a Everybody' – in other words, a gang bang, and the reader will have to decide if this one was wonderful.

"The girl was my high school sweetheart, Carla. We had met when we were both 15 and attending San Diego High near downtown San Diego. We studied privately with the same teacher. She played the piano like a goddess and I was crazy about her. But the incident at hand came toward the end of our relationship.

"Carla, bright and gifted as she was, was also very self-destructive. She loved to fuck, but she used sex for both comfort and punishment, depending on her emotions. As young as we were, our relationship was, from the beginning, an open one. It never bothered me that she fucked other guys; I was fucking other guys myself. She knew about and accepted my bisexuality.

"One summer weekend in the late 1940s, she and I, along with a clutch of friends, all male, took a trip down to Mexico.

"In one of the bars our party was joined by two attractive young sailors and they were definitely interested in Carla.

9

"Earlier in the day, Carla and I had an altercation, one no worse than usual, but she was angry with me. Consequently, she flirted outrageously with the sailors, and meanwhile, lost no opportunity to put me down. The sailors, while not knowing exactly what was going on, could sense opportunity.

"Finally, after suffering an unusually vicious thrust from her, I turned to one of the sailors and said, "Don't mind her, I've been fucking her all day and she's mad at me because my dick fell off. Maybe you can help her out."

"Before the sailor could answer, Dexter, one of our original party, irritated by the way she had been treating me, said, 'Why don't we all fuck her?'

"Carla turned to glare coldly at Dexter, leaned back in her chair, tossed her thick auburn hair, thrust her tits forward and said, 'Yeah, why don't you?

"Well, she was asking for it and no one in the group, except for me, was disposed to let her off the hook. On the way to the car, regretting my part in these developments, I took her by the elbow and told her urgently that this shouldn't be allowed to happen. But it was too late. She had committed herself and a kind of perverse pride prevented her from backing out. Meanwhile, everyone else, especially the sailors, were enthusiastic and excited.

"We all piled into the car, three in the front and four squeezed into the back. We drove around the town and at last parked in a dark alley.

"We all got out except for Carla. She took off her panties and flung them out the window, signaling her readiness.

"Alvin, a friend of hers who lived in her neighborhood (and with whom she was briefly married a year or so later), pushed in ahead of everybody.

"Dexter, who insisted that he intended to be next, turned to me and suggested that I get him ready. He dropped his pants and pushed me down on his dick, indifferent to the reaction of the sailors. So was I. Dexter's asshole was already known to me, my tongue having traveled there before. When I turned him around to glue my lips to it, the sailors watched intently and groped themselves.

"Alvin was not long in completing his business. When he emerged, Dexter took his turn. I was gratified to find that the sailors expected the same attentions that I'd given Dexter and as the game ran its course I sucked every dick and asshole present. I got no sperm, however, until it was my turn in the car.

"Carla didn't really expect that I would take a turn. That would mean I was treating her like a whore just as everyone else had, but I assuaged her by being even more of a whore than she had been. Instead of fucking her, I plowed my face into her cunt and pilfered all the cum from it...."

"Situational sex" is how Matt Damon described his character in the film "The Talented Mr. Ripley." In other words, he did whatever the situation called for. Some men put themselves in situations with only one thing in mind, however. Consider those who visit the dunes lining Herring Cove Beach in Provincetown, where nudity and public sex are illegal. T.A. King writes in Strategic Sex, that a well-rehearsed relay of male voices warns of approaching rangers. "We suit up; they drive by; we strip down again in the woods, making a space around the oak where we meet to jerk off in groups.

"In spring 1996, a friend sent me an e-mail advisory that an infamous cruising area in Massachusetts would probably come to the attention of the police, now that so many married men were going there for quick blowjobs. Those men were recognized as 'straight' by their ignorance of the etiquette proper to the space. They thought they could use the space without being changed by it....

"This is not to say that deep down they were 'really gay. ' Signals, roles, and performance techniques do not follow naturally from or mandate an identity. The fetish and the space take precedence over identity categories. These are not private spaces for and about gay men. Public sex spaces maneuver the players who pass through them into something other than their other public identities. You will not belong to the space if you do not let yourself become different from yourself there....He says, Is this the real me, or is he just tickling my fancy?"

In her book Mema's House, Mexico City, Annick Prieur explores the sexuality of Mexican youths, and shows how Federico, who lives in a shanty town outside Mexico City, began participating in homosex: "At the age of nine, he started to go into the city with his brother to try to make some money as a 'traffic light clown,' doing stunts while the cars waited for the green light and begging for money afterward. He thinks he earned ten to fifteen thousand pesos (three to five dollars) daily that way. He was fourteen when a driver said he would give him fifty thousand if he came along with him. This Federico did, but he did not know what he was supposed to do, and he had never had sex before.

"After that he understood that there was a lot more money to gain from prostitution than from anything else, since he had already tried other jobs – shining shoes and unloading crates. At first he had only oral sex, but, at sixteen, he had active and passive anal sex, too. He has also had some sexual relations with boys outside the sphere of prostitution now, but he has no homosexual friends. His family does not know that he sells sex. He has never had sex with girls. There is nothing effeminate about him. When questioned about his sexual identity, he was very open, he recognized that he is living as a homosexual now, but thought he might become 'normal. '

"In this case it seems as though his homosexual practice is partly a result of economic necessity, partly of having learned to enjoy it," Prieur says. "Homosexual practice is the only factor that could possibly have led to a homosexual identity, and the practice occurred at a not very early age. His sexual experience is not accompanied by an experience of effeminacy or feelings of being different as a little boy, nor is it accompanied by a social label as homosexual. Neither is it supported by participation in a subculture of self-identified homosexuals. And so, it is not enough to give Federico an identity as homosexual. Federico feels his future is open in that respect, that he is free to remain in an ambiguous situation. I suppose it would be the same with other factors. In themselves, in isolation, they are not determinant. A boy named Gata had the experience of being effeminate and of being labeled homosexual by others, but he needed the sexual experience to make the label his own, and needed other jotas to become one himself (in the sense of becoming a self-identified homosexual with a feminine style). 'It's not the same,' he says, 'because with a woman, one is excited, one makes love. But with a man, it's not the same, it's a carnal act, nothing more. You don't have so much pleasure. It's not the same, you just put it in and take it out, put it in and take it out. I'm a man, you know. I mean that I'm not attracted to homosexuales. I can be with homosexuales, and then I have no erection of my penis. You understand? So, if I have an erection, I'm not able to ... how can I put it, of course, it I want to, I may have an erection, because it's my mind that dominates my body. So I can have an erection, but the result is that I have no sperm, or, so that you understand, I don't have any satisfaction when I do it. There's no sperm.' Another mayate told me he reacted with nausea the first time; and several said that they could do it only with the lights out, or in certain positions which did not remind them too much of the sex of the other. They tell me they do not caress the homosexual much, and that they have sex rather rapidly.

"A boy named Pedro said, 'With a man you just put it in. You know. Then you come, and you leave.' They told me that while it is important for them to be able to satisfy a woman sexually, they do not care about this with a homosexual. Ernesto said, 'I come here, and I will have a relationship with the homosexual X. You then restrict yourself to making love to him. No caressing him or kissing him. Or, I do not like to do that. You see, with a woman it's different, 'cause I kiss her and hug her. And, vulgarly speaking, I turn her around, I put her like I want to. With a homosexual, it's just not the same.' The mayates often let themselves come immediately after penetration with a jota, while they would use more time with a woman.

"The fact that many men may have sex with jotos with other men present, as long as the other men are supposed to participate, too, or at least not to disapprove of what they see, shows that it is in no way a threat to male honor – though I do not believe it is a status marker for male honor either."

"Straight guys are always co-opting gay fashion," John F. Karr in the Bay Area Reporter says. "First it was pierced earrings, then those silly fag-tail haircuts. Then it was cock itself. Ever since Calvin Klein supermodel Marky Mark Wahlberg grabbed onto his with such defiant joy, the other straights hardly consider it queer anymore to play with theirs. With neither shame nor loss of manhood, firemen and even doctors proudly display their bulge in underwear ads, and real guys flaunt their shaved and trimmed pubes in the pages of Playgirl. What, you ask, will those straight guys get into next that gay folk have always known about?"

The answer is, surprisingly enough: assholes. Yes, Karr claims to have seen it himself at some of the city's more progressive sex parties. Karr says he has seen guys throwing their legs back so that their strap-on wielding girlfriends can satisfy the itch their boy has recently discovered due north of his anus! "Now," Karr goes on, "I'm sure he didn't get there entirely on his own. Feminism has led women toward strap-ons as they explore gender roles and assume greater dominance in sexplay. And it's likely as well that bi-boys have been spreading the word.

"Final stamp of approval comes with two videos: 'Bend Over Boyfriend' Parts 1 and 2. These videos are the first to promote and instruct straight couples in the joy of anal play. So when its box cover blurb asks, 'Do men really like penetration?' the question is strictly rhetorical."

The video was produced by Dr. Carol Queen and Karr claims it offers 30 minutes of "encouragement and helpful tips, demonstrated by several playful couples, followed by 30 minutes of the couples involved in sexy dildo sporting." One of the highlights is to see Robert Morgan, Queen's boyfriend who has a "short Caesar haircut and a lived-in masculinity" appear to be "mighty impatient to get plowed in a big way – a favor Carol aggressively provides." And Karr's favorite is Troy: "I think every home should have a buttboy toy as cute and eager as Troy. Whether you're a novice at butt play or an old hand, there'll be something novel in these videos that's just for you. Be the first on your block to know what those kinky straight boys are up to." And, logically, the next step would be to be plowed by a real dick, right?

Gad Beck, in his memoir about being a gay Jew in wartime Berlin, An Underground Life, describes many males he met who, while professing their straightness, still enjoyed his charms: "There was one boy there in particular who made an impression on me. His name was Herbert; he was slick and lived for sex alone. He would come to work horny in the morning and announce at the top of his lungs, 'Look at this! Today my dick is, once again, uncontrollable!' And whenever he had a chance, he was at it. Four or five girls worked for (there), and Herbert badgered more than one of them each day. There was also a lot of fooling around among the men, and when Herbert was in that kind of mood, it was my turn as well.

14

"I felt the same way as the girls; he was too rough for me, and the whole thing was rather unpleasant. At the time I was still pretty inexperienced, and I'm more into caressing anyway. Whenever he'd get his hands on yet another victim on the cardboard stack in the cellar, there were often tears...."

Later, living conditions become "cozy," and "by being forced together in terms of space, we also grew closer together at a psychological and spiritual level, supporting each other where we could. ...Reuwen was one of the refined people. He was tender and delicate, and he radiated a longing for hugs and closeness. He was almost a head taller than I was, and a strong 'Jewish' nose jutted out from a pretty face. He had dark hair, sparkling black eyes – it was not only his eyes, but his look and a soft, sensual mouth.

"We were sitting under a tree at the edge of a meadow where I tended my calves during the week. At some point he stretched out his hand, and what started out as tenderly getting closer to each other quickly and deliberately turned sexual. Reuwen was without a doubt gay, which is not the case with all the men I have ever had loving encounters with.

"The friendship with Reuwen, a romantically surging youthful love, continued throughout my entire stay in Skaby. I thought living there was incredibly erotic anyway – such an unfamiliar closeness to nature for an entire summer – and the other boys! I relished the sight of their beautiful bodies in the group shower after work. They were in their early to mid- twenties, athletic, an, despite the general atmosphere, forward-looking and optimistic."

Gad meets a boy named Manfred and sparks fly: "After the music we went to bed girls in one comer and boys in the other, I had evidently aroused Manfred with my 'feminine' charm, because he took the initiative. I knew that was the only way to get him. I was capable of winning someone over and taking control, but with Manfred I played the expectant, devoted woman, at least in the beginning. We were very loving with each other. Kissing was especially important to him. Whatever we did, it was not much like gay sex as one thinks of it today, but then again, Manfred was heterosexual anyway. With him, as with many of the lovers my age with whom I had relations during my youth, it was more about just having fun and sharing hugs and caresses – to feel that the other person was just as aroused as you were."

Gad patiently waited months until Manfred felt okay about himself: "Long, deep, heavy conversations, feelings of guilt, 'We can't see each other anymore, especially not at night, ' and then we would indeed get together again and the conversations continued. Finally I suggested that we just wait and see what happened. Either we would 'indulge in our weakness,' as he called it, or we would see each other and be able to abstain. Both scenarios would give us some kind of clarity. I just couldn't stand endlessly talking about it anymore. And of course, I was absolutely certain how things would progress." Later, after Manfred had gone, he looked around for someone else he liked: "My eye caught a really tall guy! I always managed to get close to him at night. When the lights were turned off, easily, effortlessly, we slid closer together. With so many people in one room the nights were anything but quiet anyway. In these huge halls, one would start moaning, another crying. Who was interested in checking out what was going on in the dark?

"At that time, I refined my method of making love when there are other people sleeping in the same room. No one should notice, but satisfaction should be possible nevertheless. Affection, gentleness, and letting go are the key words – it isn't always necessary to screw around until the walls shake!"

Then he meets a teen named Zwi: "It must have been obvious to him that I was also attracted to him physically, because things progressed with Zwi the same way they had with some others – that is, he made the first move, not me." They had gone swimming and were lying in their swimming trunks under the trees: "We were surprisingly relaxed even though bombers were flying overhead. It was an afternoon that seemed like part of a carefree childhood, I was thinking. Zwi was lying there quietly, deep in thought, Then at some point he embraced me; he was passionate, awkward, and at the same time tender. I was happy, but I held myself back, didn't push him. Our coming together was an incredibly slow process, cautious, and very loving.... We knew we could count on each other. Knowing that in the midst of the danger we were living every day brought out an overpowering feeling of attachment between us. From that fraternal trust, erotic feelings developed. That day in the forest was the first time we had sex."

16

Yes, the possibilities are endless, especially when you get outside of the U.S. and encounter how other cultures deal with sexual issues. When Bel-Ami superstars Lukas Ridgeston and Johan Paulik, who live in Slovakia (where everyone is straight, according to Bel-Ami chief George Duroy), visited the U.S. in 2000, Mickey Skee interviewed them. He reported that "the boys say that most of their friends enjoy sex of all kinds, and fucking and sucking among them as youths is fairly common in their part of Europe. And they don't consider man-to-man sex as being gay. In fact, homosexuality is linked to transvestitism, they say, and that is considered abnormal. But, that's not what Johan and Lukas and their friends think of their refreshingly innocent and carefree sex. It's common to be with a buddy who might get a hard-on while they're fishing, hiking through the fields, wrestling around or taking a shower together. Then, if they feel like they want to blow off steam by jacking off together, or sucking each other off, they do it." Basically, Skee determined, they regard themselves as straight and they don't see it as strange that they not only have sex with other guys but that they perform all kinds of what we here regard as homosexual acts. "We are sexual," Johan said. "We like to do this."

"There is no such thing as being bisexual where we are from, we are not even that," Lukas added. "We are just guys who like sex." Just how much Johan enjoys it is evident in the series of soft-core films he made for Pride's Mike Esser in the U.K. One video, "Summer, the First Time" was a sensation, pairing Johan with "straight" Sean Benedict, who, Esser said, "was really into the idea of having sex with Johan."

And consider what award-winning porn performer, the mega-hung Spike, says: "Working with straight guys bothered me at first. Being originally straight, then calling myself bisexual and now being gay, I went through it. I have background in this and I'm not just prejudging them. It made me a little angry that they can't just say they're bisexual. The bottom line is they are allowing another man to suck their cock, or they're fucking another man – or getting fucked. Whatever you call it, you're having sex with a man. At least call yourself bisexual, stop with the 'straight' thing! 'Straight to bed' is more like it. So that part made me angry at first.

"And the whole thing of looking at a titty magazine! Look, it's very difficult when you're on set anyway, and you want that chemistry between you and the other performer to help make it look really hot

17

onscreen. And when the other guy is looking over your shoulder at a magazine or a video of 'hot pussy action' – that's the last thing you want. So in that context it's hard for the gay performers when there's a straight guy on the set. But there are a lot of 'gay for pay' performers who are excellent at it and who get into the gay sex while they're there. Billy Herrington, for instance. Even though he had the video thing going, he was extremely comfortable to work with. I think I intrigued him, being a little guy with a big dick."

Yes, any boy can!

ANY BOY CAN
John Patrick

The music – the Pointer Sisters singing "I'm So Excited" – was way too loud. The stripper named Hot Rod strutted around mouthing the words. He had disastrous teeth, crooked and bucked, and there was a gap on the upper left side where at least two were missing. Every time he reached the end of the runway he flicked his tongue in and out and fluttered his black cape to offer a glimpse of his long, pale penis. I was beginning to wonder if this was all he was going to do when he raised his arms and started pumping his hips. His penis flapped around like a noodle. Even the drunk next to me began to pay attention.

"Watch out," the drunk said. "He's gettin' ready...." The old- timer was right about that: Hot Rod suddenly leapt off the stage and was dancing in our direction. But it was the fat, bald man sitting on the drunk's other side that he targeted. Two inches from the man's face, he resumed pumping.

The drunk leaned across the bar to get a better look, obscuring my view. I stood up. "I guess you get what you pay for," I said, referring to the fact that there was no cover charge. "That's debatable," my friend Derek said. Derek had been here before and added, "The last time I was here, Hot Rod said, 'For ten bucks, I'll stick it in your drink.' I wonder...."

Sure enough, Hot Rod wrapped the guy in his cape. The man's shriek was muffled. Hot Rod opened his arms, triumphant, then commenced a frenzied, complicated flourishing of his cape as he backed up the three stairs and onto the stage. Under the fixed spotlight he turned away from the audience, lifted his arms and began pumping his hips again. Faster, faster. The music stopped. Not the way it was supposed to but as if the needle jumped off the record. Hot Rod froze, legs bent, groin thrust forward. A good thirty seconds went by and then the spotlight dimmed. Hot Rod still didn't move. From where I sat, in this light, he was not too bad: great shoulders, nice tight ass, nice long dick.... The spotlight and the house lights came back on, and Harry, who owns the bar, yelled, "Let's hear it! Let's hear it for Hot Rod Reynolds!"

Hot Rod leapt back around to reveal the semi-erection he managed while frozen, just a flash of it, then he hung the cape over one arm like a toreador and strode offstage. "Show him you love him, you cocksuckers!" Generous applause followed, even a few whistles.

Even the man who had his head wrapped and his drink dipped applauded.

Now on the stage appeared two guys wearing cowboy hats, chaps, spurred boots and leather-fringed G-strings. They twirled lassoes and rode phantom bucking broncos and slapped their own asses, then each other's. I tried to lose myself in the dancers' bodies, but their outfits distracted me. I could feel my whole self folding in, retreating from the light and noise, the idiotic music, the laughing, the smoke. I ordered another beer.

The next guy was Steve, a blond, hunky body-builder who dressed in marine drag. Steve's big finale was turning away from the audience, removing his G-string, then turning back around with his white glove waving on the end of his erection. Derek laughed and applauded. The guy ended up giving the glove to Derek – for a generous tip.

"Can we go now?" I asked Derek.

In the car, Derek was silent, playing with his glove.

"Jesus Christ," I muttered as he brought the glove to his nose and sniffed. With his eyes closed he took a deep, resuscitative breath. When he opened his eyes, he saw I was staring at him.

He gave a little laugh. "I smell trouble."

Trouble was what it always was with Derek. He was the most willing bottom I had ever encountered. Sex with him had been instantly addictive. During the first six months we were living together we made love at least once a night, and once in the morning before he went to work. But it always had to be same: he would never want to top me. Never. I pleaded with him, but it was no use. I told him I was versatile – "Versatile! You know what that means?" – but my pleas fell on deaf ears. Now, we were at the point where we were really just friends.

Now, out of the blue he said, "I love you, you know."

"What you love is me fucking your ass. That's what you love," I retorted.

"Yeah," he said, nodding. "That's right," he added, as if he

could rest his case. "Nobody fucks like you do."

This wasn't the first time I had heard him saying that. He'd been saying it even before he moved in with me. But this was the first time we had gone to the Boiler Room together and now his imagination had shifted into overdrive.

"You should dance there...." he went on, sniffing the glove again.

"Me?"

"Yes, you. You know you'd be great."

At home, Derek was hot to trot – hotter than he'd been in some weeks. It made me hot just to see him in bed, getting his hole ready for me. He moaned and groaned while he sucked on my dick, from the narrow head all the way to the thick base, tickling my balls at the same time. After a bit, I grabbed his buns. Just the feel of them brought my rod up to full attention. Which caught Derek's attention. Putting my hands on his shoulders, I moved my hips back and pulled my cock out of his mouth, then slammed it back in. He played with himself while I face-fucked him the way he loved it.

When I could see he was about to shoot his load, I pushed my hips forward, thrusting my dick deeper into his face at just the right moment. His spunk shot straight up, hitting his smooth chest and torso. I gave him another minute to hang on my hard-on, then I made my move.

Grabbing Derek under the arms, I pushed him back across the bed, then took him by the waist and turned him over. He was like a miniature statue toppled – that's how perfect his rounded muscular body seemed. He looked over his shoulder at me, very excited. I had become his fantasy dancer made flesh. I imagined he was thinking about Steve or Hot Rod. Kneeling over him on the bed, I gripped his buttcheeks and bent down to take bites of that fresh young flesh. His ass was all mine and I was letting him know it. While I held Derek

21

down with one hand, I lubed up his tight, pink pucker with the other. I wedged two fingers into his tight ass. He pushed his delectable butt up at me, and I positioned my cockhead against his pliant asshole and gave a little push. A hard-on with any bend in it would have a hard time with such a tight asshole, but I was hot for this, incredibly hard and ready. Derek gasped as my thick shaft made its way into him.

Once I had a couple of inches imbedded in him, Derek stiffened up like he'd been harpooned. I held still for a minute, massaging his shoulders and back while I held him in place. Then I started moving my cock in and out, slowly sinking it deeper and deeper in the warm oven between those dreamy buns. My thick shaft made its way into him. Derek moaned and groaned, but soon he was working with me, pushing his ass up as I sank my rigid cock down. Before long, we hit the perfect rhythm and I was getting close. Looking down, I watched every inch of my long dick disappear into his ass.

Pounding away at his ass faster and faster, I felt my balls tighten as my desire peaked. I held his shoulders in a vise-like grip and came. Derek bit down on a pillow as his tight ass-ring was draining every drop of my cum.

I kept going, slow-fucking him for a few selfish minutes before I finally pulled out and collapsed onto the bed on my back. Derek rested his head on my chest. "God, that was hot."

"You were just thinking of Steve."

"Ha! He's straight. All the dancers are straight at that bar."

"Yeah, sure."

"It's true. They're all straight. Nobody scores with them."

"I bet they're gay-for-pay then."

"Yeah, maybe." He was quiet for a moment. Then, looking up at me, he added, "He sure is a hunk though, isn't he?"

"Yeah, a real stud."

He looked off into space. "Yeah, I'll admit I did think about him at one point."

I didn't really want to know what he was thinking at what point, so I kissed him. I could feel his heart pounding as he kissed me back and I wrapped my arms around his sweaty body and held him tight.

He lay there with a big smile on his face. "You should, you know."

"Should what?"

"Dance at the Boiler Room. Think of the money you'd make. You'd be the only gay guy there. Really...."

"Dream on."

About a month later, there I was, at the Boiler Room, getting ready to go on stage. I had gotten laid off at the advertising agency where I worked as a copy boy when they lost their biggest account, and was at loose ends. Always self-centered, Derek had taken up with an older man whom he said could help him advance his acting career and had moved out. I was desperate. The Boiler Room was dark, sexy, dangerous, filthy, and enticing: everything temptation should be. Everything I wanted it to be.

I had only been working there a couple of weeks when I met Ricky. I had arrived early that night and, pulling out my favorite G-strings, I discovered a couple of wadded one dollar bills I had missed from the week before. Starting the night with a little money always lifted my mood.

I shucked off my shirt and pants, placing them neatly at the bottom of the broken locker to protect them from the smell of smoke and sweat that permeated everything by the end of the night. Harry, carrying two beers, and a big smile on his face, came down the stairs on his way to his office and paused to give me a quick up-and-down look. Mostly down. 1 couldn't tell if he liked me because of my legs, my package, or because I took the job seriously, showing up on time and staying sober through the whole shift. Probably a little of all three.

"Hey, babe, you ready for a great night?" he asked.

"Always!" I replied, mustering as much enthusiasm as I could manage.

Hot Rod and Steve arrived a few minutes later, discussing how wasted the cowboys, James and John, had gotten at some party the night before. This usually meant that they would be arriving an hour late for their shift, and we'd have to shift the dance schedule around to work them in. I threw my leg up on the counter, mostly to stretch and limber up, but also to give Rod and Steve something to look at. Which they always did. Straight – but still curious.

I was contemplating what costume to wear when I heard:

"Hi, guys!" I turned around to lay eyes on a delightfully nervous little muscleboy.

"I'm Ricky. Harry said to come in here and meet you guys."

Hot Rod and Steve gave him the quick once-over, and, satisfied that Ricky wouldn't horn in on Rod's clownish caped- crusader or Steve's muscle-stud themes, said "Hi," and went back to their conversation.

"Hi, Ricky," I said. "You done this before?"

"Um, no, I haven't," he said nervously.

I put two and two together. Harry had just auditioned little Ricky in his office, and now the kid was ready for the big-time. Harry, I knew from my own experience with him, was harmless. All he liked to do was suck cock, and one of the best ways to get him to shut up was to shove your dick down his throat. All was forgiven as your cum splashed all over his face.

I smiled. "No sweat! You'll do fine. Pick a locker and get dressed."

Ricky opened the locker next to mine and stripped, revealing a crisp, tightly packed musculature. And he had a nice ass too – a match for Derek's.

I had an idea. "Say, Ricky, you want to do the first set together? It's usually pretty slow."

Ricky seemed relieved at the idea. "Hey, that'd be great! Then you can show me how it works."

I thought to myself, Oh, I'll show you how it works all right! but I held my tongue. "What kind of 'theme' do you want to go for?"

"Well, I don't have much...." he replied nervously. A quick glance showed he had a couple of G-strings but nothing much in the way of costuming.

"Well, I have some extra things, if you don't mind wearing a collar and a jockstrap." He looked like he might get into the submissive role, and I was testing the waters.

"Sure! Sounds like fun!" Ricky replied. Like a nervous stray puppy, he was eager for a little affection.

"Okay," I said, handing him the leather collar and the jock, "Lemme go talk to Jake, the DJ, about our music."

I threw on some pants and headed upstairs with some cash. My little spat of last week with Jake was going to end now with a bribe. I could care less about my music, but I wanted something good to work this kid over on stage, and I wanted him to have a good experience.

"Okay, you bastard, here's five bucks. I'm dancing with the new guy, and I want my special tape." He knew what I wanted: Ravel's "Bolero," which begins slowly and quietly and gradually builds to a loud, intense conclusion.

"Sure, stud. But five bucks?" He tossed it back at me. "You know what I want."

"Later," I said, smiling. I should never have fucked him the first week I was there, but I was feeling depressed and he started out giving me a superb blowjob – even better than Harry's – and then I just let nature take its course.

I hopped back downstairs and put on my top harness, leatherjock, boots and gloves.

"So, how rough do you like it?" I asked Ricky playfully.

Ricky smiled. "Oh, I think I can take whatever you dish out."

I broke into a broad, wicked grin and pulled out my flogger and handcuffs. This was going to be fun, and really wake up the early crowd.

As the rhythms of "Bolero" began to quicken, I teasingly swished the crop above Ricky's head. At first the strokes were symbolic, but soon, as I became more certain of the power welling up inside me, slowly and swiftly, I began stroking the crop up and down his body, as if I was brushing him with a feather. He got on his knees before me and I tapped the flogger lightly along his backsides and thighs, and as the

25

music swelled, I tapped him harder and harder. Soon he began to squirm and breathe heavily, and I hit him harder. Finally, as the music peaked, I gave him two last hard whacks, and finished by rubbing his rear gently, and he writhed on the stage. I stripped him, then did a quick strip myself, and we rushed off the stage. A beaming Harry came to the dressing room and told us he wanted an encore for the second show, but we needed to have a better finale. I understood what he meant. At two in the morning, we could get away with a lot more. Ricky agreed, then went upstairs to circulate and collect some tips from customers who wanted to grope him.

We reprised the whipping session, then, with the song starting over and wrapping around us, Ricky looked at me and smiled quickly. I smiled back. I could see beads of sweat had gathered in the hollow of his throat and began to slide down his chest. I licked the sweat off his flesh, and the guys at the bar watching us went wild. I was soon fitting myself into him, my thigh between his legs, his thigh between mine. I moved my head into the crook of his neck. He put his hand in the small of my back and pulled me deeper into him. I went back to licking the sweat from his Adam's apple up to his chin. He tilted his head back and closed his eyes. I put one hand on his waist and the other at the back of his head. Grinding, dipping, he bent his knees to help me ride his thigh. He pulled me into the smooth slickness of his chest. He kissed me suddenly, hard on the mouth. He moved into me relentlessly, rubbing my hardening dick. I turned him around and began to batter his ass with my dick. "Mmm, baby, I can feel your heat," I whispered to him. "I want to give you some lovin.'"

He didn't reply; but his hips ground a little faster and a little harder as I kissed his neck from his ear down to his shoulder.

With one hand working his cock, the other hand came around to pleasure the nearest nipple.

As the temperature rose dramatically, I told him, "Ooh, Ricky, we'd better go back downstairs now."

We took our bows and, since we were the last to dance, the locker room was vacant.

I tossed our costumes on the floor and reached for my erection. "There's something I've just got to give you."

26

In an evil voice, Ricky asked, "A tip?"

"Uh, huh."

At first, I simply had to lean back and admire the natural wonder that was Ricky's ass. He lay on his back on the bench and spread his legs. I opened my locker and got some lube. I rubbed some on his asshole and all over my cock. That sent shudders through him and me.

I began drawing my fingertips lightly across his puckering skin. Keeping it going, I repositioned myself over him and then dragged my erection across his genitals towards his asshole, just barely touching his skin with it. Slowly, ever so achingly slowly, I shoved my now-fully hardened cock down into his ass, and his hips began really grinding. His heat rose higher, and his hips moved more furiously, sucking me deep into him.

He protested heartily when I pulled out of him, but he quieted down as I shifted to a better position and settled into a nice rhythm. He screamed, and his asshole was unbelievably hot and seeping when he thrust upward. I slid in and out with shuddering ease, letting him really feel the penetration as I move against his ass walls, which begin to lengthen and deepen and open wider.

The fuck was so good, I couldn't imagine ever wanting to stop, but I was close. He moaned out his pleasure as I fucked him more and more feverishly, his asshole clutching and shaking.

Fixing to boil, he blurted out, "Give it to me, stud. "

And I did. My cock was charging in and out with a great heat.

As he thrashed and came, copiously, in his hand, I continued to fuck his ass with gentle force and, screaming and clenching, he grabbed my ass and pulled me into him. "Oh yeah, stud. Give it to me," he chanted over and over again with mantra-like intensity, and I responded by fucking him for all I was worth.

I came, gloriously, and I couldn't have been happier. With my cock still inside him, I bent down to kiss him, feeling the radiating heat flush my awestruck face.

"Mmmmphh, " he half sighed as I gently withdrew from him.

I gave him my best toothy smile as I rushed to the bathroom.

When I came out, he had vanished. The next night, Harry told me that he had called in to say his lover wouldn't let him dance again. I chuckled, thinking maybe when he got home he told his boyfriend all about it....

Ricky was replaced three days later by a different type altogether: Carlos, who was built like a marble statue. I stood in the doorway, mesmerized by him. As he disrobed, I began to breathe heavily. When he stripped off his boxers and began touching himself all over, my fingers were shaking. His uncut cock was semi-hard and incredibly thick. He saw me standing there just staring at him. He smiled and took my bag off my shoulder and started unbuttoning my shirt. Once it was on the floor, he knelt down and opened my pants and unzipped the fly with his teeth. As my shorts slipped down and over my boots I reached down to caress his cheeks and lips. He sucked on my cock a bit, but I couldn't stand it, I had to have him in my mouth.

I dropped down and swallowed him whole. His body tensed for a moment as the head of his shaft bumped the back of my throat. My lips skated over his skin, and the cock began to harden. He put his hands in my hair and controlled the sucking. Carlos, hard, possessed one of the biggest cocks I had ever laid eyes on: over nine inches long and really thick, with a head that was bigger than the shaft. He seemed to be amazed that I could take the whole thing down my throat. While I was sucking him, he told me that most guys didn't like to suck his cock because he was uncut. I thought for a minute that he might come, but then he pushed me back and said, "Later. You got me warmed up. Thanks."

Wiping his pre-cum from my mouth, I stood up. "You're welcome," I said.

Carlos largely ignored me for the rest of the night, but when I finished my last set and went downstairs, he was waiting for me. He said nothing, just pushed me to my knees to continue where we had left off. This turned me on and I stroked my cock to full attention while he fucked my face with his lusciously thick prick.

Finally, Carlos told me to get on the bench. I obeyed, although I really didn't think I could handle his thickness. Still, it had been so long since I had bottomed that I just lifted my feet over my head, and placed my knees on either side of my head so that my ass was splayed open and eager for him. That was all he needed. He just shoved it right in, not giving me a chance to get used to it. I screamed, but he wouldn't stop, and before long he was fully in me and he began the fuck. Tears came to my eyes as I grabbed my cock and began to jack myself.

Just then, Hot Rod and Steve came into the dressing room. Their whooping and cheering only added to the intensity of the session as Carlos was thrusting his cock into me.

When we finally finished we were drenched from the exertion. As he lifted himself off, I collapsed back to the hard, flat surface, breathing heavily from my exertions. A hand moved softly down my chest to my belly. I opened my eyes to see that Hot Rod was stroking me. He had never touched me before. My cock responded against my will to his caresses, rising tall, hard, and firm against my wishes and better judgment.

His hands stopped briefly and he got some lube. His slick hand moved down my prick to my balls, rubbing and caressing them. His exploring hand moved farther down, under my balls, and into my soppy hole. His fingers started by making small circles around the outer rim. My legs, splayed wide open by Carlos, left no part of my body unavailable to his groping hands. His probing fingers massaged the rim of my anus.

Steve now moved in, bringing his erection to my lips. Remembering how Derek had reacted to Steve's dance and the glove so long ago, I was flying high. One of Rod's hands worked my shaft, the other pressed into my ass. As the finger moved deeper into me, I experienced a stabbing pain. I tensed up, and the he stopped. But, after I moment, I could feel the heat of him as he climbed onto the bench and positioned himself against my ass.

I relaxed to accommodate his cock, and he started to rock back and forth, slowly thrusting it in and out of my hungry hole. The tempo of his fist pumping my rod and his cock fucking me had me writhing on the edge of climax. As Rod came inside me, Steve was ramming my mouth and the discomfort was great at first because his cock was so thick, but soon intense pleasure spread over my entire body. I couldn't believe I had been fucked in the ass and was now being fucked in the mouth by two guys who had told me they were straight and had avoided any closeness for so long – and I was really getting off on it! I came with an intensity I seldom felt before in my life. Rod left my cock throbbing on my belly, pulled out of me and disappeared.

I began writhing in feigned pain and grunted in protest the fact that Steve was still fucking my face after I had come. Steve seemed to understand my plight; he removed his cock from my mouth. I flexed my aching jaw. Then he lifted my head from the hard surface and raised it to meet his pelvis, then he plunged his now fully hard cock back into my mouth again, knocking my head back and forth as he rammed it in and out. I could feel his dick growing even larger and I could tell he was close to orgasm.

Suddenly, he stopped pumping and withdrew his cock from my mouth. I could feel the enlarged, swollen cockhead and taste his pre-cum as it slid across my tongue. I could feel the heat of him as he climbed onto the bench and positioned himself against my ass. I started shaking my head and thrashing my legs, attempting to avoid what I knew damn well was to follow. My ass ached, and I really didn't need any more fucking, but I could do nothing more than groan. He shoved the head of his prick into me and I cried out, begging him not to continue, but he ignored me, and his body slammed against mine. I pushed back, but my protesting only seemed to ignite his fire.

"Oh, shit," he groaned suddenly, and he began fucking me frantically until I could feel his cum pumping into me, filling me. Then he just collapsed on top of me, his energy spent.

After a while, Steve climbed off me and disappeared as well.

I was groggy, but I was sure that Steve had kissed me on the forehead; it was only for a second, but there was no mistaking it. I didn't know what I thought about what had just happened, because, for once, I didn't want to think at all.

I dressed and slowly made my way home. I couldn't get the images of Steve's cock sliding in and out of my mouth and Rod's jacking me off out of my mind, and I remembered Derek's sniffing of the stud's glove. God, I thought, if Derek could have seen me in that dressing room!

Thinking about Derek standing there watching us got me hard again, and then I remembered Steve's kiss. And, somehow, I knew he would do it again. Maybe they would all do it again!

A WILD AND CRAZY RIDE
Jack Ricardo

Back at the beginning of gay liberation, I joined the Gay Activist Alliance in New York City. We had meetings, we demonstrated, we partied, we fucked. At one of our meetings, I met one weird dude. I'd never seen him before. He was good looking, not cute, but you just knew when he matured he'd be one handsome dude. I was 19 at the time ,and I'd guess he was about the same. I was a dirty blond (still am, for that matter), had long curly hair (not long anymore), a firm body (yeah, still got that), and was slightly taller than him. He had dark hair, a cute wee body, and bubbled when he talked. That is, his energy level was at a peak, constantly.

After the meeting, he came over and started talking to me – and talking and talking and talking. He said the subways were unsafe because he never saw rats down in the tunnels and if rats wouldn't go there, it was unfit for humans. I'd seen rats in the subways and told him this, but he ignored my comments and continued his tirade against the subways. Basically he was doing a monologue.

During his harangue, he popped up with, "Why don't you come up to my place and talk? I don't wanna have sex with you, but I like talking to you." He liked talking, period. And he continued talking. About eggs now, and how good they were for you and that's all he ate. And about rats in the subway. And all the time, sailing around like a whirling dervish. Even standing still, he was active, shifting from foot to foot, swiveling, poking his neck back and forth, flapping his arms. I decided this dude was either so horny he was burning up, or he was crazy. I opted for horny. We walked to his place. No, I walked. He hopped around like his pants were on fire.

His place was a half-room dive near the docks. A bed, no bathroom, no closet. And when we got there, he again assured me he didn't want to have sex, but suggested, "We might as well take off our clothes and be comfortable though. It gets hot in here."

I was hot already, and not only from the heat of the night. This guy had this frisky little body and had so much pent-up energy, he gave off

31

sparks that were almost frightening. I was intrigued. I was fucking horny. We stripped to our shorts. White briefs, both of us. And he, all the time, chattering like a chimp. Rats, eggs, everything but sex.

I decided he was a closet case, maybe even terrified because he couldn't admit that he did want to have sex. Badly. So badly, I could almost smell his need. It emanated from his body like musk from a moose. The dude was burning up with desires he was trying to suppress. And now that he had another dude in his lair, he couldn't suppress those fierce cravings for long. We were sitting on the bed and while he continued his one-way conversation, he dropped a hand in my lap and started playing with my cock through my shorts. He wasn't saying he didn't want to have sex anymore or that he did want to have sex either. He kept talking absolute nonsense, on and on and on ... until I told him....

"Shut the fuck up for a goddam second!" I shouted. The only way I could get his within. My attention was centered on the stiff cock clamped around his fist. He was startled. "If you wanna keep that fucking mouth busy, stop your fucking yakking and get down there and eat my fucking shorts." With that, I grabbed him by the neck, pushed him to the floor between my legs and planted his face in my lap.

He began protesting but the words came out as complete gibberish. After all, he was also gnawing on one hard dick probing through white cotton. And doing a good job of it, a damn good job, mouthing my fucking cock, chewing my cock with both a ferocity and a gentleness that was fucking amazing. And after he feasted on my covered cock, he went to work on my balls. He began licking over the large pouch of nuts, trying to swallow each of those fuckers through the cotton material, holding onto my hips and mashing my balls, my cock, all over his face. He was one starving cocksucker who wanted cock so badly, he wasn't about to give it up now that he had it. And I wasn't about to let him give it up. I grabbed his ears with both hands and fed him, telling him, "Come on, faggot, put that fucking mouth to good use for a goddam change. Eat it, fagboy. Enjoy that fucking meal. Have yourself one fucking blast." My words made him more hungry, more starved, more desperate.

He gobbled up the front of my shorts until they were soaked with his drool and his spit and pre-cum juice that was leaking from the head of my cock like sap from a tree. He was both thrilling me and exhausting me with his ravenous hunger. I fell back against the wall, my feet still spread wide and hanging over the side of the bed, his hands on my knees and his tongue swiping over my pulsing cock like a lizard testing his lunch. He lifted his eyes to watch me watching him. His eyes were wide and delighted and crazed. I said, "You are one wild cocksucker, you bastard."

He backed up, sat on his heels, his hands dropped to his thighs. His hair was a tangled mess, his mouth was wet and glowing. His cock was straining against the pouch of his shorts. His bizarre grin lit up the room like the moon on a dark sea. The look in his eye was one of greedy longing.

"I never did that before," he said through gasps. He wiped away the dribble from his lips.

"Bullshit," I told him, catching my breath.

"I never did," he protested loudly, like a kid caught lying. Then quietly added, "I always wanted to but I never did, I was afraid. But you ... you .. .I wanted to do you but was afraid and yet I didn't know if you ... but yeah I did want to...."

And then he started rambling again, about me, about my underwear, about my cock, about rats in the subway, and eggs for breakfast, lunch and supper, and was off to the moon. I closed my eyes until I couldn't stand his idiotic rambling anymore. I pounced off the bed and pushed him to the floor. He fell back, shocked, shaken. I pulled off my shorts. My cock snapped out and bobbed up and down, and my nuts hung low and full. I stood over him, naked, one foot on each side of his waist, holding onto my hard cock and waving it over him. A warning, a promise.

"What are you gonna do?" he squeaked, like a meek little mouse in a trap of his own making.

I smiled. No, I sneered. "Give you what you fucking need, what you fucking want, you cocksucker. My fucking dick!"

He started talking again about how he never had sex with a guy before and about how afraid he was and about how horny he always was and about how he's always jerking off, and about rats in the goddam subway and goddam eggs to eat. He only stopped his fucking prattling when I knelt down, sat on his chest, fisted my fucking pole with one hand, snatched his hair with the other, lifted his head, and stuffed my cock between his lips.

Yeah, he wanted cock, he needed cock, and he finally had fucking cock. One stiff fucking cock with a big round cut head that filled his mouth. He started sucking on my cock-knob with a vengeance that was savage. At last he had the opportunity to use that mouth for something besides talking. And he was using it, and using it fucking well. Swiping his tongue round and round that big fucking cockhead, twisting his neck, piercing his tongue into the pisshole, groaning and moaning loud and sloppy and happy. My rod was fucking burning. This guy was the neediest and hungriest bastard I'd ever been with. He was a born cocksucker.

Without even thinking about it, I fell over his head, held myself up with stiff arms and started to fuck that little bastard's face, ramming my cock into his throat, pulling it out, wet and warm and rock hard, then ramming in again, and pulling out, fucking that cherry cocksucker's face. A cherry cocksucker who needed to suck cock like other men need to breathe. The guy didn't gag. In fact he wanted more, harder. He grabbed my hips and held on while I screwed my fucking cock down his throat, while my balls banged over his chin until they were sore and I was panting louder than he was, until I couldn't hold back and I rammed my cock deep inside that cocksucker's throat, with my balls smashed on his chin, and stayed there because my nuts were fucking exploding and my cum was splattering from my fucking cock like a volcano exploding. I was shaking, he was taking it and loving it, his fingers biting into my hips with a grip that pained, and moaning with such fucking joy it was a pleasure to hear.

I emptied my nuts and dropped next to him, spent, and damn near passed out. Maybe I did, for a while. I became aware of the crazy dude again when his voice intruded, still chattering away. I opened my eyes. He was sitting next to me, still in his shorts, legs to his chest, arms over his knees, chattering away like a goddam baboon. He saw me staring at him. "Hi," he yelled, then became oddly quiet. His eyes were shining. So were his lips.

That mouth looked fucking beautiful. Never, never, have I had such a ravenous blowjob. I closed my eyes again, still savoring the moment. And he instantly started up again, chattering away about absolute drivel. My mind was still filled with that exquisite sensation of my hard cock down his soft throat. I could say my cock got hard again, but I would be wrong. It never got soft.

I opened my eyes and leaned up on one elbow. I swiped the sweat from my brow and strung my fingers through my hair. He was leaning back on his arms, his legs were spread flat. I was staring into his lap. His cock was making one high tent inside his briefs, the rounded peak topped with a grimy splotch of slime. He stopped talking for a second, then continued, more feckless, talk for the sake of talk. He was still afraid, yet he wanted more. I could see it, I could taste it, I could feel it. I was fondling my balls and flipping my cock back and forth. He watched me play and still blubbered away, drooling like a wacko.

I knelt up beside him, my cock again bobbing in expectation. I rolled him over onto his stomach. He went willingly and didn't even ask what I was going to do. He still talked now, but this time about getting fucked. "Nobody ever fucked me before. I fucked a girl once but I didn't like it. I thought I'd like getting fucked by a hard cock like yours but I don't know. I fuck myself with my finger when I jerk off sometimes, but I don't think I can take a cock up my ass. I think I'll try...."

I let him chatter while I spread his legs, knelt between then, and pulled his shorts down and off his legs. His ass was exposed. One fine ripe white ass that fucking steamed. I grabbed both cheeks. They were hard, they were hot, they were sweaty, they were round as two melons. He was resting his head on his arms. I spread his cheeks wide until that mouth-watering little rosebud popped into view. A sprinkling of dark fuzz was a map that led down the divide where the tiny, wrinkled hole sparkled. I leaned down and licked that little asshole. The dude clamped his mouth shut and moaned quietly.

I teased, licking round and round the rim and felt a small pressure against my face as he lifted his hips ever so slightly. I again lapped over the exact center of his asshole like a horny dog. Another moan, more passionate, a little louder, another tiny lift upward. I again rimmed the edge of his asshole. My nuts again started bubbling up another load of cum. I opened my mouth full wide and smothered the outside of his asshole with full sloppy lips. He lowed like a cow. I pulled his legs wide apart and speared my tongue inside his asshole. My tongue flittered all around the cavity of his ass, touching, tasting, feeling pure smooth untainted asshole. I ate out and slobbered over that dude's asshole until my jaw was aching, until I was satiated, until my cock was so hard it was painful, until my balls were near boiling over.

I sat up and admired. He stopped talking, for once. He was breathing, loudly, dreamily. I slopped my hand with spit and oiled my fucking cock. It throbbed in anticipation. I slipped one hand under his hips and pulled his perky little ass up. I aimed my cockhead directly at the tiny asshole and pushed it inside. He didn't yelp, he didn't cry out. He swooned. Fucking swooned! He oohed, he ahhed, he mooed.

My cockhead was warm and cuddled inside that asshole and I goddam near swooned myself. I watched as the shaft of my cock widened that tight puckered hole and slowly disappeared inside his ass. When I pulled his hips back and when my cock had pronged that little fucker all the way, when my cockhairs were scratching his pure lily white ass, the guy groaned fervently, aggressively, and rammed his ass back. He startled me this time and almost toppled me over, but I hung on. And it became one wild fucking ride.

The guy was shaking under me. Every muscle in his body was pulling my cock into his ass. He hunched his ass back while I started fucking him, pulling my cock to the brink then plugging back in. He was growling like a mad dog, he was snarling like a wild wolf. So was I. I screwed him, and he screwed my cock with a boundless energy. Soon he was crying out in agony, in delight, in pain, in so much pleasure it damn near blew the ceiling apart. He was squirming under me like one lone living muscle that was devouring my fucking cock until I thought I'd fucking drown. Bouncing up and down. Bouncing me up and down. The muscles in his asshole were grasping my cock, tickling my cock.

Then he yelled, and literally flipped me over backwards until I was on my back with him atop me and my cock buried so far up his ass I thought for sure it would pierce his stomach. I started groaning, moaning, and grabbed him round the waist, fisted his cock, fisted his balls. He snapped his head back and nuzzled it into my neck. I bit it, I sucked it. I was dropping one heavy load deep inside his ass. I could feel his fucking cock quaking, his balls one hard rock of cum spouting, his ass muscles gnawing my cock. He was shooting off, great globs were detonating, splashing down on my fist, my hand, his balls, both of us salivating and wailing like rabid banshees.

When I woke up, he was sprawled on his bed, snoring. I was on the floor. I had never felt so wasted yet so glorious in all my life. I was floating on a cloud.

After our one time together, I told that dude I wanted to see him again. Rats and eggs be damned, that was one wild and crazy ride. He said he wanted to see me too. But he never came back to G.A.A. When I went to his room at the docks, he was no longer there. I often wonder what happened to that little fucker. My guess is, he simply went totally crazy from too many bottled up feelings that can explode in a torrent of unbelievable sex!

READY PLAYMATE
R.J. Masters

I awoke and looked around at the unfamiliar surroundings. For a moment, I couldn't figure out where I was. Then I remembered. I had gone out drinking with my best friend, Joey.

I rolled over in the bed and my hand made contact with the warm body lying in the bed next to me. I instinctively pulled away when Joey sat up. "Good morning," he said softly, his eyes meeting mine.

"Morning," I replied, suddenly becoming aware that I was stark naked beneath the sheet. My mind began to race, desperately trying to piece together the events of the previous night. Joey was gay, and here I was in bed with him. What had happened between us?

I looked around the room, hoping I would spot my jeans lying close by. My heart pounded in my chest as I realized that I would have to get up naked and hunt for them.

He snuggled close, letting his hand reach out and caress my semi-hard cock. Every muscle in my body tensed, as I tried to think about how I should react, what I should do. I couldn't believe that I was responding to his touch, but my cock hardened and lengthened as he stroked it.

"Joey, I don't know what happened last night," I began, squirming away from him.

"What do you think happened?" he teased, inching even closer than before.

"I don't know. That's why I'm asking you," I replied, quickly growing impatient, though I was certain I already knew the answer.

"You really want to know?" he taunted, while his hand continued to run along my throbbing cock, teasing and arousing as it moved. His thumb circled the rim sending erotic shock waves through my reluctant flesh. I could feel my body slowly surrendering itself to his expert touch. Though part of me was resisting, was unwilling to take this any further, the rest of me was putty in his hands, anxious to be molded into whatever he wanted me to be.

"Just tell me," I demanded.

"Okay, Adam, I'll tell you. Nothing happened. We got drunk, came back here and went to sleep. That's it."

"Nothing? Then why are we naked?" I asked, still not sure I should take his word.

"You spilled a drink in your lap. I rinsed your jeans and shorts and hung them in the kitchen. You can go see, if you don't believe me," he replied, a sadness showing in his dark eyes.

I didn't know if I was relieved or really disappointed. I thought about pushing his hand away, of getting out of bed and running from Joey. But that wasn't really what I wanted to do. Instead, I leaned back and closed my eyes, just enjoying the feel of Joey's naked body next to mine.

I let his hand continue to play with my horny cock, while he humped his hard prick against my bare thigh. I was taken by surprise when his hungry mouth sought out mine, but I didn't pull away. My head was spinning and my pulse raced as his tongue pushed its way between my parted lips. He was unrelenting, delving ever deeper into my moist, warm mouth.

My initial apprehension was quickly replaced with anticipation. I was as driven by my animal lust as he was. I let my tongue slither between his sexy lips, probing the inside of his mouth and flicking against his tongue. Jolts of inexplicable pleasure shot directly to my aching cock.

My bloated balls churned, eager to expel their heavy oversized load. He captured my hand in his and guided it to his long, slender boner. I could feel each beat of his heart as the blood rushed through the pulsating vein. I had never imagined it would be so thrilling, make me tingle with excitement as I held another man's cock in my hand.

He pulled his lips away from mine and blazed a trail down my neck. He kissed and nibbled his way to my stiff pink nipples. His tongue lapped and flicked against them in turn, then his teeth lightly scraped the tender skin. I moaned and humped upward, repeatedly driving my cock into his fist, as I neared eruption.

Pre-cum oozed from my gaping piss-slit, drooling onto my smooth, hairless abdomen. He smeared the warm, sticky juice down my length so that his fist slid easily up and down the slippery shaft.

"You're so hot," he groaned. "I've wanted you in my bed for so long."

"Suck it ... please," I pleaded, unashamed of the desperate need that had overtaken my body. He looked up at me with his warm brown eyes and that disarming smile.

"Yeah, I'll suck you all right. I'm going to make you feel so good, you'll never want to get up and go home," he purred.

The heat of embarrassment flooded my cheeks, when he pulled the sheet from my body. He let out a soft whistle. "So beautiful," he whispered as he retrieved a box of condoms from the night stand.

I watched, mesmerized, as he eagerly tore open one of the foil wrappers and unrolled a bright red sheath down my hot, thick cock.

He slowly lowered his lips, flicking his tongue against the sensitive head. Chills swept up and down my spine and goose bumps spread over my muscular thighs.

He drew the head into his mouth, letting his tongue caress it, swirl over and around the rim. I thrashed and moaned, trying to force my horny cock into his throat. But he would not allow it. Instead he focused on the swollen head, poking into the covered piss-slit and driving me crazy with desire.

"Take it all, please," I begged.

Instead he let my cock slide from his mouth. He lapped and sucked on my tender balls, drawing first one, then the other into his moist, warm mouth. My cock jerked with uncontrollable desire, but he ignored the pulsating beast.

He drenched my balls in his saliva, then let his tongue sweep across my tight puckerhole. I thrashed wildly on the bed, grabbing handfuls of the sheet as my excitement grew. No one had ever sucked my balls or licked my ass before and the new sensations were nearly more than I could endure. My entire body was on fire. I desperately needed to get my rocks off, but he refused to give my cock any of the attention it was so hungry for.

His tongue wormed its way past the unyielding ass-ring that stood guard at the entrance to my body. It wiggled and squirmed as it slithered in and out of me.

"Oh, man, that's so good," I groaned.

His teeth grazed the sensitive tissue, sending sudden jolts of pleasure through me. The pressure was building up and I thought I would explode, that my hot wad would erupt on its own. I had never been so completely turned on.

Tiny beads of perspiration formed on my skin, as my excitement became overwhelming and I humped against his face.

"Oh, man, suck my cock, please," I begged again.

I was relieved when he finally returned his attention to my aching boner. He flicked against it, then finally parted his lips and allowed the head into his mouth. Slowly, inch by inch, he swallowed up my quivering flesh. His throat muscles contracted around it, squeezing and massaging until I could hold off no longer. I humped his face like a madman, my body driven by the need to shoot off. A low moan escaped from deep down inside me. My muscles tensed and my waiting load exploded with surprising force into the tip of the condom. I gasped for air as a second and third smaller burst followed.

His lips remained locked around my pulsating cock, until I had finished coming. Then he released the still-hard intruder from his mouth and looked up into my eyes with a mischievous grin.

Without saying a word, he pounced on me. His large, muscular body covered mine. I could feel his heart pounding in his chest. He mashed his lips against mine, while his wet, sticky cock head poked into my curly blond bush. It contacted my bare skin causing me to tremble.

His kisses were filled with a hunger – a desperate desire – that was overpowering. I couldn't resist, only surrender to his urgent need.

I shivered with excitement as he cloaked his cock in a blue latex sheath and approached me. He dangled his cock before my eyes, then lowered it to my lips.

I hesitated for a moment before pursing my lips and planting a kiss on his sensitive cockhead. I kissed and lapped at the twitching stock, then let it slide into my mouth. I caressed it with my tongue, thrilled by the sensation of the smooth hardness sliding over it. I could feel the heat of his arousal through the latex protection.

His cock pushed into my throat so that I gagged and gasped for air. He retreated quickly, allowing me to catch my breath, then plunged back into the warm, wet cavern.

"Oh yeah, you like my cock in your mouth, don't you?" he groaned, his voice hoarse with his uncontrollable lust.

I couldn't speak, but I readily nodded my agreement. I hadn't known what I was missing before this morning. My sex life had been adequate, but there had been a need, an unspoken emptiness that I now recognized. There was nothing like a horny cock sliding in and out of your mouth to fuel the fire already raging inside you. I had never imagined it would be so satisfying to pleasure another man, to siphon his oversized load of creamy goo.

I worked my mouth happily up and down the long, throbbing shaft. He moaned and humped ferociously, his big, hairy balls slapping against my chin each time he slammed forward.

I could see his balls pulling up close to his body, and eagerly awaited the moment when his wad would explode into the condom. He banged harder and faster and I knew it wouldn't be long.

Suddenly, without any warning, he had yanked his cock out of my mouth and was moving between my thighs. He grabbed for a bottle of baby oil sitting on the nightstand and quickly squirted some of the cold liquid onto my tight manhole. His cock was not as thick as mine, but it was big enough. I wasn't sure I could take it. I had never even finger-fucked myself when I jerked off. Taking his horny eight inches seemed impossible.

He pushed the spongy head against the tight muscle ring. I gasped and writhed beneath him.

"Oh, I can't take it," I groaned. "It's too big."

But he didn't cease his relentless invasion of my virgin manhole. He pushed deeper into me, overwhelming me with the sensation of incredible fullness.

When I had taken it all, he remained motionless allowing me to become accustomed to the feel of a stiff cock inside my body. He retreated slowly, massaging my inner walls as he moved.

He slammed forward, banging against my prostate and sending waves of pleasure through my body. I eagerly received him, humping upward so that he could jab that much deeper into my gut.

My cock slapped against my belly, bobbing between us as he rammed into me. His long, slow strokes caused my cock to jerk and twitch. I was only moments from blasting his chest with another steamy wad.

His hands caressed my chest, searching out my stiff nipples. He tweaked and tugged the rosy nubs while his cock plundered my body.

His breathing was loud and ragged as he thrust into me again and again. The pace picked up and he began banging into me with quick, short jabs.

"You're so hot," he moaned. "I've wanted you for so long."

I watched his face, the intense, determined expression as he made one final desperate lunge. I felt his cock wiggle and squirm inside me, filling the condom so that it swelled in my belly. His eyes were squeezed shut, his head thrown back as the convulsions continued to rack his muscular body. A deep guttural growl broke the silence of the room.

At that moment, my own cock jumped and my hot, sticky wad erupted. My muscles tightened as the stringy goo spattered my chest and abdomen.

He hovered over me for an instant, apparently mesmerized by the pulsating beast between us. His fingers smeared the white cream over my muscular pecs, then approached my lips

"Open," he whispered.

I hesitated, then complied, allowing him to push his cum-drenched fingers into my mouth. I sucked them clean, tasting my own cream for the first time. It was not what I expected and I was not repulsed by the taste of the salty cum.

He rolled off me, his cock sliding from my body, and picked up a towel.

"Care to join me?" he asked casually, as though he naturally expected me to hurry after him.

I surprised myself when I quickly bounded out of bed and followed him into the bathroom. I couldn't get enough of his hot body. He had given me more pleasure than I had ever dreamed possible, taken me places I had never even thought about going.

"Are you sure nothing happened last night? I mean, all this just seemed too easy."

"It was easy because you wanted it. Getting drunk and getting naked with me last night just set the stage. We slept in the same bed, snuggling close to each other all night. This morning, we just did what you've always wanted to do."

I thought about that for a moment. He was right. I had wanted to be with Joey for a long time, but my inhibitions had held me back. Now it was all out in the open. I couldn't deny it, and I was relieved. We could have hot, horny mansex any time. I knew what I wanted and I was going to get it, and I was certain Joey would be more than happy to oblige. MY SEXY NEW NEIGHBOR R. J. Masters

"Oooh, he's so cute. I hope he's the one moving in," I whispered to myself as I watched the moving truck at the apartment building across the street.

The neighborhood was full of couples and older people and I was desperate for some young blood. A hot, sexy blond was more than I had dared hope for, but there he was carrying boxes into the duplex apartment.

I licked my lips, as I stared at his bulging biceps and incredibly firm, round asscheeks which were squeezed into a pair of skin-tight jeans. My dick hardened as I imagined how it would feel to ram my stiff pole into the crevice between those mounds of flesh. I wanted him.

It had been so long since I had gotten laid, I knew I couldn't wait much longer.

I watched as the two older men who had also been carrying boxes walked toward a red Ford pickup. The cute blond followed them. My heart skipped a beat as he embraced each one of them before they got into the truck. It wasn't a platonic, "good buddy" type hug, either. He was obviously as gay as I was.

The truck drove away and the handsome stud stood alone in the isolated driveway, staring after it. "Yes!" I cried enthusiastically. He was my new neighbor.

I reached down and stroked my cock a couple of times, finally pulling it from inside my jeans. The thick uncut head was oozing pre-cum juices, making it wet and sticky in my hand.

I was still standing in the window, my hand furiously fisting my meat, when I felt his eyes on me. I thought about stuffing my dick back inside my pants, but then decided it might be best to be straightforward. I thrust my hips toward the window, exposing myself to him, and continued to yank my throbbing boner. I waited to see what his reaction would be. He didn't take his eyes off me. Instead, he smiled and his hand dropped down to give his basket a quick grope.

That was all it took. I beckoned to him. "Come here," I yelled through the glass, desperate not to let him get away. I even thought of running outside, but decided to wait and see whether he was really interested.

He looked a little surprised and hesitated for a moment, then began to stroll toward my building. I was on the second floor, so I opened my door wide and stepped back into my parlor. I heard the downstairs door slam and then the footsteps bounding up the stairs.

My heart raced and my pecker ached in anticipation of what was to come. I pulled back the foreskin and let my thumb lightly circle my deep red cockhead as I waited.

He slowly stepped inside my apartment, as if he was not sure he was doing the right thing. When he saw me standing in the next room with my dick in my hand, he closed the door behind him. He stood, staring at me for a moment, an awkward silence creeping between us.

"Hi!" he said softly.

"Hi. I'm Jesse. Welcome to the neighborhood."

"Thanks. I'm Brandon."

Brandon seemed nervous, but the bulge of swollen manhood struggling to escape from his stiff jeans told me all I needed to know. He was definitely as hot and horny as I was.

I couldn't wait to get him naked – to check out his oversized basket. I approached him and slipped my hands under his blue tee shirt. With one swift movement his smooth, muscular chest, with its large, pink nipples was exposed to my hungry eyes. I let my fingertips circle his pretty buds until they were as hard as my dick, then pinched and twisted them until he cried out.

He wrapped his arms around me, crushing my body against his and clamping his mouth over mine, obviously as hungry for this as I was. His tongue slithered between my parted lips and danced around my own, while my hands cupped those firm asscheeks. We ground our bodies together, my raging hard-on thrusting against the solid bulge that was still concealed by his jeans.

I tugged roughly at his button-fly – my need becoming more urgent with each passing second. I ached to feel his hardness sliding alongside my own. I shoved my hands under the waistband of his Levi's and white jockey shorts and pushed them to the floor, revealing his imposing pecker and oversized nutsac in one quick swoop.

"Oh, you're so hot," I gushed, letting my eyes drink up all his beauty.

He stepped out of the crumpled pile of clothing while I shed my own jeans and dropped to my knees in front of him. For a moment I just stared at the eight-inch beer can dick with its flaming cockhead oozing pre-cum juices from his slit.

I wanted to flick my tongue against the sensitive glans and devour his sweet cum, but the threat of disease had robbed us of that pleasure. Instead I reached into my desk drawer and removed a box of condoms. I tore open a crisp wrapper and applied the latex sheath to his horny member. Such a waste, I thought, as I let my tongue run the length of

47

his throbbing meat, caressing the pulsating vein. All that sweet cum and I couldn't swallow up a single drop.

I could feel the heat of his arousal through the second skin. I knew he wanted this just as much as I did. So I continued to tease him, alternating between licking him like a lollipop and flicking savagely at his tender flesh.

He gasped as I wrapped my lips around the thick pole and let it slide into my mouth, then swirled my tongue over and around it. His knees trembled and goose bumps spread down his hairless thighs as I tortured the massive intruder.

He grabbed a handful of my hair and forced the spongy head into my throat. I swallowed, contracting the muscles surrounding his horny stick.

"Oh yeah, that feels so good," he moaned appreciatively.

He thrust harder and faster, slamming into my eager mouth with reckless abandon. I was so hot I could hardly stand it. I reached down and gave my wand a quick yank from time to time, a little surprised that I hadn't popped my load yet.

He banged into me, his balls pulling up close to his body as he neared a powerful explosion. I knew it wouldn't be long before I would feel his load erupt, causing the condom to swell in my mouth.

"Suck it man. Take it all," he commanded, forcing my nose into his golden bush and the swollen cock head deep into my gullet. His body tensed and I knew he was about to explode.

"Oh shit," he growled, as his body convulsed with spasm after spasm of ecstasy.

When he was finished coming, he pulled off the used rubber and tossed it into the trash. I handed him a paper towel and he wiped up, while I continued to stare longingly at his naked form.

"You give great head, Jesse," he remarked, looking in my direction.

"I've had a lot of practice, but that's not all I'm good at," I replied, grinning mischievously.

He pretended to be shocked, but leaned over the back of a chair and seductively spread his creamy white butt cheeks. I could see his tiny pink nether mouth winking at me and could hardly wait to get at him.

"You like what you see?" he teased, fingering the tight chamber.

I quickly cloaked my stiff weapon, lubed it with some baby oil, and approached the inviting tunnel. My heart was thumping in my chest, as I pushed the tip of my cock against his stubborn ass-ring. He was tight, but the muscle reluctantly gave way and allowed my length to invade his body.

"Oooh, wow, it's so big," he groaned. "It feels like you're going to tear me apart. Just take it easy," he moaned, as I pushed further into his chute.

I retreated, so that only the very tip of my horny pecker stretched him wide, then slammed back into him. He groaned louder as I repeatedly pulled out, then re-entered him. I plunged deeper into him each time, finally claiming his entire body as my own. My balls were churning, begging for release of their long pent-up wad, but I desperately wanted to prolong this moment.

"Oh yeah, I'm going to fuck you so hard you won't be able to sit down for a week," I growled into his ear.

He continued to groan and beg for mercy, as I banged him with long, slow strokes – driving my meat into his belly with deliberate roughness. I knew I wasn't hurting him nearly as much as he pretended. It was all part of the game. Each time I jabbed into him, I felt his body pushing back, eagerly meeting each movement.

With each thrust, I was getting closer and closer to the moment when my load would be launched into the latex sheath. I slammed harder and faster, while he humped against the back of the chair.

He contracted his ass-muscles around my aching pole, squeezing me until I could hold back no longer. I felt my hot cum coursing through my length, filling the condom within him so that it swelled with its load. I collapsed on top of him, crushing his body against the chair, satisfied at last. "Oh, that was so good," I whispered, kissing his neck. "Yeah," he eagerly agreed. He squirmed beneath me, causing my softening tool to slide from his stretched asshole. "Is it my turn now?"

he asked, smiling. I had been a sexually active gay all my life, had been fucking since I was fifteen, but I'd never been a bottom. I wasn't sure I was quite ready for it. But my sexy, young neighbor was anxious to do it. "I don't know. I've never done that before," I confessed. "Oh man, you don't know what you're missing. It's the most incredible feeling. C'mon, let me show you," he coaxed, slithering out from under me. I stood up and eyed his thick dick, which he was hastily cloaking in a new condom. I wanted to let him fuck me. But I was still a little apprehensive. "I won't hurt you. I promise," he vowed solemnly. "I'll be gentler with you than you were with me," he added, smiling. I smiled back, knowing I could not refuse my handsome Adonis. I took his hand and led him into my bedroom. "I think we'll be more comfortable in here," I said, lying down on the bed and spreading my legs. He stood for a moment, just looking at me. "You've got such a hot body," he remarked, kneeling down on the bed and crawling between my thighs. I closed my eyes, expecting to feel the searing pain as the monstrous cockhead invaded my virgin pussy. Instead I felt his index finger sliding across my uninitiated hole, then pushing gently against the tight muscle-ring. "What are you doing?"

"Stretching you so it doesn't hurt so much. But it'd help if you would relax a little."

"I'll try," I reassured. I took a deep breath, and just as I did, he shoved his finger into my body. It didn't hurt at all. In fact, it felt really good. I relaxed, as he inserted a second, then a third digit into me. "Oh, wow, this is so good," I murmured. "I know," he replied.

He probed my insides, wiggling his fingers and separating them in the confined space. I was enjoying the sensations so much, I was anxious to feel his stiff young cock burrowing into me.

When he had decided I was adequately stretched to receive his massive member, he withdrew his fingers and I watched as he inched closer. I gasped when I felt the cloaked cockhead pushing against the ass-ring. He didn't have to force his way in, though, as the muscle quickly relaxed and allowed him admittance.

"Oh yeah, you're so fucking tight," he moaned. "This is going to be incredible."

He retreated, then carefully re-entered me. As he began to fuck me with slow, deliberate movements, I felt my dick hardening and bouncing against my belly.

"Oh yeah, fuck me hard! Harder!" I pleaded.

I scarcely couldn't believe I was getting so hot. He plunged deeper into me with each thrust, bringing himself closer to climax. Soon his breathing was becoming more ragged and his chest was heaving. I knew it wouldn't be long before he exploded.

The oversized intruder began to slam more recklessly, jabbing harder and faster as the excitement built up within him. His bulging biceps were quivering. The snake within me twitched and jerked. Then his entire body tensed and convulsed as a powerful climax rocked his solid frame.

I shuddered and my juices erupted onto my belly, as I came a second time. He slumped down on top of me, crushing my softening cock between us and smearing the wet, sticky cream.

He mashed his lips against mine, and let his tongue dart into my mouth. I eagerly kissed him back, enjoying the momentary closeness we were sharing. Our kisses were hot and full of passion, and I could sense that he was as reluctant to end our time together as I was. When he finally rolled off me, he looked into my eyes. "I sure am glad I took the apartment across the street. I had my doubts."

"So am I," I replied. "It's been a long time since there have been any young men in this neighborhood. I could hardly believe it when I saw you moving in."

"If you think I'm hot, wait until you meet some of my friends."

"I saw the guys who were helping you move in. If they're just a sample, then I'm really impressed."

He smiled and got up, gathering his clothes from around my apartment. When he was dressed, he turned to me. "Next time, my place. I'll invite my friends over and we'll all have a really good time."

"I can hardly wait," I answered, as he opened the door and headed out.

I watched him out the window, as he crossed the street and went into his apartment. Things were definitely looking up for me. I had already been in heaven. I couldn't imagine how it could get any better.

MAKING EMIL
David MacMillan

I realized just how much Emil had got to me when I opened the door to him that late November afternoon. It was more than simply being happy to see him there, smiling at me as his face swam closer to mine. It was more than his kiss and the feel of his body in the open doorway. It was more than just the sex he so willingly shared.

I was in love with him.

That was dangerous.

I couldn't understand how it happened. I had thought myself so careful.

I was alone and far too aware of it. He was by far the best- looking man I had seen on the promenade the beginning of October. That he was a student at university made him even more attractive – organized intelligence and good looks were a winning combination for me.

It had been his body I wanted that first night I met him, however. His slim, warm body against mine. The pleasure of it accepting my possession of it. The sexual gratification I could give him – that we could give each other.

We lay pressed together beneath the bed cover, a sheen of perspiration on his naked skin the aftermath of our sex. He wiggled his backside against my now subdued manhood and grinned over his shoulder at me. "Am I good?"

"Good as a sexual partner or as a person?" I asked, wallowing in satiation. In less than two months Emil had become my nightly companion. We took long walks. We discussed the world and I learnt from his knowledge. And we always found our way back to my bed to celebrate Eros.

He looked over his shoulder at me, his eyes questioning. "I hadn't thought of how you saw me before," he mumbled doubtfully. "I guess I just assumed...." He hesitated, pulling his thoughts together. "What do you think of me?" he asked finally.

"You're intelligent, handsome, honest, honorable...." I touched his cheek with my fingertip and smiled. "You're independent but willing to share yourself. You see what needs to be done and you do it. And you're someone...."

I looked away. "You're someone with whom I've become very comfortable." I wondered if I could tell him. He was everything I had just named and I had come to love him. But could he accept me? Would he still love me when he knew?

"You mean it?" He turned and reached out to me, pulling me to him.

"I don't lie, Emil." I smiled back at him. "I don't feel I have to."

His lips found mine as his body turned to press closer to mine. His kiss was not one of hunger but a simple, heartfelt thank you.

"You are also someone I've come to care for these two months," I told him moments later when he pulled his face back to smile at me. My fingers absently caressed the closer mound of his buttocks.

"You'll love me yet," he said softly and nuzzled the tip of my nose with his.

"I already do. But will you love me?"

He snorted and pulled away to look back at me. "You've already infected me, Karl von Muribor. I love you. I even want to move in with you."

I gazed at him for moments, studying him and attempting to understand the man who existed beneath the flesh and bones.

I sighed. It was now or never. "If you want to live with me, there's something you have to know." I sat up but held his eyes with mine. I needed to learn if I were going to have to live more years alone. I needed to know my fate now.

"You have AIDS?" he cried, his face draining of color as he stared at me. "Jesus!"

"Worse – or better, depending on how you look at it." He relaxed slightly, but I still felt his tenseness. "I'm a vampire," I told him.

After a long, pregnant pause in which he studied me closely, he forced himself to laugh. "That's not funny, Karl. You frightened me there."

I pushed myself off the bed and stood up, hoping I was doing the right thing. He needed to understand why we never met for lunch or had dinner together. Why I had not already invited him to live with me. Immediately, hair grew over my face as my nose and lips elongated into a snout and my forehead sloped backward to meet my ears.

"God!" He sprang to his feet, dancing to the head of the bed to press against the wall – unable to take his rounded eyes from the wolf I had become. "If you can understand me, change yourself back right now, Karl!" he demanded as he fought to control the fear that surged everywhere through his mind. "Don't do that again!" Meekly, I sat back down on the bed, a nude human male to his eyes once again. He still stood and hugged the wall, tensed for flight, looking as if he'd fly from me if I said a word. I understood it was not the time to pull him to me and hold him. "You're really a...."

"A vampire," I finished for him.

Moments stretched into minutes with him cowering at the head of the bed staring at me in disbelief, mingling with fear. He shook his head now, forcing his rigid, cramped muscles to relax. I nodded.

"You go out in the sunlight...."

"In late afternoon, in the winter, when the heat is minimal."

"You drink blood, do you?" I nodded. "From humans?" I nodded again. "You haven't touched me."

"1 love you, Emil. I feed on derelicts, men already mentally and emotionally dead."

He collapsed then, crumpling defenselessly on the bed. "I loved you," he groaned, tears welling in his eyes. "I gave myself to you – you're the first man who ever ... I didn't even believe all that stuff about God and Satan." He looked at me, shook his head as if to clear it, and said: "And look what happened, I fall in love with somebody who's sold himself to the Archfiend."

"But I am not evil. I'm just a human who's transformed into something different. Something more advanced."

"Is that all?" He calmed slowly, his fear receding before the reality of my placid demeanor. "You aren't going to take my soul or anything?"

"I wouldn't hurt you if my life depended on it."

He slowly moved to sit beside me, watching me carefully as he did so.

"I don't want your soul or your life – nothing but your love," I told him and only then touched him, two of my fingers drawing circles on his thigh.

"Do I need a cross or something?" he asked hesitantly.

"If you wish to wear one." I grinned in spite of myself as I continued: "Would you permit me to buy it and give it to you?"

"Jesus," he groaned and fell into his own thoughts and, I hoped, sought a way he could accept me.

"One of the American writers makes it seem sex can be a lot more fun with one of you nipping at a guy's neck," he offered finally, trying a smile that was much too tight to fit his face.

I chuckled. "I wouldn't know. I've never fed and made love at the same time, but I expect that writer wasn't overly accurate."

"I'm going to have to learn to live with this, aren't I?" I nodded. He shivered and shut his eyes. "Hold me, Karl. Show me this is going to be all right."

We strolled the Platt promenade along the east side of the Stihl in the old town of Zurich across from the university. The air was brisk even for the beginning of December. Emil huddled in his parka, his hands deep in its lined pockets. I wore my great coat open, relishing the wet chill against my thin clothes.

"Why haven't you bitten me?" he asked, breaking the silence that had held us since leaving the flat. His eyes were on the river, his neck stiff in his refusal to turn to face me.

"Because I love you. Because I don't want you to die."

He turned then. "Die? I'm going to grow old, my skin wrinkling, my hair falling out – arthritis even. I'll die all right – and you'll still be young, won't you?"

I nodded and we lapsed back into the silence that held us together but which kept us so far apart.

We passed through the small park at the northern tip of the Promenade, the bow of this small island splitting the river in two. We moved along the side that faced the great buildings of government and business across the river.

"I don't want to grow old, Karl." He stopped and faced me, his eyes finding mine and holding them. "I don't want to die." His eyes shut and he turned away from me again. "Make me like you."

"There's so much of life ... don't make a choice now that means you give it up."

"Do you really love me?" He whirled back and faced me. "Really?" I nodded. "Then, make me like you."

I smiled. "Enjoy your youth, Emil, share as much of it with me as you will, but see your world before you decide. Experience life. Taste the warm haze of a summer day here in this park. Enjoy good food. I'll be here when you know you want what I am."

He frowned. "What happens if you aren't around when I'm forty and old?"

I chuckled. "I'll be with you."

"Yeah...."

I sensed his doubt but chose simply to put my arm about his shoulders and was rewarded by his hand slipping inside my greatcoat to circle my waist.

The sun of late December had set beyond the windows when I awoke a fortnight later. Lust filled Emil's eyes as it did his member when he slipped under the covers to lie naked beside me.

"I've been wanting this all afternoon," he breathed against my ear as he straddled me and melded his body along the length of mine, his teeth nibbling at my ear lobe, his body moving sultrily against mine. "You're going to be my Yuletide present tonight."

Our lips met and his tongue darted between them, between my teeth, into my mouth. He began to worry my fangs with it.

Smiling, he pushed up on his knees. "Bite me while we're doing it, Karl. Drink my blood."

"You're way up there," I observed, sloughing his request away.

My erection pressed against his entrance and my hand formed a fist around him. He smiled down at me. "Bite me." His voice was insistent as he forced our coupling.

"Why?" It was increasingly difficult to think logically as my member pushed into his warmth. I pulled the prepuce over his wide knob and held it closed there.

"It's supposed to make sex even better. I want to know if it's true." He ground his backside against my thatch and sighed.

He achieved as much union as I was capable of providing and bent along my body to kiss me, groaning: "Bite me now, Karl. Drink from me."

He pressed himself against my chest, his nipples hard against me, and moved his head that I could reach his neck easily. My fangs scratched across the exposed skin and he groaned. "Do it. Do it now," he mumbled near my ear. His lower body ground around my manhood inside him, his bollocks hard against my abdomen, his cock tight against his.

I bit him, shallow punctures just above the clavicle.

He gasped. His arms went around my chest, holding me tighter, forcing his neck closer to my lips. His hips grew still around me and I humped his spread asscheeks to take up our sex where he had left it. "Let's turn over, Liebchen," he whispered against my ear. "I want you real deep tonight. I want you on top of me."

We maneuvered about, him falling in beside me and me rolling onto him, my manhood penetrating deeper into him as I settled over him. His hips moved against me, grinding his pole against me as I pushed into him. My hips instinctively worked against his open backside. My body relished the touch of his along the lengths of our bodies.

My fangs dug deeper as the rest of my body took over the mechanics of our sex; that he not move, that he lie beneath me and I drink from him.

My hips moved against his open backside, my buttocks flexing. My manhood ploughed him slowly and deeply.

Emil ground against my every thrust and tightened the walls of his canal to grip at me each time I pulled from him. His knees rode his ribs as he leaked his anticipation. My lips covered his wound and I drank as greedily as my organ possessed his lower regions.

His body shuddered against mine and his seed erupted between us. Mindlessly, I continued to plough his spasming canal and drank from him. "Keep doing it, Karl," he gasped against my cheek. "I want to come again."

I was beyond thought. The pleasure of our union consumed me. His hard member riding my stomach pushed me to greater heights. The taste of him pulled me into our coupling further than I had ever known a man.

I smiled in victory as he came the second time, his seed spreading between our joined chests.

I slipped from him and collapsed against the bed, exulting in what I knew was the best sex I had had in a hundred and fifty years.

Emil's continued gasping pulled at me slowly, demanding my attention. In nearly three months of daily sex, I had never seen him so excited that his breathing continued to be labored. I studied him more closely, the languid aftermath of sex evaporating as I accepted his ashen pallor.

I had drunk too much. I bit him as he had first begun to ride me. I had licked and slurped as he worked his way through two orgasms. How long?

More importantly, how much?

I was no longer hungry as I lay beside him and studied him. Yet, our afternoon sex normally left me craving the hunt – though I always forced the desire from me that I could be with him. The deeply bruised skin of his slender neck, the jagged wounds no more than two centimeters from his clavicle told me what I did not want to know.

I had drunk far too much. There was nothing wrong with Emil's breathing, except his lungs were instinctively laboring to pull more oxygen into them to compensate for the loss of blood that normally carried it to the cells of his body. I had taken that blood. Far too much.

His color was waxen, his breathing remained rapid and labored. I sensed his thoughts becoming kaleidoscopic, whirling about dizzily.

I concentrated upon my study of him, attempting to avoid what I knew was true. I had known these physical reactions since I first fed on fresh blood – as I had the feverish pitch of his increasingly jumbled thoughts. He was dying – slowly enough he had yet to realize it.

Lieber Emil, what have I done to you?

I had stolen his innocence and his youth. Never again would he walk along sunlit paths and enjoy mortal beauties. Never again would his seed spray over another he loved enough to give himself. I had given him mortal death.

I knew what I must do. I had to give him a new life before his old one was completely gone. I had to give him what he once asked and tie him to me for eternity.

Without thinking, I pushed myself up on my pillows until my chest was even with his face. With the middle finger of my left hand, I pulled back skin and flesh and cartilage, opening a hole between my ribs so close to the sternum it too was partially exposed and I felt the chill of the room's air upon the exposed bone.

I leaned toward him, lifting his head with my right hand and bringing his lips to my breast. With my fingernail I nicked the vein behind the bone and pressed his lips to the hole now open to my heart. To my blood now seeping out onto my chest.

He sucked greedily. Instinctively. As a newborn baby sucks at its mother's breast. I became weaker and looked to see if his pallor had begun to change. This was my first effort to create another vampire; I only knew he had to have my blood to survive. I didn't know how much he needed – or how weakened I must become that he be saved.

An effervescent glow developed quickly on his skin, the coarseness of his mortal derma smoothing out and becoming even as he ceased being human and became more. I shuddered as the room dimmed perceptively to my eyes while weakness continued to grow over me.

I listened in the silence of the room and found his breathing was not as labored as it had been. I willed my vein closed and pulled away, falling against my pillows. Emil moaned as my blood transformed him, raising his head slightly and opening strangely clouded eyes. I moved closer and helped him lay his head on my chest.

I watched his transformation in the last rays of the weak winter sun. My strength returned as his breathing slowed and became shallow – normal for a vampire at rest.

I held Emil and hoped he would love me tomorrow as he had today. He would have much to forgive when he awakened – beginning with the mortal youth I had stolen from him

.

MEMBER OF THE TEAM
Thomas Wagner

We had just won the championship volleyball competition for our state. Since I was captain of the team, the guys lifted me on their shoulders all the way to the locker room. I'd always been wary about revealing my horny proclivities, so I got a little jittery in response to my excitement, feeling all those well-built shoulders under my ass gave me a wicked hard-on.

One guy in particular drove me wild: my blond, all-American teammate, Rob. His body is muscular and hairless, and he is well-hung to boot. I was always afraid to come on to him and ruin our friendship, but many a night I spent whacking off imagining his full mouth sucking me off.

At that moment, I lost my balance as they lowered me onto the cold locker-room bench. My pronounced erection jabbed right into Rob's face. I didn't know if he would clobber me or not, but Rob didn't look a bit angry. I thought I noticed a horny look instead, but I wasn't sure but what was pure wishful thinking on my part.

All the guys except Rob and I were in a hurry to go celebrate our big win with their waiting girlfriends, so we lingered in the showers together. My heart beat wildly long with my growing woody. I was also growing confident he wanted to celebrate with me in a much more personal way. And so I took a chance that I was right.

"Rob, you didn't mind the way my boner got in your face before, did you?" I asked, turning around and fully exposing my cock's stiffness as the hot water created a steamy atmosphere for the two of us.

"No, not if you give me a closer look at it, now," he quipped with a devilish smile.

He took immediate advantage of our isolation and moved toward me like a tiger stalking his prey. His glistening body brought out my deepest animal instincts. And a virtual growl emitted from my throat just anticipating his touch.

Rob was now so close that I could hear his heavy breathing as he bent to give my earlobe a nip. He licked his way down my neck, and I reacted by pulling his sizzling body close to mine and digging my fingers into his taut back muscles. Our nipples wrestled with one another like two hot pokers.

"Jeez, I've wanted you for so long. Your body's been driving me so crazy, I can't think any more," I said, wrenching my neck back as the water flowed down my aching body.

"I've wanted you just as much but I was afraid you were straight and then you'd kick the shit out of me. Let me make it up to you. You'll forget about it," he answered, making hickeys all along my torso.

Then his eager mouth sucked in my right nipple as his left hand tweaked and pulled at my right one. My limbs went limp and I bent over making nasty bites along his broad shoulders. Rob groaned with pleasure as he licked his way down my torso to my burning groin

Finally, he lowered himself to his knees. The steaming water washed over us like a sun shower. Rob brushed his hands all over my shaky legs. His hands caressed my upper and inner thighs and steadied them so I wouldn't fall over.

But this massage-like touching quickly wore on my patience. I got hold of his head and ran my fingers through his sweat- matted hair, nudging his head towards my by now painful erection. I thrust my hips into his face.

It was then he got the fantastic close-up view that he'd asked for. My blue-veined shaft glistened with a dewy drop of pre- cum and seemed to grow bigger by the moment. The dark fuzz that covered my balls looked matted like a playful otter bouncing up against his adorable face.

Rob's nose nudged my hairs, as the water cascaded over him making his body shine in the dim light. His tongue flicked ruthlessly along my bloated base and then returned to the reddish, swelling balls. He tongued my juicy nuts into his mouth, munching on them gently at first, then more hungrily.

His fingers got their first touch of my drenched ass crack that had the feel. Rob sighed as he felt my crevice. He spread my cheeks roughly with his other hand and continued to tongue my bobbing dick.

"Oh, yes, Rob. Do it hard. Swallow it, man. Swallow it all!" I hissed, then let my voice trail off in a series of loud grunts.

"I'll do you the way I've been dying to since I set eyes on you, captain."

In response, I smashed my groin into his upturned mouth while he was in mid-sentence. He sucked the pre-cum off of me, savoring the fresh tang, and constantly poked at my tender tip with his energized tongue. He was so cock hungry he could have eaten me alive.

This was not enough for me. I rammed all my weight into him, shoving my fat prick farther into his throat further. He took it down with a stronger gulp, sucking and licking it. I thrust my hips with a quick rhythm, like his mouth was my instrument.

"Yea, you got it. Suck it deep, college boy. Nothing like sex education instead of all that sports stuff."

In no time he took up the pace. I fucked even faster, holding his head as he pulled at my hairs, pounding his face with my meat. Then my thrusts became unpredictable like his ragged breathing. He wedged his finger at the rim of my hole. Then as I rammed him again, he shoved it into my contracting chute t as far as it could go.

He definitely hit a bull's eye because I groaned and thrashed my head back and forth like a madman. After that he gave my balls a tough fist squeeze and I felt them start to unload in his tightening grip.

"I'm there, man. Don't stop. Oh, yes! Yes! Yes!"

Just as I started to yell, my load let loose deep into his slime -thirsty throat. He swallowed load after load of my warm jizz that deluged his throat in spurts and then in more continuous streams. I kept up the volleys, unloading so fast he almost gagged. But I still kept up the tempo.

He guzzled and slurped my juices until I'd totally emptied out. I kept fucking his wet throat though, just for the feel of it. It was like some moist tropical rain forest for my private use. I just kept fucking.

I slowly pulled out of his mouth and squirted my last drops of cum across his face as I stared at his purple swollen dick. It bobbed back and forth like a cobra enchanted by the snake charmer. His enormous bloated balls gleamed.

I wiped my dick all over his boyish face. And he became pliant as a kitten this time around, waiting for me to touch him. I felt heady with the power my head had over him. I bent over as Rob kneeled at my feet like a beggar praying to be given something to get him through the night.

Then I heard him groan; he made small spasmodic pushes and his groin rose to meet my manhandling, like a horse to its master. I could feel the hot blood whirring through his bloated limb, filing him further and making him grow with every jack- off move I provided. Rob's little movements quickened as did his rapid breathing.

I jerked him of with harder strokes with my right hand. With my left hand I clamped on his balls, gripping them roughly in a tight squeeze. Then he managed to glide my now re- hardened dick back into his mouth. He grunted like a wild pig in between his fervent sucks.

I gripped him as tightly as I could and went the length of him, using all the increased power my weight lifting had developed. His skin almost flew off from my intense exertions. His knees dug into the concrete.

But every painful sensation only increased his dick power and he fucked my hand like the wild beast he was, bucking and twisting and thrusting away. His tight ass bobbed up and down, his fat balls smacked up against his flesh.

After that, I saw the pre-cum began to trickle down his inflated rod. Rob held on to the back of my thighs in order to balance himself. His grip became stronger as he grew closer to coming.

My dick had inflated in his skillful jaws once again as if I hadn't come seconds ago. I started to pound his face for the second coming and I liked the way my body took over my entire spirit. I held onto his shoulders and pumped like crazy, until I felt a giant load descending.

"Yes, Rob. I'm there. Suck it up, man. Faster, Rob, faster. Now! Now! Now!"

Then I blew my load into his mouth. He sucked me down hard. Rob worked even harder this time. He just had to have my juices oozing down him for another go. I felt his throat contract and swallow wad after wad. I couldn't believe I had any left, let alone a whole water-slide of the stuff.

I kept jacking him off in the meantime. Then in seconds his cock went off like a geyser which blew all over all over his chest and neck and even on his chin and face. Some of his jizz flew onto my balls as well.

I pulled off his mouth. He started to rasp, "Oh, yes! Yes! Yes," until only a dribble dripped down his softening dickhead.

He dutifully licked off my balls and dick one last time without my even asking him for special favors and then looked at me with a cum-stained face – all smiles, as if he'd just won the championship all over again.

I got hold of his ears and brought his head into my groin for a hug. "You're unbelievable. Promise me we can go on with this and you won't back away from me."

"Spike, there's too many positions I need to get right before I stop spiking you, which reminds me...."

Rob started licking my ass to prepare for the spike he had in mind, and that was only the beginning of a winning season of a different kind!

STUDY BUDDIES
Chad Morgan

Not many of the guys where I go to school are gay. Or at least they aren't out enough for me to tell who they are. Last year there were a couple of guys I'd see around, and we'd meet up once in a while to get off, especially when our roommates were gone for a weekend. But this year when I walk across campus, I'm always on the lookout, but I don't see them. So now I watch faces as much as anything else, looking for eye contact that will let me know there could be more to it. I want to make a connection with some of them. And stuck out here with no car and no easy way to get to town makes it hard to find men who want the same things I do.

So last Friday it was raining, and I was on my way to the library. Yeah, on Friday, and I was going to do some work. That tells you what my social life is like. Nowhere. It was raining, pouring, in fact, and I had no umbrella. I headed for the library doors with my hand against my forehead, trying to shield my eyes from the rain. I looked like I was scouting for the Indians to come over the hill with my favorite sidekick. All of a sudden I felt a poke in my arm. Some guy was putting his bumbershoot down and I was in the way. "Oh, excuse me," he said. I looked at his face, then closer at his eyes. Brown, deep-set, friendly. He looked straight into mine.

"Not a problem," I answered as I tried to shake off some of the water. I felt like I should shake like a spaniel that's just retrieved a duck from the lake.

Holding the door for the guy, I went in behind him and walked to the second floor. When I got to my study carrel, I took off my soaking-wet jacket to let it dry. I looked for the book on economics my professor recommended. There was nearly no one else in the library. And why should there be? Friday was either for going home or going to parties on campus. The parties, with their overindulgent freshmen and sophomore drinkers, didn't interest me, and going home meant changing buses three times, then walking the last couple of miles. No,

I'd tough it out at the library, and worry about socializing in another lifetime.

I sat down in my study space, and who should come along but Mr. Umbrella, soggy wet in spite of his precautions. His back was to me, a wide-shouldered torso in dripping jacket, also wearing sodden shorts and squishy sandals. He was browsing the shelves and, maybe, glancing toward me.

"Hey, man," I said. "What are we doing here on Friday afternoon when the rest of the campus is either going home or headed for a fiesta?"

"Oh, yeah," he said, recognizing me. "Right. Well, I've got a paper due Monday and nowhere else to go, so why not?" Where has this guy been? I thought. He's a hunk, and he's got nowhere to go? Maybe his tootsie dumped him. Hmm, no, couldn't be. No, he couldn't be gay. I'd have seen him somewhere. He turned to look at me and our eyes locked. "Have I seen you around here before?" he asked.

Great line, I thought, but I couldn't think fast enough. "I just transferred here from out of state. I doubt that we've met. I'd remember if we had."

An opening so wide I could drive through it. "Well, I'd remember you too. Uh, you want to get a pizza when you've finished your work here?"

"Sounds good to me. I've got to find a book my history prof wants me to read."

He went off to search the shelves, and I tried to study, but my imagination was racing ahead of me and I couldn't concentrate. We'd spend the night in my room, since my roomie had gone home for the weekend, and I'd let loose some of this jism I've been saving far too long. I was up and hard already, just thinking of sticking my tool up that obviously tight butt of his. Legs like those should be wrapped around my neck, not doing mundane things like walking around libraries. I almost smacked my lips just thinking about it.

I got up to go to the john, hoping no one would see the stiff pole under my pants. I'd have to relieve myself a little while I was in there. It had been far too long since I'd had an encounter. I thought to myself that I'd better check while I was there to see if I had any supplies with me.

The doors were open except for one. And there, under the door, were those soggy sandals of Mr. Umbrella's. "Hey, man, is that you? The umbrella guy?"

He opened the stall door, and there he was, sitting on the throne, his scepter in hand. "Come on in. I was hoping you'd find your way in here."

The size of that scepter was simply amazing. I fell to my knees in awe, taking it out of his hands, swathing it in a rubber I fortunately had in my wallet, and putting it into my mouth, way in. Oh, yeah, oh yeah, much too long.

His cock filled up the rubber so that it was taut, and I could feel the ridge of his cockhead, no problem. I ran my teeth up and down lightly, then got to work.

I took some time toying with his piss-slit, which I could feel flexing and gaping underneath the sheer latex. He groaned as I flicked my tongue surely and silently along the long underside of his cock and felt ripples of sensation echo throughout his hot body as he moaned and humped his hips to the beat of my cock-worship.

With a gasp, he yanked my face right up against his crotch and slid his fingers through my hair. At that point, I finally gave in, opened my mouth wide, and gradually inhaled every throbbing inch of that fleshy baton. I slid my throat over his cockhead like a sheath taking its sword, all the while curling my tongue around his flange, along the underside of that softly pulsing vein, and then back down his shaft until I felt his rigid bulb shoving the condom down into the depths of my throat. Fighting back a gag, I began to bob my head up and down along its rocky, pulsating length.

"Oh, man, that's the way," he cooed, scrubbing his hand up and down the back of my head while I sucked and sucked, taking him into my mouth and throat as far as I could, massaging him with every muscle I had in my gullet.

Meanwhile Mr. Umbrella was moaning in pleasure. He'd spread his legs far apart and pushed his body forward, holding the sides of the stall. He was having a good time. He dug his hands under the neck of my shirt and massaged my shoulders.

"Man, oh man, that's good," he said. "Suck me harder, will you? Bite down on the tip."

I did more than that. I reached back and stuck my longest finger in his anus and probed until he responded with a louder moan. It was the magic button.

When he finally got off, he bucked and jumped, and I could feel the hot cum fill up the tip of the rubber. I wanted to rip it off of him and wipe it all over my chest right there in the can.

Straightening his clothes, Jim (I couldn't go on calling him Mr. Umbrella) said, "Hey, that was OK. What are we going to do for you?"

Just then some skinny guy who looked like he worked in the library came in, tried to ignore us, and went into one of the stalls.

Out of earshot, I said, "I want you to ram that pole up me. I want to feel that chunk of flesh up my ass." His orgasm had done nothing to reduce the size of my own shaft, which now thundered for relief. I didn't know how we'd make it to my room before I exploded.

"I'll certainly try to accommodate," he said with a big grin. "Shall we leave now? "

"1 thought you had to find a book. Maybe we could go between the bookshelves and get it on, even though that would be risking discovery even more than in the bathroom. Probably it would be some bitch; she'd report us and we'd get bounced out of school."

"First things first."

We walked back to my carrel. I could see out the window that the already dark day had already gotten darker. It was nearly night. Six-thirty, I thought. The library would close by eight. A sofa at the end of the big room was empty of course, since no one else was around. "I've got an idea," I said. "Let's go down here."

Jim looked at me skeptically, but followed. I threw down my jeans and kneeled on the sofa, my ass sticking out toward the book shelves. He didn't need any other invitation. His thick rod was out of his pants and sheathed in rubber before you could say turn the page....

72

He spit on it for lube and entered me, pumping gently at first and then thrusting harder as my asshole became more used to him. I wanted to scream with pleasure, but we were in a library, after all. The rhythm of his thrusting was rocking me back and forth, and I got higher and higher until I shot off a wad that slopped off onto the sofa beneath me. Meanwhile, I could feel Jim's movements getting jumpier, less steady. I knew that he was about to get off too, and all of a sudden I felt the man's pole heat up inside me. He jerked and spasmed and then pulled out, leaving me wanting a whole lot more but temporarily satisfied. I rolled over onto the sofa and dragged

him down on top of me.

"Well, I guess if we get caught, we get caught. We haven't thought too much about that so far," he said. I wondered how much longer we'd be alone, if I could get him face down on the sofa while I banged his poop deck.

"Can't you just imagine what someone's going to think finding a big unidentified stain on the sofa?" I asked.

"Yep, if they knew what it was, the freshman girls would think they'd get pregnant if they sat here."

We both laughed at that.

"I don't think I'm going to get a lot more done tonight," I said. "Let's stop for a pizza and go to my room."

"Hey, that sounds like a plan to me."

No sooner had he stood up than the skinny librarian strolled through the room, watching Jim zip his pants and me look for my shoes.

"Well, at least we weren't making noise or disturbing the other library patrons. I don't think there are any explicit library rules about 'No Screwing' in the library."

"Let's get out of here before that guy invents one. I don't think he likes us," Jim offered. "On the other hand, maybe he wants to play too."

"Oh, no thanks. I don't think he's my type."

He smiled at that.

We walked back by my carrel so I could pick up my books. Jim grabbed the volume I'd been reading. "That's it," he said. "You've got the book I was supposed to find."

"Great! We can share it," I offered, slinging my still-damp book bag over my arm.

The rain had finally stopped, and as we walked back across campus through the puddles, it seemed like I'd always known Jim. But, too, it was going to be good getting to know him. It was even better that I wasn't alone on campus. Somebody else here shared my interests – and not just in books! Yeah, maybe this wouldn't be such a bad year after all.

CHERRY FARMER
Jason Carpenter

I climbed down off Dad's new 1974 Ford tractor and wiped the sweat from my face with an already soggy handkerchief. My blue coveralls were pasted to my ass and my balls were tingly with sweat. The green beans had provided a good crop, but now it was time to ready the soil for fall planting. I unbuttoned my fly and took a whiz, never suspecting I wasn't alone in the field until a voice called out from behind me. "Hey, can you tell me where the nearest gas station is?" I turned, startled, my uncut cock still dangling from my fingers. The dark-haired, good-looking stranger appeared exhausted. He carried a gasoline can. His eyes drifted to my meat and stayed there for an instant. "Uh, sorry," I said, folding myself back into my denims. He nodded. "Ran out of gas up the road and started walking. Saw your tractor and thought I'd better ask directions." I ran my callused fingers through my thatch of shaggy, straw-colored hair. "Closest place is five miles."

"Damn!" He spat, wobbling in his tracks. I handed him my water jug. "Have some water before you get a heat stroke." He gulped greedily. "Whoa! You'll get sick," I told him, taking the jug from his hands. Water spilled down the front of his white shirt. It clung to his muscled chest. "Tell you what... I was about to go back to the house for lunch. You can ride with me and I'll fill your gas can from our supply."

"Great. Will we both fit on the tractor?"

"Tight, but possible." I helped him up first. He slipped a little and I pushed his tight butt with the palms of my hands until he got into the concave seat. I could see his wad of balls through the cloth of his pants. When I got up beside him I noticed a bulge in his slacks. His eyes followed my gaze and he smiled. "Amazing, isn't it. An inch away from a heat stroke and still able to get a boner."

"Maybe you need another kind of stroke," I suggested, reaching over to rub his prick.

"Oh, shit, man, I've never been with a guy before," he sighed.

"Mmmm, good," I said, putting his hand on my own cock.

Happily, he stroked me as diligently as I stroked him. I kissed him deeply.

We unzipped and unbuttoned each other until our cocks were standing tall and hard. I bent and took his salty meat in my mouth and gobbled him down until his pubic hair touched my lips. I came up slowly and ran my tongue all around the head and down the underside of his lovely circumcised poker. He wasn't real long, but he was nice and thick.

I let my fingers trail beneath his shirt, pinching his nipples and caressing his flat, hard stomach. He pushed my head down and fucked my mouth with long, fast strokes. No problem. I took all of him down my throat and, when he arched upward and I knew he was about to come, I ate him greedily, bobbing up and down until the first flush of creamy jizz spewed out of him. Then I sucked as hard as I could, pulling cum from his balls and cleaning his pipes.

"Ahhh! Ahhh!" He cried out as I blew him expertly. He fell back against the metal seat. His cock was red and well-used. "Fuck,' that was good!"

"Well, slip your pants down and pay me back," I told him, unfastening the straps on my coveralls and pulling them to my knees.

"Is it gonna hurt?" he asked, his brown eyes wide with fear.

"Just for a second, but I'll be careful getting your cherry, sugar.

When he got his pants down I scooted beneath him and wormed my seeping, throbbing nine inches up his incredibly tight rectum until the crown was way up in his hot guts. "Dear heaven, you've got a big dick!" he said, at first trying to pull up off my monster sword, then relaxing and letting his bubble ass settle into my lap. He began to move up and down on me in slow strokes. I switched on the tractor and shuddered as it roared and vibrated mightily, sending a pleasant sensation up through my balls.

"Hold on!" I yelled, popping the clutch and starting forward down the rows.

I steered with one hand and held my new friend around the waist as the tractor bounced along. Every jolt slammed my erection deeper up his dark passage. The heady smell of man-shit mixed with the rich scent of the freshly turned soil.

"Je ... Jesus!" He cried out as my cock speared far up his taut hole.

I moved my hand to his jizz dribbling cock and fisted him, straining to stuff more and more of me up him.

Then an idea struck me.

I turned the tractor so I would be running over the heaped rows instead of between them. The big tires bounced and fell, making the tractor jump inches above the ground with each row I crossed. My cock pistoned fast and extraordinarily deeply up my friend's cum-chute, reaming out every inch of his sweet insides. His virgin ass stretched to accommodate my cock.

Unable to hold back, I arched my bare butt off the seat and nearly passed out when an enormous gush and spurt of hot, liquid fire spewed out my cock-slit and up his clenching asshole.

At the same instant, I felt his load spew out over my fist and I jacked him off hard. We melded into one, connected by our flesh.

I stopped the tractor and stayed up his hole until my cock shrank out of him. He turned and kissed me on the lips, his tongue reaming the inside of my mouth.

"So, how was it?" I asked, pulling up my coveralls.

"Wonderful. I'd always wondered ... He smiled shyly.

I helped him get his clothes together and headed for the house. The truck was gone from the yard, telling me Pa was off on one errand or another. Ma passed on a couple years back, leaving her two men to care for themselves.

As we climbed down from the tractor I stuck out my hand, thinking it funny that I'd fucked the guy before we even introduced ourselves. "I'm Jack Crown."

He took my hand in his. "Tom Billings. From Waco, Texas."

"What are you doing in Spring Up, Nebraska, Tom?"

"I have relatives in Oregon. Thought I'd visit them for a while."

We went up the stairs to the porch and walked into the house. The screen door banged shut behind me. Within minutes I'd fixed us both a huge ham sandwich and a tall glass of iced tea. We scarfed the food down ravenously.

"Listen," Tom started, hesitantly. "Could I maybe, uh, do to you what you did to me?"

"Screw me, you mean?"

I nodded.

"Well, sure. Why not. Come on up to my room."

Minutes later we were both freshly showered and naked. Tom admired my high school mementos, trophies and such from my football days. I stepped up, took his balls in my hand and kneaded them gently. "Come on ... do me."

"Can I fuck you straight up – like, facing you?" He asked, a bit uncertain of the mechanics involved.

"Sure. Look," I said, laying on the bed, atop the down comforter Mom made. I lifted my legs and held my nuts out of the way until I knew Tom could see my blond-furred asshole.

"It's so small, and sexy."

"It'll stretch ... even to take that big hunk of meat of yours."

Tom crawled up between my thighs. He held his cock in his fingers and rubbed his crown around my ass-ring until I opened enough for him to get an inch up me. He braced himself on both palms and thrust forward, pushing his love muscle into my dark desert. I squirmed beneath him as his thick cock slid against my prostate, making my cock swell to its full length.

Suddenly he shoved hard, burying his bone all the way. I draped my knees over his strong shoulders and tightened my sphincter muscles. He cried out in delight. My cock rubbed against his belly and I gripped his ass with my fingers and pulled him deeper until I felt his hot cum splash my insides, bathing me with his cum. Simultaneously, I shot a creamy ribbon of cum up between our sliding, writhing bodies. The scent of cum filled the air. Tom collapsed between my legs, kissing my nipples and licking at my flesh.

"Eat me, Tom! Please, show me you can suck cock," I taunted.

He tugged his cock out of my ass with a sucking sound and went down on me, licking away the cum that bubbled out my slit. His full lips engulfed me and I felt my cockhead rub the back of his throat and beyond.

I rolled, taking Tom with me, until his head was on the mattress and I straddled his face. I slowly fucked his mouth, rubbing the crown of my cock around his lips, then into his mouth and deeper. He stuck out his tongue and I squeezed out a drop of jizz for him. He savored it then said, "Give me your big load!"

I started slowly, not wanting to choke him with my nine inches, then increased the speed and depth of my thrusts. His brown eyes went wide when I put all my meat down his gullet and throat-fucked him until my balls ached. A load of cum built in my nuts, surged up my dickshaft like a raging torrent and gushed in a splattering explosion of spunk down his throat. He sucked and gulped, drinking down every drop and drawing more and more from my nuts until I thought they would collapse.

He finished me off with a few gentle licks and a kiss on the tip of my cock.

We lay side-by-side, embracing, our cocks touching, as Tom pushed my hair out of my eyes. "Thank you," he said, looking into my eyes as though he could see my thoughts.

"You're very welcome. Not every day I get a cherry. Especially not off a guy as cute as you," I told him sincerely.

Just then I heard Pa's truck pull into the yard. Tom and I rolled out of bed, hurriedly dressed and dashed down the stairs like a couple of kids playing tag. We reached the hallway just as Pa walked in.

He looked at us for a second then said simply, "Fields ain't gonna plow themselves, Jack."

"I know. Pa. Just came in for a bite to eat and to get some gasoline for Tom here. He ran out on the road and was about to croak from the heat when he saw me. Being neighborly, Pa ... the way you taught me."

"Okay, son, go about your business. I'll see you at supper."

I filled Tom's gas can from the tank out by the bam and took him back across the field to his car.

Looking to make sure no one was coming, I took him in my arms and kissed him, fondling his golf ball-size cods in my hand. "If you're ever back this way...."

He slipped his hand down my coveralls, caressed my cock and balls then withdrew his hand and took a long sniff of his palm. "I'll be back and, until I return. I'll save my asshole just for you."

I waved after him as he drove away, a veil of dust hiding

him from view.

There was still plenty of light left and the fertile soil had to be tended to properly, so I cranked the tractor and started where I'd left off earlier, but this time filled with pleasant memories to help me pass the time.

MARRIED BILLY
Mario Solano

I usually don't get involved with married men, I like my men a little more innocent. Actually, I like my men a lot more innocent, I like to pick my men from the tree like I would pick a ripe juicy peach. I don't like to send my men home to their wives with my dander on their dick and I don't like the possibilities of where they may have put that thing last. As a confirmed homo, pussy turns me off. The mini-affair with Billy happened by accident. Maybe it was his gold hoop earring, or maybe it was the fact that he teaches children's theater, which makes him behave and appear youthful. Blame it on the Bossa Nova. Blame it on my youth. Blame it on the fact that I am a sexophile. Actually, there is no blame, and no apologies. It happened and I'm deliriously happy that it did. From now on I am not going to think twice about having sex with married men. Billy has converted me. I am now the other woman, so to speak, the mistress, the home wrecker – and the only difference between me and those other two-timing gals is, I have a big dick!

Now you have to understand the relationship here; Billy and I are "summer neighbors." We rent small cottages by the beach. I live alone and Billy lives with his wife and young daughter. On the property, directly outside my kitchen window, is an outdoor shower which is delightful. The shower area is enclosed by a rickety picket fence with an even more rickety swinging door. There's a rule about the shower. Whoever is taking a shower has to lower a bamboo shade which actually covers my kitchen window. That is, unless they want me to watch them. Up until today that has never happened. Today, I guess Billy wants me to watch him, because he left the shade up.

There's nothing quite like taking a shower under the summer sky, after a hot day at the beach, at sunset time or beneath a sky full of twinkling stars. A few feet away from the shower is a communal clothesline. I go outside to hang my bathing suit and beach towel on the line. I notice that Billy is watching me with that hungry look in his eye. I walk into the enclosure.

"Nice dick," I comment. Billy looks down at his cock, up at me and smiles. "I write erotica. I have described many penises, in great detail. And I must say, yours is something to behold."

"Think so?" He bends his knees and holding his dick out to look at it.

"I know so. It's big, fat and perfectly cut. In the biz, we call that a mushroom head. Does it get bigger when it gets hard? Or does it stay the same size?"

"It gets twice as big and twice as fat."

"I'd love to see that."

"I'll show you," Billy says as he yanks on the head and strokes the shaft.

"Here, this might help." I hand Billy a plastic bottle of liquid soap.

Water streams out of the shower nozzle. Billy turns his back to the water and gives me a side view of his body. He is right. His dick has grown into a huge cock with a juicy looking mushroom head. My towel drops to the slats. My cock is so hard it hurts. It throbs, slaps my belly, then dangles like a sausage in a butcher shop. Billy turns his head to look at me.

"You ain't so bad yourself," he says. His tongue hangs out of his mouth as if he is hungry.

I had spent the day at the nude beach and I was horny. I love going there and what turns me on most is when guys look at me with lust on their lips. It was like that today. Guys were staring at me and whispering to each other about me. I could tell. I guess I'm not too bad to look at. I'm pretty athletic so my body is good. Not buff, but not bad either. I'm five-ten and a hundred and fifty pounds. My hair is normally dark brown but I've been rubbing lemon juice into it so there are blond highlights. My eyes are dark brown and set very far apart. My nose flares a little at the nostrils and my lips are perfectly round. Thanks to my expensive dentist, my teeth are pearly white and I like to smile and show them off. My cock is one of those dicks that starts off small but, as it gets hard, it gets bigger and bigger until, at full readiness is about seven inches and fat. I'm perfectly cut and I have a perfectly proportioned head on my dick.

At one point I walked up to the bluffs and watched an elderly gentlemen giving blowjobs like they were candy. He sucked off a very young, very white boy with a small cock and big balls, and he sucked off a guy that was black as the Ace of spades with a huge cock and small balls.

Two blonds, who looked so much alike they could have been twins, fucked the guy's mouth brutally, taking turns pounding his lips and trying to shove both of their cocks in his mouth at once. I was going to stop the assault but the old guy seemed to be enjoying it.

At one point the guy on his knees looked over at me and beckoned for me to go over to him. It was too bizarre. I turned and walked away.

After that little show in the dunes, I am ripe for sex. The open shade to the shower and Billy's lust is too much for me to resist.

I look Billy in the eye and say, "Look, I'll suck yours if you suck mine." I hold my cock out toward him as if it is a prize. We take a step toward each other and grab each other's meat. Billy tilts his head back toward the nozzle, fills his mouth with hot water and goes down on me. My cock feels as if it is in a soft warm womb. Billy's mouth clamps down on the shaft of my cock and my cock swims in warm water.

As he tries to deep throat my cock, he gags and the water gushes out of his mouth, cascades down and around my balls, down the inside of my thighs to my bare feet. Billy looks up at me with doe eyes and a dimpled chin. I lift him by his arms and kiss his lips. Billy goes wild.

"It's been so long since anyone worshiped my body from head to toe. Would you do that for me?" He pleads.

"You do me first," I say.

I push him down again and place my cock near his puffy lips. He licks it. I massage his head, yank gently on his shoulder-length brown hair, squeeze his ears, and fondle his ear lobes. I bend over and kiss the top of his adorable head, chew on his hair, lick his forehead, eyebrows, eyelashes, inside his ear. Billy moans.

I place his lips on my belly-button and massage his broad, tanned shoulders, run my fingernails up and down his tanned back and pinch his big brown nipples. Billy's tongue licks whatever part of my body that goes anywhere near his mouth. Once again I lift him by his armpits, kiss his lips and slowly go down on one knee as I lick his chest, his belly, which is not tight. Billy has lovely love handles. I squeeze them, kiss them, lick them. His hands roam my neck, ears, head, back. I lick the shaft of his cock. Run my tongue around the mushroom head, into the piss hole. I chew on his big round balls and bury my face in that space between his balls and his asshole. I take a deep whiff and smell a soapy clean hole. I run my hand around his thighs, calves, bite his knee caps, rub and massage his hairy legs. I lift one of Billy's feet. Billy reaches out to steady himself. I suck each of his toes as if it is a cock. I lick between each one, then run my tongue along the bottom of his foot.

Billy's head hangs loose and he says, "Yeah." I do the other foot. At that moment I realize that I am going to fuck a happily married man. I turn him around and jam my face between Billy's ass cheeks. My tongue darts in and out of his hole like a pool player's cue stick smacking the cue ball and making a break. I aim, lunge, whack with my tongue. I do this over and over as I hold onto his love handles and pull his ass cheeks backward onto my face. I feel the hole open, and layers of flesh surround my tongue. I pry Billy's hole open with my fingertips and fight for it like a fisherman fights for a forty pound fish. I am determined to hook this one.

When I feel the time is right, I stand up and place the head of my cock near Billy's hole and pull him backwards toward me. My cock slides in. Billy tenses. "Relax," I say.

Billy laughs and thrusts his ass cheeks backwards, impaling himself on my throbbing cock. He yelps when it slides in. I cover his mouth with my hand. His daughter is not far away. I saw her lying in a hammock while I was hanging my things on the line. I have no idea where his wife is. I am pretty sure that she is not in the vicinity. If she was, he would not be doing this.

I jab. Billy digs his teeth into my hand. He wiggles and moans. I fuck him, fuck him, fuck him. I grit my teeth. Billy reaches back, grabs my hips and helps me fuck him.

"I want to see your face," he says as he pulls away from me. Billy lies on his back on the wet wooden slabs. The shower pours water on his chest and he raises his legs in the air and holds back his thighs with his hands. His hole is big and red and raw looking. I take the bottom of his feet, get on my knees and once again place the head of my cock near his hole. Billy wiggles and, like a Hoover, his asshole swallows my cock up to my balls.

"Now fuck," he says, demanding and gritting his teeth. I fuck him and fuck him and fuck him. The shower water is getting cold but as soon as it hits our bodies, it heats up. We are like two wild men. We don't care about anything but this fuck. Not his wife, nor his daughter, nor if we get caught. Billy and I are having great sex! We claw each other's backs and squeeze each other's pecs.

"Oh, don't be so selfish," I say as I release my cock from his hole, straighten out his legs and lube his cock with my asshole juice. I sit on it. No preliminaries needed now; no foreplay, no lube, other than the shower and the soap on his cock.

I grimace as the head of his mushroom head forces itself into my tight hole. It enters like a plunger and the rest is easy- almost. The shaft slides in easy enough but there is that fleshy wall inside my hole which Billy's fat cockhead has to pass through. "Oh god!" I gasp. I feel like I'm going to give birth. Billy rams it all the way in again. My eyes fill up with tears.

When I eventually open my eyes, I see Married Billy's boyish face and impish smile. I know what he is going to do. He pulls his cock out a few inches, smiles mischievously, and slams it home. There is so much pain and so much pleasure, I feel as if I died and I am shot down to hell and then I am instantly catapulted up to heaven.

I grab Billy's face with both hands and pull his face toward mine until our eyelashes are intermingled and our lips are as close as a kiss. I grit my teeth and whisper, "Fuck me, Billy. Fuck me. Fuck me silly!"

I dig my fingernails into Billy's neck. I bite his lower lip, and then I bite his upper lip. I bite his ear lobe so hard I draw blood.

I keep on begging him: "Fuck me. Fuck me. Fuck. Fuck. Fuck."

And Billy he does – fast and furious. He knows how to fuck, I have to give him that. And I know that anyone anywhere near us can hear our howls. We sound like two cats in heat thrashing each other.

Billy shoots so much cum up into me that I think I can actually feel it in my mouth. I can smell it, taste it, feel it. Billy plunges my ass so hard, his thighs feel like paddles on my cheeks. I'm sure my asscheeks are bright red from his pounding. Every time I think he is finished, he shoves his cock back in once more and I feel another load shoot up inside of me. Finally, Billy falls in a heap on top of me, my legs are still in the air. Billy lies so still, I think he fell asleep or passed out. I try to push him off of me. "No you don't," Billy says. "I've only just begun...."

A KILLER OF A COCK
William Cozad

The new mall opened with a lot of fanfare. It was a cluster of mostly franchise stores around the rotunda of a huge six-story building, with escalators going to the various levels. There was even a live band playing.

I checked out some of the stores, everything from a sweets shop to a record store, bookstore, clothing specialty stores, shoe stores, you name it. After a cup of coffee and a cookie, I needed to take a piss.

There were rest rooms on each level. But the crowning jewel as far as I was concerned was the men's room on the concourse below the street level. That tea room was designed with me in mind. Narrow gray metal shields between urinals that hid nothing, but possibly prevented splashing piss. Sinks lined the adjoining wall with sensor-activated water faucets. The mirrored wall gave a magnificent panoramic view of the urinals.

On the opposite side of the room were the gray metal stalls. The stall next to the handicap one was directly in line with the urinals. That's where I camped out. I sat on the throne with my shirt unbuttoned and my jeans and briefs down around my ankles. I left the door ajar. I watched the guys come in to pee. I got a gander at a variety of dicks. I lewdly stroked my prick. I coughed and tapped my foot but didn't attract the attention of anyone who was interested in a little furtive, mutual jack-off or quickie blowjob.

The toilet wasn't a very busy place and was now quiet as a mausoleum. Looking at my watch, I noticed that it was approaching closing time.

The grand opening of the mall might have been a success, but the superbly designed tea room on the concourse level was a dismal failure as far as I was concerned. I didn't want to just look, I wanted to reach out and touch.

I was about ready to hike up my britches and call it a night. I could have whipped off a quickie load to christen the new tea room, but my dick went limp.

Glancing through the crack in the stall door, I noticed the janitor had come in with a bucket and mop. He was better dressed than I, with his black jeans, long-sleeved white shirt and black bow tie.

He was short and muscular, with slick black hair and brown eyes. He couldn't have been over eighteen. The sight of him made my dick spring to life, and I clutched it.

He scanned the room and spotted me in the stall. So I decided to give him a show. He had a walkie-talkie in his hip pocket. Maybe he'd notify security and I'd get busted for lewd conduct, whatever. They say that a guy has a brain and a penis, but not enough blood to fill both of them at the same time. My dick was fully engorged. Leaning back, I lewdly stroked it.

Frozen in his tracks, the youth was gawking at me. Damned if the lump in his black jeans didn't thicken. I looked into his soulful brown eyes and ran my tongue slowly over my lower lip like a porn star bitch.

He left his mop and bucket and came over to the door. I opened it wide.

Reaching out, I grabbed his crotch and pulled him over. It was more like an alligator leaping out of the water to snatch a drinking wildebeest in its jaws.

I unbuckled his belt, unzipped his fly and slid down his black jeans. He was wearing bright yellow bikini briefs that were sexy as hell. I clutched his skimpily clad buttcheeks and licked his satiny undies. I saw and felt his dick throb inside. A patch of black fuzz led from his belly button down into his crotch. His bulging thighs were smooth. There was no outline of his crown, so I figured he had uncut instead of processed meat. I licked and nibbled on his dick bulge.

Hooking my fingers into the waistband, I slid down his briefs. His uncut dick was plump and his fat balls dangled. His black bush was lush and fanned out.

I sniffed his crotch and smelled his sweat, body musk and ripe aroma. I licked his balls and his rosy dickhead peeked out of the hood.

I grabbed his throbbing pecker with the veins bulging in his shaft. His dick had expanded into a fat, throbbing eight-inch cock that was wrist-thick. I slid the cowl of foreskin over his crown and pinched it. I lapped at his balls in their chicken-skin sac. I stuffed both of them into my mouth and hummed on them while I stroked his dick.

He moaned. I spit out his nuts and continued to masturbate him, glancing up into his smoldering brown eyes.

I skinned back his dick and rolled my tongue over his cheesy cockhead, which had turned purple. I darted my tongue into his wide piss-slit and tasted his sweet, oozing pre-cum.

I clutched his bare, smooth buttcheeks and literally devoured his dick, taking it all the way down to the wiry pubes, which tickled my nostrils. Then, clasping the thick base of his dick, I bobbed my head up and down on it.

"Oh yeah, man, suck it! Suck my big dick," he hissed. "Suck it really good!" He tore at my hair, then held my head while he rocked on his heels. Finally, he slapped my hand off his dick. He roughly mouth-fucked me, ramming his dick down my throat. I was loving every minute of this!

With his concentration on his dick, I pulled a sneak rear attack. I ran my fingers into his sweaty, hairy asscrack and stuck my middle finger up his hot hole, which was so tight it had to be cherry. I fingered his hole while he fucked me in the face.

"Always heard queers were the best cocksuckers. Take my big dick all the way. No bitch could do that."

His wet, bloated balls slapped against my chin.

He was moaning and groaning while he drilled his dick down my throat. I was busy fingering his bunghole. My own dick was quivering and leaking like a sieve.

"Oh, shit... I'm coming!" he bellowed.

He crammed his exploding prick so far down my throat that he practically smothered me with his pubes. His dick gushed wads of cum down my throat.

Suddenly his dick deflated and the last drops filled my mouth. He backed away and his dick slid out of my mouth. The head was back in the hood. My finger slid out of his hole.

"Stand up, cocksucker," he ordered.

Well, I wasn't sure what to expect. Yeah, he was strong as a bull, but I figured I could handle him if he flipped out and started to bash me. But he didn't.

I stood up and he sat down on the toilet. He grabbed my boner, something I didn't expect that. And darned if he didn't roughly wipe off the pre-cum, which made me wince. Next thing I knew he took a couple slides on my dick.

"Always wondered what this was like." He chuckled. "Shit, they say that eating pussy is sucking dick by proxy." I didn't know what the hell he was blabbing about, but my dick was hard as a rock. He wrapped his sweet lips around my cock and started to suck up a storm. His teeth grazed my sensitive dick, but I wasn't about to stop him. All too soon my balls were rumbling. My dick began to dribble. Inexperienced cocksucker that he was, he couldn't handle the onslaught. He choked on my spurting prick and let go of it. Like a loose cannon, my dick shot volleys of cum all over his face. He licked his lips like the cat who got the cream. Looking down at the first-time cocksucker whose curiosity got the best of him, I decided to go the whole nine yards. I had to taste his ass. I yanked him up and reclaimed the throne. I shoved him spread-eagled against the stall door. "What the fuck!" he said, glancing over his shoulder. I spread his buttcheeks and dove into his crack. I darted my tongue up his cherry pucker. "Oh, yeah, dude, eat me! Whoa! That feels fucking great." Coming up for air, I poked my fuck-finger in his asshole and pried it open. "Want me to fuck you, don'tcha?"

"Shit, no! Your dick's too big. You've got a killer of a cock, man."

"Hey, no bigger than yours." That seemed to persuade him. "C'mon, it'll make a man outta you." He chuckled again, as if amused by the idea that by having a cock shoved up his ass would somehow make him even more of stud than he was already. He didn't try to escape when I eased him back down on my dick. "Oh Jesus! Fucking Christ! It's killing me." His crack was slathered with spit. He sat down on my "killer' dick, facing away. My dick snaked up the tightest hole it had ever been in. He lifted up and slowly humped his butt on my dick. I clutched his waist and held on while he set the rhythm. "Hurry up, man! Your big dick's like a fuckin' telephone pole!" Well, I couldn't hold off any longer if I tried. His cherry butt

gripping my dick like a vise, plus the feel of every nook and cranny of his chute took me over the edge. "Oh, Christ! Oh, Jesus! I can feel it shooting up my fucking ass!" My dick went off like a rocket, shooting my payload deep into his bowels. "Oh shit, I'm gonna blow!" he grunted. His dick exploded, squirting globs of cum that landed on the gray metal door and dripped down it. He lifted up slowly off my dick. Before he could stop me, I licked his crack and tasted my own salty cum. I spun him around and cleaned off his dick, tasting his sweet juice. He pulled up his sexy yellow bikini briefs and black jeans. I pulled up my pants. "Well, I'd better get outta here. It's closing time," I said. "Yeah, see you around, big guy." As I left the men's room, I noticed a sign had been hung on the door: "Closed for Cleaning."

A LAST FLING
John Patrick

Their summer of flirting had led them here: a half-built office building – a construction site that had been walled off from the street by a makeshift door that Rich had padlocked from the inside. It was seven o'clock at night. Rich was trying to explain what needed to be done to Ned, the youth who was to replace him as foreman.

The summer of flirting was over. Rich had to fly back to Chicago in the morning to get married. The more he joked with Ned, and lied to him, and led him on, the more protected Rich felt from the unpleasant, nauseating, impending upheaval that was going to be the rest of his life. Why was he getting married? To please Mom and Dad, that was it. But now Ned was his reward. He had wanted Ned from the moment the kid walked onto the site, but he couldn't bring himself to make the move. No, he kept telling himself, he was straight. Well, maybe he fucked around, but he was going straight. This was it. So tonight was the night and the wrongness of it, the wantonness, excited Rich beyond words.

At one point, Rich made a lewd little joke and pushed Ned away. Ned laughed and pushed back. A shoving match ensued, followed by a strange silence. Ned was eyeing Rich's crotch. Rich had an obvious hard-on. Rich saw where Ned's eyes were riveted. When Ned looked up. Rich gazed into his eyes. He knew Ned wanted him. Yeah, it was there for the taking. He deserved it; he deserved a little bachelor party of his own. Their bodies came together and their arms went around each other.

Their lips were as close as they could be without actually touching. All the muscles in their bodies were tense, rigidly controlled. Rich could feel Ned's breath on his face as Ned exhaled. Rich brushed his resting lips against Ned's, gently teasing his mouth. He let the tip of his tongue run along the inside of Ned's lips; Ned's mouth opened wider, beckoning Rich's tongue to enter it. Rich plunged his tongue into Ned's mouth, probing Ned's tongue as it responded to him. Rich closed his eyes, and Ned pulled him toward him. Their bodies collapsed against each other. Ned kissed Rich deeply, pushing his lips hard against

Rich's; their tongues invaded each other's mouths. The taste of cigarettes and the beers they had enjoyed together earlier, after work, mingled.

Rich grabbed the back of Ned's head and clasped his fingers into his hair, pushing Ned's lips harder against his. Ned's moan was absorbed into Rich's mouth, and his arms wrapped around Rich's waist and pulled his body harder against Rich's.

Finally Rich stood back, in order to breathe, pretending to smile, to free himself from the boy's body. Rich couldn't help it; the kid turned him on. He always liked small guys, with cute buns. Rich was big, big in every way. And dark and hairy. Ned was blond, blue-eyed, and adorable. Ned had a curious look on his face – one of vacancy and desire. He licked his lower lip. Rich thought about going back to kissing Ned but that didn't seem right, so he stood still, thinking of what to do next.

Ned was way ahead of him. Ned went right for the groin. He had been wanting to do this all summer. He kneeled before Rich and ripped open his jeans. Rich's cock sprang into view. Amid the dusty smell of glue guns, tar sealant, and Sheetrock dust, there was man-sweat rolling off Rich. Ned loved it. He was glad they were doing it this way and not in a motel, in a bed. This was the way he always dreamed it would be, here where they worked, side by side, for weeks.

Ned pushed the jeans down around Rich's ankles so he could get the full effect. Rich was everything he thought he would be. The cock was magnificent, at least eight inches long and thick, and the balls were huge. "Oh god," Ned moaned as the big prick throbbed in his face. He reached out and pulled on Rich's nuts, which hurt Rich, who pulled away.

Ned looked up at him, his sad eyes smiling. Ned's daddy owned the construction company and Rich wasn't in a position to push the kid away. While they worked together, he could feel the vast inexperience of a kid of complete fragility, shielded by daddy's wealth, and used to getting his way. Now he was finally getting his way with Rich.

"I'm getting married in three days and you are disgusting" was what Rich wanted to say. But he couldn't, because Ned wasn't disgusting. Ned was fuckin' beautiful.

"Suck it," Rich commanded, and pulled Ned's head to his groin. "You've been wanting it ... take it."

And Ned did. He was so expert that it scared Rich. He suddenly wished he'd not wasted all that time flirting with the kid. This was the best damn blowjob he'd ever had.

It went on for several minutes, Ned feasting on the cock, Rich loving every lick, every kiss, every caress.

But just when he thought he might come, Rich was in for a surprise. Ned wanted it in him. Rich let out a small puff of air, a slight moan, like someone tired from a long day of work. But his work really hadn't begun yet. Rich saw the burning need in Ned's eyes. Rich's cock was warm, and a fire raged deep inside him. Wanting, needing, and in heat.

After Ned got out of his jeans, Rich cupped Ned's asscheeks in his hands, pulling the mounds up and slightly apart. Ned's hips pushed hard toward Rich and they began imitating the movement of penetration. Ned moaned in want. Rich bit Ned's neck as he entered Ned, and Ned groaned as his ass yielded to the invasion. The pain was excruciating for Ned; he never thought it would be this difficult to take, but he was willing to put up with the pain to please Rich. Once he was in Ned, sex flooded over Rich, his body filling with excitement. He bit the back of Ned's neck and licked up to his ears.

After a few full thrusts where the cock's shaft was consumed entirely in Ned's ass, Rich went from cautious probing to slamming. Hard, fast, he plunged into Ned. His sweat fell over Ned's back like baptismal water. The nerves in Ned's ached with sensation. The fuck was so intense that it threatened to consume them both. Ned loved having it deep inside him, and he met every thrust of Rich's, getting closer.

Ned made so much noise while getting fucked that Rich worried that a passerby, a cop, a homeless person, might hear them and rush onto the site – arrest them, shoot them, beat them to death with the spade beside Ned's writhing head. What really worried Rich was the sound of the yelling itself – a lonely yell, from a kid who didn't have many friends, who would have to be satisfied with this degraded scene for months, who didn't need to care what Rich thought of him because he knew they wouldn't be calling each other ever again.

At the end, Rich crammed his cock into Ned with a fearsome power, Ned's body like a vise, and Ned yelled and yelled. Ned pushed his ass toward Rich with each thrust until suddenly Ned felt a popping sensation, followed by a severe emptiness deep inside his ass. "Oh, no," Ned groaned with displeasure. Rich had slipped out, but he was soon re-entering him with one strong stroke. Ned was close. He was pushed to the edge. "Harder," he gasped.

And Rich responded as if the idea had been his own, and his next downward stroke into him was harder than Ned had imagined possible.

"Arrghh!" yelled Ned, coming violently as the cock slid roughly in and out of him, his cum splattering on the floor. Rich came too, then collapsed on top of Ned, sweating, breathing heavily.

Soon they were on the floor; Ned was mostly on the concrete, Rich was mostly in the dirt, and, as they lay spent next to each other, Rich felt like crying. He pushed Ned away. He regretted it the moment he did it, but it was too late.

Angered, rebuffed, Ned jumped up, pulled on his jeans and ran to the door. He unlocked the gate and ran out, leaving the door hanging open. "Damn!" Rich cursed. To think he'd been dreaming about this, a last fling, and it had to end this way. Now he felt like crying again. • • •

In the bridal suite, Rich hugged his new bride. Honey, where am I? he wanted to say. Neither of them could speak. She seemed ashamed and agitated. Staring at her, Rich suddenly remembered his dream from hours earlier on the airplane; he'd slept soundly, and not until this instant – not after waking, not while driving – had this wild, foggy, sweet dream from the plane come back to him: he was screwing Ned in the dirt. And, although he didn't think so at the time, now when he thought of it, when he dreamed of it, it was impossibly good. The image of Ned's face as he orgasmed stung him, and he froze, baffled, and forced it from his mind.

Rich unzipped his suitcase.

"That's your side of the room, those are your drawers," she said.

Rich pulled out some clothes and looked at them. "Why did we do this?" he asked.

She sighed, spent. "What?" Did she have to answer this question for him, too? She started to tell him the truth: "Because nothing better came along after we graduated from high school." But she thought the better of it. In his presence now she felt small and tired and afraid. She said instead, "We're on the grownup train now, and we don't get off until the graveyard."

Rich held up his folded shirts. He said he was talking about the clothes. As in, "Why not leave them in the suitcase and forget the dresser?"

But Joy knew something was different. Something was terribly wrong. At home, over the last six months, when she felt bad, her mind had traveled to Rich, working hundreds of miles away for the summer, and she wondered why he didn't call every night. Oh, he'd call, but there was no rhyme or reason to when. Now she thought she knew: he was sleeping with someone else.

"Everything is okay with you?"

"Yeah." Rich smiled pathetically. "I'm just tired."

She didn't accept that, not totally. She asked, "Are you mad at me?"

He said, "Are you mad at me?"

She smiled. "Hell no. You're the best thing that ever happened to me in my whole life." She waited for him to speak. "Well, the only good thing."

"Are you kidding?"

Finally Rich lay down beside her, and they put their faces together and talked, and after five minutes they felt lucky and were able to kiss. The amount of work connected with a wedding and the excitement and the well-wishing had overwhelmed them, Joy explained to Rich. Rich said, "Yeah, that must be it."

By the time Rich started fucking his bride, they'd finally quit talking. When the two of them got tired doing it one way, Rich fell over, and they did it on their sides. After a while, they rested, and then resumed. Joy was on top for a long time. Their coming was still on hold, prolonged to make them both crazy with need. Their moaning was exciting to both of them. And when they were done, Rich sighed with relief. He'd done it. He was safe. But then, as he slept, he had that same dream he'd had on the plane, that dream about the blond boy in the dirt, and he woke up in a cold sweat.

Looking around from a safe spot against the wall, Ned was able to reassure himself that, yes, he had dressed correctly. Leathers, combats, jeans with a white or khaki T or vest were just about all that anyone was wearing in the bar. It was too hot for shirts, although some guys had tied them round their waists. The musclemen were bare chested, sweat dripping down their firm chests as they danced.

It was eleven o'clock and Ned resolved to wait until midnight before braving the backroom that he had heard so much about. He ordered another drink and when he looked in the smoky mirror behind the bar he saw the reflection of a handsome stud rushing toward the backroom. He blinked. It was Rich! No, it couldn't be. Not here, not tonight. His eyes were playing tricks on him. He had fantasized about such an occurrence, but what were the chances of it happening? It was in the back of his mind, though, when he made his plans to come to Chicago for the weekend, to get out of town, away from his folks for once.

Ned had not heard from Rich since that encounter in the dirt. Still, he had thought about it many times. He could not easily forget the man who had taken his virginity.

He finished his drink and slowly made his way to the backroom. It wasn't midnight, but it was close enough.

Ned went over to a small group in the center of the room. He could barely tell the men apart in the dark, but gradually his eyes adapted enough to see that one man was licking the balls of another while he fucked a third who was being sucked off by the fourth. Ned watched, mesmerized.

In one comer, two guys had stripped to their underwear. In tiny briefs, their youth seemed emphasized. They began kissing.

Ned was only going to watch but one of the boys drew him close and encouraged him. "Get your cock out," he said.

As he thought of the possibilities, Ned felt his dick stiffen, and he gave in to his fantasy of fucking two guys, one after the other. Soon one of the boys had rolled on his back for him like a dog wanting to be stroked, and Ned got in his ass straightaway. He was skinny and had shaved his body smooth. The boy took hold of his cock and said, "This is my fantasy."

"What is?" Ned asked.

"This is. Being fucked while Joe watches us."

"Yeah, I'm fucking you now all right."

"Yeah! Oh yeah!"

He stayed in him while the boy tugged on his dick, moaning in delight.

"You like that?"

"Oh! Oh, yeah!" was all he could manage. He was coming, his body jerking off the floor in quick spasms as his jism spurted all over his chest.

"You're done," said Ned, pulling out. "Okay, now it's your turn," he said to Joe. "Get yourself ready...."

Joe got down on the floor next to his friend and Ned entered him. The two youths kissed each other while Ned fucked Joe. Then the first boy sucked Joe's cock while Ned continued.

Suddenly the man whose reflection Ned had seen in the mirror was there behind him, stripping off Ned's bomber jacket. Ned was suddenly thrown, unprepared for all this anonymous sex he had yearned for back home. The man reached down and fingered Ned's ass. Ned shuddered with the thrill. "Fuck me!" he told the man in a deep voice.

"No," the stud said, "you fuck me!"

Ned nodded in consent. He withdrew from Joe and let the new stranger take his hand. The man knew his way around the room, leading Ned over to one wall. The man leaned against the wall. He was lubed and ready for Ned.

Ned stroked himself, then pressed his cock against the man's hole, which opened a little, then a lot, so he could slide himself fully inside him. Power surged through Ned as he fucked the wonderfully tight ass.

It was much tighter than the two boy's asses. He looked back at them, lost in their own world of 69ing.

Then Ned felt someone's warm hands on his waist, a moist cock being slid up and down his asscrack. He was doubly thrilled now, letting the flirtation continue while he fucked the other man. Soon he was feeling a finger pressing into his hole. As that finger slipped inside him, Ned bucked his hips back to envelop it. This continued for several minutes, with Ned bucking between the finger in his ass and the ass he was fucking.

The finger in his ass slipped out, but the man behind him had not given up, as Ned realized when the man whispered in Ned's ear, "I'm gonna fuck you now." He smelled of leather and citrus cologne. Ned was soon grabbing the ass of the man he was fucking to steady himself as the tip of the new stranger's cock pressed against his eager asshole. He pushed hard against him and he grunted in discomfort as the thick cockhead shoved at his hole.

The man he was fucking was moaning now, close to orgasm, and all Ned's concentration went into pumping his ass.

Ned moaned as he relented and let the man in, feeling his cock filling him up in battering thrusts. Ned was afraid to shout out, but holding it in just made him more excited, a ball of tension waiting to be released. But soon the man Ned was fucking was shouting out, caught up in his own fantasy, and it was only seconds before he came, thrashing about as Ned pushed twice more into his depths, then came himself. Ned's whole body shook, sandwiched between two strangers, the second man coming deep inside him with great shouts of triumph. They pulsed against each other, all three in the thrall of something bigger, part of the shouts and groans and moans that went on all around them. Finally the man withdrew from Ned, slowly and with long groans. Ned gasped as he was freed from his cock.

Following his example, he pulled out of the other man's ass, holding on to it as he slid out inch by inch, until the head of his cock burst from the hole.

Suddenly another man appeared, his hard cock ready, and he started to enter the man Ned had just fucked. Ned thought he said, "No more...." then he clearly heard "No, please ... please don't...." yet the other man continued. Ned realized it was part of the game.

Suddenly someone was on him again, this time grabbing him by the shoulders and powerfully pushing him to the floor. The man unzipped his fly and forced his fat cock into Ned's mouth before he could gasp for air. He nearly choked as the stranger started to fuck his mouth as if it were his ass.

Then someone was between his legs, diving to his crotch.

"Hey!" said a familiar voice. Ned looked closely at his face, in the darkness. A horrible recognition dawned. "Rich?"

The man pumping with all his strength said gruffly, "Shut the fuck up, can't you see he's busy?"

"Not anymore," said Rich, shoving the man away from Ned. "He's mine." Ned gulped down air.

"What the fuck are you doing here?" Rich asked Ned angrily.

"Same as you." Rich shook his head in disgust.

"My god, what were you doing letting that scumbag in your mouth?"

"I didn't have much choice." Ned looked at him apologetically.

"You shouldn't be here, Ned. We're leaving."

"Well," he said sheepishly, "okay." And then Rich pushed Ned out of the club and into the street. For Ned, the thrill of being in the back room was dissipating as they walked toward his motel, but it was soon replaced by a new rush of desire. By the time they got to Ned's room and shut the door, Rich was beside himself with need. Rich had never expected to see the kid again, let alone here in his backyard. Rich pushed him down on the bed and pulled off his boots and his new camouflage pants.

"No," murmured Ned.

"I can't do this."

"You don't want me?"

"No."

"Why don't I believe you?" Rich took Ned in his arms and kissed him. Pulling away, Rich said,

"I'm gonna fuck you."

"No. I can't take any more."

"But I have to fuck you."

"No!"

"I think you mean yes, don't you?"

"No!" Ned shook his head from side to side as Rich stood and dropped his jeans.

"You do want me...."

"Oh yes! I know you have to do it. But I have just fucked three guys and I liked it. I was also fucked and I hurt. So I want to fuck."

"Oh, I get it now. Well, it doesn't matter to me."

"It doesn't?"

"No. As long as it's you doing it, you can do whatever you like. You fuck me then. Finish what the hell you started back there if that's what you want. Fuck my ass."

"Okay." Rich got on his back on the bed and spread his legs. "I saw everything, you know, Ned. I thought, 'God that kid fucks like a jack rabbit. Where'd you learn to fuck like that?"

"From you."

"But...!" Soon Ned was thrusting his cock deep into Rich in long, slow movements that made Rich shout out, "Fuck me! I need it." Ned tried to hold back but it was hopeless; he was coming now and he held Rich tight, his hands on Rich's shoulders as he plowed into him. "You liked that, didn't you?" Rich asked as he kissed Ned's face. "I needed to do it to you."

"No, I needed you to do it to me. For what I did to you. That night
"

"Don't sweat it," Ned spit. Then Ned fell down between Rich's legs and licked gently at his huge cock, making it throb and soon Rich was groaning with release. As Ned took Rich's cum, he felt free. They had given each other everything now. They could finally rest. "God, I've missed you," Ned murmured in Rich's ear.

"I've missed you too." But even though Rich had missed Ned, he had to leave him. He had to go home:

"My wife worries about me. Friday's supposed to be my poker night, and ... well, if I'm too late, she starts calling around...." Ned nodded that he understood. The next morning, before he left the motel, Ned called the number Rich had given him. A woman answered the phone and Ned was surprised to hear a baby crying in the background. Rich had had to get married. Poor Rich. Ned hung up. His hung-over brain was finally realizing that he couldn't meet Rich again. Never again. It was as simple as that.

IT STARTED WITH A HANDJOB
Anonymous

Our college had "suites" where four guys shared a common hallway entrance and a bathroom. One of my "suite" mates was Joe, a guy who was average-appearing in the face but with a truly lovely, smooth, swimmer's build. I secretly lusted for him for weeks into the first term.

We would occasionally go into each other's alcoves for study breaks and just to break the sometime boredom of weeknights during the school year.

My most vivid memories of Joe are when he was lying on his bed, clad only in a pair of black bikini trunks which accentuated his prominent basket. On different occasions, I would go into his space and pretend not to notice his crotch. I would try to make conversation, all the while trying to cover my raging hard-on.

Finally, one night late into the term, I went into his room just to kick back and listen to a new CD he had gotten from his girlfriend. He seemed melancholy that night and I asked what was bothering him. He told me that his girlfriend had been gone for a few days and somehow the conversation came around to other women he fucked, sex in general, and what turned us both on. I told him what turned me on most was "giving other people pleasure." This intrigued him, and, as we continued chatting, I began to notice a definite growth in his briefs, until finally you could see the developing outline of his thick and long cock.

Soon the cock slowly started peeking through and then up beyond the elastic top of the briefs. He noticed my stares and just stared back. He then asked if I wanted to come over and sit on his bed with him while we looked at a couple of Penthouse magazines he had acquired from a friend. I said sure, and after sitting there, pretending to be interested in the magazine's pictures, I couldn't help noticing his hard-on. Almost absent-mindedly, he would reach down and rub this magnificent dick (still with his underwear on). He caught me looking and again just stared back at me. The cock, I noticed, was oozing pre-cum by this time. Finally, he said "So you like giving to pleasure to others, eh?"

"Yeah," I said casually.

"Well, you could really pleasure me if you rubbed it, okay?"

I decided that since he caught me looking anyway, I might as well have some fun. I reached over and palm-rubbed his dick through the underwear slowly and then up the underside that was sticking out of the elastic waist band. I also massaged his balls through the underwear. This went on for about ten minutes and the entire time I couldn't take my eyes off that magnificent set of dick and balls!

He was moaning softly and sometimes bucking his hips to try and prolong the hand contact.

Finally, he pushed my hand away and quickly pulled off his underwear. That revealed a contracted ball-sac that, along with his dick, was turning a darker shade of red. He had some lotion in a bedside drawer and squirted some on his cock. I reached up and started a light-alternating-with-firm grip on his cock, going very slowly at first, then speeding up. I also would throw in palming the underside of his cock its entire length up to the piss-slit. Pre-cum oozed out and I rubbed it away.

I would do this until his bucking became very pronounced and then would back off in my strokes. I would let go altogether for a short time and then tease the entire length of his dick with a very light touch of my fingertips. I also would lightly tease his balls all the way down to the area near his asshole. After about a half hour of this, I thought he had enough, so, with both hands I squeezed and stroked his dick with increasing tempo and incorporated a little "twisting" motion at the head. All of a sudden, he had a look of agony on his face and stiffened his arms and legs. His back was unbelievably arched and he was straining for my hand contact. He started moaning and whimpering. At last he bellowed, "I gotta shoot! Oh, please don't stop!" He let out a yell, and let a jet of cum that must have been 3-4 feet long spew from his cock. He kept bucking his hips and gushing cum. Finally, he collapsed.

After I satisfied him, he just lay there breathing heavily, and looked at me with an interestingly grateful but exhausted gaze. I excused myself and ran back to my own room to jerk myself off.

The next day, he mentioned nothing about what had happened. However, a week or so later, he mentioned that he really could use some of my special "pleasuring." Out came the Penthouse magazines again. I repeated the process, but I added some tongue action. He didn't appear a bit startled by it. In fact, he moaned, "Suck it. I know you want to." Oh, boy, did I! What a cock to suck! I had never had one thicker or longer, or as beautiful. Before he came, I came myself, soaking his sheets. When he came, I swallowed it all. Again, he lay helpless on the bed, and I rushed back to my own room.

From that time until he moved to another dorm, I gave him a blowjob almost every night. Near the end of our rooming together, he took to face-fucking me, and I would slap his ass and even shove a finger up there when he got close.

Then one day in the fall of 1985, I happened to see Joe in the campus bookstore and he seemed very happy to see me. He bought me a cup of coffee and while I enjoyed the brew, he suggested we go to movie over the weekend. He said his girlfriend was going to be out of town, and I told him I understood perfectly.

All during the film, which was, appropriately enough, "A Room With a View," I was working on him, turning him on. It was almost too easy. And I told him I wouldn't disappoint him. In fact, when I told him I would reward his paying for my ticket by giving him the best damn blowjob I had ever given anyone, he laughed nervously and said that might be the best bargain he'd ever heard of.

He agreed to go with me to a special spot I had found-as if he had any choice by that time. It was a warm, cloudless Indian Summer night, and he eagerly followed me to the secluded spot where I would often go, I told him, to "commune with nature," and jack myself off.

That night the air was filled with the sound of crickets, a few chirping night birds, and the constant noise made by the cars on the highway on the other side of the ridge.

After kneeling before him and really working him up, I got down on the grass on all fours. I pushed my pants back and began rubbing my asscrack with my fingers, acting like a bitch in heat. I had lubed my ass earlier so my fingers slid in easily.

He didn't seem a bit shocked at my behavior. He swiftly knelt down behind me and began inserting the spit-slicked head of his cock into my ass as if it was the most natural thing in the world. In fact, he took to it so keenly that I was sure now he was not the stranger to boysex he pretended to be. I began to move back and forth as he just held his cock there. I continued to grind and buck against it, wanting more and more of what he had to offer. And he gave it to me. All of it. After he got all eight inches in me, he came, and it was the most explosive climax he had enjoyed in all the times we had been together.

I moved out from beneath him and watched him collapse onto the grass, utterly exhausted, a contented smile on his face.

I smiled then too, and lay my head on his thigh so that I could take his semi-hard cock back into my mouth and suckle it while I jacked myself off.

For the next two semesters, he would occasionally permit me to give him a quick blowjob, but never were we to repeat that glorious night under the stars. Perhaps I'd gotten too close to the truth for him.

THE PROCTOR
Anonymous

In my youth, I was a dorm proctor at an Ivy League prep school. The dorms were the old academic style, sprawled around quads (courtyards) and were not tightly packed high rises like some today. Each section was like a private enclave. They were also totally male. The place was like a fortress and guards at gates kept women out at all times except Saturday from 12-5 PM in designated lounges.

I was about six years older than the twenty college freshmen who were in my charge. They lived two to a room off a dark, twisting hallway. As a senior proctor, I got a spacious two room suite. It was all very cozy and we all shared one smallish bathroom which made for eye-filling shower scenes and lots of towels snapped at cute butts. Like in every frat house there were the two inevitable well-built and hung exhibitionists who most of the time wore only the bare minimum or just a smile inside. Karl was a hard bodied gymnast with an eight-inch, uncut cock; the other, Brent, was the ultimate blue-eyed blond tennis jock. He had a perfectly proportioned physique with smooth, luscious skin and a big package. About half the boys were from Eastern prep schools.

Things were a lot different in those days. There was no concept of anyone being "gay". That word meant only "merry". AIDS did not exist. The boys went where their urges led them and no one sweated anything at all. Many enjoyed each other all week and had girlfriends on the weekend. The word "queer" was occasionally used but only in jest. Lube as known today didn't exist. There was only Vaseline or baby oil. The little old lady who ran the local sandwich and sundries store always asked me what the guys did with all that Vaseline, she had to reorder twice monthly. They told her they used it to clean their leather shoes for dates! Frequently the room doorknobs were slippery from Vaselined hands.

In the evening, my section was very casual. The guys were lucky they had a relaxed tolerant proctor. Most of the others were quite uptight and officious. In my area many doors were always wide open no matter what lascivious scene was ongoing inside. I had the only phone on the floor and if there were messages for guys I went and got them. This had me walking, with relative ease, into and out of all those horny scenes nearly all the time.

A particular group used to congregate in one room frequently to drink lots of beer and enjoy water sports. There were no computers or games back in those days so they practiced playing with each other and being "fireman" which meant hosing each other down with used beer. The poor maid used to come to me in tears until I went out and got them rubber sheets with which to drape the entire room. Forests of wood were grown nightly and the action was everywhere abundant. Guys walking around the halls with hard-ons presented a stimulating sight. Since I never flinched at anything, they were relaxed and fully uninhibited around me.

Of course, I needed my proctorial free room and board and so could only observe the scene, or find myself in possible difficulty. But there was so much to observe!

One night a sign was posted over our bathroom piss-trough by two nearby proctors who were third-year medical students asking for two guys to volunteer as "body models" so they could practice doing physical exams. They said it would be informative and the guys would get a free complete exam. Both of these med students liked boys...of that there was no doubt. I had twelve pre-meds in my group and they quickly asked if they could watch and learn something about the human body.

Of course the two exhibitionist studs, the muscular gymnast and the hunky blond tennis champ, quickly put their names on the notice as the "body models." Another jock, from across the quad, who was a big-time collegiate wrestler in his second year heard about it all and joined the list of body models. Then I was asked if the whole thing could take place in my large living room, and the med students told the guys they would supply plenty of beer. Now you know that I just had to help education along by providing my large room, myself as host, and anything else that they might need. Someone had to do it!

This whole thing was set for Saturday night. It was quickly evolving, with an anxious and growing excitement among the boys, as a "for men only" instructional demonstration examining the hot bodies of those luscious jocks in front of twelve all-too-eager pre-meds and me! Knowing the personalities involved... the "doctors"... the jocks... the sexually curious boys... everyone sensed that an unusual event was unfolding and I felt that my involvement was okay since it was billed as "educational."

On a cold snowy Saturday night, my twelve pre-meds came from dinner excited and eager to enjoy another "all-male" evening. Rick and Don, the med students, came in green scrub suits, brought big chests filled with iced beer and also their doctor's bags. Beer went down, boys relaxed and discussed what med school would be like. Our jock "body models" arrived. Karl the uninhibited gymnast, cute, hunky and with a seductive smile, was in tight-fitting white sweat pants and top which showed off his broad shoulders and muscular ass. Brent the tennis jock was barefoot in a bathrobe indicating he had little on underneath. At five-ten with blue eyes and thick blond hair contrasting with the gray robe, Brent had the look of a male model. They were the center of attention as I relaxed them with beer before the "show" in which they would be the main feature.

After two hours of beer and locker room talk, Karl said, "I want my physical." I led him over to my cleared-off, oversized work table centered in the room under a cluster of spot type ceiling lights. Rick then bolted the hallway door. It was chilly and knowing he'd be striping the "examinees," he upped the thermostat setting.

The "audience" sat in two rows of folding chairs in front of the table. "Dr." Rick looked hungrily at Karl and told him to remove his sweats as he pulled stethoscopes, blood pressure cuffs, jars and shiny metal instruments from his and Don's doctor bags. Karl, enjoying all the eyes on him, peeled off the top and slowly pulled off his pants leaving him in only socks and tight fitting, ankle length white, ski-type underwear. The wide elastic band hugged and outlined his hard ripped stomach muscles below the navel. The strong light glinted off his muscular shoulders and emphasized the large bulge in the white fly front pouch.

Hoisting his latest beer can overhead with one hand, he looked at the guys, grabbed his crotch thrusting it forward and yelled "Yeah ... penis power ... suck it!"

As Rick and Don prepared, three young men, loosened up by the beer, went up and ran their hands all over Kurt's hot torso and biceps, enjoying the feel of that smooth, hairless skin while two other guys groped his crotch.

Rick asked if the guys wanted to see how a "complete physical examination" is done or just ask questions. The group, now excited and horny, demanded complete exams and I told them not to be embarrassed to ask anything at all about the male body or men's health during the physical examinations. "Dr." Don looked slyly at Rick and said "Okay, then, no-holds-barred exams it'll be."

The shirtless Karl sat on the table and Rick motioned for Brent to join them up front. Don removed Brent's robe under which he had on only a small swimmer's jockstrap with the mesh pouch well stretched over his half visible cock and balls. His pretty ass framed by the leg straps was hot! Brent stood about six-foot with nice slender muscles, an appendicitis scar, and light blond fuzz accentuating his abdominal midline and extending down into the jock. Both models sat on the table. The guys split into two groups around them as Rick got started.

I watched Rick work on hot Karl as he checked his eyes, ears and mouth permitting us to look through the lighted ophthalmoscope at Karl's retinas and eardrums. He had each of the guys feel slowly around Karl's neck for lymph nodes, which resulted in a noticeable swelling in Karl's fly front pouch. Rick thumped the protruding muscular chest and showed how to apply stethoscopes he had given the guys to hear heart sounds. They enjoyed playing around with Karl's chest and nipples. Boys then took turns trying to take Karl's blood pressure. As each performed this their eyes were on his crotch and thick thighs.

Explaining reflexes, Rick demonstrated several. He tapped a knee, the leg jerked. He laid Karl on the table, pulled his socks off and stroked the soles of his feet making the toes curl. He stroked across the stomach making the exquisite abs twitch instantly. "We'll see other interesting reflexes a little later." Rick announced, "Next we examine the male sex organs and anus ... Karl I'll need you completely naked."

A nervous murmur went through the group seated again in the wooden folding chairs in front of Karl. I heard a lot of throat clearing and swallowing around me. Karl sat on the table edge, removed his fine neck chain and watch, then pulled down his skivvies as slowly as possible gradually revealing a nice pubic bush. Continuing until his cock sprang out, he pushed the white pants to his knees exposing naked thighs which looked good enough to eat. The pressure of the table edge accentuated the roundness of the big quad muscles above his knees. He savored the moment as two boys pulled his pants all the way off. Karl stood up, a cute dark-haired lad, he was, I thought, every gay guy's wet dream. The light modeled his thick neck and well-developed gymnast's shoulders, full pecs with pointed nipples on large brown aureoles. A wide deep cleft ran down the middle of his eight-pack abs. He had classic V-taper lats and a sexy vein over each bicep. His beautiful, uncut penis curved down over hefty balls. The tight lacy foreskin molded to the large glans revealed its shape and encircled the tip just short of the piss slit.

Reacting to the staring eyes, Karl turned, posed and flexed, showing the guys his muscled back and delts. His haircut squared off at the neck accentuated thick trapezius muscles running from his shoulders up onto the neck. He swiveled his hips, displaying the unbelievable round gluteus muscles of his ass. Then as he turned again, with everyone clothed and him standing there stark naked, it was suddenly an erotic scene and Karl looked tense.

To break the ice, Rick explained the groin fold and ligament where the spermatic cord comes down to enter the scrotum. He pulled over a tiled coffee table and ordered Karl to stand on it with legs spread and hands clasped behind the neck. This thrust his dick, now at Rick's eye level, forward. To prepare for an "interesting reflex" Rick massaged Karl's lower ab muscles down to the pubes with one hand, and his balls with the other until the tense sac loosened completely. Then, the boys watched in amazement as Rick stroked the inside of the thighs with a pencil causing the balls to instantly pull up. "This reflex, the cremaster, exists to protect your testes during fucking and when they get cold." Rick then sensuously ran his hands down the inner edge of the ab oblique muscles where they frame the rectus six-packs and converge into the pubic hair. These muscles actually extend down into the sac, and that raises the balls.

Seeing all this, a kid asked: "Do guys have erogenous zones?" Rick had Karl turn away and bend grasping his ankles. He then slowly ran two fingers over the back of Karl's scrotum, up and down the perineum between balls and his anal opening, all around the hole and then massaged his pucker. "That's a main area, there are others." When Karl reversed, his prick was two thirds erect.

A guy asked about average penis length. Rick replied "about six inches... hard." Rick then lifted Karl's soft dick, and proceeded to measure along the top: "4.5 inches flaccid." He then looped the tape around both balls: "9.5 circumference." As the men watched, Karl held his dick up while Rick examined the balls and cords in the sac, describing what was where. He then took the penis, pulled the foreskin back on the shaft, spread the lips of the slit and inserted the metal cone of a lighted instrument for an inch as Karl winced. Peering in, Rick describing the healthy pink urethral lining.

Since every guy there was cut, with Karl up on the coffee table, legs spread and pelvis pushed forward, we all got in line to examine his foreskin, feel his balls, and look into his cock. By the time I got there, his cock was quite a sight. Fully erect, it throbbed in my hand as I felt its heat. I noticed the swollen veins in the foreskin from all the handling and Rick had to wipe pre-cum from the tip before I inserted the scope for a look. Poor Karl clearly was struggling, trying not to shoot all over us.

Rick, now really uninhibited from more beer, gleefully showed how to measure a fully aroused cock. He fingered Karl's prick for a while then held it down level to the floor and measured along the top... "8.25 inches erect." He quickly wrapped the tape around the shaft, steadying the sensitive organ which was flexing and lurching.... "5 inch circumference ...God, Karl, the girls must really love this thing."

Karl laughed: "Yeah, and some of the boys like it even better!"

Then Barry, yelled "Hey, Brent, let's see yours."

Brent walked up, pulled his jock off and Rick measured the slender lengthy cut unit. "4.75 soft." He then got Barry to stroke Brent's dick with one hand and fondle his balls with the other. The shaft quickly reached full length. Taking advantage of the situation Barry wet two fingers and massaged the head until it expanded and was ready to shoot. Rick took over, measuring: "8.75 fully hard beats Kurt by a half inch!" Kurt said "But don't worry guys mine tastes and fucks much better." Brent stood there with his perfectly formed, smooth cockshaft jutting out and curving upward gracefully, as the engorged mushroom cap flared out. I saw several men licking their lips unconsciously.

With Karl still on the coffee table, a question came up: "Is it tricky to pee with a foreskin."

Karl replied: "Oh fuck ... don't remind me ... I've had 4 or 5 beers!"

The kid, in jest, placed a small empty pretzel bowl on the table between Karl's spread legs. Karl, still glistening with nervous sweat from all the handling, retracted his foreskin, arched his back and put both fists on his butt pushing his half erect cock forward for a healthy "no hands" piss. To the delight of his turned on "audience" a thick yellow stream burst from his hose and descended in an arc which glittered from the strong overhead light. The room fell silent except for the splashing piss. It splattered guys in the front row as Karl squirted all over the tile table top. The raised rim retained it as he fully emptied his bladder. Standing barefoot and naked in his own piss he yelled, "Yeah ... that's much better."

The guys were a little shocked at this "Animal House" kind of behavior, but enjoyed every second of that long, ninety- second urination.

On another Saturday night, we had yet another "for men only" party doing physicals on naked jocks. Dr. Rick said he'd finish Karl the gymnast's exam and also invited the third jock who wanted to be examined in front of these boys. This was Phil the wrestler from another quad, who had an unbelievable body. Phil made expenses working for the art department as a nude model. He also got paid plenty by the Urology department because of his large dick. They used him as a male research subject in several projects including an involved study on nerve endings in the penis. Rick worked there weekends and said that wrestling turned Phil into a total exhibitionist and that he had arranged with him to show us "interesting techniques" tonight.

I iced several 6-packs of beer and Rick brought cartons of med equipment. All twelve of my pre-meds came, turned on by the wild session the week before. This time they were noisier and much less inhibited as they quaffed my beer.

Karl and Phil arrived in sweats. Eyes followed Phil, a real hunk, and I knew that this night would get very hot! At five- eleven and muscular from wrestling, he was as cute as they come with black hair, turned up nose and "come fuck me" brown eyes. He simply oozed sexuality and charm and was well aware of his effect on men. I couldn't wait for him to take his clothes off!

Rick and the guys discussed male body types, dick structure and many questions on erection mechanisms and ejaculation control.

After a couple hours of drinking, Rick turned on the strong light over my big work table in the room's center, locked the door, and said "let's examine." With the boys again in 2 rows of folding chairs he told Phil and Karl to "get undressed", while he covered the table with white towels and removed his instruments from a bag.

The horny, beered-up crew kept yelling, "Get those dicks out... take it off!" as our hunky body models peeled off sweat tops and bottoms. Karl got down to white briefs and Phil stripped to a well-worn jockstrap. The bulges in Phil's stretched pouch revealed that, as rumored, he was indeed a well-developed male.

An excited Dr. Rick called: "Karl, your anal exam is first, so take off your underpants."

Phil, in true jock style, grabbed Karl in an armlock and let the randy boys get him naked pulling off his socks and jockeys. Karl responded with "this is for you later fucker" as he wagged his half erect cock at Phil. Phil said, "Yummm...." The he licked his lips and gave Karl the finger.

For maximum eroticism, Rick bent Karl over the table with his left knee pulled up onto it in order to spread those sizzling ass cheeks. This gave the thrilled boys a direct view of both his pretty hole and his big uncut dick and heavy balls dangling down over the table's edge.

After putting a latex finger cot on his index finger, Rick lubed Karl's pucker and gradually penetrated the hole describing the healthy tight sphincter and smooth lining. He lingered and rotated, showing how to go beyond and down, to massage the prostate as Karl groaned. Then he handed out finger cots rolled like small condoms and we all took turns putting one hand on that hot ass as we used the other to finger fuck this hot stud. Strings of fluid streamed down from his cock and everyone had erections pushing their pants out!

A kid asked, "Karl what's it like to jerk off with a foreskin like yours?" Karl: "fuck man...I don't need lube...I'll show you" The hungry-looking boys encircled the table, and Karl lay down on it just as I handed him a fresh beer. He looked at me and said, "You do it."

With two fingers I kneaded the meaty half-erect cock, fully covered by his long skin. It stiffened in my hand as I grasped it at mid-shaft and started slowly and rhythmically sliding that luxurious skin up and down. Gradually the head emerged. I wet two fingers and gently massaged the head a little. As I pumped, the shaft telescoped out. The boys watched in fascination as the prick pushed out to Karl's full eight-plus inches and the skin stretched smooth except for its attachment at the frenulum just below the groove of the glans.

I lightly massaged his balls as I continued the slow pumping. He was starting to move his hips more. Two boys held his arms back and two others were rubbing their hands all over his chest.

Each time I felt the prick tensing and nearing climax, I moved down and worked only the bottom few inches then resumed sliding the skin fully up and down the shaft. Periodically I stopped to push the skin over Karl's cock head and squeeze. By now he was leaking a lot of pre-cum and moaning. This prick now got hotter in my hand. After about fifteen minutes of this, I pressed firmly on the prostate area under his balls, which he had told us earlier he liked, and stroked the slippery shaft near the head with the same steady slow rhythm. Karl arched, his toes curled back, his delicious abs got rigid and I counted seven spurts of hot juice propelled from his weapon. The first few shot at least three or four feet and came down on my hair and shoulders. I jacked until my hand was covered with Karl's fluid, then put his cold beer back in his hand.

To strip for his exam, Phil pulled off his socks and jock and aware that all those men were staring at his dick, he shook it to primp it out. He was a sight: naked under the light, tanned with perfect musculature, zip skin fat, rock hard abs and sexy brown nipples on the lower curve of his hard pecs.

Rick sat the two nude athletes on the table, quickly took blood samples, then handed them cups for urine. Karl, as one of our section's water sports enthusiasts, pulled over my plastic waste basket. While the crew chanted "Pee! Pee!" the two nude men stood there, filled the cups, and to delight the boys continued pissing together into the waste basket. It sounded like Niagara Falls! They put on a show with the final squirts and with great fanfare shook the last drops from their hoses.

Dr. Rick ordered the naked wrestler to get on the table and stretch out along its length. Phil said he had received nasty hits on the mat to stomach and crotch and wanted a thorough going over. Rick sensuously moved his hands and stethoscope all over Phil's chest. Then he pressed around the abdomen telling us where various organs were. He went to answer a phone call. Phil relaxed and folded his arms behind his neck which thrust his chest out displaying that hot jock-stud physique and smooth hairless skin. Guy's hands were all over his torso, biceps and leg muscles. I got euphoric getting him to do crunches while we felt up the muscle blocks of his 8 pack abs and watched his genitals bobbing up and down from the action.

Rick had returned from the telephone and now massaged Phil's abdomen, working his way down to the pubes. "Looking for signs of injury," he said. He kept pausing to look at Phil's long, smooth, circumcised dick capped with a head much larger than most men piss through.

As Rick examined the muscles beneath the pubes the cock started to swell. He squeezed along the shaft and said "no scarring." Then he fingered the swelling head and opened the slit. He held the penis against Phil's stomach and slowly massaged the large round balls in a firm scrotal sac as Phil groaned with pleasure. "Ball's look fine too." Any questions?

"What's the most sensitive area of a dick?"

Rick replied, "lit just so happens that we have a perfect virile male specimen here so I'll show you!" He placed a thick pad of folded towels under Phil's hard ass, arching his back and pushing his genitals up higher for best access and for our viewing pleasure, then spread his legs wide.

Grasping the penis, he said, "Yes, this is the circumcision scar, the skin from here to the head is the most sensitive on the shaft. He fingered it until the prick extended to full erection. It was a perfectly straight rod with a solid, virtually vein-less shaft. The big round cap pointed straight to the overhead light. Rick measured the cock...a full nine inches, then he put his tape around the shaft, five inches circumference. Rick took my soft sable artists brush, very delicately ran it up and down the shaft and then circled around just below the glans. Phil squirmed from the sensations. Rick brushed over the scrotum.. .Phil shivered. Rick finally concentrated on the "sweet spot" of the cock's underside just near the groove in the head. The big prick suddenly flexed and the scrotum tightened up on the balls. "With this perfectly formed penis you can feel the two large blood filled cylinders and the third one underneath for the urethra." Lucky us, all the men there got to check out and palpate the anatomy of this magnificent rigid sex organ.

Rick stopped just short of getting Phil off, moved him to the end of the table, rotated his hard muscular butt up and got him to hold his ankles. Guys reacted to this amazing scene. This incredible ass looked like it was being prepared for fucking. Rick loosened up Phil's sphincter with his finger in there and then took a speculum like a gynecologist's, greased it and worked it through into Phil's rectum. Then he opened it about an inch and a half wide, gave us a light and we all looked into Phil's glorious body at the pink lining and folds. Guys were amazed that Phil seemed to be enjoying all this.

"Now we'll do something interesting." He placed a 4-inch- long probe on a wire up into Phil's rectum and withdrew the speculum, letting the sphincter close on the probe. He then cemented a small sensor just beneath the balls and another just above the penis after trimming away a small area of pubic hair. With piles of towels under Phil's knees he ordered two guys to keep his legs spread apart and told Phil to keep his hands folded under his neck. What a fucking hot display this was with this muscular stud and his sexual apparatus all splayed out and wired!"

"This monitor shows all the muscle contractions before and during orgasm...The top line shows the first wave about just before the balls tighten up. If we manually stimulate the penis and stop at this signal, theoretically we can masturbate him all night without him shooting his load."

The guys reacted with, "You've got to be kidding!"

Rick said, "Hey, just you watch."

119

Rick applied baby oil to Phil's cock and carefully jacked it to its full hardness, nearly nine inches. As he watched the screen he slowly pumped, stopping short of the head. "The trick is to avoid the sweet spot for more than a second or two." He jacked for several minutes and then got the signal. He immediately curved his thumb and switched to rubbing only the upper surface of Phil's amazing penis. Then with two fingers he stroked all the way up and down the sides only. He applied his thumb underneath hitting the sweet spot a few times and the beeper sounded. Then he curved his fingers and returned to the dick's upper surface. Now he came up onto the head with each stroke. The signal. This time he stayed on the head and the shaft pulsed and flexed like it was going to shoot. "That's what happens if you go pas the first signal."

He did this back and forth for an hour. Guys were feeding poor Phil beer. Finally Phil said, "Fuck it, just get me off." Rick showed one boy where to keep his hand pressed against Phil between his anus and balls. When I say "now" you'll feel that area contract due to muscle action and a second later Phil will shoot.

The boy simply massaged the sweet spot and held a glass over the cock. "Now!" Rick shouted.

"Jeeez!" Phil yelled out and came with such force we could hear the splats as the shots fired into the jar. Eight in all. Rick leveled the jar and said all the stimulation produced 4 times the fluid he'd shoot in a normal jack off.

As the party broke up Phil remained on the table cooling down from ecstasy. Karl, still nude, stood there worshiping Phil's chest and feeding him beer with a strange look on his face.

Rick and I, full of beer, walked the boys down the hall and stopped to pee. At the piss trough Rick told me that Phil, a total stud, does this stuff all the time for the Urology studies, plus sells semen whenever they need it. He had been trying to get Phil to spend a weekend with him in the mountains. Now I knew for sure that Rick was gay.

We returned to my room shocked to find Karl and Phil, still buck naked, up on the table kissing. Karl was working up his erection. The boys asked for coffee; I made some fast. Phil said they'd enjoy it more if we watched! Rick and I gleefully sat down in front of the table with coffee and for two and a half hours got the hottest sex show ever seen by mortal man. Sucking, body worship, and then flip-flop fucking. Seeing those big units in action was almost too much to bear.

A few months later, I got to share a room with Phil for three days on a science field trip, but that, as they say, is another story.

THE HUNTER AND THE HUNTED
Thomas C Humphrey

The icy rain lashing our backs, we raced the hunting dogs across the narrow slough and up the pine-blanketed hill. By the time we got to the dilapidated cabin, I was soaked to the skin and trembling so violently that I could hardly turn the knob and open the sagging door.

I had cautioned Mr. Westerfeldt several times that we needed to turn back as a low, dark ceiling of clouds roiled in from the northwest, gravid with rain, the advance edge of a front that would plunge the middle Georgia temperature into the low teens before morning. But if I hadn't already guessed it when we first met that morning, I learned in a hurry that Glen Westerfeldt believed neither in caution nor in taking suggestions, especially from an eighteen-year-old kid he was stuck with against his will.

While I bustled around kindling a blaze in the fireplace from the pile of tinder-dry wood stacked in a comer, Mr. Westerfeldt slumped morosely in a tall-backed kitchen chair with a broken splat and a caved-in bottom. As cold and wet and uncomfortable as I was, I couldn't help but be pleased with this picture of him. Despite an undeniable strong sexual attraction toward him, I had almost instantly disliked him when we first met that morning.

I had already been told that he had founded a computer software company in Atlanta and quickly had become a millionaire several times over. I had been instructed to cater to him and make sure that he had a good outing. When I first saw him, I had been more than willing to do anything he wanted, anything. I had expected some potbellied old man, too out of condition to walk more than a hundred yards without resting. He strode into the Sand Creek Hunting Lodge dog kennels and immediately set off a melting sensation in the pit of my stomach and a weak tremor in my legs. He was a big, strikingly handsome, virile man in his early forties, wearing a brand-new outfit, complete with matching hat and shined boots, but he obviously would have been more at home in an expensive imported three-piece suit.

"This is Tobias Cameron. He'll be your guide today," Mr. Denham, the Lodge manager, introduced me.

I stepped forward with a smile and stuck out my hand. Mr. Westerfeldt ignored me, and I had to let my hand drop awkwardly.

"Hell, he's nothing but a boy," he said to Mr. Denham, as if I were deaf, or wasn't even there. "Be damned if I'm going to pay an arm and a leg to get in some good shooting and have a barely weaned kid spoil it for me. Get me a real guide, or I'll make some calls and move somewhere else. You're not the only place in the area, you know."

I was taught to respect my elders, but this man got my dander up, and when Mr. Denham didn't defend me, I jumped headfirst into the breach.

"My dad's the best quail hunter in these parts, and he's been teaching me everything he knows since I was eight years old," I said. "That makes me the second best. Now, I'm missing school today to fill in for my dad, who has the flu. But I'd rather be in school or anywhere else than spend the day with you. The guides at Rolling Oaks Plantation, about ten miles south, are all old men. Maybe you should give them a call." I turned on my heel and started for the door.

"Tobias!" Mr. Denham called frantically, followed immediately by Westerfeldt's deeper, "Wait a minute, kid."

I turned and watched him approach, hoping the contempt showed in my face.

"You've got balls, kid. I like that," he said. "Come on, and let's see if you're as good as you think you are."

Although we found plenty of birds and got in some good hunting, things were all business between us the rest of the morning, and the strain was almost palpable. Then the storm hit us out in the middle of a field, despite my continued warnings.

Now he sat in the icy cabin, his new clothes disheveled, to say the least, with cockleburs and beggar's lice covering his pants up to his knees, his once-shiny boots caked with mud from our dash across the slough, and a steady drip-drip of water from the brim of his hat onto the rain-stained shoulders of his jacket. I hoped he was as miserable as I was.

In nothing flat, I had a roaring fire going and the heat began to fill the room. The dogs, who had been licking and grooming themselves, huddled as close to the hearth as possible and curled up to sleep. Soon the tiny cabin smelled of wet dog, burning heart pine, and ancient dust.

"I've gotta get out of these wet clothes and hope they'll dry some," I announced, still trembling from the wet cold.

"That sounds like a good idea," Mr. Westerfeldt said, leaning down to unlace his muddy boots.

I sat in the other chair, took off my boots, peeled off my dripping wet socks, and squeezed water out of them onto the floor. Then I stripped off my nearly threadbare army fatigue jacket and flannel shirt, leaving myself bare-chested. As I backed a little handmade wooden bench up to the fire and hung my clothes across it, I felt Mr. Westerfeldt's eyes following my every move.

"Good thing you knew about this place," he said.

"Yes, sir," I answered. "A friend of mine and I discovered it when we were little kids. We used to camp out here sometimes and skinny-dip in the pond out back and fool around on weekends."

"Ever bring a girlfriend out here?" he asked, a note of lewdness in his voice.

"Naw, nothing like that," I said, glancing away self-consciously.

"Just you guys fooling around together, huh?" he teased.

"Yeah," I answered, flushing a deep red. I leaned against the bench and kicked off my jeans, which were soaked from mid-thigh down. Then, wearing nothing but my briefs, I sat in the chair across the table from him and watched as he stripped down to his boxers and tee shirt and arranged his clothes in front of the fire.

"I should have listened to you when you wanted to turn back," he said unexpectedly. "But at least we got in some good hunting before the rain."

"Yes, sir," I agreed.

"Why don't you call me Glen. The misters and yes sirs and no sirs make me feel ancient," he said with a low chuckle.

"Okay, Glen, if you'll call me Toby. I hate Tobias," I said.

"Deal," he said. "You're a damned good shot, Toby. That four-for-two display was mighty impressive."

Although they carried shotguns, guides were not supposed to shoot along with guests, but he had kept goading until I rose to his challenge. Too small and slightly built for team sports in school, I was proud of my marksmanship and had a shelf full of trophies from skeet and trapshooting competitions throughout the South. Considering that my honor was on the line with this man I disliked, I walked in front of the dogs on point, flushed the covey, swung to my right, and waited for two birds to cross paths before I squeezed the trigger. I quickly swung left and homed in on another one. Just as I fired, a second one cut across my line of vision, and, again, I downed both with one shot. I had seen my dad do it, but it had been a first for me. It had obviously impressed Mr. Westerfeldt.

"Aw, I was just showing off – and I got lucky," I said with false modesty. "Please don't say anything about it back at the Lodge."

"Don't worry. Whatever we do is strictly between us," he said. "Whatever we do." There was a peculiar glint in his eye, and I got the feeling he was communicating something beyond words.

"You're a pretty good shot yourself," I said, responding to his new friendliness. "Of course, I could give you a few pointers," I added, with a big teasing smile.

"There's only one pointer I'd want you to give me," he said, and, again, I sensed that the conversation had shifted to another level.

"What's that?" I asked in all innocence.

"I didn't say that," he chuckled. "Forget you heard it." A long, uncomfortable silence followed, a silence in which his eyes roved up and down from my face to my bare chest, completely disconcerting me.

"I've got to take a leak something fierce," I said, taking a deep breath in hopes of stilling the insistent quiver in my stomach.

I moved to the back door of the cabin and swung it open. Just as I reached in my briefs to free myself, he crowded in beside me, his huge frame filling the narrow doorway. I squeezed myself against the opposite door jamb to make more room.

"Mind if I join you?" he asked as his heavy stream splattered against the rain-drenched wooden steps below.

Momentarily, I was afraid that I wasn't going to be able to piss, but then I started to gush out. Glen directed his stream over toward me and began playing it slowly up and down my stream. It was if he were physically caressing my thighs, flirtingly advancing toward my crotch. I had never experienced anything quite as intensely provocative. My legs almost buckled, and I leaned heavily against the door jamb to support myself and to try to get my suddenly ragged breathing stabilized.

I was too embarrassed to look down at him, but I glanced upward and met his eyes. For a split second, his face displayed a predatory hunger that frightened me. Then he caught my gaze, the feral cast faded from his eyes, and he smiled warmly. I hurriedly tucked myself back in and moved away from the door, wondering why my legs felt so weak.

I had seen predators in action, especially hawks scouting a flock of chickens. Somehow, the chickens know when the hawk alights on a nearby tree branch and patiently awaits his opportunity. But instead of running for safety, the chickens mill around, squawking and clucking nervously, until the hawk selects his prey and suddenly swoops down to claim it. As the flock noisily scatters, the chosen victim seemingly accepts its fate and quietly crouches down until the hawk's shadow obscures the sun and its sharp talons bite in cruelly.

Like a member of some anestrous flock, I busied myself with a flurry of activity, punching up the fire and repositioning the smoldering logs, kneeling down before the hearth to add fresh fuel, all the while trembling with a completely alien and fearful visceral excitement. Suddenly, I was still. Without turning, I sensed that Glen was close behind me, I could feel the hawk's wings shadowing me. When he grasped my shoulder with his thick hand, I gave a sudden start, as though talons had sunk in, and then I sagged back against his hairy legs, surrendering to the predator.

Glen lifted me by the arms and turned me toward him. He had removed his tee shirt. He hugged me tight against him, my cheek pillowed in his thick, wiry chest hair. His erection throbbed insistently against my belly. His hands roved restlessly, frantically, across my back. He nuzzled into my neck and nibbled and sucked at my skin, every cell of which was electrically attuned to his touch. His hands trailed on down and he cupped my buttocks, kneading and squeezing and lifting.

"Beautiful! So smooth and tight and flawless!" he whispered against my neck.

He hooked thumbs in the sides of my briefs and peeled them down my thighs with aching slowness, his fingers lingering on my ass cheeks. My dick was on the verge of explosion. When he had it exposed, Glen shifted one thick hand to my crotch. His other hand continued to shove at my briefs, his fingertips gliding down through the cleft of my ass cheeks. He cradled my tight nutsac in his palm, pulled my cock away from my belly, and wrapped his fingers around its base. His touch was almost more than my aroused flesh could bear.

He backed up and slid his boxers down. Grabbing my hand, he led me to his cock and curled my fingers around it. I gasped a quick breath of surprise and looked down at an unbelievable trunk thrusting up from a forest of dark undergrowth. He was huge! My thumb and forefinger would not close around his shaft, and inches upon inches remained exposed on either side of my palm. The deep blue veins coursing its length and crisscrossing like tributaries were nearly as thick as my little finger. It was darker than my own and even darker at the scar of his cut skin. The thick flared head swelled and subsided with every heartbeat, angry and red. It both intrigued and frightened me.

Glen slowly moved my palm on his shaft. He took my rock-hard dick in his other hand and slid up and down, pinching my foreskin closed over my dickhead. The sensation was so keen I threatened to shoot my load at any moment. After a bit, he turned my hand loose and reached around to toy with my buttocks. One finger searched for an opening and eased inside me. I leaned in and rested my head against his chest and wrapped one arm around his waist to help support my violently trembling legs.

He lifted me effortlessly, turned, and set me on the end of the rickety table, my legs dangling inches from the floor. He stepped between my thighs and pushed me onto my back with one palm on my chest. He again took my dick in his hand and leaned down to kiss and chew at my erect nipples. His mouth slid downward, and his tongue reamed my navel. Lower and lower his lips crept until he was licking the head of my dick and nibbling and pulling at my foreskin. I trembled in excitement and expectation. A couple of friends and I had jacked each other off several times, but only once had a mouth been on my cock, just for a moment, before my friend jerked his head away and grimaced with distaste. When Glen took me in his mouth and plunged down to my pelvis, I arched my back and almost climbed off the table, moaning at the new, exquisite pleasure of his warm mouth.

He raised my legs and draped them across his back. As he sucked my cock and attempted to swallow my tight ballsac, he eased a moistened finger up my ass, to the first thick joint, then the second, then all the way inside. I was a complete virgin, and though his finger stimulated my sensitive anus, his moving and probing around also hurt, especially when he eased a second finger alongside the first.

What followed was rape, pure and simple. He spat on his huge knob, pulled his fingers out of my ass, and attempted to substitute his huge cock.

"Don't," I begged. "I can't."

"I want to, Toby," he said with finality. "I'll be easy. Just relax."

When the huge crown of his cock parted my sphincter, I let out a yelp of pain so sharp that the dogs roused up and milled about to see what was happening. I tried to move my legs off his shoulders and wiggle away, but Glen wrapped one thick arm around my thighs and tugged me back to the edge of the table. Crying and begging, I pushed and hit at his chest and tried to sit up, but he shoved me back against the boards and held me immobile with his forearm. Helpless to do anything but yell and curse at him, I lay impaled on that huge timber as he slowly but relentlessly shoved deeper and deeper into me.

In the midst of my agony, I remembered having read about a barbaric torture in which the nude victim was bound and set atop a sharpened, greased stake driven into the ground. His own weight and gravity shoved him farther and farther down the stake until his innards were punctured and he slowly bled to death. Underneath Glen, I felt a very real kinship with such a victim.

Oblivious to my acute pain, he journeyed deeper and deeper, until he was embedded full length, his chest pressed firmly against mine, his lips and tongue caressing my neck, ears, cheeks and, finally, my mouth. Then he started to move inside me.

Fortunately, his assault ended quickly. Just when I decided I could not stand any more, he gave a few short, staccato thrusts, pulled almost all the way out, and then shoved full length back into me. He went rigid, and his huge pole throbbed deep inside me. He collapsed onto my chest and gently nibbled at my neck. His cock softened and finally eased out. He lifted my legs off his shoulders and stood up.

"I'm sorry I hurt you," he said, wiping at my tears with a thumb. "But you're so beautiful! I wanted you so much!" His eyes refused to meet mine.

I wiped at my ass and came away with traces of blood mixed with his come, which was dribbling onto the table.

"You bastard, you split me open. I'm bleeding!" I complained, a note of panic mixed with my anger.

He slid me farther onto the table and dabbed at my ass with his tee shirt. He spread my cheeks and peered closely to determine the damage.

"You'll be okay," he concluded. "There's just one tiny tear. You're okay. I'm so sorry I hurt you!"

Leaving the tee shirt pressed between my cheeks, he bent down and took my flaccid dick in his mouth and rolled it around with his tongue. Despite my pain and anger, it stiffened and lengthened immediately. He gave it and my swollen nuts full attention, and, before long I was writhing and moaning with pleasure, twining my fingers in his hair and tugging him ever deeper on my cock. Much too soon, my back involuntarily arched, my legs thrust straight out, my toes curled, and I let loose a tidal wave of spunk deep in his throat. He lapped and swallowed it all down and gently licked and suckled my oversensitive cock until it completely softened in his mouth.

It quit raining soon afterward, and we got dressed in our half-dry clothes and went back to the Lodge in awkward silence. I let him out at the Lodge entrance without even saying good-bye and went on to the kennels to groom and feed the dogs before driving on home.

In my bedroom, I stripped, checked to see that the bleeding had completely stopped, and drew a warm bath. As I soaked in the steaming tub, I seethed with anger and a desire for revenge. Reporting his abuse never entered my head. In my little country town, I could not have borne the humiliation which would have come with an admission that I had been fucked. Maybe I could trash the Mercedes he had driven from Atlanta. As soon as the thought formed, I rejected it. I was not the kind of person to do something like that.

I settled back in the tub and tried to clear my mind of its anger. I almost dozed off. Then a curious thing happened. Glen appeared before me vividly, with his thick arms, his hairy chest, his sculpted abdomen, and, most of all, his mammoth cock, standing erect and ready for action. Disturbed by the significance of this vision, for a moment I fretted that Glen had detected something in me that I was not fully aware of, or did not want to admit to myself. But the overpowering image of him and his cock blocked out all thought. Holding the vision clearly in mind, I reached for my dick, which was already stiff and clinging to my belly. With rapid flashes alternating between Glen pumping away inside me and his ravenous mouth on my cock, I frantically stroked myself and in nothing flat gushed a heavy load across my chest and onto my chin.

When I calmed down, I toweled off and liberally applied a soothing ointment to my sore ass. I was hardly dressed when Mr. Denham called from the Lodge to report that Mr. Westerfeldt had nothing but praise for me and wanted me as his guide the next day. Knowing what probably would be in store for me, I could have refused, but, my bathtub jack-off fantasy still tingling my groin, I quickly agreed. The prospect of being with Glen again dominated my thoughts all evening and fueled another hard-on and frantic release in bed that night.

The next morning set a pattern for our new relationship. We both shot every time the dogs went on point until we had a respectable number of birds as quickly as possible. That necessary chore over, we rushed to the cabin, built a fire, spread a blanket in front of the hearth, and wrestled around kissing and embracing and exploring until our lust reached a frenzied peak. Glen lifted my legs and slowly, agonizingly

131

entered me, using liberal amounts of a lubricant he had brought along. The lube maybe made it easier for him, but it did not help me. His huge cock still felt like an endless heavy timber as it inexorably inched deeper and deeper into me. But overriding the pain was a sense of rightness at lying beneath him, securely blanketed by his heavy body, feeling him move inside me. After he climaxed and withdrew that first morning, again I was bleeding, and again he was profusely apologetic, but I experienced a joyous awareness that, through our coupling, I was being defined to myself, and, for the first time in my life, was content with the definition.

Then came the good part. He sucked and swallowed my dick like a starving newborn calf. He was satisfied to come once a day, but he wanted to stay on my cock until he drained me dry. I began to think he could spend all day sucking me without a rest. For someone who had never done anything but jerk off, it was great! But after the fourth time that first day, I had to protest that my dick was getting sore from all the attention.

The pattern was repeated every day the rest of the week, after I said to hell with returning to school. Glen reminded me of a few guys I knew who had mooned about and become totally fixated on some girl after she finally consented to help them lose their virginity. Daily gifts flowed in – a bottle of highly prized and exorbitantly expensive cologne, trendy designer jeans and coordinated shirts, a pair of boots, a leather jacket, a thick, heavy gold chain. Any time we were alone, his hands were all over me, and he couldn't tell me often enough how much he cared for me. A couple of times, he insisted that I drive into Macon with him for dinner at an expensive restaurant. He persuaded me to sneak into his room at the Lodge, where we lay in each other's arms until almost daylight.

As the week passed, we did a lot of intimate talking, and I came to like him as a person, as well as a sex partner. He confessed that he had gone into a sexless marriage of convenience, knowing he was gay, but was continually longing for what he had found with me. He asked all kinds of questions about me and my plans for the future. I had to admit that, although my high school grades were excellent and my SAT scores were quite respectable, I would have to settle for a nearby community college, if I went at all, because my family could not possibly help with my education.

By Saturday, when we went to the cabin for the last time before his departure the next morning, he was ready with a proposal. He would use his influence to get me into Emory

University and set up a trust fund to guarantee my education no matter what happened between us. He would hire me in his business for the summer, furnish me a car, and move me into an upscale apartment where the two of us could be together whenever his work permitted it. It was an undreamed-of offer which I immediately accepted.

As I lay in front of the fire with my dick tunneling deep into his mouth that last morning, I did not know whether I was selling myself. I did know that the distinction between predator and prey, hunter and hunted, had blurred, and my own shadow loomed larger and larger.

THE INTERN H.
A. Bender

"Okay, you asked for it, kid..."

One-time beloved, now reviled U.S. President William Jefferson Clinton isn't the only one who had trouble with interns. I knew I was in trouble the minute I laid eyes on Mickey. Given our relationship, I knew I needed to keep my hands off him – even if he turned out to be gay – but he was too good to pass up.

His red hair was a touch unruly – not in the manner of someone too careless to comb, but clearly his hair had a mind of its own. He wore it shaved almost to nonexistence on the sides, the way so many kids today do, but there was plenty of it on the top, and it was tousled with that just-got-out-of-bed look that made me think of fun and games between the sheets and made me wish I'd been under the sheets with him!

His nose was just the perfect length and width, his cheekbones high and strong, his eyebrows about two shades darker than the hair on his head, and his skin totally innocent of any sign of blemishes, although a few freckles graced the landscape of his otherwise unmarked face. His skin was so whisker-free as to make me wonder if he even shaved yet, though at 18, he had surely made the acquaintance of a razor by now.

The face was so unbearably cute that I had to tear my eyes away to survey the rest of his body. What I found there was equally fine. His muscles weren't the major bulk that suggests hours in the gym, but rather the fine-and-easy ones that suggest a guy who isn't afraid of a little hard work. I could imagine that perhaps he'd unloaded produce cartons for a supermarket after school, back in high school, or perhaps helped out his dad in some sort of business that required some degree of brawn.

All that was conjecture, though. The only thing I could be sure of was that the result was one fine body that was around five-nine, strong in build – and altogether delicious to look at. So delicious that I wanted to start right in chowing down on him, beginning with the part that, though tucked behind his fly, was making such a mouth-watering bulge in his crotch.

He had a package that made me salivate, and once I'd torn my eyes from his face and noticed the grapefruit-sized bulge in his chinos, it was hard to drag my eyes away from raping his dickmound so I could look him in the eyes to talk to him. Although, when he turned around, I had to admit that his butt vied with his basket for Most Desirable Body Part. When he shifted his weight, his two taut cheeks wriggled like he'd hidden something live in there. My dick swelled and throbbed in response, pretty alive itself.

The other thing I knew for sure about Mickey, besides what my eyes told me, was that he was interning in the store for the summer. And, as my temporary employee, he definitely came under the category of "Forbidden Fruit."

I was as temporary in the store as Mickey was. By profession I teach English (and coach basketball) at a small college (which will remain unnamed here). The store is my older brother's. But when Bob and his wife got a yen to take a trip to Australia for their tenth anniversary, he asked me if I'd come in and run the store for three weeks while they were gone. Add another week before those three, just to familiarize myself before he took off, and there went four weeks of my summer. Like a schmuck, I agreed. Bob's been a good brother to me; how could I not help him out?

When Mickey showed up for work, the day after Bob took off, I had more reason than ever to regret agreeing. How was I going to keep my hands off the new intern for three weeks?

Mickey went to the local college, where he was studying merchandising. He was part of a program in which he would spend July working at one local business, August at another, and divide his days between doing grunt work and planning out a merchandising campaign for the business.

I got through the first four days okay, playing mentor and keeping my hands off. It was a struggle, and I went home to beat off furiously to mental images of Mickey sucking my dick, but I managed to keep my dealings with him on a proper business plane.

I had worked at Bob's store once before this summer, so I was able to answer most of Mickey's questions, and his gratitude was unabashed when he thanked me for giving him so much of my time. The truth is, business was a little slow, and I was glad to spend the time with Mickey, helping him out by answering questions while stoking my imagination with plenty of fantasy fodder for later jerk-off sessions.

In a rush of helpfulness, in response to Mickey's latest effusive thanks, I offered to take him to dinner Friday night after work. "Burgers and brews," I clarified. "Nothing expensive on my budget."

"I can't order beer-I'm only eighteen!" Mickey chuckled.

"Then come to my house. I'll barbecue and stock up the fridge with some cold ones."

As soon as I made the offer, I regretted it. What had I done? I'd have Mickey alone at my house ... now how would I keep my hands off him? But it was too late. Mickey had already accepted. With alacrity.

It turned out he had an ulterior motive himself that evening, and essentially the same one I was trying to avoid – but with a twist. You see, Mickey didn't just want my body crawling up his. Oh, no. There was more to it than that. Mickey was cherry – and he wanted me to bust his cherry! Of course, I declined. It simply wouldn't be appropriate.

"Then don't plan on my staying late this evening," Mickey said sadly. "I'd made up my mind tonight was the night, and if you won't do it, I'll just have to go to the adult store. They have gloryholes in the booths. I'm sure there's a willing cocksucker there who'll suck me off and let me suck him."

How could I let that be his introduction to gay sex? It seemed almost charitable to offer to be his first, if it saved him from such an inauspicious beginning.

Or was I needlessly rationalizing? I only know that when Mickey put his hand on the well-swollen lump in my crotch, I let my hand drop to squeeze the protrusion in his own chinos, then unzip his fly and fish for dick, yanking – with difficulty – his fully engorged meat from the opening of his pants.

Already swollen to its maximum potential, it was crimson with want and oozing crystalline dick-honey. I smeared the natural lube across his taut-skinned glans and worked it into his corona with my thumb. Meanwhile, I hefted his balls with my other hand and squeezed his sac gently while I watched his taut belly rippling with waves of desire beneath his T-shirt.

Mickey's face was eager; Mickey's body was tense; Mickey's whole being was so into this experience that he was ready to jump out of his skin with wanting and needing and being so, so ready to fuck, get fucked, suck, get sucked – which did he want to do, anyhow?

So I asked him.

"All of it!" he responded eagerly. "All of it!"

Very well then, where did he want to start?

"Let me suck you!"

"What?"

"I've always dreamed of sucking a dick!" His voice was that of a kid in a toy store who's been told he can carry out anything his heart desires. I gave him my "toy" to play with – properly wrapped, of course.

"How ... just how does one do it?" he asked, quite unsure of himself. He was so cute!

"Well, just wrap your lips around and let nature take its course. Just follow your instincts." I led him to the couch and fell to my back on it. The kid crouched over me, and did what he was told.

Well, I must say that he possessed very good instincts indeed! Even before his lips had encircled my thick prick, his tongue was swirling around my dickhead, laving my crown and tantalizing all the nerves that populate my sensitive glans. I quivered at the feel of this novice sucker exploring his first-ever dick.. .and doing one damn fine job of it. My body began little hunching motions as his tongue flickered oh-so-knowingly across the tip of my dick, across the landscape of my glans, down the side of my column.

If I hadn't known better, I could have sworn this was a kid with experience. Much experience! But the rapturous, wondrous, overjoyed look on his face told the tale. There was no mistaking the joy of the first-timer! The kid was good ... but he was doing it on pure instinct, not experience.

"You've watched a lot of porn videos, haven't you?" I surmised as his lips tightened around my shaft and began traveling downward slowly, teasingly, tauntingly.

"Well, no. Maybe one," he admitted, taking his lips off my cock for a minute, "but I've seen it about half a dozen times now." Then he resumed the job he was so delighting in, pleasuring my dick.

I began teasing his tits. With both hands free, I was able to molest both his tits at once. I flicked at them, pinched them, twisted them lightly. I ran the edge of my thumbnail teasingly across the nub of both. I did everything I could think of to make them feel hot. And he returned the favor and added a few tricks I hadn't thought of.

The kid had some wonderful instincts. My dick surged in his mouth, my balls filling fast. I wondered how long I could last. And I didn't want my hard-on gone yet. I had something else I wanted to do with it.

"On your hands and knees," I directed him.

His eyes lit up with joyful expectation. "Are you going to fuck me?" He scrambled to assume the position.

"Oh, boy!" I sighed. My rod was already sheathed in latex. All I needed was some lube, but a glance at my shaft showed me his slobber coated it well enough that I thought we were all set in that department too. "Let me know if it hurts too badly," I told him. "It's bound to bum a bit. But I don't want it to be unpleasant. Yell and I'll stop if it gets to be too much."

"I can take it – believe me! I have waited for this for so long!" He exhaled the words in a wondering, unbelieving voice. Again I was reminded of a kid, this time one who's found a whole electric train set-up in his living room. Mickey was something else! How could I feel guilt over fucking my intern? How could I feel anything but joy at this situation?

He had scrambled to get in position, so now his rosy pucker was winking at me, his clean, wrinkled hole pulsating as it waited for me to take his anal cherry. I gazed in awe at the never-before-breached aperture and positioned my dickhead at the wrinkled bung. Then I gave a forceful thrust and breached his first line of defense. The tip of my dickhead was within the grip of his bunghole, and the rest of my cock was slowly edging in. When the full tip was inside, I came to a momentary stop. "How's it feel?" I asked, ready to pull back out if it was more than he could handle.

"Oh, it's okay," he said through gritted teeth, clearly trying to be brave. "Give ... give ... Please, give me more." He turned and looked over his shoulder at me, wanting to watch as I drove my meat home in his ass.

"Okay, you asked for it, kid," I said, and punched my hips forward again, driving more of my solid cylinder up within the snug, hot confines of his asshole. I saw a grimace cross his face, but he immediately replaced it with a smile.

Soon more than half of my cock had been swallowed up, inch by inch, by Mickey's compliant asshole. I pulled slowly back out, feeling the gripping sphincter sliding along my shaft as I eased out till only my dick-plum was left inside. Then I rammed back in as hard as I could, as far as I could.

Most of my dick slid into him this time. He was still tight as hell, but now he was moving in concert with me, slamming his buns back against me as I thrust forward. So more of his searing assault gobbled up my meat than before. I watched my mottled red flesh disappearing into the blazing inside of his anal cavity, and I felt his heat surround my pulsating tool.

Reaching around, I grasped one of Mickey's nipples and began tweaking and pinching it. His body shuddered with an exquisite ripple of sensation that coursed through his body and shook him in its grip. Then he started really hunching back and forth, no longer even in rhythm with me but driven by his own desperate need. I molested his nipple some more, and he bucked his ass back at me over and over, hungrily gulping every inch I had to offer. The boy's dick-hunger seemed insatiable, but I crammed every inch into him repeatedly.

Bending down, I bit his shoulder. Mickey let out a groan of such despairing delight that I thought he was coming right then, but a quick feel of his distended rod told me he was not yet disgorging his jizz. As long as I had my hand on his dick, though, I began jacking the shaft, not too quickly but in a gentle, encouraging rhythm. My efforts were met with another groan.

My balls kept thumping against his taut asscheeks with every forward thrust. The feel of our contact made me that much hotter, and I realized I couldn't hold back much longer. With an increased sense of urgency, I speeded up my jacking of his dick and coaxed him to give up his load.

As my own load boiled up in my balls, I felt Mickey's rhythm subtly change, and I knew he was almost there. "Do it! Shoot it! Come my hand!" I begged him through clenched teeth.

My body tensed to deliver my load. Then a buzzing filled my head and I punched forward one last time, filling the

rubber deep in his bowels with a searing load of juice.

As I spurted, I felt Mickey's dick quiver, throb, and spit gobbets of cum onto the couch below us. I caught a modest handful and brought it up to Mickey's mouth. "Here ... you've probably never tasted cum before," I said. "This is the only safe way to drink it these days ... your own."

"Ha!" Mickey leaned down to my hand, slurped his own stuff from my palm, and groaned with delight.

As we separated and flopped onto the sofa, I removed my rubber and tied off the end. Mickey snuggled up against me. "They didn't tell us in school that we'd learn about gay sex while we were interning... but I'm awfully glad you made this part of my learning experience!" he said with a twinkle in his eye.

I was glad too. Former president Bill Clinton's experience with his intern had come to a sorry end, but I could see there would be nothing but good out of my experience. I was only sorry, now, that my brother hadn't signed up for a longer cruise.

SHOOTING SEBASTIAN
Mike Johnson

I. The Solo Shoot Tuesday Evening – First Contact.

I have been photographing lads in the nude for several years now and have developed quite a reputation in the industry. People always ask me, "How do you find such gorgeous guys?" Well, I get my models in a variety of ways. Some respond to adverts I place in magazines, particularly the free-sheets that circulate round most of the bars and clubs these days. Others contact me because, their friends put them up to it.

Others get in touch after seeing some of my work published in either a magazine or book. I would say about 25% of the guys I eventually work with come to me in this way. The rest come to me by word of mouth. In other words, one of the guys who has posed for me gives them my number, or I see them on the street and give them one of my business cards. And finally, there are the guys who are referred by other photographers. Such was the case with a lad known as Sebastian. I had been given his phone number by John Horseman, another photographer who knew what types I preferred to shoot. (By the way, Horseman lives up to his name, I have heard, but I have no first-hand knowledge of it.)

I rang the number I was given by Horseman again and again, always getting a busy signal. Finally, it was ringing. "Hallo," a woman answered. She had a slight accent. Possibly French. "Could I please speak to Sebastian?"

I then heard her call out in the distance. "Sebastian ... A call for you."

Shortly after, Sebastian came to the phone. "Yes?"

I explained who I was and what I wanted, quickly and a little nervously. Despite doing this job for nearly ten years, I always am nervous on first contact. I am never too sure how the lad will react.

"Horseman told me he was going to mention my name to you and that I would be getting in touch. I hope he did."

"Oh yeah, he did." I could almost hear the smile in his voice. "You do pictures for mags and things?"

I sighed internally – with relief. I hated phoning someone up out of the blue. I explained that John had shown me his own photos of Sebastian taken at the Camera Workshop and that, based on them, I would like to do some work with him. I had to explain that it was for possible publication and he'd have to sign a model release, but he would be paid.

"What sort of stuff do you want me to do?" he asked.

"I generally do full nudes...." I paused before going on, waiting to see if he said anything. There was no response. I knew he'd done nude work at the Camera Workshop, but it was one thing posing for photos which will only be seen by a hundred or so people and totally different to be seen by thousands in a magazine or book. "Is that okay?" I asked hesitantly. "I won't ask you to do anything you feel uncomfortable with."

"Oh, yeah, I guess." He chuckled. "But you probably won't be able to find a publisher who'd want to use pictures of me!" I laughed. "Remember, I have seen what you look like, and I am sure they will be lining up to get their hands on pictures of such a handsome guy!"

"Flatterer." And he laughed again.

We chatted a bit more about the sort of images I wanted to get and what he thought he would be comfortable with and what he didn't think he could do. We then agreed the fee he would receive and the date of the shoot? "Okay, Sebastian I will see you on Saturday. One last thing, can you please avoid wearing anything tight before the shoot. It leaves marks on the skin which always show up in the shots."

"I'll keep bollock-naked until you get here then," he said, and I could hear the smile in his voice. I was sure this was going to be a fun shoot. Pity he was straight. Saturday Afternoon – The Shoot I had been keen to work with Sebastian as soon as I had seen his pictures. He was only nineteen then, nearly six foot tall, with a well-defined body. His hair was so dark it was nearly black and his eyes were a deep brown.

He also had a bit of chest hair. Best of all, he also had very hairy legs. I'm afraid hairy legs are my big weakness. A hot summer with guys just walking around in shorts can be very frustrating, to say the least.

We had arranged to do the shoot at his flat on a Saturday. His girlfriend was away in Paris visiting her parents. I was right when I guessed she was French. Although Sebastian had what I thought was a French accent himself, he was from a small village just outside Luxembourg City. Then again, nearly all towns in Luxembourg are small.

I arrived at his place at shortly after one. I was a bit early, mainly because, despite being a Saturday, the roads had been fairly clear. We'd agreed I would get there nearer one-thirty. Anyway, as it was raining, I didn't feel like sitting in my car for another half an hour. I got out of my old Ford Escort went to the side of the house where the entrance door to the first and second floor flats was located. I rang the door buzzer. It was one of those security panels.

Soon after, I heard the crackly voice of Sebastian. I identified myself and there was a buzz and the door latch opened. I pushed on the door and it opened to let me into the bright hallway. There was uncollected post that looked very old and wrinkled lying in a pile in one comer. Presumably the spots of a long-gone occupant of one of the flats. Other than that it was completely empty. The floor was tiled in a black and white checkerboard pattern and the stairs looked original Victorian/Edwardian. They were painted white but where it was chipped you could see a dark wood underneath. Obviously this building had always been flats and not a later conversion.

I went up the first flight of stairs and Sebastian stood by the door to his flat smiling, and wearing only a pair of jogging pants and looked slightly disheveled. Jeez, I thought, he's even better in the flesh. "I thought you weren't going to wear anything," I said.

He grinned and held out his large hands. "Oh, don't worry, they'll soon be off," he said, almost in a whisper, but still smiling.

We shook hands and he led me into the large, slightly untidy flat. "Sorry about the mess. I had a couple of friends over last night. I only woke up a short time ago." He flashed a little embarrassed smile.

"Don't worry about it." With that we set about putting the cushions straight and taking cups and glasses into the kitchen and just generally tidying up. It actually only took a couple of minutes before it was tidy again.

"Do you mind if I have a quick shower?" he asked, not waiting for me to answer. He quickly disappeared into the bathroom.

At first I could hear the distinctive sounds of Sebastian cleaning his teeth and rinsing out. Then there was the sound of cascading water as the shower was turned on. I heard the shower door slide open and close as Sebastian stepped in. I could just imagine the soap foam forming on his body. Round his chest, on his legs. In my mind's eye I saw him rubbing every inch of his arms, butt, legs and, of course, his cock and balls. Oh to be a bar of soap! I smiled to myself.

While Sebastian was in the shower, it gave me time to set up my camera equipment and plan the shoot. I had brought two cameras – one for black and white film, the other for color. As well as that I had a couple of reflectors and flash guns. I checked the batteries in the flash guns and made sure I had spare batteries for my camera. Although I always checked to see that I had everything I needed before I left home, I usually fear I have forgotten something – especially the batteries!

I remember one shoot with a lad named Shamus, when just as he was beginning to get relaxed, and I turned on the battery in my camera, it died and I hadn't a spare with me, so I shot into town and picked up a new set of batteries. But, alas, the moment was lost. So now I always have spare batteries.

After twenty minutes or so, Sebastian re-emerged looking even better than before, still wearing his jogging pants. But now he had also put on a figure-hugging white vest. "Shame you are straight," I whispered under my breath. Before I had even made first contact with Sebastian, I had been told by John at the camera club, that the lad was 100% straight. He knew this because he'd tried. Then again, John made moves on nearly everyone who posed for him. Me, well, I just flirt, and if something happens that's a bonus.

"Do you want a coffee before we start?" Sebastian asked with a grin.

I wasn't in a particular hurry. With his girlfriend away there was no rush. "Sure," I said.

He made the coffee and we sat chatting. He told me about his girlfriend, Louise. They had met shortly after they had started university. He was studying economics, she was doing politics. She had moved in with him six months ago after his flat mate had moved out. So far things were good, but he didn't want it to get too serious. He smiled a very sexy smile when he said that.

"If you see most girls for more than a week they think you've made a lifetime commitment. Louise is not like that. We have a very, how do you say, open relationship? Yeah, open. Very open." He took a sip of his coffee. 'We have a good time together, but we are not tied to each other. Do you understand?"

I nodded. We chatted then about his studies. What he wanted to do once he had finished university. He even told me about his grandfather and that he (his grandfather) had fought in the Second World War. Sebastian was an interesting young man, both easy to chat to and look at.

As soon as we finished our coffee, we started the shoot. I had him standing and sitting in various parts of the room still wearing his pants and vest. I must admit neither left very much to the imagination, which made it even sexier.

"Okay," I said, "I want you to start lifting the vest with your right hand and rub your crotch with your left."

He obliged, whilst keeping a smoldering sexy look on his face. Boy was this guy hot! My lips went dry and I had to keep licking them. He seemed to enjoy the effect he was having on me. He also seemed to be having an effect on himself because a definite bulge started to appear in the front of his jogging pants. He lifted his vest higher and started tweaking his nipples and rubbing his chest. From this point on he needed little or no further direction from me. He pulled off the vest fully and stood facing me with his feet apart whilst he stroked his chest and rubbed his crotch.

He then turned his back to me and whilst looking over his should started to ease his pants down. My camera clicked away, capturing every revealed inch. He bent down as he pushed his pants down to his ankles so that his round, firm, hairy butt was presented to me like an offering. His thighs and calves were beautifully shaped – strong but not stringy. He was muscled without being over-muscled like a bodybuilder. This guy was so horny I had difficulty stopping myself from shaking. I had to keep reminding myself, over and over: "He's straight. He's straight. He's straight. Dammit!"

He then seemed to get a bit embarrassed and wouldn't turn round to face me. I realized then that he had a very impressive erection. I must admit it is not an uncommon response even for the straightest of guys to get a boner when they strip off in front of someone else for the first time. It doesn't mean they are in anyway interested. However I was a bit surprised, because John had said there had been no stirring at all in that area when Sebastian had posed for him in the Camera Workshop.

I smiled. "Don't worry about it. I've seen plenty before. The more you try to hide it the less likely it is to go down. We'll just carry on as though it wasn't there." Always easier said than done. But it sometimes works. I must admit my own cock was getting hard just watching him. I licked my lips again. My throat had gone dry and I had to take a drink of water before we resumed.

He grinned an embarrassed grin and turned to face me. He needn't have been embarrassed. He was a good seven, very straight, very thick inches. A pearly drop of pre-cum could just be seen forcing its way out. I carried on taking the pictures as if nothing extraordinary was happening. Inside I felt that someone had just turned the heating up to full power and I was perspiring.

"Could I have a another glass of water?" I asked.

He obliged and went to get me one. I watched him walk naked past me with his great hard-on. I wanted to reach out and grab it, but resisted the temptation.

For the next hour and a half I had him sitting, standing, lying in various locations round the flat, ending up with him on the sofa. His erection went down occasionally but never for very long.

At the end he said, " I really enjoyed that. Much more fun than doing the session in a studio. It's warmer as well." He smiled his sexy smile again. 'Want another coffee before you go?" Before I answered he got up and went into the kitchen. When he brought the coffee back he was still nude. He gave me a cup while I carried on packing my camera gear. He sat back down on the sofa.

"What you doing now? Have you got another shoot lined up for this afternoon?" he asked before taking a sip of his coffee.

"No, just back home and get this film in to be processed." I responded

"So you're in no rush then? I thought you might have another shoot lined up with someone else."

"No, not this afternoon." I carried on packing my gear away without really looking up. I then realized he had sat back and opened his legs wide to reveal his erect cock. I looked at him slightly surprised.

"So you don't have to go for a while yet?" He was like Bacchus tempting me.

"You sure?" I asked.

He nodded. I went over to him, and I could still smell the odor of fresh soap mixing with his own underlying aroma of pure male lust.

I took the head of his cock into my mouth and let my tongue explore the glans and the slit. It was like letting a ripe strawberry slip into my mouth. The pre-cum oozed onto my waiting tongue. He groaned and pushed my head down farther onto his shaft. I nearly gagged as it hit the back of my throat. I had to get used to his length before I could take him all the way to the base of his shaft. I soon got into a rhythm pleasing to us both.

While he slowly pumped my mouth, my fingers started to explore his body. His nipples. His legs. Oh, his wonderfully hairy legs. They were covered in thick almost black hair. His balls, too, were densely covered in thick black hair. Finally his ring. It was warm and inviting. I pushed in one finger. He groaned deeply and pushed my head down on to his cock.

As I took more of his cock into my welcoming mouth I slowly worked my finger in and out of his relaxing warm moist hole. A second finger soon followed it, then a third. Sebastian groaned in pleasure and put his legs over my shoulder so I could have easier access to his ass.

149

Sebastian then started to increase his thrusting into my mouth. He gave little or no warning as he shouted, "Christ! Oh ... I'm gonna shoot ..." as he spewed his hot salty spunk into my mouth. I swallowed as much as I could, but it was quite a load and some trickled from my mouth onto his pubes and balls. My fingers were still up his butt as he gave a final shudder.

I sucked him dry, but he was still hard.

Between gasps he said, "You got a rubber?" I bobbed up and down on his still-hard cock in answer. "Great, 'cos I want you to screw me."

"Hmmm, ' I said, leaving the cock. My pants were soon off. He stroked my shaft, admiringly I thought. Then he smiled. "Oh, this'll be nice. God, that Horseman! I hurt for three fuckin' days!"

I ignored that, but filed it away for future reference. Now I had second-hand knowledge that I could trust. He put the condom between his teeth then slid warm, moist lips down my shaft. Obviously he had done this before. He then sat back on the sofa a lifted his legs in the air, presenting his stunning warm hairy ass. Just waiting to be plundered. I eased in slowly while I wanked his still-hard cock.

He was so relaxed and well-lubed that I entered with little to no resistance. The snug interior of this stunning youth soon engulfed my entire shaft. We kissed deeply. I gently thrust into him. I could feel his hard cock pressing against my stomach. I wanted this to last forever but my cock had other intentions. I could feel my resistance weakening and the speed of my thrusts increasing. I had been turned on since the beginning of the shoot, and this was better than anything I could have dared dream.

"Oh, yeah, fuck it," Sebastian groaned as I finally shot my load, then collapsed on top of him. "Oh yeah," he sighed.

We rested a few minutes before I could feel his hard cock pressing between us.

"Suck me again," he begged, almost pleading. "I've plenty more cum for you."

As I pulled my cock out of him, my mouth once again found his hard cock and I immediately went down on him. Soon after, I was rewarded with another huge mouthful of warm, salty spunk. All I could think of was, "He's straight! He's straight! Yeah, and I'm a Dutchman."

Since the session that first Saturday, Sebastian has posed for me several times. It always ends the same. So the next time someone tells me, "There is this good-looking straight lad...."

II. The Duo Session

About two months after Sebastian's first solo shoot with me I arranged with him to do a duo session with one of my regular models, the comely lad Mike Green. I had worked with Mike on about half a dozen previous occasions and he had appeared in several magazines and graced the cover of a couple. Mike wasn't as muscular as Sebastian but he was fit and had a very thick, eight-inch, uncut cock. He was about the same height as Sebastian and had similar hair color, although his was cut much shorter. He also had great legs, covered with dark hair. His pubic hair was also quite thick, but his buttocks and chest were completely smooth.

On the day of the photo shoot, I finally found a parking space and put my money in the meter, which allowed me to park for up to four hours. I was sure that would give me enough time for the shoot. Fortunately I had managed to find a parking spot which was not too far from the flat where the shoot was to take place. Within about five minutes, I was standing outside the front door and ringing the bell for Flat 2. I knocked and Mike came to the front door. "Sebastian's not here yet, but he has called to say he's on his way," he told me as we walked through the foyer into the ground floor flat. Once inside, Mike gave me a quick tour because I hadn't been there before.

Mike had arranged the location for the shoot. The flat wasn't his but belonged to a friend. It was quite large – the lounge/dining area was about twenty by fifteen. There were also two good-sized bedrooms, a large, mirrored bathroom and a compact kitchen not even big enough to swing a cat. Mike looked at me staring at it and said, "Yeah, it's small, but Frank hates cooking anyway. He nearly always goes out."

"It's nice," I said, going back into the lounge.

"Frank said we can work anywhere except in his bedroom." As Mike told me this, he opened the door to the room in question. I looked in to see a large four-poster bed and fantastic tapestry wall hangings. It looked like something out of a medieval castle. It was a major contrast to the rest of the flat which was very minimalist, white walls and modem art. "Shame. It would have made a great setting," I said as Mike closed the door. He nodded in agreement then asked, "What do you think of the rest of the place?"

"It's great. I think if we start off with you both having a shower together, then move in to here," referring to the lounge area, "and see where we go from there."

Just then the doorbell rang and Mike left to answer it. He came back with Sebastian who was wearing black jeans, a white T-shirt that hugged his muscular chest, and trainers. Mike was also dressed in black jeans and a T-shirt. The only difference was his T-shirt was dark blue.

As neither of them had met before I thought it would make sense for us all to sit a chat a bit. I am always a bit tense when I set up a duo shoot because I never know if the guys will get on or not. In this instance I need not have worried. Mike was also at university so they started talking about their courses, the problems they were having with their professors, and so on. It was also obvious they found the other attractive.

After about half an hour of listening to them, I said, "I hate to interrupt but we really need to get started," and led them both into the bathroom.

I photographed them undressing. They did not take their eyes off each other while they stripped.

Sebastian climbed into the bath first and turned on the mixer tap and then the lever for the shower attachment. He started to soap up when Mike climbed in with him. Mike put some shower gel in his hands then applied it to Sebastian's chest. Within minutes the two teenagers were exploring each other's bodies with water cascading down their well-defined torsos.

Both were already hard and their cocks kept on rubbing against each other.

Mike finally knelt down and took the head of Sebastian's cock into his mouth. They had become almost oblivious to my presence and the clicking sound of my camera. Sebastian grabbed the sides of Mike's head and started to pump his cock in and out of Mike's mouth. Occasionally he pulled back so far his cock came out totally, but within seconds it was re-encased in Mike's mouth. This went on for several minutes then Mike stood up and forced Sebastian down into a kneeling position.

Sebastian didn't immediately take Mike's cockhead into his mouth. Instead, he licked Mike's balls whilst his hands grabbed Mike's bum cheeks. Mike pushed his hips forward and his cock rubbed the top of Sebastian's head. Mike then said, "Suck my dick. I want your hot gob on my cock." Sebastian looked up, licked his lips and then licked the head of Mike's cock. He then ran his tongue down the length of Mike's cock to its base in the mass of thick, black, curly pubes. Mike tipped his head in pleasure, savoring the sensation. Sebastian then ran his tongue back up to the head then engulfed it in his lips. Mike groaned in pleasure. "Ohhh... that's good," he sighed.

Sebastian's head bobbed up and down. Taking Mike's shaft to the back of his throat then back up again. I got some close- ups of the hard cock plunging into Sebastian's mouth. The two guys were really enjoying themselves.

Mike then pushed Sebastian off. He looked down, breathing heavily. "Shit, you'd better stop or I'll come now."

Sebastian immediately plunged back down on Mike's cock. Mike couldn't resist any more and started pumping quicker until he groaned, "Here goes," and shuddered as he obviously came into Sebastian's eager mouth.

Both youths now clambered out of the shower and started to dry each other off. Sebastian's cock was still hard, and despite shooting a load Mike was also stiff. Once they were fully dry we all moved back into the lounge. Mike and Sebastian sat on the sofa and started kissing. By this time I was on my third roll of film and carried on, clicking away.

Mike leaned into Sebastian's lap and took the hard cock into his mouth. Sebastian swung his legs round so that they wrapped round Mike's back. Whilst Mike sucked on Sebastian's cock I could see his fingers probing into Sebastian's ring. Sebastian closed his eyes and moaned in pleasure. I moved around the two to get shots from various angles. Mike rolled a condom onto his cock and plunged into Sebastian, then pulled right out before plunging back in. Sebastian groaned and played with his own nipples and cock. Then unexpectedly he grabbed my trouser belt and pulled me towards him. When I was close enough he tugged down my zip and pulled out my hard cock and started sucking on it.

Fuck the pictures, I thought to myself and put the camera down. In moments my trousers were off and the three of us were on the floor. Sebastian was on his back with Mike plowing his ass.

I was astride Sebastian and, while he sucked on my cock, I sucked his.

I could feel Sebastian increasing his thrusting speed and could taste the pre-cum that was oozing out of his slit. Mike pumped harder and faster. My own hips were humping faster as well while I face fucked this gorgeous guy. I then heard Mike groan as he shot his second load of the day in the youth. I was soon rewarded with a delivery into my mouth of hot salty spunk This triggered me to fire my own load and Sebastian swallowed all he could.

Eventually we all collapsed on to the floor.

"Not bad," Mike said smiling. "Wouldn't mind doing that again" then to me he grinned as he said, "Did you get everything you wanted?"

"And more..." was all I could say.

Mike then leaned across to Sebastian and took his flaccid cock into his mouth. His fingers played with Sebastian's balls. Sebastian leaned back against the sofa. Within minutes his cock was hard again. I moved across towards them both and joined Mike sucking of Sebastian's cock and balls. Mike then moved round so he could suck on my cock. My tongue flicked over the firm strawberry head of Sebastian's cock. I could taste the creamy salt and smell his musky odor. As I took more of Sebastian's cock into my mouth, Mike swallowed more of my stiff cock into his mouth. He also played with my balls.

Both Mike and I then pulled Sebastian up and got him down on all fours. Mike moved round to Sebastian's face and sat down in front of him. I moved around to his ass, which was still well-lubricated from when Mike had fucked him. Sebastian looked back over his shoulder to see me putting a condom on my stiff cock. He then turned to face Mike and took Mike's semi-hard cock into his mouth.

I gently eased my cock into Sebastian's arse. He didn't flinch and his head continued to bob up and down on Mike's cock. I pressed in deeper until my cock was buried in his warm hole up to its base. I left it there enjoying the warm sensation. Sebastian ground his hips, wanting me to start pumping his arse. I started to pull out then plunged back in and soon found a rhythm. While I fucked him, he carried on sucking Mike. I reached underneath him and grabbed his hard cock, which was slick with Mike's saliva. I was soon building to a climax when I felt Sebastian shudder beneath me and felt my hand filled with warm spunk. I kept on jerking his cock and he just kept on pumping.

Mike then called out as he shot another load. This time it splattered Sebastian on the face. Seeing this really set me off and I came deep inside Sebastian.

As I pulled out of him, he lay his head in Mike's lap. Mike leaned back on his elbows. We were all pretty well shagged out.

Finally, we all had a shower and then got dressed.

I left Sebastian with Mike; they said they wanted to go over some course work.

I managed to get back to my car with five minutes to spare on the meter. I climbed in, turned the ignition key and soon began the long drive home. As I passed the flat, I slowed down, looked up at the building, as if I could see them, "working" hard. I smiled, took a deep breath and said to myself, "I really must do that again sometime. Sometime soon."

FLORIDA FLAMES
Peter Gilbert

Michael was bored. The copy of The Racing Cyclists' Weekly that he'd bought on his way to work did little to lift his depression. Des Simons of the 'Preston Pedals,' whose picture was on the front cover, was an extremely beautiful young man. There was another picture of him inside, a side view that showed off the rounded contours of his butt to perfection, but Michael was used to publications of a much more explicit sort. In London he could get them but not in Southcliff on Sea.

He'd been excited when they told him he was being sent to manage the Southcliff on Sea branch of the Easy-Fit shoe company for two months in the summer. After seven years in Head Office he'd almost forgotten the thrill of gently massaging a young man's toes and imagining what the rest of him was like. Sadly, there weren't that many young men in Southcliff on Sea. It was the most moribund place he'd ever been in. The directors were sure he could do better than Mr. Rowers. He wasn't so sure.

It soon became apparent that nobody in Southcliff bought shoes – and, as for the holiday-makers the directors had such high hopes of attracting the few that spent their holidays in Southcliff were middle-aged and unlikely to spend money on brightly colored beach shoes. On that particular day there had been just one customer: an elderly woman who wanted a can of gold spray to paint her shoes for a tea-dance at the Pavilion.

"What on earth did Mr. Flowers find to do in this dump? he asked. Lynn, his over made-up, solitary sales assistant stopped polishing her nails. "He always kept himself busy, did Mr. Flowers," she said.

"I can't think how. His window displays were dreadful. The stock room is crammed with 'Florida Flames'. That's disgraceful! All managers were asked to return those when we realized that salt water attacks the glue."

Lynn sniffed and carried on with her manicure. For the third time that afternoon, Michael went outside to inspect his window display. It was, he thought, a hundred times better than Mr. Flowers' pathetic efforts. Michael had taken out the faded shoes on plastic stands. He had covered the display area with gravel, hung up a fishing net and some floats and filled the window with the very latest 'Easy Fit' beach shoes. Brightly colored 'Sandflies,', 'Beachcombers' and 'Rock-pool Roamers' looked really good displayed on the inverted plastic beakers that he had covered with sand to make them look like little sand castles. There was no doubt about it, he thought. It did these local managers good to have someone down from Head Office – even though he'd got the worst branch.

He was still concentrating on the 'Beachcombers', wondering if perhaps they might look better in a greenish spotlight when he became aware of two young men standing on his left and, with a thrill, he realized that they were not only looking at the display but talking about it.

"Doesn't look as if they've got any," said one. He was tall, blond and – much more important – he, like his companio, was wearing very brief shorts. Michael didn't look directly at them but at their reflection in the newly polished plate glass. He hadn't seen anything as beautiful since he arrived in Southcliff. The blond one had remarkably smooth legs. The other, a much darker boy, had what looked like very hairy legs indeed. He glanced down at their feet. The shabby trainers they wore were size elevens at least. Size eleven! Long, supple toes! The sort of toes that could wrap round a pencil and gave promise of something else that was long and equally supple until it was manipulated into stiffness! Michael's cock gave a twitch of appreciation. A part of his mind hoped that they would lose interest in the display and turn round so that he could study the reflection of their buns. They didn't. They seemed fascinated by the window display. That was understandable. It was good. He doubted if any Southcliff residents had ever seen anything so artistic.

"Those 'Beachcombers' would be all right," said the dark one. "How about them?"

Michael turned to face them. They were really beautiful. "One of our bestselling lines," he said, taking control of his thoughts, "Designed and handcrafted especially for us." The fact that the craftsmen concerned were children who worked for a few cents a day wasn't important. "I'm the manager here," he added, noticing the startled expression on their faces.

"Oh. You must be Mr. Flowers," said the blond youth.

"Mr. Flowers is on vacation at the moment. I'm down here from Head Office."

"We were looking for 'Florida Flames.'. Have you sold out?" the dark one asked.

Michael thought of the hundreds of boxes in the stock room, each one with its brightly colored label. The letter 'F' in both words had been made to look like a palm tree.

"Florida Flames?" he asked, frowning. "I think I may have one or two pairs in the stock room. They sell so well and we have so few left that I didn't put them on display." He held the door open for them. He'd been right, he thought, looking downwards as they passed him. Their cocks were only just discernible, nestling limp under the shiny material of their shorts but those bumps were definitely not cigarette packets or billfolds. Once he'd got them in the fitting chairs he might get a better idea. It was always a thrill to kneel in front of a good looking young man and look up the length of his legs to where his treasure lay.

Lynn put her manicure set aside. "Could you have a look in the stock room and see if we have any 'Florida Flames' left, Lynn?" he said – and made a mental note to speak to her about leaving open manicure sets on the chairs.

"That shouldn't be too difficult, but I thought you said they...."

"Just have a look," said Michael. "Eleven's I should think but bring me some eleven and a half's as well." He smiled at them. "If you would care to sit down...."

"We haven't got time," said the blond.

"Oh but size matters a great deal," said Michael. The words seemed to echo in his head and, once again, he had to force himself back under control. "Easy-Fit is one of the few companies with its own patented foot gauge," he said, bending down to bring it out from under one of the chairs. "Now, do you want a pair each or are they for just one of you?"

"Oh, just give us the largest pair you have for Christ's sake!" said the dark young man.

Shocked to the core, Michael looked across at Lynn. "You heard the gentleman," he said. She went into the stock room and returned seconds later with one of the all-too-familiar boxes. "You are quite sure? We wouldn't be able to replace..." said Michael but the lad had almost snatched the box from his hands. The other one paid for them and they left the shop. "Well! Absolutely amazing! I can't get over it! Total lack of manners and what sort of person in their right mind   ?"   said Michael. Lynn resumed her seat and took an implement of some kind out of the manicure case.

"Mr. Sinclair-Evans' boys," she said. "They're all like that?"

"And who is Mr. Sinclair-Evans? I wish you'd stop doing that. It puts the customers off."

Lynn didn't look up but continued to pick and file. "There aren't that many. You said that yourself. He lives in Cinderella's Castle."

"Who? What?"

"Mr. Sinclair-Evans. He lives in Cinderella's Castle. You know. That big place with all them turrets on top of the cliff. Its real name is the Villa Alhambra but everyone here calls it Cinderella's Castle."

"And the boys are his sons?"

"No. He has boys staying with him. He's a sort of tutor. Something like that. He always sends them down for beach shoes but I've never seen one wearing them." She giggled.

"And what is so funny about that? A person living in a big house would naturally want the best shoes and Easy-Fit is renowned for high quality."

"And high prices," said Lynn. "No, I wasn't laughing at that. It's just that my friend Suzie and me..." and she giggled again.

"Your friend Suzie and what?" said Michael. "Do stop doing that! It's most irritating!"

Resignedly, she put the implement back in the case. "We was walking along the beach. Last summer it was. Suzie was a bit keen on one of the fishermen so we went out ever so early so we'd see the boats come in and we got to the part of the beach where Cinderella's Castle is and, well, there were two of the boys playing volleyball...."

"And? There's nothing wrong with volleyball."

"They never had a stitch on. Honest! Nothing at all, let alone sandals. We was so embarrassed, we didn't know where to look!"

"I'll bet you did."

Lynn picked up yet another instrument. "I'm not like that," she said. "Anyway, they were too young for us. You could see that. Not that we was looking. I mean...." She blushed and set to work on her thumbnail.

Michael called in at the paper store on the way back to his flat. "Like your new window display, dear," said the old lady that ran the place. The fishing fleet, she said, always came in on the morning high tide and the tide table was on the back page of the Southcliff Sentinel. He bought a copy.

At six thirty on the following morning, clad in shorts, a shirt and, of course a pair of 'Beachcombers' he set out. His business suit was in the back of the car. He drove the entire length of the promenade. It ended in a car park. There was a public toilet there – the ideal place to change before driving to the store.

He parked the car and went down a flight of steps, unnecessarily posted 'TO THE BEACH.' The towers of the Villa Alhambra came into view as he rounded the headland. It really did look like something out of a Disney film. He'd never seen anything like it. Towers sprouted out of every wall making the place look like some sort of gigantic stone cactus. He walked on. There was nobody about. He couldn't even see a fishing boat. A summer haze hung over the sea. He stopped. The only sound was the hiss of water lapping over the shingle. Lynn had called Southcliff "The Town of the Living Dead." She was right, he thought – and then he heard voices.

"Yours," said one.

"Sod you!" said the other, and then they both laughed.

Ahead of him, the large rock outcrop the locals called 'The Knuckles' took up most of the beach and the rising tide was already lapping at the seaward end. They had to be behind it, he thought, and the only way past it was a narrow gap between it and the cliff face. They were bound to spot him if he walked through that and if, as Lynn had said, they were naked.... He walked to the rock. It wasn't too difficult to clamber up, but 'Beachcombers' were not designed for rock – climbing. The surface was rough and there was seaweed on the lower parts that made him feel doubtful about tackling the ascent. The tide was coming in fast. There had to be a way, he thought and he continued climbing. It wasn't very high, not more than eight feet. He reached the top, got down on all fours and very carefully shuffled across the surface to the other side. He lay down on his belly and looked down.

Lynn hadn't been lying. The net was stretched across the beach, supported by two steel poles. The dark boy had his back to Michael. He was attractive enough but the blond one was breathtakingly beautiful. Just as Lynn had said, neither wore shoes of any sort. Neither wore anything. The dark boy's creamy white buttocks contrasted with the dark hair on the lower parts of his legs. Looking down at him made the long walk worthwhile but the blond one was even better. His cock looked stubby but remarkably thick. It was almost as thick, thought Michael, as the pole they used to drag out the sun awning at the store. He wondered what it was like when it was erect. As stiff as the pole almost certainly. Michael's tool hardened under him. The lad had a good chest too, he thought. Even from that distance he could see the brown aureoles round the nipples. He was hairier than Michael had guessed too. Every time he raised his arms to pat the ball back across the net, Michael got a glimpse of the golden hair that sprouted under his armpits. The hair at his groin was darker and glittered like polished bronze in the morning sun.

Suddenly, the dark boy let the ball fall to the ground and trapped it under his foot.

"Already?" his companion called. He walked round the edge of the net. Michael shifted forwards, cursing the pebbles that high tides had thrown on top of his rock. The blond one, he thought, was probably the most beautiful young man he'd ever seen. Not that the dark one was to be despised. Those hairy legs

"You can't see the fishing boats this morning," said the blond boy.

"No. Too much haze. It's going to be a hot day."

"Which means they can't see us. How about it?"

"Could do. Have we got time?"

"Just about. Have you got the spunk? That's the question."

"Don't you worry about that. There's enough for you and the boss won't be disappointed. The horn of plenty, that's me."

In here then. He can't see us in here."

About six feet to the right of Michael there was a triangular cleft in the rock. It was almost as if some giant had cut a segment out of it. The two young men walked towards it, their cocks dangling – and then vanished from sight.

"Oh yeah! Go slowly."

"...ly" The echo rose from the fissure.

"Do you want to suck it?"

"...uckit?"

"Oh yeah! Go for my balls. Hang on. Ah! That's better."

"...ter." Crab-like, Michael moved in the direction of the fissure. "Go slowly."

"...ly."

Michael moved forward again and stopped.

"Oh yeah!. Yeah! Aaah! There!"

Echoes of liquid noises emanated from the cleft and then there was silence. The dark one went out first, followed by the taller blond. They stopped and looked towards the house giving Michael his first chance to appreciate the blond boy's backside. In that field, Michael was a connoisseur. His career in the retail trade had started in men's swimwear. His extensive library back in London contained pictures of butts of every possible shape, size and color. Nonetheless, he'd never seen anything like the blond boy's jutting, soft-looking cheeks. They were rose-pink. The rest of him was the color of rich cream. Very carefully,

Michael inched forward and then stared again. The pink formed a pattern of intersecting curves. He shifted forward again and then there was no doubt about it. He couldn't see the 'Easy-Fit' logo but he could make out the double 'F' palm trees.

"Any minute now," said the blond. That puzzled Michael. There was no doubt at all as to what they'd been doing. The 'minute' had come and gone. Then the sound of a whistle drifted down from the top of the cliff, four staccato blasts.

"What did I tell you? Always on time," said the blond boy. They stood up and, with cocks still half-hard like fleshy water divining rods, they went across the beach to a small opening – obviously the bottom of a flight of steps that zigzagged upwards. Michael watched them until they were out of sight.

The images, the blush-pink palm trees on creamy skin and those two delightful cocks, stayed with him for the rest of that day. He had to see them again. There had to be some way of making a surprise visit to the Villa Alhambra without causing suspicion. A man with two gorgeous gay boys as guests, and who smacked naked butts with sandals, could be a very interesting person to know...

Surprisingly, the Easy-Fit Store Managers' Manual provided the answer. It was in the section headed 'Customer Complaints.' In the extremely unlikely case of a product being found faulty after being put on sale, store managers should do everything possible to contact the customers, explain that a very small percentage of the product had been found to have slight faults, and to issue a credit note.

"I'm going out, Lynn," he said, emerging from the stock room.

"Again? You went out this morning. Where to this time?"

"Visiting a customer," Michael replied.

"Mr. Flowers never visited customers. He had enough of them in the shop. That's what he used to say. He...." but Michael had left the shop.

The Villa Alhambra looked even odder the closer one got to it. Michael had difficulty in finding the entrance. It was surrounded by a high wall. Finally, ignoring a sign that said 'TRADESMEN: PLEASE USE REAR ENTRANCE' he stood on the doorstep and rang the bell.

The door opened. "Could I speak to Mr. Sinclair-Evans?" asked Michael.

"You are. I was expecting you to call."

Dumbfounded, Michael didn't know what to say. The man confronting him was very tall, wore glasses and had silvery hair. Michael's practiced eyes scanned corduroy trousers and a pair of very-down-at-the-heel brown shoes.

"I'm the manager.... acting manager. I'm from Head Office actually. Easy-Fit Shoe Company." He pulled out his card case. "My card," he said but Mr. Sinclair-Evans waved it aside.

"You'd better come in," he said. Michael followed him down a corridor and into what was obviously a lounge but furnished quite differently to Michael's expectations. There was no expensive antique furniture. Most of it looked shabby. Mr. Sinclair-Evans beckoned to him to sit down and sat opposite him on a long settee. Michael's composure was thrown completely. Mr. Sinclair-Evans had anticipated his call and that could only mean that he had discovered the fault in the 'Florida Flames' and should, by rights, show some sign of annoyance. But he didn't. He sat there smiling as Michael launched into a description of Easy-Fit's testing methods. It was the sort of smile that said, "I know all this but I'm letting you continue."

Then Michael saw it. It was on top of a bookshelf, of all places to put a beach shoe: a Florida-Flame, minus it's strap. "Ah! I see it's happened already," he said. He stood up, walked over and picked it up. "It's the effect of sea water," he said. "We will, of course, issue a credit note to the full cost." Like some mystic oriental god, Mr. Sinclair-Evans continued to smile. "There is no need. I am quite satisfied," he said. "However, comma, let us talk of other things. The real reason for your visit has nothing to do with shoes, has it?"

"Of course it has. As I explained, 'Easy-Fit has a   "

"Oh come, come my dear sir. You know exactly what I mean. This morning, up on the Knuckles...."

"You saw me?" Michael felt his face reddening.

"I was watching you much more closely than you could have imagined. I have a camera obscure up in the tower. It's a device that

165

throws an enlarged picture onto a screen. I found your antics quite amusing. Like me, you find young men objects of beauty. That you are a man with the heart of an artist I don't doubt. Your window display is excellent...."

"Thank you."

"However, comma, shoes and young men are not designed purely to be looked at. We are blessed with other senses." The man's pedantic manner and his superior, supercilious smile infuriated Michael. He wasn't used to being talked down to. Mr. Sinclair-Evans continued. "One could draw a parallel with shoes," he said. "A shoe must look good and feel good as I'm sure you will agree."

"Yes, but I don't quite see...."

"You have already appreciated the good looks of the two youths I have here at the moment."

"Yes."

"But you haven't yet felt them. There is nothing, my dear sir, that feels so good as a young man. One could wax poetic if one wished. The smoothness of skin moistened by perspiration. The delightful texture of their pubic hair. And as for the object in the center of that hirsute escutcheon – 'objects' I should say, for there is as much inherent delight in their ball bags as in their rising cocks." Michael shifted in his seat. The conversation was beginning to have a visible effect on him. "And the other senses?" he asked. "Smell. The scent of recent perspiration. That's why I like them to take exercise before breakfast. It gives me an appetite." Michael couldn't resist smiling at the memory of the exercise he had overheard. "But for something rather more substantial than a slice of toast, I imagine?" he said. "Indeed, yes, but I reserve the feast for the afternoon and evening. Where was I?"

"You've covered sight, feel and smell," Michael replied. "Mentioned. Not covered. That would require a library of books."

"Hearing?" Michael suggested. "Aha! Hearing. That is where your excellent sandals come in, what are they called, Florida Fires?"

"Flames. Florida -Flames."

"An excellent piece of work. The sole is so delightfully supple. The slap of the sole on a buttock is the overture to the most beautiful symphony in the world. The young man's gasp. His heavy breathing ... Not enough research has been done on the correlation of pain and sexual stimulation, but I assure you that it exists. As indeed, I observe, does a conversation such as this." Michael parted his legs to let his imprisoned member spring up beneath the expensive worsted of his business suit. There was no further point in disguising his interest. He blushed slightly. "I see what you mean," he said. "I also saw the marks you left on the blond boy."

"David. He was delightfully responsive. You merely saw the aftermath. Rather like looking at a field that has been plowed after the com has been seeded. The moment of his seeding was memorable indeed." Mr. Sinclair-Evans licked his lips. "And you sowed your seed in his furrow?" said Michael. Mr. Sinclair-Evans obviously enjoyed all these metaphors. "Alas no. My doctor advises against any form of physical exercise. A few slaps with a beach shoe deprive me of breath these days. Old age I fear. It comes to us all. It's a tragedy because it does them so much good. In the old days I could reform a boy in days by fucking him regularly. The current regime of nakedness and spanking them till they ejaculate is all very well but believe me, my dear sir, there is nothing so effective as penile penetration."

"I can believe it," said Michael, suddenly remembering one or two incidents with Mr. Entwhistle when he'd been a teenaged trainee swim-wear salesman.

"It takes time for them to appreciate my methods," said Mr. Sinclair-Jones. "Just as a violin needs a good bow to make it sing, youth needs a beach shoe. Thus I have to send them to your excellent store. A pair of young men needs a pair of shoes; a new pair every time. The one you picked up was used on David last night. Neil's is here, still in the box. He'll delight me today. However, comma, we come to the last and most important of the senses. That of taste. I have found, over the years that that every young man is...."

There was a knock on the door. "Enter," said Mr. Sinclair- Evans with all the pomposity of a judge. The door opened and the boy with the dark hair boy entered. Not that Michael noticed his hair. Not at first anyway. He had no more clothes on him on that late afternoon than he had early in the morning. He took one look at Michael, attempted to cover his dangling cock with a piece of paper he was carrying and retreated behind the door.

"Oh. Sorry. I'll come back later," he said.

"Come back!" said Mr. Sinclair-Evans. Gingerly, still with the paper covering his middle, the lad stepped back into the room.

"Neil," said Mr. Sinclair-Evans and, turning to Neil, he said "You know this gentleman I think."

Neil looked over. "Oh yeah. The guy from the shoe store," he said.

"He is not the guy from the shoe store. He is the acting manager of the shoe store and is from the company's Head Office."

Michael nodded. In any other circumstances so correct an introduction would have required him to stand up and shake hands. In this case it seemed inappropriate and, in any case, standing up would have been difficult. His cock made up for any apparent impoliteness in the rest of his body.

"The gentleman was watching you this morning from the top of the Knuckles," said Mr. Sinclair-Evans.

Neil turned distinctly pale.

"When you were playing volleyball," said Michael. "I didn't want to embarrass you in view of your ...er... unclothed condition."

"Oh," said Neil. He turned to Mr. Sinclair-Evans. "I've written it again," he said.

"Then you'd better show it to me hadn't you? Don't worry about this gentleman. He and I share the same tastes."

Neil had his back to Michael when he handed the paper to Mr. Sinclair-Evans. Nonetheless, Michael got his first close up view of the young man's cock. It had looked appealing enough from the top of the rocks; long and thick, it drooped forward from a thicket of black hair. At close range, it was truly stunning.

"This is good," said Mr. Sinclair-Evans. He was reading the paper. "Very good in fact. Neil has problems with spelling. However, comma, he's improving all the time. I'm delighted with him, and he will delight me even further."

"You sort of teach them then?" Michael asked, vaguely remembering what Lynn had said.

"I do not sort of teach them. I teach them. I teach them very thoroughly and very well. Neil will be university material in a couple of years. I only take on boys with real academic potential. They are the only ones that interest me. Strangely enough they are often the most beautiful. Neil is a case in point. I'm sure you would agree that he is strikingly good looking. Turn round, Neil. Let the gentleman see all of you." Neil turned.

"Oh, yes. Definitely," said Michael, feeling embarrassed. Des Simons and the young men in the picture books back in his London flat faded from his memory at that moment. Neil had what Michael would describe as a 'real mouth waterer.' "Once they have become accustomed to my methods, they work hard which is a reward in itself," said Mr. Sinclair-Evans. "Neil is a good example. I found Neil in a bus station...."

"Stoned out of my mind," Neil added.

"He's pretty typical. Shop lifting; street brawls; drugs; thrown out of his home and as arrogant as can be."

"That's right," said Neil. "I told you to fuck off."

"So you did. Well, I brought him down here. We have a house rule that you will have noticed. I don't allow them any clothing in the house or on the grounds. It's the first stage in making them appreciate their inferiority. Self-confidence fades with every article of clothing removed. They start learning again just to get permission to go down into the town."

"I see," said Michael.

"You mean you understand. But, indeed, you see as well. A delightful sight wouldn't you say?"

"Very." Michael's voice suddenly became strangely hoarse. "He has a very beautiful bottom. That's what attracted me when I first spotted him."

169

"I was bent over spewing my guts at the time," said Neil, inadvertently dampening some of Michael's ardor.

"It seems to me that a lesson is in order," said Mr. Sinclair- Evans.

"I've done six hours, boss," said Neil. "I was hoping to go out."

"Not for you. For our guest. You can still go out afterwards."

"I'm not quite sure I understand," said Michael, secretly hoping that he hadn't misunderstood.

"We shall enjoy a chorus. A duet for the senses," Mr. Sinclair-Evans replied. "A pleasure shared is more rewarding. Come and sit next to me."

That was easier said than done but a butt like Neil's was worth any amount of effort. Michael had been gazing at it like a starved child in a candy store. The hair on the young man's lower legs thinned out above his knees and there was just a faint hint of darkness running up the inside of his thighs and vanishing between the tightly clenched cheeks of his ass.

He grinned as Michael lowered himself gingerly onto the couch beside Mr. Sinclair-Evans. He'd obviously noticed the state Michael was in.

"Let us begin with his visual impact," said Mr. Sinclair- Evans. "Pleasant. Would you not agree?"

"Very," said Michael, faced with a close up of Neil's cock. Neil himself had referred to it as 'the horn of plenty' that morning and there was something very reminiscent of a cow's horn (albeit upside down) about the way it stood out from its bed of black hair before curving and tapering to a puckered point. Sparse, long hairs grew from the wrinkled surface of his well-filled scrotum.

"Remarkably tactile," said Mr. Sinclair-Evans. "Move to one side Neil. We must allow our guest access to your treasures." Neil took a step sideways and Michael's nostrils caught the first whiff of his odor. There was perspiration there; a faint hint of some sort of male toiletry and something more elusive and indescribable. It brought back faint memories of the various flats he'd occupied in London, and the boys he'd picked up to share a number of beds. The brass bed in Sycamore

Road and Tony. Then there was 125A and the mahogany bed – he could remember that but not the names of the young men he'd shared it with.

"The olfactory delights of a young man are enhanced when the foreskin is retracted," said Mr. Sinclair-Evans, "like a rose when it emerges from the bud. Go ahead."

"If Neil doesn't mind," said Michael, whose hand was already moving towards it.

"Neil is not in a position to mind. In fact, Neil will adopt any position I choose for him."

Michael closed his fingers round it. It had been a very long time since he'd had a cock in his hand. It was warm and very much alive. It twitched in his hand and he felt the lad's pulse racing. Very slowly and very carefully, he slid the skin back. Like a ripe, purple plum, Neil's cock-head slid out and into view.

"Nothing like it, is there?" said Mr. Sinclair-Evans. Michael didn't answer. Neil's cock was hardening in his fingers by the second, swelling to such an extent that he had to relax his fingers to accommodate its diameter. Neil breathed deeply. Michael looked up at his face and smiled encouragingly but Neil's gaze was on the wall behind him. Michael put his free hand against the inside of the boy's thigh and slid it slowly upwards. The hairs there were as soft as silk. His fingers touched Neil's balls. As delicately as he could he lifted them on the side of his finger. Neil gasped.

"He is possibly a little too hairy;" said Mr. Sinclair-Evans. "Possibly because of my having been a school teacher I prefer my boys to be a little less hirsute. However, comma, he has a very pretty bottom. It will look even prettier tonight I assure you."

Michael was breathing heavily, and was too angry to answer. Lynn's constant, empty-headed chatter was bad enough, but at least Lynn had the good manners not to discuss the customers in their hearing. It was difficult to imagine what Neil felt. He didn't seem to object to what Michael was doing he must have felt like some sort of exhibit in a museum.

171

Michael slid his hand further between the boy's warm thighs, turned it palm-upwards and hooked his middle finger. Instinctively, Neil clenched his ass-cheeks but not before the tip of that questing finger had found a tight knot of muscle. He squeezed the steel hard shaft in his other hand. Neil began to breathe more heavily.

"It won't be long now ... but don't let him make a mess," said Mr. Sinclair-Evans.

"Oh, don't worry. I won't." said Michael.

"David is very good in that respect. I have rarely seen a lad produce so much. There comes a time, you know, when they stiffen at the sight of a beach shoe and before you can say 'Jack Robinson' their cocks are streaming.

"Ah, the nectar of excitement and the ambrosia of their coming. The Bible, you know. What does it say? 'From out of the strong came forth sweetness. ' David is delightfully strong. I think I'll...."

He stood up and left the room. Michael was so astonished that he let both hands fall.

"I thought that might happen. He's gone to find David," said Neil.

"What for?"

"What do you think? Watching you turned him on – as much as a guy that age can be turned on. You were doing all right. Better than him. Carry on."

"Are you sure you...." Neil didn't let him finish. He stepped forward, took his rigid cock in his hand and pressed the tip against Michael's mouth.

No further persuasion was necessary. Michael let it slide in until the head was pressing against the back of his throat. Neil hung over him, supporting himself by putting his hands on the back of the couch. Michael reached round him, put his hands on the boy's soft ass cheeks and pulled him further towards him. It had been a long, long time since he'd had a cock like that in his mouth, a long time since he'd had any cock in his mouth.

At last Neil began to respond as a young man should respond. His panting breath stirred the hair of Michael's head. His ass tightened and relaxed in Michael's hands. For a brief instant Michael thought he might choke but the expertise of past years hadn't deserted him. He paused briefly with the palms of his hands deep in the dimples of Neil's buttocks, took two deep breaths and it was all the way in. Not for long unfortunately, but the pleasure it gave Neil was worth the inevitable sore throat he'd suffer for the next hour or two. "Oh Christ! That's great!" Neil gasped.

Michael concentrated on breathing through his nose. He held it for as long as he could and then, very gently, let it move upwards and out of his gullet until the tip was touching his teeth and he could breathe normally again. He licked it for a few minutes, worked the tip of his tongue in and under the soft foreskin. Then he let it all into his mouth again and sucked as hard as he could. He would have liked it to have taken longer but all that preliminary manipulation in the presence of Mr. Sinclair-Evans had obviously taken its toll. A series of little spasms ran through Neil's body. His backside quivered in Michael's hands then tightened and the first jets spurted into Michael's mouth. He swallowed as much as he could and let the rest run round his mouth. What had Mr. Sinclair-Evans said? 'From out of the strong came forth sweetness'. There was a lot of truth in that.

Pompous old idiot, he reflected. Neil's cock slid from his lips and a few drops of his spunk landed on the carpet.

"He's not that bad," said Neil.

"Neither are you. You were right this morning. You really are the horn of plenty."

"Christ! Did you see what we were doing?"

"I heard. I couldn't see."

"Don't tell the boss for Christ's sake. He'll beat the hell out of us if he finds out. We're supposed to keep it all for him."

"Don't worry. I won't. Neither will I tell him about the visits to my flat."

"But I don't even know where you live."

"125A Beach Road. It's the flat above the bank. An ass like yours needs something else apart from a beach shoe."

Neil leaned forward and traced the line of Michael's cock through the material of his pants. "I see what you mean," he said, grinning. "Can David come too?"

"Your tutor assures us that he can," said Michael. That assurance was soon verified. Mr. Sinclair-Evans returned, sat down and wiped his mouth with his handkerchief. Neil had gone upstairs to get some clothes on, Michael having offered to take him into town. "Most satisfactory," he said. "I trust Neil was too?"

"Very," Michael replied. "Perhaps you would care to return this evening. We could have a spanking good supper if you know what I mean." Michael declined with thanks, but stayed for some time talking. "You're in a good mood this morning," said Lynn as she applied scarlet paint to her thumb nail. "Had a date for your return to Head Office have you?"

"I shall not be returning to Head Office. I'm staying here," said Michael, carefully shredding the Racing Cyclist's Weekly into the waste paper basket. Lynn was so astonished that her hand shook. Tiny dots of red varnish spattered onto the floor. Michael was so happy that he didn't even notice. "Another thing, Lynn," he said. "I've found a buyer for those 'Florida Flames.' Special cheap price, but they'd only get thrown away if they go back to Head Office."

"What ... all of them? There are over a hundred pairs in there!"

"Oh, I know," said Michael, envisaging over two hundred individual shoes. Over two hundred young men! With his help, his new business partner could take on many more students. Southcliff on Sea was a good place to spend the rest of one's life.

THE FACE OF APOLLO II: LEAVING PRESENT
Barnabus Saul

There was generally a bit of a scramble for the washroom before English lessons. It kinda marked off the kids who hadn't done their assignments from the ones who had. The slackers arrived late for class and all together and all wearing shorts. College allowed shorts for summer wear and there was nothing in regulations that said they couldn't be worn in winter. So in winter if you weren't keeping up with English work, you took your shorts with you and changed for English lessons.

Redvers Blunden paused dramatically at the blackboard as the troupe of six lads entered the room, as if this almost scheduled interruption were pushing him beyond the limits of human tolerance. With heavy gaze he followed the progress of twelve hirsute and sturdy knees to their places. There was a wolf whistle followed by an outbreak of sniggering and Mr. Blunden moved quickly to silence indiscipline in the ranks. "Stand up, Davis!"

A boyish-looking guy stood up and looked progressively more sheepish as Blunden railed against his childish behavior and asked him if he wanted his little bottom spanked. He sat down blushing furiously much to the amusement of his colleagues who had already mentally stripped him and placed him across Blunden's lap. With heavy sarcasm Blunden asked if he might be allowed to continue. Blunden took very much to heart the old teachers' motto 'Never smile till Easter', in fact he took it so seriously that he never smiled at all.

He completed the short list of dates and titles on the board and began to dictate his outline notes on nineteenth century English poetry. Talking from memory, on autopilot, Blunden's mind was free to pursue the aesthetic qualities that presented themselves. He paced to one side of the classroom and back noting the views and eventually positioning himself where a hunky relaxed inner thigh displayed itself to his sight. Its owner, slightly uncomfortable as students are meant to be on the undersized furniture provided, sat splay-legged as befits a guy with

175

much to squash between beefy thighs. The boy was concentrating on his dictation work, a task which did not come easy, yet some subtle nuance of communication told him he might expect an awkward question any moment. The way to avoid this inevitably shaming experience was to adjust his stance, placing his foot on a rung of the chair so that his solid knee pointed more directly at Blunden and afforded a clear view into the tunnel of his shorts leg. Blunden stood for some time in appreciation of this enticing sight. He licked his lips and in his mind ran his tongue the length of the inner thigh. But there was no view to be gained of the youth's scrotum, and Blunden today was feeling decidedly scrotal so he moved on. The youth, still without looking up from his scrawl, returned his foot to the floor confident that he had achieved a satisfactory grade.

Blunden paused at the front of the classroom to ask a question. He raised his eyebrows to the lad seated to the far left of the front row. Unable to answer, the guy shifted his position in his chair and adjusted his shorts to afford a clear view of his knob head. Blunden paused silently to contemplate the enormity of this student not knowing an answer, and moved on to the next youth, who displayed himself likewise, and the next, and the next, until, with a whole row of gleaming helmets exposed, Blunden arrived, disappointingly at a youth in jeans who knew the answer.

Blunden resumed dictation and moved in search of other knees and lower thighs which hinted of glorious upper thighs and magnificent genital organs. No boy looked up from his urgent dictation yet as he moved around the room bare knees followed his progress as if each boy unconsciously sought to recommend an intimate view of himself for his teacher's approval. Blunden found what he required, a single ball cuddled in a long relaxed sac, and remained to contemplate it as he dictated the major part of his notes. At length he progressed to the back of the room where Robinson struggled with the writing task. "And what precisely would have been the motive for that, seemingly eccentric, act on the emperor's behalf?" asked Blunden. "Let's see those hands up. Is your hand up, Mr. Robinson?" A muffled remark somewhere, evidently about a hand being up Mr. Robinson, caused a few titters which Blunden ignored. Robinson took the hint, though clueless about the answer and raised his hand, accidentally nudging the hem of his shorts in the process and exposing a couple of inches of shapely penis. "Well done," said Blunden approvingly, "so we don't need to ask you." He asked one of the guys in long trousers, who always knew the answers. "Perhaps you know the answer to this one then, Mr. Robinson." Robinson eased the hem of his shorts yet higher, displaying a now stiffening cock and its attendant ammunition sack. Blunden asked his question of someone else.

For the remainder of the dictation session Blunden remained at the back of the room keenly observing Robinson's private parts. When he had said all that could be possibly said and recorded on the subject, he bent forward to peer disinterestedly at the illiterate scrawl in front of Robinson, placing an approving hand on the youth's dick and balls, and said, "Well done Mr. Robinson."

"Thank you sir," beamed Robinson, and Blunden returned very reluctantly to his own desk.

"And now your assignments from last night," he announced, casting his eyes around the classroom. Downward looks are a teacher's usual indicator at such times, a sudden interest in a small area of flooring. Blunden looked down the register by way of pretending to pick a random name, and happened upon the name of the youth with the cute left bollock. "Would you like to come out and read your work to the class?"

The boy picked up his papers and faced the class beside Blunden. A pile of books on the desk served as a rest for his essay, and to obscure the lower half of his body from the class. He knew that all he had to do was to keep talking more-or-less sense in order to escape the results of having done no work. "The works of Lord Byron can be viewed in several perspectives...." he announced.

Blunden's fingertips stroked the very lightest of circles around the hollow behind the youth's knee. The youth's voice took on a slightly more husky tone and there was a discernible muscular tremor in the thigh muscle as Blunden's fingertips brushed very gently upwards, tickling the hair and rounding the boy's leg so that the whole palm was soon able to appreciate the firm, muscular column. Blunden's hand gently inched its way upwards, pausing to give an encouraging squeeze when the youth stumbled in his narrative, tickling and probing with delicate caresses of the fingertips as it went. The youth's shaft by now was fiercely rigid, trapped downward- pointing by the shorts and forming a huge tent there. The hand explored it only cursorily. On other days it might have rested there. It would have slid the tube of satin skin back and forth and teased with thumb and fingernail at the cleft of the helmet, a move all but guaranteed to bring the youth to a breathless climax, which he would try to cover with a coughing fit, shooting hot sticky jets over Blunden's hand and provoking knowing grins around the classroom. On still other days the hand would have wedged itself firmly into the hot moist cleft where the legs met and where the thumb could tease and probe at the soft lips that guarded the puckered little hole until it gained entry. Today, however, the hand had balls on its mind and curled grateful and appreciative fingers around a magnificent pair of juicy, spongy plums.

Until now Blunden had snapped the fingers of his free hand to draw attention to any weakness or mistake in the youth's reading, but now there was a more direct way of drawing attention to his errors. After such a mistake the youth began to exclaim loudly and struggle to correct himself. All around the classroom other youths swapped knowing grins and mouthed in a satisfied way that he had him by the bollocks.

By now the clock was ticking towards the end of the lesson. Blunden summarized the work they had heard. "You're all over the place boy," he said, "you raise a topic in one paragraph which raises the expectation of explanation in the next and you do not supply such explanation. You're off gathering nuts in May. What are you off gathering?"

The class sensed a comic interlude and sat forward attentively. The word had a tactile accompaniment so that when the youth pronounced "Nuts in May, sir," the first word arrived in a high voice, with a little jump and a distinct wince, which made the class fall about with mirth. Blunden, unsmiling as ever shouted fiercely for silence and repeated this little ventriloquist's trick in order to provoke the mirth yet again. At last he released the boy and allowed him to sit down.

Blunden concluded the lesson on a serious note. "Before you go I might as well let you know that this will be my last week in school. There has, I gather, been some complaint, the nature of which need not detain us here, and rather than become embroiled in unpleasant proceedings of a formal nature, I have agreed to leave the school. I would like to thank you for your attention over the past months we have shared and wish you well with your new teachers. Good day, gentlemen." The bell rang on cue and the class dispersed.

Allen, Clyde and Raymond headed for the washroom. "What about that? Who snitched do you think?"

"No idea," said Raymond kicking his shorts aside, "but I'll be glad not to have my nuts go through the crusher anymore." Which brought on a chorus of Here we go gathering nuts in May. "No really guys, look at that," the youth continued his complaint, holding forward his ballsac for the others to examine. "They're almost squeezed out of shape. I'll be the only guy around with round nuts."

Allen's hand flew forward and grabbed them. "Hey stop whining, will ya? It's easy enough to squeeze 'em back into shape,"

"Ow, ow. Leggo"

"Sing Nuts in May"

Raymond gave a grudging rendition of the chorus and Allen let go. "Anyway, it could be worse. Look at Clyde. He's got scratches from Blunden's moustache all over his arsecrack. Show him Clyde."

Clyde grinned and in sliding off his shorts turned his back and bent low to reveal twin globes of peach-like sheen. There were no scratches nor were there any blemishes of any kind whatsoever to mar the breathtaking beauty of this boy's tail. Allen whooped 'yeah' and grabbing Clydede's hips, pressed his rig against the crack and performed a series of mock thrusts. "Tell you what, though," he said, thoughtfully continuing to rub his stiffening rod along the length of Clyde's crack, "this is going to play hell with our grades. At least you know with old Blunder that you can trade a pass for a few touch ups. I mean, what would you rather do, write an essay or get wanked in class?"

"You're right," agreed Raymond, "I guess we owe him quite a lot. What do you think Clyde?"

"No way. He had his fun up my shorts. My balls are black and blue from him fumbling about up there,"

"Let's see,"

"Fuck off you pervert, you ain't looking at my balls. Give him your own nuts to play with. I don't owe...." But Clyde's mouth was precisely at the right height to be silenced by a length of Raymond's shaft. All that followed were incoherent strange noises.

"Glad you agree, Clyde. I think we ought to get him a leaving present."

A bell rang. Raymond and Allen jumped. "Hell, I'm going to be late. I can't go into class again with a boner. I gotta beat off."

Clyde fetched his trousers and put them on while watching the other two beating their rods. "What you gonna get him then?" he asked.

"I know what he'd like best," said Allen panting from his exertions and continuing to pump his rod back and forth, "there isn't much time to have a collection. I know one thing he'd like. He'd like that juicy little tail of yours. You heard him going on about spanking Davis' sweet little ass. Perhaps we should gift wrap it for him!"

"Why my tail?" snarled Clyde, "give him your tail."

"Well, perhaps you're right," teased Allen, "perhaps Davis has got a cuter tail than yours. Hey, any of you guys seen Davis' tail?"

"Yeah, I have," Raymond caught the mood, continuing to pump his wood. "That is one firm, smooth, peachy, tight, shapely little pair of buns. Clyde wouldn't stand a chance beside that. Davis could sit on my face and I'd die happy."

Clyde sneered. "He ain't. I bet he ain't as taut as I am. I bet he's carrying loads of fat round there. There ain't no fat on my butt."

"Yeah?" gasped Allen, "now why don't you just remind us both? Help me finish this off real nice," he indicated his rapidly moving hand.

"Yeah c'mon, Clyde," pleaded Ray. "It's just what I need too."

Clyde shrugged and muttered "Things I do for you sick pair of perverts." He turned his back, dropped his jeans and boxers back down and touched his toes. "And don't get any splash on me," he warned from beneath his draped jacket.

Allen blew a kiss in the direction of Clyde's curvaceous ass.

"Lovely tail, Clyde, lovely tail," he gasped, suddenly tensing all his gut muscles, causing his helmet to almost double in size and turn a radioactive luminous purple as he kicked a gob of cum from his cockhead. It dropped with an audible plop onto the floor.

"Oh, you got the prettiest little tail of the group," added Raymond. "You know, we should do a photo, tell the guys it's for art project, they'll do it. At the swimming pool, get them to drop the backs of, ooh, aah..." and he too delivered a long string of spurts of cum.

Quickly the guys tucked away their yet-engorged dicks and headed for class.

Friday was Blunden's last day in post. His farewell interview with the principal was a muted affair, a muted drink and some stilted pleasantries that studiously avoided the reason for Blunden's enforced resignation, his career prospects, the large golden handshake the college had found itself forced to provide or the little-short-of-glowing references the principal had to write. Blunden took the long way back to his room via the sports changing rooms where occasionally, just as the eighteenth century ha-ha gave way to an edifying landscape view, a door left ajar might likewise offer a scene of sudden delight. But there was no activity on this Friday afternoon, sportsmen were either playing away or had stayed home. Lessons were erratic on Friday afternoons, most of the time being given up to individual creative activities. Blunden headed for his room to collect, for the last time, his briefcase and effects.

He opened the door and his jaw dropped. Never in his life had he, pedestrian, boring old Blunden, been the subject of a surprise party. Yet here in his study had collected a large group of his students, all on their feet, beaming and crying "Surprise!"

Blunden took a moment to collect his thoughts. It would not be in his character to go along with such festivities, yet today was his last day, there would be no class discipline implications, and, he thought wryly, if they wanted to celebrate his leaving, why not. There was a modest buffet spread out on his desk, and cans of lager contrary to school regulations. Blunden's face broke into a grateful smile, which occasioned a further cheer of delight from the assembled youths, for whom this outcome had been in no wise certain.

Blunden sat down in the place of honor. Stacking chairs appeared. Everyone managed to be seated in the somewhat cramped circumstances of a lecturer's office and food and lager circulated. Blunden counted some twenty heads around him among whom, he noticed with a minor pang of disappointment, was not young Clyde with the silken soft thighs that promised perfect buns he had never alas encountered. He luxuriated instead in the enforced proximity of the virile youths around him.

The first to speak was Allen: "We didn't know what to get you as a present sir, but we thought you might like something like this."

As if on cue, the door to the next room opened and, to cheers and whistles, Clyde was there after all. Blunden watched entranced as the youth entered for, apart from a length of blue cloth encircling his hips and tied at the front like the bow on a ribbon, Clyde was stark naked. He scowled at the boys who were whooping, grabbing at his nipples and making lewd pumping gestures at their crotches and got on with what he had agreed to do. He moved his limbs, lithe and catlike towards Blunden, tempting and teasing and rolling his supple hips. He took Blunden's hand and rubbed it over his firm, warm belly and chest, and along the length of his inner thighs. Finally, he settled himself on Blunden's knee with his arm around his neck.

There was much applause at this performance and even Clyde had been won over; his scowl turned to a grin. Allen called out above the noise of revelers, "Undo the bow, sir." and when Blunden did, the ribbon fell to the floor leaving Clyde bare-naked on his lap. Now Blunden played up to the crowd who encouraged him as he kissed nipples and made extravagant licks across armpits. To further cheers he buried his head in the youth's lap, nuzzling and kissing the stiffening rod and seizing the contents of his purse.

Blunden tried to address the youths but for once his words stumbled. "Boys I ... this is ... I mean...." he buried his head again for a moment in Clyde's groin before continuing. "Wonderful," he gasped. There was another light cheer as Blunden turned Clyde over on his lap and contemplated at long last those magnificent ripe peach globes. As he kissed and licked he barely noticed the surrounding youths enjoying this vision almost as much as Blunden himself. Allen had taken on the role of Master of the Revels, and now quietly muttered "We'll just leave you to it for a minute shall we sir? Don't go away." And he ushered the remaining lads discreetly into the adjoining room.

For how long Blunden worshiped that faultless flesh he knew not. Time stood still for Blunden as he stroked and probed and tasted delicious boy essences. He rolled Clyde over again and nuzzled the bouquet of teenage armpit, then licked the little puddle of sweat that accumulated in the navel. He took each ball into his mouth, one by one as there was too ample a provision to take both at once, and he tasted every crevice of Clyde's firm young prong. When something distracted him, he looked up; there was yet more surprise for him. The youths had returned, there was a cake. But more than that, they were all, every one of them, stark naked as Clyde on his lap, and every one of them sported a beautiful erection. Brandon for once in his life, was lost for words as he surveyed the roomful of boy-babe bottoms, boy-babe bellies, boy-babe breasts, boy-babe bollocks, and boy-babe boners. It was Allen who broke his reverie; "We got a cake sir. Are you going to blow out our candles sir?"

Clyde slipped effortlessly off Blunden's lap and hovered near, knowing that he might be required again. Allen continued, "And we got something else for you sir." He nudged Davis who stood close by but who held back. "Go on Davis." He and several others offered encouragement to the reticent youth who took a few steps forward and placed himself tail-up across Blunden's lap. There was a mass movement of the spectators to be at the rear end of Davis, and some jostling for position.

"Go on sir, spank him sir," cried one youth, a cry joined by several others, "tan his little butt, sir," for nothing engenders such delight as the sight of such misfortune in others.

"Not too hard sir," pleaded Davis, his fresh little buns clenching and wiggling in anticipation. Blunden raised a hand and allowed it to fall a couple of times upon each buttock, each time accompanied by a yelp from the hapless Davis and gasps of amusement from the audience. Blunden paused a moment to knead the firm mounds with outspread hands. He could feel Davis' rod clamped tight between his thighs and Davis was swiveling his hips to take advantage of this. As Blunden pulled the buns wide apart every head in the room craned to view the secret jewel hidden in between. Every head except Davis' of course; he wailed in embarrassment: "Oh no sir, don't let everyone see my snatch sir." But it was too late. Many lips pursed in whimsical imitation of that tight little hole, many a sigh was exhaled, and Davis' pucker shot to number one in the top ten chart of most wanked about physical features, remaining there for many months. Blunden delivered a few more light slaps, and a few lingering kisses, and Davis was allowed to stand up. A few fans assembled round him, keen to admire the blushing effect and to press their respective attentions.

For a while the guys enjoyed the buffet. Blunden leaned against his desk as each youth came in turn to say his personal goodbye. Blunden placed his hands on firm, athletic hips as Kramer wished him well and allowed him to kiss a muscular neck, he twirled Waterman's nipples, stroked Castle's six- pack, tweaked Andrews' helmet, rolled back Farson's foreskin and weighed everyone's balls.

And so Allen organized everyone into the last event of the occasion, the games. He arranged the youths in a wide semi- circle so that Blunden had a clear view of all of them and shouted "Go!"

The lads set to in a grand prix, or "Grand Pricks," as they insisted on pronouncing it, wank race. Every boy had his own technique, some teased, some tickled, some manipulated only the helmet. Some held on with both hands and hammered their hips back and forth, but most lads used a tight fist and a well-sprung wrist. There were gasps and grunts and groans; this was a race and no boy could afford the smoothness of a luxury wank; every youth heaved and strained.

It was a close-run thing but everyone agreed that Jeff shot first. Other lads followed close behind. The yells came almost as thick and fast as the goo; now a youth to Blunden's left would cry "Me, sir! Look, sir!" then one to his right, "Here I come sir, look sir," then one before him.

One by one the youths climaxed and sat down on the floor. Their raw engorged pricks, smeared with glistening juice, bounced slowly downwards or draped nonchalantly across their thighs. The atmosphere in the small enclosed room, already heavy with the odors of armpits and boy-pubes, rapidly became heady and exotic, like the overpowering scents in an orchid house.

Finally there was only one youth left standing, a boy who always did his homework and never wore shorts. He continued to work hard at his muscle as his mates broke into a slow handclap while chanting "Come on, come on, come on come on!" He flushed, "Hey, this is my fourth time today! I didn't know we had to bring a bottle to the party."

"Come on, come on, come on ... come on   "   ˙

And, finally, he arrived, thin and watery but better than nothing, to cheers and applause. He took a bow and smeared a palmful of juice across his chest.

Blunden sat in his chair watching as the lads pulled on their clothes and left one by one. When the last boy had zipped up, adjusted a prominent bulge, wished him farewell and closed the door behind him, he took a deep breath and shook his head. If only every teaching day could be like your farewell party, he thought.

Well, perhaps at his next appointment he should learn from this....

YOUNG LOVE IS A BEAUTIFUL THING An Erotic Novella
by PETER GILBERT

"Their good looks, their exquisite youthfulness, the sensitive love they shared were refreshed, livened, invigorated by the sixty pounds on the card table.... And when the expensive drinks were finished, and it was close to four in the morning, happy they gave themselves to love. "
– Constantine Cavafy, 1927

"Meet Rex. Rex is a recent addition to my 'stable.' That sunburn is all over and I do mean all over, folks. Rex is just 19, and he's been around but not too much if you know what I mean. Rex says he's open to as many new experiences as possible. I can offer Rex in 10 by 8 natural color (10 separate studies). If you'd like to see Rex in action, send for the 15 minute video. Boy! Does that boy explode! It took a long time to clean his spunk off the camera lens."

Ivan sat back and lit up a cigarette. The notice on the wall said 'NO SMOKING' but nobody took much notice of that – especially early in the morning. The audio-visual aids block was rarely visited at that time. That was just as well. A visitor might well be shocked by what he was typing but, if your employer provides a computer fitted with the very latest desktop publishing program, it might as well be made good use of and what he was doing was considerably more profitable than the endless lists of who had booked which studio or rehearsal room, and which item of equipment was out on loan to whom.

He read through what he had written and added a bit about Rex sunbathing at that moment by the pool outside the window. He scrolled back a bit further to the previous page to tell the readers that Terry still sang in the church choir. He rummaged in the desk drawer for his notebook packed with 'space fillers'. "Why do so many of my customers like blond boys?" he typed. "Because they get dirty quicker! So long folks. See you next month. You keep the orders coming and I'll do the same with the boys" – and soon another issue of 'The Pepper Pot' was streaming off the printers.

"What a bloody laugh," he muttered as he pulled up the Venetian blind to reveal the back yard of the plastics factory. No 'Rex'. No swimming pool. Just an oily puddle. As for 'Terry' – the last time that lad had been in a church, the priest had poured water over his infant head – if, in fact, he'd ever been christened. If he had, there were no signs of it having had a lasting effect. That lad did everything Ivan asked him to do – everything. He did it well too. Michael (alias Terry) was a big earner and, in a matter of moments, Ivan was going to find a few more just like him.

The printers stopped. He bundled up the copies and stacked them in a cupboard. He locked the door and took the floppy out of the A drive and slipped it into his pocket. He looked at his watch. Just nine fifty-five. Time to go fishing...

There were just over a hundred of them in the lecture theater. He couldn't make out many details. Just faces. White faces and brown faces. Blond hair and dark hair. He wondered who would be the first. He'd given this lecture to new students for something like ten years. There was no trace of nerves now. In fact he found some of the things he told them quite amusing.

"My name is Ivan Pepper," he began, "and I am the college audio-visual aids technician. Hence the jeans. I don't get paid on the same scale as the lecturers and there are times when, unlike them, I actually have to do manual work." He paused for the laughter to die down. "Another difference is that I am here till nine o'clock every evening. I do not bugger off to my converted windmill at four o'clock in the afternoon. Neither do I write poetry," he said. That raised a terrific laugh. He hoped the Vice Principal could hear it. The man was completely useless. He had only been taken on because of 'Whispers from my Windmill' and 'Mill Musings'. They might have sold more copies than 'The Pepper Pot' but he hadn't made anything like the money Ivan had made from his enterprise.

That thought bolstered him considerably. The students listened to him attentively, laughing at his references to the academic staff and making notes. He continued.

"As you go through this place, learning to be teachers, you'll need my services more and more. Just why anyone would want to spend his life doing that is beyond me but I guess you have the consolation of knowing that if you are a total failure you'll be able to join the academic staff at this place. I can supply you with just about everything you need. You want to make a video? There are two video studios. (And some of you are going to be in there, as naked as the day you were born with your cocks straining to splash it out, he thought) "You want a slide of some weird ancient monument? Come and see me. There are over ten thousand slides in the collection. (And some that are not part of the college collection.) "Basically, if you're stuck – come and see me. Thanks very much. Now I must get back to work and you can have a break."

Applause rang round the theater. He'd got them. He'd managed it again. "That," they would say, "is a really nice guy. He's like us."

As always, he hung around the door as they streamed out. Each one smiled at him. Some made complimentary remarks. Years of practice enabled him to thank them and smile automatically while he appraised their potential – and there were some very nice ones in that intake, some very nice ones indeed. He wondered how long it would take for the word to get round. They were at their most vulnerable in the first month at St. Christopher's. They all had implicit faith that their grant checks would arrive promptly. They went out and bought everything they could lay their hands on – and it wasn't very long before they were in the audio-visual aids block. "I'm in a bit of a jam and so and so says you might be able to help."

He left the theater and strolled happily down the corridor. The Vice Principal's door was open as usual: "I'm always available. Come and see me at any time." Ivan smiled. Not one student ever took the Vice Principal up on the offer. They found the atmosphere in the audio visual aids block rather more congenial.

Just as he passed the open doorway, the Vice Principal looked up. "Ah, Pepper!" he called. "A moment of your valuable time please."

Furious, Ivan strode to the door. He stood on the line where the plastic floor of the corridor gave way to the newly installed thick carpet. "For your information, I answer to Ivan or to Mr. Pepper. Ivan is reserved for my friends. The Principal also calls me Ivan. From you, I'll accept Mr. Pepper," he said, as loudly as possible. By sheer good fortune, two students walked by at that moment. Another pro-Ivan story would be going the rounds.

'The most significant poet since T. S. Eliot' looked distinctly ruffled. "Ah! I haven't got used to these silly little college conventions yet," he said. "Come in." Ivan stepped into the office. No expense had been spared on doing up that office. He could have replaced all his video cameras with just half that money.

"Sit down," said the Vice Principal.

"I'd rather not. It makes me feel uncomfortable to be on the same level as a person of your status."

"As you wish. As you wish. How did your little talk go?"

"Pretty well."

"I thought I detected a lot of laughter. They weren't playing you up I hope?"

"Not in the least."

"It might be an idea in future years for you to have a member of the academic staff in there with you – just to keep control. One has to bear in mind that you are not academically qualified."

"I think I can just about manage, thank you. When you next play a tape to your students, let me know won't you? One has to bear in mind that you are not qualified to operate a tape recorder."

"Yes. I mean no. That will be all Pep ... Mr. Pepper. There are going to be a good few changes in this place shortly. I think your attitude might improve then."

"I doubt it. I doubt it very much," said Ivan. Undoubtedly, he thought as he strolled back to his office, the V.P. would be in the Principal's office as soon as the man arrived. He had nothing to worry about. The Principal thought the world of him. They'd got on well from the day he'd arrived for his interview.

One sniff of the air outside his office was enough to tell him that he had a visitor and who it was. Raymond Moncrieff – known to thousands of clients as 'Garth'. A body of solid muscle surmounted by an almost empty skull.

"Hi, Ray. How's life?" asked Ivan, opening the door. Raymond was sitting in the old aircraft seat Ivan had purloined when the R.A.F. station closed down. He exhaled a cloud of smoke. "Not bad," he said.

"Lying toad. You only come down here when things are getting on top of you. What is it this time?"

"A hundred quid. Is that possible?"

"Everything's possible if you're prepared to play ball – if you'll pardon the expression."

"Can you keep my face out of it this time?"

Ivan looked him up and down carefully. Raymond was in the financial shit so often that there was a danger the punters would get tired of him. There wasn't an inch of Raymond that hadn't been photographed or filmed in close up. It was high time that Raymond had a co-star. This might be the opportunity.

"Why the sudden shrinking violet act? The punters have seen your face enough times."

"Well, I know but I was thinking. One day someone might recognize me."

Ivan smiled. There was some intelligence there. It had taken six months to manifest itself.

"Got gay friends in Canada, have you?" he asked.

"I've got no gay friends, full stop," Raymond growled. "Then you have absolutely nothing to worry about, have you? They're the people that appreciate your pictures. The only problem is...." He flicked through the pages of his appointments book. "I've got another one booked for tonight and I guess your need is urgent. It usually is."

"Got to have it by tomorrow."

"Then I'll have to fit you both in. We'll manage somehow." Raymond murmured something, levered himself out of the chair and left. Ivan opened the window and took a few deep breaths of chemical-laden air and then went out to find the most unusual young man in the college. As he had anticipated, Michael Maystone (alias 'Terry') was with his football buddies in the refectory. "Am I to blame if the referee is blind?" he said and all the others laughed. "That guy's eyes are so bad that he couldn't tell tits from tassels. Talking of tits, have you seen....?" He looked up and saw Ivan.

"If it's about the football video, you weren't in your office. I'll bring it in this afternoon," he said.

Michael Maystone had never borrowed a football video. There were some others, not part of the official college collection, that he borrowed regularly. Football didn't feature in any of them.

"Thanks. I was going to ask you about it. Incidentally, have you got a moment?"

"Sure. Back in a minute, lads," he said. The swinging doors closed behind them and they were alone in the corridor. "So... what brings you sniffing round your old auntie so soon, dear?" said Michael. "Didn't the church shots come out properly?"

"They were good but I need you for another job this evening."

"Auntie's busy tonight, lovey. New students' disco. Can't stay away from that."

"I only need you for about half an hour. Look, we can't talk here. Let's go to the A V block."

"I'm not sure I can do it, love. I'll need to wank about three times and even then I'm not sure it'll work. Anyway, I've got to be seen as the college stud at the disco. I can't dance half the night in my new stretch pants with a dick like a wet wick!" He bent his fingers, gazed at his fingernails for a few seconds and then polished them on his eyebrows. "Who is it anyway, anyone I know or aren't you prepared to say?"

"You're going to meet anyway. Ray Moncrieff."

"No! Come on dearie. Auntie likes a joke occasionally. Tell me honestly."

"You heard. Ray Moncrieff. He's continually short of the ready stuff is our Ray. I've done some stills and a video. Now he needs a partner. Tonight he gets one. You."

"Lovey, there is no way I can keep calm with him. I come over all unnecessary even thinking about him."

"Well you're going to have to try. And keep the masculine Michael persona. Tonight Terry meets Garth."

"Garth!" Michael chortled. "Garth! Oh that's too much!"

"So for that matter is church-going Terry, but the punters love him."

"It was the robes, dear, the robes. All that lovely lace brushing against my cock. Just as well it had to come off. You'd have had some explaining to do to the vicar. Here's your surplice back, dear. Sorry about the spunk stains."

"No clothes at all tonight," said Ivan. "You can wear your disco outfit to get here. That'll save going back to your room to change."

"Good idea. God, these affairs bore me. I shall have to drink too much, dance until my legs ache and then bed some daft teenager and she'll tell me all about Mummy and Daddy and her bloody horse."

"Go on. You'll enjoy it when you get there."

"That's the odd thing. I will," said Michael. "See you at eight thirty then."

Raymond was the first to arrive. Ivan didn't need to be told he was walking down the corridor The cigarette smoke preceded him.

"Here I am," he announced. "Everything ready? "

"I've got one more to do before you and he's not here yet," Ivan replied.

"Do me first then. Which studio?" He took off his jacket. "No. That wouldn't be fair. Besides, he's in a hurry too. He's going to the freshers' disco."

"So am I. Come on Ivan. Let's get it over."

"No. That wouldn't be fair. I did tell you I'd got another one tonight. Aha! Here he comes."

"Who is it?" Ray asked.

"You know I never give names away. You just stay here in the office out of sight. Get undressed. This won't take long. I'll come and get you when I've finished with him."

Ivan was just in time to stop Michael from entering the office. "Straight into the studio," he whispered. "He's here."

"Auntie is not at all sure that her dear nephew's advice will work," said Michael. "She's just had a triple wank and she's trying for all she's worth to think about other things but the Moncrieff body sort of intervenes."

Ivan put his finger to his lips and opened the studio door. "My word! What have we been doing?" Michael exclaimed.

"It's the scenery from last year's pantomime," Ivan exclaimed. In one corner of the studio was a roofless but cozy-looking bedroom. The window looked out onto a garden. A branch, laden with apples swung slightly on its spring support. He'd augmented the chintz-covered bed with a desk and a computer. A pair of muddy football boots lay on the floor by the bed and 'Baby Bear's' kiddie-wallpaper had been just about covered with Techno concert posters.

"Are we going to be photographed in that?" Michael whispered.

"It's all right. He can't see or hear anything. I've made sure of that." Ivan took the key to the control panel out of his pocket and held it up.

"But where's the camera?" asked Michael. He was already starting to take off his clothes.

"There's one hanging perpendicularly from the rafters above you. Another is peeping through a crack in the wall and there's yet another inside the 'o' of 'Techno' on that poster. He'll never notice it. The still camera that he's expecting is there, already loaded. When you're ready, just sit on the bed and think unhappy thoughts."

Michael folded his clothes carefully, peeled off his mauve boxers and did as he was told.

"Now what?" he asked.

"We wait," said Ivan. He tried hard not to look at Michael's limp cock but couldn't help it. It was pretty big, even in that state and he liked the way the foreskin covered the tip as if it had been sewn with minute purse strings. One of his clients had written in to say that 'Terry' had the nicest cock he had ever seen. That was another letter due to be answered. There were loads of them. The man that fancied 'Terry's cock. The man that wanted a date with Garth. The one who wondered if 'Robert' had a younger brother – preferably aged about sixteen – not to mention the fantasists who claimed to have done the most amazing things with his models in the past and the people who were 'genuinely interested in photography' and wanted to visit. He'd have to get down to some letter writing tomorrow.... He looked at his watch, nodded to Michael and smiled.

"Ready. I just hope I can hold out," said Michael and Ivan left the studio.

"About bloody time!" said Ray, putting out his cigarette. "Has he gone?"

"No. We have a tiny problem. Well, not really 'tiny' "

"What is it?" Ray asked, alarmed. He made a grab for his clothes.

"Nothing too serious. He can't get a hard on. Unlike you." Ray's mighty cock had thickened and hung, half hard from the dense bush of hair at its base.

"Silly sod. Tell him to come back another day."

"I can't. I've got to get these shots done today. I wondered if you could help."

"What can I do?"

"Finger him up a bit. Get him excited. I leave it to you."

"Fuck that!" said Ray, angrily. "What the fuck do you think I am? I'm no fucking queer. Why can't you do it if you're that keen?"

"For the simple reason that my arms aren't long enough. I can't keep one hand on a camera lens and the other on a cock.

Come on Ray. Nobody will ever know."

"He will. I don't want some fucking pansy boy saying I wanked him off."

"Perhaps you ought to know who it is. Michael Maystone. He's no more queer than you are – or me for that matter. Like us all, he's in it for the money."

"He's too good a bloke to be in this business. His dad's loaded too. Don't tell me he's short of money."

"Well, I don't know why but he is. He wants a hard on. I want some pictures of it and some of you. Separately of course. So we need your help."

"Not with you looking on. I'm not getting into that," said Ray.

"Of course not. I'll stay in here. You go in, do your thing and tell me when he's ready. How's that? I'll up the money a bit."

Ray sat thinking for a second or two. Finally, he stood up. Ivan suppressed a smile. Despite Ray's protests, his cock had lifted appreciably. "I never even did this at school," he said, and he stalked out of the room.

Ivan unlocked the console cover and flipped switches, mouthing the commands to himself as he did so. "Camera one – on. Camera two – on. Camera three – on. VCR one – on. VCR two – on. VCR. three – on. Mike – on. Intercom from control – off." A blurry image appeared on a monitor screen. He turned the knob. Gradually the picture became clearer and then both of them were there in glorious color. Ray's suntan contrasted with Michael's white skin. Ivan smiled. He couldn't have got a better color combination if he'd hunted all the shops in town for bedspread and curtain material.

"Those apples look good enough to eat," said Ray, looking out of the window.

"I wouldn't. They're wax. Did Ivan tell you about my...."

"Yeah. What are you doing posing for porn pictures? I thought your old man paid you enough."

"Birds, my old mate. Birds. If I don't get a good shag regularly I go to pieces. Pussy in this town is expensive."

"Is it? Is that what's caused the problem?"

"I guess so. Worth it though. Tits like water melons and a cunt like silk and I've got another one lined up for tonight."

"Lucky sod. Do you reckon you could fix one for me?"

"I could ask. I reckon I could. One look at your dick would send a girl into a frenzy."

"Do you reckon?"

"I'm sure. And you're nearly there already and look at this useless article of mine."

"Shall I wank it a bit?"

"Go ahead. It might do the trick." Michael lay back so that his head touched the wall. The wall, the apple tree and the garden all wobbled slightly. Ray put out a hand and gently touched Michael's flaccid penis which, almost at once, twitched slightly.

"Close up," Ivan whispered, hoping that they wouldn't hear the lens motor. Michael's cock head emerged, purple and shining from its protective sheath. Ray's hand moved slowly and carefully up and down. At one point he stopped and tentatively put a hand between Michael's legs to tickle his balls. For one with no experience, Ivan thought, he was doing extremely well and his cock was hardening visibly as he worked. Michael, he concluded, must have had the most fantastic concentration. He would have liked to know what was going on in the boy's mind. Time and time again, his cock rose, only to sink immediately the moment Ray paused in his ministrations. Not only that, although he had his eyes closed and appeared to be entirely relaxed, he was carefully keeping a tiny space between the back of his head and the thin wall to prevent it moving again.

"It's no good," he said at last. "It won't work. You could try sucking it."

"Fuck off."

"It's the only thing that would work."

"How do you know?"

"Birds. Nothing like having a bird give you a blow job."

"I'm no fucking bird."

"Then don't get your feathers ruffled. Anyway, about the only thing that's the same between birds and blokes is that their mouths are the same and with you I wouldn't have lipstick marks on my cock."

"Well you can find someone else. That's the one thing I am not doing. Fucking filthy, that is."

"You don't suck naked cock, you fool. You put a rubber on it. All you get in your mouth is rubber, not cock."

"That's all very well but...."

Ray was still wanking Michael as he spoke. That, thought Ivan, was a good sign.

"Well what?"

"What if Ivan comes in and finds me doing it?"

"The moment you hear him at the door, you whip your cherry lips off it and give him a big smile."

"Do you reckon he's queer?"

"Ivan? How should I know? I doubt it."

"Well... all this photography and stuff. It's all a bit odd to me. We had some queers at school. I don't want to get mixed up with anything like that."

"He makes a bit of extra pocket money. So do we. Now, are you going to get down on this or not?"

Ivan was not accustomed to praying but, at that moment, he did the next best thing. There was a pause. He watched the expression in Ray's eyes and waited.

"Might as well. Let's get it over," said Ray.

"Leave off a minute. There's a rubber in my pocket. It was meant for later on." Michael walked off the set and returned a second or so later with the packet in his hand. He tore it open and, with considerable difficulty, put the rubber over his half- hard penis. With all the practice of an experienced actor, he found the exact place on the bed where he had been lying and resumed his position.

"Now then," he said and, once again, he leaned back.

"Providing you never tell...." said Ray. And those were the last words he uttered for some time.

"You, Raymond, alias Garth, had more experience at that posh school of yours than you let on about," Ivan muttered as at least half of Michael's cock went into Ray's mouth. Deftly, Ivan managed the controls, adjusting the focus occasionally, dipping the set lighting very slightly to avoid excessive reflection from Michael's glistening saliva-soaked cock. Most of the sound effects came from Michael.

"Ah! That's better! Oh, that's great. Christ! You're good at it! Oh yeah. It's working."

It was. It was working almost too well. The camera secreted behind the poster was getting a perfect close up of a cock rising and swelling by the second. Ray stopped for a moment to draw breath and then went down on it again. He'd had to twist his body in order to get it into his mouth and it was unfortunate that his huge pectoral muscles obscured the tip of his own mighty member but it was as stiff as a steel rod.

Michael put out a hand and touched the back of Ray's neck. "Careful!" Ivan muttered. "Don't rush things," but Ray didn't appear to notice – or, if he had, was too far gone to care. Michael's fingers slid up and down then began to tickle the skin. Ray moved his head further down. Michael spread his legs wider and his hand moved down Ray's back.

"Oh yeah! Yeah!" he gasped. "Keep on...." but Ray didn't. For a moment or two the nodding of his head speeded up. Then, suddenly, he pulled his head away. For a frightening split second he appeared to stare, wide eyed, right into the camera lens and then he fell sideways onto the bed.

"Shit!" he shouted, but it wasn't shit. It was semen. It seemed to leap out of his cock, rose some ten inches into the air and spattered down on Michael's legs and belly. Another spurt followed the first. The rest ran down the rampant shaft.

"That was your fault!" he gasped. "What did you want to tickle my neck for? I'm sensitive there."

"You should have said," Michael replied. "No harm done."

"That's what you think. That's a hundred quid down the drain."

"More like a hundred c.c. all over me," said Michael. "I'll have to have a shower now. I don't want the birds to smell your spunk." Ivan left them to talk for a few minutes and didn't go into the studio until Michael was wiping himself dry with a handkerchief. "Ready?" he asked brightly and then, with a look towards Michael's still erect penis, he added "I can see you are but what's happened to you, Ray."

"He shot." said Michael. "Shame. I would have liked to get a photo. Why didn't you come and let me know you were ready?"

"I didn't know it was going to happen," said Ray in a pleading tone. "What about the money? I really am in a jam."

"No problem," said Ivan. "I'll pay you tonight and you owe me a session some time. How's that?" Ray beamed. "That's great! Thanks a lot. Any time," he said. "He's a good guy isn't he?" Ivan heard the words distinctly as the two of them, immaculately dressed, walked up the corridor. "He's great," said Michael. "Incidentally, you're not so bad yourself." Ivan closed the door and locked it from the inside. A long night's editing lay ahead of him. 'Terry and Garth' was going to make money; a lot of money.

"You're just trying to wind me out," said Dr. Burton. "I'm sure you could do it."

"It's 'wind me up' Meg, not 'out' – and no, I'm not winding you up this time. I'm not saying I couldn't do it. It's just that it would take too long."

Meg Burton was one of Ivan's favorite lecturers. He was one of the many hundreds of people that enjoyed pulling her leg. There was the glorious moment, captured by one of the students on video, during one of her field trips to the coast: "Dr. Burton! Dr. Burton! Come here quick! I've found a shark!" the student cried. "I don't think so, dear. To find a shark in a rock pool on the English coast would be rather unusual," but she went over to look at it all the same.

Ivan's had been the best. Everybody said that. Meg had been out with her students and came back with a jar of tadpoles that they'd caught in the duck-pond in the cathedral close. On hearing from Ivan that they were the personal property of the Dean and Chapter and protected by ancient statutes, she'd gone back at the dead of night to return them and spent the next few days in fear of immediate arrest.

To be asked to make an hour-long, time lapse film of a caterpillar changing into a butterfly when there were already two professionally made films on the subject in the A V collection was too much. Ivan had more important things to attend to.

"Well, if you say so, Ivan dear," said Meg. "I'll have to make do with one of the others but I'm sure you could do a better job. How are you getting on with Windmill Willie?"

"I'm not."

"I guessed as much. The man's a pain. I can't think why they took him on. I mean to say – a poet! What does a poet know about training teachers? They should have recruited a biologist. The awful thing is that the Principal is handing over more and more of the reins to him. It's understandable, I suppose. The Principal's due to retire in three years but I don't fancy working for that man at all."

Ivan was dying to get away and Meg could gossip for hours if one let her. Fortunately, a group of students arrived for a lecture. They were first years ... and rather pretty first years at that. Most of them sat down immediately and got out their brand-new files and books. Three hovered.

"Oh, Dr. Burton," said one, an extremely good looking, fair- haired young man. "I saw a most interesting lizard on the way to college this morning."

White jeans, decided Ivan, were not ideal wear for a day in college but they set his butt off perfectly and that bulge in the front looked promising....

"Did you, dear? What did it look like?"

"Well, it was green...."

"That's not unusual. How big was it?"

"About thirty-five feet – and there was fire coming out of its nostrils." The lad's two friends sniggered.

"I shouldn't think so, dear. I think you're winding me ... up. Now go and sit down and we'll start."

"It doesn't take them long to get the lay of the land round here," Ivan thought as he walked back to his office. He wondered how long it would be before they heard about his little sideline. A shot of that boy, topless and with the white jeans pulled down at one side to expose just a bit of bush would go down well with the customers...

Back in the office, he dealt with the request slips first. Dr. Walsh wanted the video on gas chromatography. Miss Stanton wanted the sound of early morning bird-song. Dr. Page wondered if Ivan had a slide of Stonehenge. Ivan had thirty- two slides of Stonehenge. He packed them in a padded envelope, put everything outside in the basket for collection, locked the door and settled down to the real work of the day. The letters came first.

'I wonder if Robert has a younger brother....' He could have, Ivan thought. Wonders could be worked with digital photography but, like making biological time-lapse films, doctoring photos took time. Several people wanted more photo-sets and videos of his various stars. They were no problem. Then came the usual batch of 'background spotters': people who thought they recognized the ruined building, the forked tree or even (wrongly) the farmyard in which 'Tommy' had been photographed. "So what?" Ivan muttered but they all got replies.

The letter from G. D. Morris was half way down the pile. G. D. Morris had a standing order for everything Ivan produced. He always paid in advance and he never, ever queried post and packing costs. He would have been the perfect customer if it weren't for his constant requests for letters from Ivan's stars. The boys would have been shaken rigid if they knew about Mr. Morris's letters. He always wrote using an Asian news store in Birmingham as an accommodation address.

"I enclose a twenty pound note for young Tommy," he wrote. "Do make sure he writes to let me know he's got it. You can't trust postmen these days. Of all your boys, I like him best. I'd like a close up, in color, of his ass. Get him to part his cheeks to show me his tight little hole. How often has

he been fucked? Is there a picture of him being fucked?"

"No, there isn't," Ivan muttered, "and you, my friend, are a nutter but here goes.." and he composed a suitable reply. There should be no problem, he explained, in getting the rear view Mr. Morris wanted.

Unfortunately, although 'Tommy' delighted in being screwed, he drew the line at being photographed at the time. He especially enjoyed being fucked by mature men.

Ivan was pretty sure he was right in that respect. 'Morris' was almost certainly not the man's real name and he probably lived some way from Birmingham but everything about the letter indicated that he was getting on – if not actually old. 'You can't trust postmen these days' and the extraordinary way he wrote the date: '8th of September, 1999 – and the ending 'I am, dear Sir, sincerely yours, G. D. Morris.' All his letters were beautifully typed on thick, cream paper in contrast to the cheap stuff most of Ivan's correspondents used.

So the morning went by. He was contemplating an image of 'Robert' on the computer screen, wondering if it would be possible to get rid of the hair on the boy's legs when there was a knock on the door: the secret knock. Ivan swung round in this chair and unlocked the door. It was Michael Maystone. "Hi, Terry. Come on in," said Ivan.

"Terry in the photos. Michael in the flesh," said Michael. "You're getting senile dear. How old are you?"

"Thirty two."

"Hmm. Early for senility. Perhaps it's Alzheimer's disease." Ivan swung round to face him. "Do you wonder?" he said, irritably. "I'm answering letters from people that use false names and accommodation addresses. I reply using a false name and an accommodation address and use false names for the people I'm writing about. Schizophrenia is nearer the mark."

"Don't tell me dearie. I know just how you feel. Look at the other day. One minute I'm in your divine little dolls' house with the best-looking boy in the college's cock in my hand and getting a lovely spunk shower. Three hours after that I'm in bed with the prettiest girl in the first year, giving her the fuck of her life. And she doesn't have a horse. She's got a pet rat but fortunately that wasn't visible. What we both need, dear, is a break. How about a weekend at your place by the sea?" The thought had already occurred to Ivan but he was in two minds about taking Michael with him. The little house at Garmouth was becoming more and more his private territory. Few people even knew about it. He'd taken Michael down there in the previous year, ostensibly to help in the redecorating and he'd found Michael's company fun then. Sex with Michael after a hard day's painting had been great and, in the village, Michael kept to his macho persona. He made eyes at the girl behind the bar in 'The Cabin' and teased the sex-starved spinster who ran the village Post Office unmercifully.

But that was in the time when Ivan's business was just getting under way. Since then he'd come to regard Garmouth as 'home' – the place where he could be himself and the pressures of running a mail order business could be forgotten. For that reason, the studies he had taken of Michael on the beach that summer had never been released.

"We could go down on Friday night and come back on Monday morning," said Michael. Ivan kept his eyes on the gradually changing picture of Robert on the screen. "I'll think about it," he said. "Here, have a look at these. One or two mention you." He handed over the sheaf of letters and continued to work – and think.

'Lighten the pubic hair a bit' – odd about pubic hair. The people you thought would be covered like gorillas never were, whereas the ones you guessed to be sparingly endowed had what felt like coconut matting round their cocks. Michael was just right in that respect. Ivan remembered sliding his hand down under the sheets on that first night at Garmouth. Smooth torso and belly flesh suddenly gave way to a crinkly, wiry bed of hair, and that, in turn, led his wandering fingers further until they made contact with eight inches of steel-hard flesh.

'Narrow the mouth a bit and make the lips just a bit thicker.' That made him think of Michael's lips. They felt like one of those suckers you used to stick posters to glass surfaces. He'd never experienced anything like that frantic kissing session. Michael's tool, still stiff, was pressed against Ivan's cum – soaked belly. Ivan's tongue explored his mouth and then paused before their lips joined and stayed joined for a very long time.

"Dirty old men!" said Michael from the aircraft seat. "Do you let the others see these?"

"What do you take me for?" Ivan asked.

"It might do some good. They might realize how much they could make by going just that bit further."

"There is one hell of a difference between having your picture taken and having a cock in your ass," said Ivan.

"Don't tell me, dearie. I know. You taught me. Remember? What about Garmouth this weekend then?"

"Oh ... okay."

"You don't sound very keen. Auntie could feel quite hurt. What does one of her many admirers say ...?" He shuffled

through the letters. "Ah yes. '...Terry's lovely long back and tight little butt, not to mention his superb cock.' See what you'll miss if you don't take me?"

"I wouldn't describe it as superb. I've seen bigger ones."

"I'm sure you have dearie, but this one is available. So is my tight little butt. What about it?" Pleasurable memories of the last time flashed through Ivan's mind. "Okay. I guess so," he said. "Friday evening at about six?"

"I'll be ready."

"I've got something else at Garmouth to show you, too," said Ivan. "Don't tell me dearie. Lovely photos of delightfully young students gasping as mammoth cocks impale their tender asses is it?"

"No. Nothing like that. You'll see. And now you can let me get on with my work."

"Doesn't look much like work to me," said Michael. He got up from the chair peered over Ivan's shoulder at the picture on the screen. "Looks a bit like that guy in the second year. The runner," he said. "Do you think so?"

"Yes. That's him a few years back. Long before we knew him."

"I rather hoped you'd say that. Friday at six."

"Auntie will be there, lovey. Bye for now," and Ivan was alone again. • • • Michael's ability to change character was amazing. Throughout the journey he'd kept up a stream of his high camp chatter: "Ooh! Look at that one dear! What couldn't your auntie do with that?" The moment he was in 'The Cabin' at Garmouth, he became macho Michael again. "I really like this place," he said, when he came back

205

from the bar and put two beers on the table. "'The Cabin' or my place or Garmouth generally?"

"All three really." Garmouth was a small village on the east coast that had been discovered by the yachting community. Yachting – not sailing. These were the big, ocean-going jobs, not the little dinghies one associates with seaside resorts. They lay moored alongside the new jetty glittering with chrome and new white paint. Long before this revolution, when Garmouth was a quiet little fishing village, Ivan's aunt had bought a cottage

there. At the time, everyone in the family said she was mad. When she died, it was worth more than a hundred times the price she'd paid and when her will revealed that she had left it to Ivan his first thought was to sell it. He hadn't thought and, every time he came to Garmouth he had grown more and more fond of the place. It was home – the place he could really relax in and, unlike the flat he occupied near the college, every stone of it belonged to him.

The village people were friendly. It amused him to wonder how they would react if they knew about his little business. They didn't even know what his full-time job was. They were the sort of people who didn't ask questions like that.

In the days of Ivan's aunt 'The Cabin' was called 'The Jolly Miller' – a rather run down pub patronized mostly by the local lads. The name was changed. The smoke-stained walls were hidden by yards of fishing net, ships wheels and photographs of sailing boats. The menu had changed too: not the food. Just the menu and the prices.

"I think I'll go for the succulent pieces of prime steak, marinated in a savory sauce, and served in a crisp pastry case with seasonal vegetables and fries," said Michael, sipping his pint of 'Bosun's Bitter' reflectively.

"And I'll have the organic eggs, fried in fresh farm butter, garnished with herbs with fries," said Ivan.

The waitress went to the hatch between the bar and the kitchen. "One steak pie and chips, and one egg and chips!" she shouted.

Not everything had changed though. The proprietors had kept the pool table and the dart board and, though one would never know it from their demeanor, the pool table (or rather the players) was sufficient inducement for Ivan and Michael to suffer the pretensions of the place. A boy and a girl were having a desultory sort of game, stopping repeatedly for a quick sip of their drinks and a lingering kiss.

"Wouldn't mind trying his savory sauce or his succulent pieces of prime steak," said Ivan, looking over in their direction.

"I get the best of both worlds. I was thinking similar thoughts about the girl," Michael replied. "Mind you, I tend to agree. He seems to have a nice straight cue...."

"And a pocket full of balls," said Ivan. The waitress brought their food.

"You really ought to come here more often," said Michael, looking over at the pool players again. "If you did you'd know who these people are and be able to introduce me."

"That would be counterproductive. I want you for myself."

Michael grinned. "That's the nicest thing I've heard for a long time," he said. "Let's get going. Your bedroom calls."

"Not quite yet. There's something I want to show you first. It's not far. We can walk from here."

They finished their meal, paid the bill and with friendly nods to the young pool players, they went out into the autumn sunshine.

"This had better be worthwhile," said Michael. "I'm getting quite horny. It must be the sea air."

Ivan led him along the newly built jetty. Some of the yachts had been covered up in readiness for the winter. They stopped near the end.

"There!" said Ivan proudly. "What do you think of that?" 'Peppercorn' was a fifteen-foot motor cruiser. Ivan had bought her second-hand but, nonetheless, the purchase had made a temporary hole in his finances.

"Amazing!" said Michael. "How the hell could you afford it?"

"Photos and videos of you and all the others."

"I think I shall ask for more next time. Can we go down and look inside?"

"Sure." Proudly he showed Michael the engine, the cleverly designed cabin with its dining table and benches which converted into a double bed. He showed him the cooking stove and the refrigerator and the cunningly disguised toilet and shower cubicle.

"Brilliant! I love it!" said Michael. "When do we go out in it? I've never had sex on the high seas before."

"Tomorrow, maybe. Now let's go home."

Undressing somebody, Ivan decided, was much more fun that watching them take their clothes off. And the bedroom in the cottage was a much more suitable place than the studio at college. He would have liked Michael to show a bit more enthusiasm but then, that was typical of Michael. He was probably thinking about some girl as Ivan's fingers worked on his laces, buttons and zip fastener. He said nothing. He just lay there. He did go as far as to raise his butt off the bed so that his jeans and shorts could be dragged off him. Finally, he lay naked and with his penis pointing up to the rafters. Rapidly, Ivan stripped off, slinging his clothes onto the floor. It was an odd thing, he thought. Literally hundreds of people had seen Michael's cock in photos and videos. They'd seen it limp. They'd seen it as it was now, stiff and rearing up in anticipation. They'd seen it shooting its load but none of them had seen it in the flesh – hard flesh. Neither had they smelt that musty aroma or handled it. There was a hell of a lot of difference between a photo and flesh... He took it between his fingers and bent over to kiss the tip.

To Michael, it seemed, there was no difference between this and being photographed. He lay, passive and with his eyes closed as if having his cock kissed and licked was the most ordinary thing in the world. Ivan contemplated the body stretched out beneath him. Michael was twenty-one years old. He wasn't really handsome but there was something about that snub nose and the freckles on either side of it that sent the punters crazy for more pictures. As for lower down – Michael's chest was superbly muscled. His belly was flat and hard. His legs were long and, although hairy, they were not so thickly covered as to look too fuzzy in photographs. Every line of his body seemed to draw the eye to that magnificent eight- inch cock, uncut and capable of a hardness that didn't seem possible.

Ivan lowered his head further and opened his mouth. Michael opened his eyes, put his hands behind his head and closed his eyes again. Ivan moved his tongue from side to side to savor Michael's unique taste. Then, closing his lips as tightly as possible on the shaft, he began to suck. Michael made no sound – even his breathing remained even. Ivan could see his chest rising and falling. It was as if Michael was asleep. If it had been possible for Ivan to smile, he would have certainly done so. It had been like this on Michael's last visit, he thought, until....

He took his mouth away. Michael's cock, gleaming wet, swayed slightly. "Turn over," he said and Michael did so.

Ivan opened a drawer of the bedside cabinet, tore open a packet and slipped the rubber over his already moist cock He applied a dollop of jelly and wiped all his fingers except one with a tissue. Now was the time for bisexual Michael to forget all thoughts of the opposite sex. Ivan spread the fingers of his right hand as wide as he could and placed his thumb on Michael's left cheek and his little finger on the right. Michael's skin felt cool and smooth. He pressed downwards and thrilled at the softness of Michael's buttocks. Then he started – moving his middle finger rapidly back and forwards – exactly as he had done before. For a moment there was no reaction but then Michael gave a gasp and instinctively parted his legs. The finger went deeper between his cheeks. Michael spread his legs even wider and the little puckered opening touched the tip of Ivan's finger. He kept on straightening it and bending it. Michael gasped again, louder this time, and his hands gripped the pillow.

"Oh, yeah! Oh, yeah! Do it. Do it!" Michael panted.

Ivan grinned. It was a tempting prospect. He tried to remember the exposure table to prevent himself from coming too soon. His finger worked deeper and deeper between Michael's snow-white buns. As it did so, his thumb and little finger moved inwards, leaving snail-like glittering trails of grease on the skin.

Michael wriggled violently. "Do it! Do it!" he panted. Ivan kept working. The muscle was beginning to relax. At least he thought it was.

It felt softer and more ... what had G D Morris written? 'He looks like the sort of boy that has a delightfully responsive ass.' That was ages ago, long before Ivan had experienced it. Maybe it would be an idea to write back and tell the guy he was right. It was definitely beginning to respond. He pressed it with the tip of his finger and Michael groaned.

"Do it! Do it, Ivan!" he gasped, and Ivan knew that the barrier was down. Michael's imagination had been emptied of feminine images. He climbed up on to the bed, placed his hands on either side of Michael's shoulders and slowly lowered himself. It was as if his cock had eyes. He felt it touch Michael's open cleft, slide between the soft buttocks and position itself right on target. He licked the back of Michael's neck and, as he did so, lowered himself some more. It opened up for him like a soft mouth anxious to engulf its prey. Centimeter by centimeter, he pushed in. Michael gasped. Then he groaned and gasped again. Soft, warm tissues opened up as his cock head reached them and then closed again, pressing against the shaft. Finally, breathing heavily, he was in – right in. His chest lay against Michael's shoulder blades and his groin pressed against Michael's soft buns. He put his hands on the boy's shoulders and thrust hard.

"Oooh! Yeah!" Michael gasped. Another thrust. "Yeah!" then another. "Yeah!" and Michael wriggled again. Soon he was writhing, moving so much that it was difficult to keep greasy fingers on his shoulders. Ivan put them under Michael's heaving belly and soon found what he was seeking. He gripped it as hard as he could and kept on thrusting away. He wondered who would be first. It had been him last time but Michael's cock was already beginning to ooze. He could feel it, warm and viscous, creeping between his fingers. He thrust away again. All thoughts of camera exposure times fled from his consciousness. He could only think of Michael and Michael's ass and how great it felt to be in it.

"Ah! Yeah! Ah! Yeah!" Was that Michael or was it himself? He paused for a second, gathered all his energy and gave one mighty thrust. Michael yelled and then lay quite still. Ivan's fingers were soaked as one jet after another flooded them and

Michael's belly. At exactly the same time – indeed it felt as if the jets were synchronized – he came. He felt his body go rigid as successive spurts filled the rubber. Then, he sank, exhausted onto

Michael's back. "Bloody great!" he murmured. "Just what auntie wanted," said Michael – the first time he'd used the camp voice since stepping out of the car.

"Stay where you are. I'll go get a paper," said Michael.

"What's the time?"

"Nine o'clock."

"Christ! Have I slept that long?"

"No, dear heart. You haven't slept much at all. Nor have I for that matter. Where are your car keys?"

"On the hook in the hall but the paper store isn't that far. You could walk it."

"Yesterday I might have been able to. I might even manage it later today but at the moment it's quite impossible," Michael replied. "Having your cock in my ass most of the night has numbed my enthusiasm for walking. See you in a minute."

"Give me a kiss first," said Ivan. Michael bent down and their lips met. Ivan struggled into a sitting position and put his arms round Michael's back. Michael did the same to him. For a long time, they stayed like that clasped tightly to each other. Michael's tongue tasted odd, Ivan thought, but on reflection, that wasn't so mysterious. As far as he could remember he'd come twice in Michael's mouth during the preceding night and no doubt Michael was thinking the same thing about his tongue!

Finally, they broke apart. "I'd better go now or they'll have sold out," said Michael, brushing his lips with the back of his hand. Ivan lay back again and listened to the sound of the front door being opened and then shut, and then the car engine starting. Suddenly, Ivan felt threatened. His work at the college, his secret sideline and now the cottage at Garmouth had all merged together. In the past, without knowing he was doing it, he'd kept them all separate. Now, thanks to Michael, there were no more secrets. Not even 'Peppercorn'. What sort of stupidity, he wondered, had led him to show the boat to Michael and promise to take him out in her? He could at least have kept that aspect of his life to himself.

"You've got yourself lumbered," he muttered to himself. What would happen if Michael gossiped? True, he hadn't yet but he might. Worried and miserable, Ivan turned over and went back to sleep. He was in the middle of a terrifying dream in which hundreds of college students were queuing in the street outside, demanding to be let in to the cottage and threatening to report his sideline.

"God! Still in bed!" He woke with a start. Michael stood at the foot of the bed with a shopping bag in one hand a newspaper in the other. "I got some shopping while I was down there," he said. "Stay where you are. I'll do you breakfast in bed. Smart little darling in that shop. What couldn't I do to her!"

"Name of Jane. Father is a lay reader at the church," said Ivan. "The best sort. I shall be down there again as soon as possible. Fried eggs or scrambled?"

"Whichever you do best," said Ivan, yawning. Michael put his hand on his hip. "Your auntie is skilled at almost everything," he said in his camp voice. "Well if you scramble eggs as well as you suck cock and fuck, I'll have them scrambled, but I'll get up and come downstairs," Ivan replied. Michael vanished downstairs and Ivan went into the bathroom. Soon the smell of bacon and eggs began to drift up the stairs. When he was alone in the cottage, he never troubled to eat breakfast. In some ways, he thought, it was nice to have Michael there. "You'll never guess who I saw when I was out," said Michael when Ivan finally got downstairs. "No. Who?"

"Dr. Burton,"

"No!"

"She drove off from the shop just as I got there."

"You're sure?"

"Fairly sure. Not many people drive Minis of that age and in such good nick."

"Did she see you?"

"I think she might have done. I'm not sure."

"Fuck!" said Ivan. "That's all I need!"

212

"What's got into you? I thought you liked her."

"I do but.... This is difficult to explain...." It had to be explained. Michael listened attentively and said nothing as Ivan tried to put his feelings into words. Finally, he spoke. "I don't think you can live like that," he said. "You can't keep a huge chunk of your personality under wraps. I guess it's easier for me. I am your genuine hundred percent bisexual so I can be a heterosexual in college and gay here. Open up, Ivan dear. Open up to the world. Obviously you can't let all and sundry at St. Chris's know about the photos but most of the students know about that already. The news spreads. They like you. They're loyal to you and that's all that matters." Ivan felt better. Not entirely convinced but better. They both did the washing up. "And now what?" said Michael. "What do you feel like doing?" Michael laughed. "I know what I want but you're the boss,"

he said.

"Let's take the boat out then. It's a nice day and the tide's about right."

"Oooh! A mini Bijou cruisette!" said Michael, "and who knows what might happen to a boy on a boat miles from the shore?"

"Anything ... and I do mean anything," said Ivan. "Ready?"

"Entirely at your disposal," Michael replied. • • •

"Be careful. Somebody might see," said Michael.

"They'd have to have bloody powerful binoculars. We're two hundred yards out from the shore in case you hadn't noticed." Ivan continued to fiddle with the string at Michael's waist with his right hand whilst his left kept 'Peppercorn' cruising slowly in a reasonably straight line.

"I've never done it on a boat. It could be fun. All that lovely up and down motion," said Michael as his trunks finally succumbed to Ivan's manipulations and made their crumpled way to his ankles. He stepped out of them deftly and kicked them to one side of the cockpit. "Don't you think we ought to go down into the cabin?" he added, looking over towards the beach. There were just one or two people there, looking like tiny black ants against the gray shingle.

"Maybe later. Let's get some fresh air first."

"Perhaps they'll think we're fishing," said Michael., still gazing towards the beach.

"Perhaps. This is beginning to feel something like a fishing rod already."

Michael laughed. "My 'superb dong', that is. That's what that guy wrote in the letter. Go a bit slowly or I'll come all over your boat."

"You bloody dare. You're going to come in my mouth."

"I still think we ought to go down in the cabin. What happens if another boat comes by?"

"You'll have a queue of cum-hungry sailors. That's what. G. D. Morris was right. It is superb."

Ivan had seen and recorded a lot of cocks in the course of his business but he'd had very few of them in his hands. Actually holding one as big and as superbly proportioned as Michael's and feeling the hard flesh pulsating in the palm of his hand was quite different. He'd gotten to the stage of being able to photograph and video-record penises in every possible condition with total disinterest, but actually holding one and sliding the silky foreskin gently back and forwards had a very rapid effect on his own member. He took his hand off the wheel and pulled his shorts down.

"You're pretty well built yourself," Michael commented, clasping it in his long fingers.

Any watcher on the shore would have been confused at that point. Their bodies came closer together and merged and for a few minutes, 'Peppercorn' cruised round in a circle. After that, the mythical spectator would have seen it stop, seen the anchor being thrown over the side and the two 'fishermen' disappear from view.

"Gone inside for a cup of tea, I expect," the watcher would have said. He couldn't have been more wrong. They lay, closely entwined, on one of the benches which lay along the sides of the cabin. It only took a few minutes to convert the benches into beds but there was no time for that. There wasn't time for anything except to take as much of each other's cock as possible into their desperately salivating mouths.

Ivan's feet hammered against the bulkhead. One of Michael's legs was on the bench. The other was wedged between the bench and the little folding table but he wasn't aware of any discomfort. Far from it. Ivan's smooth cock against his tongue was warm and somehow comforting. He felt Ivan's head pushing between his thighs and tried to part his legs but that was impossible. He was still a bit sore down there from the previous night's activities anyway. Ivan gave up and began to suck on his balls, taking first one and then the other between his lips. That felt great. He continued to suck happily. The boat, riding up and down on the wavelets did all the work for him. He could feel the foreskin between his lips retracting and moving forward again without any effort on his part. It was a great feeling. He wished it could go on and on forever.

But it didn't. Ivan, who had come several times in the night, came again and with just as much force, it seemed, as when his cock was buried several inches in Michael's ass. The boat gave another lurch – and then another – and that was enough for Michael to surprise Ivan. Each slap of the water against the hull seemed to produce another spurt.

"Wow!" he gasped as Ivan's cock slid from his mouth. Ivan continued to suck hungrily.

"Bloody hell! That was great!" said Michael again and this time Ivan answered.

"That's the boat well and truly christened," he said – but there was no elation in his tone.

They cleaned up, went back into the cockpit. Ivan put on his crumpled and extremely damp swimming trunks and heaved the anchor off the sea bed.

"I'm going to stay like I am," said Michael. "Don't worry. Nobody will see anything." He clambered up onto the fore-peak and lay on his front.

"Mmm. That feels nice," he said. Ivan started the engine and they were off again. Slowly they cruised along parallel to the shoreline, waving to the occasional angler or beachcomber.

"That's them. Must be," said Michael suddenly. They'd been cruising for about twenty minutes and the tide, infamous in that part of the word, was roaring in towards the shore. Ivan shut off the engine and had to ask him to repeat it.

"Dr. Burton and her students," said Michael, pointing towards the shore. Diminutive figures could be seen all over the rocky beach.

"Might not be."

"When you see people on a beach totally devoid of sand in September, you can be reasonably sure that it's one of Dr. Burton's rock-pool expeditions/4 said Michael. "Can you get further in?"

"If you stay in that position I should be able to get further in than ever before," said Ivan. He spun the wheel over to the right. "C'mon down here," he said. "Naked young men on boats are likely to attract attention. I don't want her to notice us."

It might have been safer to leave Michael on the fore-peak. The course Ivan steered towards the beach was definitely erratic. It's difficult to steer straight when one hand is playing with a cock.

"I'm sure it's them. Got any binoculars?" said Michael. Reluctantly, Ivan released a cock which, although soft, was nonetheless pleasant to play with. He reached into the little hatch by the wheel for his binoculars. He handed them to Michael who clapped them to his eyes. "I was right," he said. "There's no mistaking those green boots. It's the new first year biologists."

Carefully, Ivan steered the boat nearer the shore and stopped the engine. "Let's have a look," he said.

His heart sank. There was, as Michael had said, no doubt about it. Why, he wondered, did she have to choose this particular part of the coast when there were so many other places. It wasn't as if Garmouth was near the college. It was as if there was some sort of huge conspiracy at work to invade his private life. Then, for an instant, he felt relieved. None of the students had even looked up from what they were doing. Boats cruising off the shore were not unusual.

Then he spotted them. Two students – one with blond hair and the other dark, were working some considerable distance from the others and had gone round the headland into the little cove which lay on the other side. From where she was, Meg wouldn't have been able to see them at all.

"Bloody idiots!" he said. They were both apparently unaware of the rapidly flowing tide.

"What?"

"Those two in the cove. If they don't get out fast they'll be caught by the tide and the only way out is to climb the cliff." He handed the binoculars back to Michael.

"Oh yes. I see. Oh! They're my mystery pair. Tim something and his mate. Can we go in and rescue them?"

"No, we bloody can't. It's much too risky. What's the mystery?"

"Just the freshers' disco the other night. They never danced the whole night. Just stayed sitting in a corner talking to each other. Buggered if I would spend five pounds to get in and spend the night chatting while I was surrounded by sex- hungry birds."

"Well, if we don't do something, that was the last disco they'll ever see. More people have been drowned in that cove than I've had hot dinners. I'll get in as close as I can and we'll shout. That's all we can do. Get back on the bow and steer me in. Watch out for the rocks."

"Hang about. I'll put something on."

"There's no time," Ivan snapped. "The tide races in there. We've got just a few minutes."

"They'll be frightened to death," said Michael as he climbed back onto the bow. Whether because of the incoming tide or the sight of a naked man, he didn't explain.

Ivan's mouth was dry with fear as, with the engine just ticking over, he steered towards the shore. "Left a bit. That's it. Hold it there. Watch this rock coming up. Right a bit. Hold it. That's it. Right a bit more. Now left ... Careful ... careful...."

The two lads on the shore stopped peering into pools and looked straight at them. One of them was the boy with the white jeans who had tried to wind Meg Burton up. They both waved cheerily. Slowly, Ivan steered 'Peppercorn' towards them until all that lay between the boat and the shore was a stretch of boiling surf about as wide as a suburban road. He had to keep the engine running but shouted as loudly as he could. They waved.

"It's no good," said Michael. "Oh well. Here we go." With great difficulty and holding on to the tiny rail round the bow, he got up into a kneeling position. The two lads laughed and waved again.

"Get out! Danger! Tide!" Michael shouted and pointed in the direction of the other students. Some of them had noticed his nakedness and were running along the shore.

"Danger! Tide! Get out!" he shouted again. 'Peppercorn' was now so near the shore that the two lads could have waded out and got on board. Instead, they realized the danger they were in and began to clamber over the rocky barrier which separated them from the rest.

"That's Ivan Pepper and Michael Maystone,"

"No!"

"It is. Look!" Their words echoed back from the cliffs behind them. For a moment, they stopped, waved happily and then rejoined their companions. Meg stumped angrily towards them.

"Okay. Now let's get out of here," said Ivan.

That was easier said than done but he managed it and there was only one scrape mark on the hull when they finally moored at the jetty. They both felt in need of a drink and 'The Cabin' was open and they were soon watching four rather beautiful pool-players.

"I suppose we'd better pay Meg a visit," said Ivan. "I don't want to but now she knows we're here and knows I have a boat, she'll come here searching for us if we don't forestall her. Bloody woman!"

He didn't mean that. He was very fond of Meg but he knew that Garmouth and all that it meant to him had changed forever. He wondered how long it would be before his other secret world would be penetrated. Who would be the first student to tell the authorities about the photography and the videos? He shuddered at the thought.

"Let's go straight after lunch and get it over," said Michael and so, after two portions of 'Chouxfleur au Gratin' (Florets of crisp summer cauliflower, cooked in a sauce of mature Cheddar cheese) had been consumed, they set off.

The camp site wasn't too difficult to find. A pedestrian knew where it was. The row of uniform tents, each with 'St. Christopher's' stenciled on the side was in a field not more than a hundred yards from the beach. The students were washing plates in plastic buckets. They found Meg in her tent, writing.

"You did a good job there, Ivan," she said. "How did you get involved? Why are you down here?"

There was nothing for it but to explain about the cottage. Meg thought it might be ideal for something she had in mind. Ivan didn't let her continue on that tack. "And the boat?" she asked.

"Oh, that's not mine. I sort of share it." This was true, in a sense. It was almost paid for but he still owed a little to the bank.

"Well, thank God you were there. As for you," she continued addressing Michael, "it's just as well my students are biologists but even biologists aren't used to the full frontal display you gave them. As it happens, with those two it was probably a good thing you were like that. They wouldn't have noticed otherwise. I wonder they didn't swim out to the boat."

"They could have done but there was time for them to get over the rocks," said Ivan proudly. "Not many skippers would have risked getting in quite so close."

"Not many good-looking naked young men would have risked getting so close to those two either," said Meg. "Meaning?"

"Oh ... it'll all come out in the end. I might as well tell you. Those two, Timothy Hyde and Philip Dove are gay. At least they say they are. Silly boys. It's almost certainly a silly phase they're going through. They insisted on being alone in a tent even though the tents sleep four – and that meant putting two other boys in other tents. They've spent the entire weekend telling all and sundry that they're gay. They spend the evenings together in the woods over there. They're not exactly popular with the others – hence the fact they were working so far away. I shall have to report it to the Principal when we get back of course. They've ruined the weekend for everybody. It's not just that they do whatever people like that do to each other. It affects the other students. Some of them put crabs and sea urchins in their sleeping bag last night. I was furious. They were beautiful specimens too."

219

"They ought to be told off for putting themselves in danger," said Ivan. "Where are they now?"

"Search me. I can get them." She put her head out of the tent. "Peter dear," she said, addressing an unseen student, "Any idea where Tim and Philip are?"

"In their tent but don't ask me what they're doing."

"Get them for me please, dear. Mr. Pepper's got a few sharp words to say to them."

"About time somebody did," said Peter sulkily.

"I'll talk to them outside, Meg," said Ivan. "The language might not be suitable for your ears."

"I am a biologist, Ivan dear, but you're probably right. Anyway, it's better coming from you. You're nearer their age." They said goodbye. Ivan avoided giving the address or the phone number of the cottage. Meg said they could talk about her ideas for a winter field trip when they were back in college. Ivan and Michael went to stand some way away from any of the tents.

"Oh my dear God!" said Michael. "Just look at this. How camp can you get?"

To the accompaniment of cat calls and obscene shouts from the other students, Philip and Tim walked up the field towards them. Baggy pullovers covered the tops of their bodies but there was nothing on their legs. Both wore skimpy swimming trunks – and they were holding hands.

"Is it about this morning?" said the blond boy; the one who wore white jeans at college.

"Yes it is," said Ivan, loudly. Then he dropped his voice. "Which one you is which?" he asked.

"I'm Tim. This is Philip."

Of the two of them, Philip was the better looking, Ivan thought. There was something about his dark skin and deep brown eyes that was appealing – not to mention his long, coffee colored legs.

"Can you make drinks in 'The Cabin' this evening?" Ivan asked, still keeping his voice down.

"Sure. Yes. Why?"

"You'll see. Say eight o'clock?" They nodded and Ivan continued. "Now stay looking as shamefaced as you can. I want Dr. Burton to hear this. It's all an act you understand?" They nodded again and Ivan launched into a blast which shattered Michael. He'd gotten used to Ivan's anomalous position in the college hierarchy. He wasn't a student nor was he 'staff' in the generally accepted sense of the word. But no lecturer at the college, not even Fred Ragstone, the physical education instructor, would have come out with such a torrent of invective. Philip and Tim didn't have to act. They blushed and shifted uncomfortably from one bare foot to the other and, when Ivan had finished, they walked back to their tent, still holding hands.

Meg Burton came out of her tent as Ivan and Michael were leaving. "You laid that on a bit strong, Ivan dear. People like that are very sensitive you know," she said.

"So am I when it comes to the safety of my boat," said Ivan. "See you back at college," and with that, they got into the car and drove off.

"Oh, my dear God – just look at this!" said Michael. He and Ivan were half way through the first round of drinks. Ivan turned his head towards the door. Tim was wearing the familiar white jeans – incredibly white for a person who was spending the weekend in a tent. This was topped by what would have been called a seaman's shirt had it not been an almost fluorescent turquoise color, and adorned with white toggle fasteners. Philip was more conventionally attired in jeans and a denim jacket.

Ivan stood up to go to the bar which gave him an opportunity to sit them where he wanted them – diagonally opposite to one another. He wasn't going to risk any hand- holding in 'The Cabin'. Philip took his place in the comer and Tim sat next to Michael. He got the drinks and sat down again.

"Thanks a lot for the rescue," said Philip. "We'd have looked a right couple of idiots if you hadn't come along."

"You'd have looked like strawberry jam if you'd tried to climb the cliff," said Ivan, but if you don't mind me saying so, you're being a bit idiotic at the moment."

"Why? What's wrong?" asked Tim, sharply.

"Oh, nothing here. Nothing at all. But what's this you've been telling Dr. Burton about yourselves?"

"I knew she'd tell everybody," said Philip, glumly.

"I gather it was hardly told to her in confidence. The other students know."

"It's no big deal," said Tim. "We're gay. It's the twentieth century for Christ's sake! There's nothing she, or anybody else, can do about it."

"Don't you believe it, dearie. Don't you believe it," said Michael, using his camp 'Terry' voice for the very first time in 'The Cabin'. They both stared at him. Philip put down his glass. "You too?" he asked.

"Michael is the one and only true bisexual I've met," Ivan explained.

"What about you though?" Tim asked.

"Unlike you, that's not a question I'm prepared to answer. You can say that I am sympathetic and that's why I want you both to listen carefully. You both attend a college which was founded centuries ago by the church for the sole purpose of training teachers. Now you know and I know that there is nothing wrong in being gay, but that is not the teaching of the church on the subject. Neither is it the view of Mr. and Mrs. Average Parent. Put an openly gay teacher in their son's school and they'll have the kid out in seconds and start writing to their Member of Parliament about corruption of minors. Thus, Dr. Burton will go back to the college and tell the Principal...."

"Who couldn't do a thing," Tim interrupted him. "It would be our turn to kick up a fuss. Ever heard of human rights?" Patiently, Ivan carried on. There were other, more subtle ways, he explained. Extreme academic pressure, borderline examination results, even a psychiatric report to say that they were not coping with college life as well as they should. "Whichever technique they use, you'll be out," he concluded.

"Absolute balls! I'll fight...." but this time it was Philip's turn to interrupt his friend.

"I knew it. I should never have listened to you," he said. "It's no big deal," said Tim. "Let them do it. We'll find another place that's a bit more up to date."

"You might be able to. I couldn't. My folks would just say I'd wasted my chances."

"Nobody could," said Michael, in his normal voice again. "The next place would ask for some sort of reference from St. Christopher's."

"I knew all along this might happen," said Philip, bitterly. Tim said nothing. He picked up his glass, took a long drink and then put it down again. "Suggestions?" he said, in a tone more indicative of anger than remorse. "Yes I have," said Ivan. "You have both achieved the best Burton wind-up of the century. That's the answer. For the rest of this weekend you camp it up outrageously and the moment you get back to college, you both invent girl friends at home and tell everyone about them. But no more shagging on the camp-site." Philip blushed. "We don't do that anyway," he said. Puzzled, Ivan looked at him. "But you chose to be together in a separate tent. I don't get it," he said. "Neither do we. We're happy though," said Tim. "It sounds like the ultimate in frustration to me."

"Not really." At which point, Philip, who had drunk less than a half a pint of beer in contrast to Tim whose glass was empty, decided he needed to go to the toilet. Ivan had to stand up to let him get out. "So, what's the full story?" Ivan asked. "Phil's never had any experience," said Tim. "He comes from one of these really religious families."

"But you have?"

"Christ, yes. You couldn't live a sex-free life in a school like the one I went to. Much chased and never chaste. That was me. Michael laughed and said he'd have to remember that one. Ivan was deep in thought. The conversation around him turned to all sorts of other matters. Michael suggested a game of pool. Ivan declined but the other three went over to the pool table. He sat there sipping his beer and watching them but less than half his mind was on the game. A decision had to be made. It was almost as if some fate was forcing him to make it and he resented that. The erosion had started. Whether to take action to stop it or let it carry on. That was the question. Over at the pool table, Tim's turn came round. He bent over and peered along the line of his cue. The white jeans stretched over his buttocks. "Go on, Tim. You can pot both of them." said Philip and the decision was made. "Pot both of them," Ivan muttered and he finished his drink. They came back to the table. Michael had apparently won. He went up to the bar to buy a round of drinks. Ivan leant forward. "I've a business proposition to put to you both," he said. "Oh yes?"

"I have a cottage here. I don't use it every weekend. I can't because I have to work most Saturdays but you can. Use it whenever you like."

"Do you mean that?" Tim asked. "Of course I mean it. You both need to be together pretty often and you can't do that at college."

"It would solve a lot of problems. I was going to ask if we could share a room or be put out in digs together."

"That would be a disaster," said Ivan. There had been two aggressively hetero football players who moved into digs with one another to save money. That had happened in Ivan's first year at St. Christopher's and it was still being talked about. Tim smiled knowingly. "And you'd expect certain favors in return, I guess," he said. "Well, yes."

"I thought so. I wouldn't mind. Just once or twice. Not regularly. Phil won't agree though. I'm sure he won't."

"You haven't heard what I have in mind yet."

"He's a bit over the top isn't he?" said Tim. He handed the letter back to Ivan. G.D. Morris had written "Teddy is very pleasing. I hope to see a lot more of him in the coming months. What a dear little bottom he has. So many boys these days have far too much fat on their bottoms. The result, no doubt, of all this fast food and sugary drinks. Teddy has the sort of bottom that I would take great pleasure in spanking. There is no greater pleasure than having a young and muscular boy like Teddy across one's knees and spanking his bottom until his cheeks are that inviting rosy color and one can feel his cock hardening with every stroke. Perhaps it might be possible to get him to pose in such a position. I enclose twenty pounds and should be grateful if you would give it to him with my compliments and please make sure he writes to let me know he's got it...."

Ivan had given Tim the name of Teddy because the lad seemed more and more like a cuddly toy. Not, unfortunately, as hairy as Ivan would have liked. In fact for some days he'd contemplated introducing Tim to his customers as Robert's younger brother but the photograph of Robert was well into the re-touching phase and he was pleased with it – so Tim became 'Teddy.'

The first studies sold very well. He'd done them on the boat while Tim and Philip were still on their field trip. The first was of Tim, bare-topped and holding down one side of the white jeans to expose quite a large area of white midriff, dark brown curly hair and just the top of his cock. Tim was a delight to work with. He was not only prepared to do just about everything, but he was quite happy for Ivan to help him assume the exact positions Ivan required – when Philip wasn't there.

The problem was that Philip was there. He'd been there during that evening's session standing well out of the camera's field of view, fully dressed and frowning whilst his friend lay back in the old aircraft seat, masturbating furiously with his head lolling to one side. He'd grinned happily at the lens as he shot his load with characteristic force all over his belly and chest. After that, and after he'd wiped himself dry, he'd been happy enough to turn over for the shots G.D. Morris was so anxious to buy. He lay there, alternately clenching and relaxing the cheeks of his delectable butt whilst Ivan ran a reel of film through the camera.

Philip was a strange young man – a very strange young man. He never said that he disapproved. In fact, the huge lump that developed in the front of his jeans at every session indicated that the proceedings turned him on. Ivan did everything possible to give Philip a chance, telling them "I'll develop this straight away. Let yourselves out by the back door," didn't work.

"We'll come with you. I've never seen that done," Philip had said.

There had been the time when Ivan left them alone for a whole hour. Tim had undressed and was lying on the 'Baby Bear' bed. Philip had frowned even more than usual when Ivan told them that the camera had jammed and he'd have to go into the dark room to fix it. In fact he went into his control room and turned on all three of the hidden cameras to watch them. What had developed? Nothing. They chatted about their field work, laughed at the way Dr. Burton had been taken in and how the same students that had jeered at them in Garmouth were now saying that they knew all along that it was a practical joke. But neither of them even touched the other.

"Where does this bloke Morris live?" Philip asked, picking up the letter to read it again.

"Somewhere near Birmingham. That's all I can tell you. He's got to live in that area to be able to pick up his post from the news store."

"He's weird," said Tim. "But twenty pounds is always acceptable. Do you think I ought to write to him?"

"No. It would be far too risky. Forget it." Ivan paid them, gave Tim the twenty-pound note and they left.

A month went by, an extremely busy and profitable month. No less than five of the new first years found themselves unable to pay their bills and came, shamefacedly, to see if Ivan could help. He was glad to oblige and they, in turn, obliged him. It took some persuasion. It always did but their photographs were soon on their way to Ivan's customers and his private post was swelled by their appreciative comments.

He'd gotten so used to opening their letters, scanning the contents and then putting them in the shredder, that G. D. Morris's letter nearly got the same treatment. He had been delighted with the photos of young Teddy, he wrote. He must have spent hours examining the photos – probably with a magnifying glass. There followed two paragraphs praising every possible aspect of Tim's backside – and then....

"I am glad the money reached him safely. One has no confidence in the Post Office these days. If he would let me have his address, I will send the books he wants."

Shaken, Ivan put the letter down and sat staring at it. "You idiot! You utter idiot!" he said.

"And who has upset us?" Michael's voice coincided with the sound of the door closing behind him.

"Oh it's you. I wish to hell you'd knock. I've just had one shock."

"Tell auntie and you'll feel better."

"Bloody Tim. I told him not to write to the Morris person but he has – and asked him for books. Look."

Michael took the letter and settled in the aircraft seat to read it. "Hmm. That was a bit silly," he said. "I love 'curvaceous contours' and 'cherubic cheeks.' I must use them one day in an essay for the V.P. They have a definite poetic ring."

"The only ring I can think of at the moment is to wring his bloody neck!" said Ivan. "Of all the daft things to do...."

"Don't get heated, lovey. It's not good for you at your age, but it would be wise to tell him to confine his letter writing to this non-existent girlfriend you've invented for him. That was a stroke of genius on your part. You'll run out of those pretty blue envelopes soon."

"Not before the engagement is broken off. It's working then?"

"My dear, it's the talk of the college. And all these weekends away! Philip too. Young love is a beautiful thing. Oh! I forgot what I came for. Are you free for a beer tonight?"

"Not tonight. I've got one of the first years coming in."

"Anyone nice?"

"Jeremy Samuels. Not bad looking without his glasses. Nice big cock though."

"That's the main thing, dear. When are we going down to Garmouth again?"

"Well, I'm not sure. I'll have to see Tim and Philip and see what they've got in mind. I wouldn't want to barge in on them."

"I don't know. Could be rather fun. Which one do you fancy?"

"I'll have Tim. I might get a fuck. All you're likely to get is a frown. I'll tell you what. If you're wanting drinking partners, take those two. Then you can sort out a weekend when they're not using the cottage and give a few words of advice about writing letters to dirty old men."

"Good idea, lovey. They should be just coming out of lectures now. I'll troll off and find them."

He got up and left. Ivan put the letters into a drawer and settled down to some college work.

On the following morning, Michael was in the aircraft seat again. "He didn't write. He says so and I believe him," he said. "So either he's a liar or G. D. Morris is making it up."

"The latter, little love. People like that fantasize. He wanked himself silly over Tim until it was real to him and then he conjured up the idea of Tim writing to him and that became real too. It happens."

"Hmm. What did Philip say? He saw the letter too." Michael paused for a second. "Philip wasn't with us when I asked," he said. "Why? Where was he?"

"On his way home. Tim came back to my place."

"Why?" Michael smiled. "Let's say I fancied another drink. Not something your average pub provides, and leave it at that."

"And didn't Philip mind?"

"We never asked him. It was Tim's suggestion; not mine. Your auntie has another surprising revelation too."

"What's that?"

"What do you reckon those two actually do down at your cottage?"

"Fuck? Suck? I wouldn't know."

"Hardly anything, dear. A very, very occasional mutual wank is as far as they get. Even that's rare. Philip can't get a hard-on for long enough."

"That's ridiculous. He was practically bursting out. of his jeans the last time he came in here."

"Tim's opinion as well. Apparently he can get Philip randy by just talking to him but by the time the clothes are off, Philip is left with a three-and-a-half-inch length of Playdo. Further, my dear, this situation has made our little friend so frustrated that he would welcome a visit to Garmouth by us though I fear you will be left out. Having once experienced his auntie's ministrations, he's unlikely to want to waste his tasty juices or his ass on a person of your age."

"Out of the question," said Ivan. "It wouldn't be fair to Philip. They'll have to sort the problem out themselves. Anyway, where would the four of us sleep?"

"There you go again, showing your age. Who said anything about sleep?"

"Well, you can go if you like but count me out. It would be a disaster. I know it would."

"You know very well that I wouldn't go down without you. Two's company and all that. Think about it." Ivan did. He thought about it an awful lot in the next few days. All the fences he had built were down. Garmouth, his business and his carefully built-up privacy had all merged into one. There was no doubt that Tim at least had clicked that he was gay. Tim had never said anything when Ivan had been placing his cock in the right angle or rubbing him with oil, but Ivan's erection must have been apparent. How many more people would he tell before the story got right round the college? It was worrying.

He carried on, notwithstanding. The business was growing so fast that he simply had to. There were now nine students on his list and all of them were progressing well. The first shots – the ones in posing slips were soon superseded by others in which the slips had dropped to expose a backside white from being covered up for too long. Soon the slip vanished altogether. Flaccid cocks gave way to stiff, upright ones that, after a few more studies and a little coaxing spurted or dribbled obligingly for the camera. The only studies he couldn't provide, despite his customers' clamors were duals. "Terry and Garth", the series shot in the pantomime scenery, sold well but the punters wanted more. He'd had hopes that Philip and Tim would be the answer to that problem but it didn't look very likely. None of the others would oblige. He knew that. There wasn't one of them that hadn't told him emphatically that he was only doing it for the money. Even if they hadn't fallen for the 'magazine in Canada designed for sex-crazed teenage girls' line, the pretense seemed to make them feel easier about doing it. The demand increased – notably for shots of Tim with someone else. Michael would have been the obvious person but Ivan ruled him out immediately. It would have been unfair to Philip and, as Philip was always present

229

when he photographed Tim, there was no chance that he would allow it anyway. He did the best he could. A shot of Tim lying on his front, with drops of his own semen on his buttocks and legs, entitled 'The Moment After' went down well with some customers but not with G. D. Morris. He didn't like Tim's 'cheeky grin'. He preferred, he wrote, "the satisfied smile of a boy sated with sex."

They tried again. It was slightly better that time. Philip had wiped the semen from Tim's legs, sporting a monster erection under his jeans as he did so. He left the studio to wash out the cloth in the toilet. Ivan was unloading the camera.

"When are you and Michael going to come down to Garmouth?" Tim asked, raising his head from the pillow.

"He spoke to me about it. I don't think it's a good idea. It's not fair to you or Philip. The idea was that you two could be together."

"But we'd still be together. You two wouldn't make any difference. It could be fun."

"Michael said something about it not working out too well. You and Philip I mean."

"Oh it's okay. I love the guy to bits but sex isn't everything, is it?"

"It's a hell of a lot. I guess we could come down. How does the coming weekend suit you?"

"It's your cottage. Any weekend suits me. Leave Philip to me. I'll tell him you're coming."

The following Saturday was one of those extraordinary late autumn days when the chill of approaching winter gives way, reluctantly, to an unexpected return of summer heat. The sea glinted like crumpled aluminum foil and there was hardly any wind. All four of them were in swimming trunks and all four wore life jackets. Ivan had learned a lot about the sea in the few months he'd had 'Peppercorn.'

"We're getting near the 'Devil's Eye.' You'd better put these on," he had said. "If we hit it, the boat will be thrown around like a cork. You just strap them round your waist and hitch the clip at end of the cord to the rail. Then, if you get thrown overboard, we can pull you in."

The 'Devil's Eye' was a frightening phenomenon. The transition of the shore from rock to gently sloping sand caused the incoming tidal race to split. One stream rushed in more quickly than the other causing a whirlpool to form. Ivan had never seen it but he had been warned often enough. He didn't expect to see it. He'd checked the tide tables before setting out but it was better to be safe than sorry.

"I feel like a dog on a leash," said Philip. "How do you adjust the size?"

Ivan shut off the engine. "Here. I'll do it for you," he said. For the first time his fingers made contact with Philip's body. He'd touched practically every inch of Tim during the previous weeks but Philip was a revelation. They were both about the same height but whereas Tim was slender and graceful, Philip was powerfully built – all muscle. It took a lot of self-control on Ivan's part not to slide his hands up under the life jacket and feel Philip's fleshy pecs.

Philip was hairy too. A narrow line of shiny black hair ran from his navel, widening appreciably before it vanished under the waistline of his blue trunks. Tim tightened the belt and fastened the buckle. "There," he said. "We can't lose you. How about you, Tim? Can you manage?"

"No problem. I've worn one of these before."

"When?" Philip asked, sharply. "Last night you said you'd never been out in a boat."

"It wasn't a boat. It was a classroom."

Michael, already belted and attached by the life line to the rail, looked up. "A peculiar teaching aid," he said. "Not even Ivan has life belts in his vast stock."

"It wasn't a teaching aid. He was a pervert."

"Who?" Michael asked.

"He got the sack. Mr. Powell was his name. He was our history teacher and he had one of these things in his desk drawer. He'd pick on somebody, put the belt round his waist and lead him round the classroom. He was evil."

"I don't get the point," said Ivan. "Why did he do that?"

231

"It was mostly if you made a mistake but there were some boys he picked on every time. He'd sort of say things like. Look, boys, he's got the brain of a farm animal so I have to lead him round. He said other things as well. Foul things."

"Like what?" Philip asked, and Tim; the lad that could masturbate unperturbed in front of cameras blushed.

"Oh nothing," he said.

"Come on. Tell us. It's interesting," Philip said. "Considerably more interesting than several hundred square miles of empty sea," Michael added.

"Well, he'd carry on about farm animals. Like, for instance, he might say you were a pig and then he'd go on about your nice fat hams. God! I can hear him now. I was only quite young when he left, thank Christ. Tim's a nice little piglet isn't he boys? He's fattening up nicely, and he had a favorite called Rutherford who always sat in the front row. "He's got nice fat hams. We'll have to ask Rutherford what he thinks. Feel his hams, Rutherford, and bloody Rutherford would put his hands on your ass and rub you."

"And then?" Philip had sat down and was leaning forward with wide open eyes.

"Well, bloody Rutherford would get a hard-on under his desk. Mr. Powell never seemed to notice that or, if he did, he didn't say anything. But if it happened to you, he'd start going on about sausages. What do we make from pigs, boys?' and somebody would say 'Sausages, sir.' 'That's right,' he'd say. 'It looks like Tim's got a very nice juicy sausage,' and then.... Oh! You don't want to hear all this. It's in the past. Best forgotten. When is the 'Devil's Eye' due to appear, Ivan?"

"Fuck the 'Devil's Eye! This is much more interesting. Come on. Tell us more about Mr. Powell," said Philip.

"We're all going to be teachers," Michael added. "We need to know. Anyway it's good for you to tell us. Catharsis they call it."

Still blushing furiously, Tim continued. "Well, there was this room leading off the classroom. More like a big cupboard really. He kept all his history stuff in there – a bit like Ivan's place in miniature I guess. Slides and books and maps. That sort of thing. He'd make you stand in front of the class and keep going on about your hams and your sausage and all the time he'd be rubbing your behind. Then somebody would ask 'When are you going to take him into your little room, sir?' Ugh! 'With me he said, 'I don't think his sausage is quite ready yet boys. I'll give it time. Sausages are best cooked slowly. His hams are ready though. I think I'll baste his hams. Hams like this need a good basting,' and they'd all laugh and you had to spend the rest of the lesson in this belt thing, tied up to a hook in the comer with all the others looking at you and laughing. Then, when the bell went...."

"He obviously hadn't finished," said Michael.

"Too right he hadn't. It was 'I think we've just got time before the next class comes in,' and he'd unhook the cord and lead you into this smelly little room. At first it was the usual teacher stuff. 'You have to learn to concentrate my boy! Forgetting the most important battle of the Civil War is inexcusable!' That sort of thing but he had an old armchair in there. Really old it was. There was a great hole on the seat but when he'd finished giving you verbal lashing ... God! Are you sure you want to hear all this?"

"Yeah!" said Philip in such an unusually croaky voice that Ivan and Michael turned to see if he was all right. Philip was perfectly all right. Philip had been turned on to such an extent that his cock wasn't just bulging under his trunks. It's purple head was just visible at the top of his left thigh.

Philip turned away. So did Ivan. Michael winked. Fortunately, Tim didn't notice. He continued.

"It only happened to me a couple of times and, like I say, I was still pretty young," he said. "I heard a lot from the other boys though."

"So what did he do?" Philip asked, and again his voice was husky.

"You're enjoying this, aren't you?" said Tim.

"Yeah! Nothing like that happened at our school."

"I wish I could say the same. Well, there was Mr. Powell sitting in this horrible old chair and there was me or some other boy anxious as hell to get out and he'd go on about how he ought to have you re-graded to a lower set and then he'd say that there was another way and get you to come closer.

233

"It's funny. You're right, Michael. Talking about it does make me feel better. I remember everything so clearly now. I thought I'd forgotten. I can even remember the smell of his breath. He used to smoke disgusting little cigars. Like black cigarettes they were."

"So what did he do then?" asked Michael. "Let's have the

whole story."

"Yeah!" said Philip. "You're standing in front of him. Then what? 'So, Tim, what shall we do with you? Shall I see the Head and have you re-graded or will you be a good boy for me?' and of course everybody said they'd be a good boy. Anybody would. 'That's what I hoped you'd say,' he said. 'Now undo your trousers for me.'"

"And did you?" Ivan asked.

"Of course I did. And he'd pull them down so you were standing there with your trousers and underpants round your ankles. 'Just a bit closer,' he'd say and you'd shuffle forwards and then he started feeling you. A bit like you do in the studio, Ivan."

"Oh, come off it! I don't force anyone to do anything!" Ivan protested.

"I didn't mean that. He sort of stroked up the insides of your legs and then started playing with your balls and your cock saying things like, 'You're going to be a real beauty when you're a bit older.'"

"He was right about that anyway," said Ivan.

"I had some hair already. He liked that. By the time he was playing with that he was panting like he'd been climbing a mountain and his horrible little cock making his trousers stick out in front."

"How do you know it was little?" Michael asked.

"Some of the older boys told me. They'd seen it. I never did. He got up and made me lie across the arm of the chair. He had this bit of an old belt. The buckle had come off, thank God. He gave me two or three swipes with that. Quite hard but not as hard as he did it to the older boys. After that you pulled up your pants, he gave you a toffee and sent you off to the next lesson. And that's all I can tell you from my own experience. Like I said, he was reported and sacked. Nobody missed him – except Rutherford. It turned out that Rutherford was his talent

234

scout. Used to tell him what people looked like in the showers. That sort of thing."

"Amazing!" said Philip. "What about the older boys? Did he do the same to them?"

"They were his cows."

"His what?"

"I'll demonstrate if you want. I know all about it because, well... after he left, Rutherford and me got pretty close if you know what I mean. In fact Rutherford was the first to pluck my cherry but that was much later. I don't think that made me what I am though. Anyway, with a bloke like you – seventeen or eighteen say..." He unhitched Philip's cord from the rail. "Hang about," said Ivan. "If this is leading to what I think it's leading to, I'll get us out of the danger area." He put the engine into gear and 'Peppercorn' moved forward. He could just hear what Tim was saying over the noise of the engine. He wished that Rutherford had decided to go to St. Christopher's rather than the Oxford college he'd joined after a school career during which he'd screwed Tim and several others.

Finally, having moved the boat nearer the shore and well away from danger, he shut off the engine and threw the anchor overboard. "Right," he said. "Action!"

"Like in the films, you mean? Sure you want to, Phil?"

"Yeah. It's interesting." Philip stood up.

"It's certainly turned you on," Michael observed. It was a wonder that Philip's trunks hadn't ripped open. If it hadn't been for the purple head, even more of which had penetrated between textile and thigh, one would have thought he was concealing a vegetable marrow. Embarrassed, he tried to pull the trunks down to cover it, revealing, as he did so, that the hair under his navel was a sparse growth compared to the forest it led to.

"Who's going to be Mr. Powell's favorite student?" Tim asked. "You'd better choose, Phil." His face was still flushed but Ivan got the strong impression that he was no longer embarrassed.

"What's he got to do?" Phil asked.

"You'll see."

"Ivan I think. I know him best."

Like the director of a film – and Ivan wished fervently that he had brought a video camera with him – Tim positioned them: Ivan on the fore-peak with his legs dangling in the cockpit; Michael on the bench seat previously occupied by Philip and Tim. They took off their life jackets and, all except Philip, discarded the life belts and lines.

"And now," said Tim, still holding the cord attached to his friend's life belt. "What do you mean, lad, when you say you can't remember the battles of the Civil War?"

"I never did know them," said Philip.

"Because ... do you know why, lad?"

"No ... er ... sir."

"Because of your bovine empty-headedness. That's why. You would be far better eating grass in a meadow somewhere, wouldn't he, boys?"

Ivan and Michael nodded. "A cow is a useful animal," Tim continued. "What do we get from cows, boys?"

"Milk," said Ivan.

"And steak," said Michael.

"Exactly. Nice creamy milk. By the look of things, your udder is just bursting to be milked. Let's ask Pepper for his opinion, shall we?" He led Philip the few paces to where Ivan was sitting. Ivan had to climb down into the cockpit. "What do you think, Pepper?" asked Tim. "Just run your hand over this cow's teat, would you?"

Ivan looked up into Philip's eyes. Philip nodded. Ivan put down his hand and took the bulge in Philip's shorts between his thumb and forefinger. It was incredibly hard and he could feel Philip's pulse throbbing. "More than ready I should think, sir," he said.

"Just as I thought. Well, we'll have to do something about it, won't we? We can't let all that lovely cream go to waste and I love cream. Especially cheesy cream from mature cows. How old are you?"

"Eighteen," said Philip. Ivan half expected him to moo.

"Eighteen! My favorite age. I shall have great pleasure in emptying your udder. I expect you've got quite a big udder. I think it's time we went into my little room."

Like someone in a trance, Philip allowed himself to be led down into the cabin. He didn't smile. He said nothing. He just stared. It was uncanny.

Aware, somehow, that their presence might break the spell Tim had created, Ivan and Michael hung around in the cockpit and peered down through the open doorway into the cabin. Tim sat on one of the long side benches. "Fancy not knowing the battles of the Civil War!" he said, scornfully. "Slip those down." Philip took hold of the waistline and shifted his shorts downwards. His cock leapt up as if it was spring loaded. A bead of moisture landed on Tim's cheek. Ivan had rarely seen a cock like it. It was enormous.

"Your milking time is long overdue," said Tim. He looked up. "I don't usually let other boys in on occasions like this," he said, "but in these special circumstances...."

Ivan and Michael almost fell over each other as they went in. Ivan shut the door behind them.

"God! You're lovely! I've never seen it as hard as this," said Tim, fondling Philip's cock affectionately.

"It's all that about your teacher that did it," said Philip.

"Uh huh?" Tim leaned forward. Philip took a step forward. His cock brushed against Tim's cheek. Tim took it between his thumb and forefinger, kissed the tip and then sucked it in – or at least as much as he could manage. Ivan pointed to the bench on the opposite side and he and Michael sat down. The nearer bench would have been better to get a view of Philip's front. They had to make do with sound effects but they were exciting in themselves. The sea slapped against the hull. Gulping noises emanated from Tim. Philip was breathing heavily and would have come in seconds, Ivan thought, had Tim not suddenly stopped.

237

"Go on. Keep on!" Philip gasped. Tim ignored him and, putting his head to one side so that he could see them, he addressed Ivan and Michael.

"Nice bum, don't you think?" he said.

"Very nice," said Ivan. Michael said it was 'bloody beautiful. '

"Mr. Powell always said that eighteen-year-old backsides were the best," said Tim in a perfectly conversational tone. "He reckoned that younger boys had too much fat on their butts. Eighteen-year-olds had just the right muscle tone. That's what he said."

Ivan suddenly remembered G. D. Morris's letter. 'So many boys these days have far too much fat on their bottoms. ' Philip might just be the answer, he thought. He was hardly a 'boy' and that hair on the insides of his thighs would have to come off but otherwise....

"And like all prize cattle, this one needs inseminating," said Tim, taking Philip's prick in his hand again. "Bloody ridiculous to reach the age of eighteen and not have had a cock inside you. However...."

Once again the cabin rang with slurping sounds, gasps and heavy breathing. Ivan tried hard not to make a sound. Philip seemed to have forgotten that he and Michael were there. His ass cheeks tightened and his back curved inwards. Great dimples formed in the sides. Then he'd relax and straighten up again. Tim's hands went round his backside as if to draw him in further. He had very long fingers, Ivan thought. That figured. His cock was quite a size. Ivan wished he could see it. It would be dribbling for sure. Whose wouldn't in those circumstances? Then he noticed something else. All Tim's fingers were pressing hard against Philip's flesh – except one. His right index finger was beckoning. An invitation? He wasn't sure. He glanced at Michael but Michael was staring at the scene in front of them like a man in a trance.

Then Tim took his right hand away, leaving four pink marks on the white flesh. He put it between Philip's thighs. Philip spread his legs. For a few seconds, Tim's finger-tips played with the wispy, black hairs on the inside of Philip's thighs. Then he took his hand out and, once again, put it round his friend's heaving buttocks – but not on them. His index finger beckoned and then pointed inwards, burrowing between Philip's cheeks. There was no mistaking that gesture. Ivan stood up. Tim dug his finger-tips into Philip's ass-cheeks and pulled them apart.

Ivan looked over Philip's shoulder but Tim, with several inches of cock in his mouth couldn't really be expected to look up – still less to confirm what he wanted Ivan to do. Ivan put his hand on the top of Philip's jutting and heaving buttocks, slid it down and insinuated his finger into the warm, damp cleft.

He'd gotten to know quite a lot about anuses since he started the business. Even the most cautious of his impoverished students didn't object to that part of them being photographed. His series 'Entrances to Paradise' had sold very well. Each one was different. Each one was meticulously cleaned and brushed with oil – and that was interesting. All of them claimed to be completely straight. None of them had ever had any experience of gay sex. "What do you take me for?" was the usual angry response to his subtle inquiries. And yet it was remarkable how so many 'virgin' assholes opened like little pink flower buds the moment the oiled bristles touched them. Jitendra Shah, six-feet-and-one-inch of dusky Indian beauty – a boy whose idea of further education was to shaft as many women as he could – had opened up to such an extent that it was like pouring oil into a funnel and he'd writhed around so much that he'd actually come.

Philip was not like that. Philip's ass felt like a knot tied in a piece of hairy, sisal string. It would take more than a few brush strokes to persuade it to open. That was for sure. It would have to be extra virgin olive oil too. Nonetheless, tickling it was a delight – and not just for Ivan. Philip bent forward and put his hands on Tim's shoulders. Ivan ran his finger up and down the cleft. There was no appreciable difference between the hardness of his perineum and the rest of him. It all felt as resistant and as smooth as if marble – save for that tight, hair-fringed orifice. Ivan pressed against it. That did no good at all. He tickled it again. Philip gasped. There had to be some way to persuade it to open. There was a key or a combination to the tightest lock. What was Philip's?

He didn't get a chance to find out. His fingers were suddenly squeezed so hard that it hurt. Philip arched his back. "Oh! Oh! Oh!" he gasped. His head drooped and, had he not been supported on Tim's shoulders, he would certainly have fallen forwards. Still spurting, his cock fell from Tim's lips. Beads of semen landed everywhere. Tim got most of it in his hair but some spattered on the bench, some on the bulkhead and some on the floor. And the moment Philip stood up

239

straight again, panting for breath (and Ivan had removed his finger) Tim followed suit. Ivan was used to the force of Tim's copious ejaculations. The one he'd achieved in the video 'Teddy's Torrent' had been a revelation but this one was even better. In fact, when he cleaned the boat, Ivan found dried semen spots on the cabin ceiling.

"Christ! You were good! Why can't you be like that all the time?" Tim asked, wiping his mouth on the back of his hand. "It was you talking about Mr. Powell," said Philip. "You left out something though. What about the belt?"

"Could it be?" Ivan thought. He'd never considered that possibility. He looked at Tim. Tim smiled. "That's the second act, to be staged tonight," he said. "Starring you and Ivan."

"Where do I come in?" Michael asked. "Not 'where,''Who'," said Tim. "Me, of course. That thing of yours looks just like what I need."

It wasn't just a key that was needed. It was a combination and it took a long time to get Philip to reveal it. By the time he did, Ivan's balls were aching. He had a hard-on such as he'd never had for years and frustration had made him bad- tempered.

The frustration started on the journey back to the jetty. Ivan stood alone at the wheel. The other three were on the bench seat behind him and he dared not look round. For starters, the approach to Garmouth jetty was difficult because of the tides, and what was happening behind him was extremely distracting.

"It's really nice. Sort of silky," said Tim.

"Go on. Go ahead if you want to," Michael replied.

"You're sure you'll be able to make it later?"

"Love, with a technique like yours, I could shoot again in seconds. Oh yeah. A bit slower. That's nice. Oh! That's great."

"It makes a change to have one that doesn't go soft all of a sudden. Up to a few minutes ago weekends in Garmouth were sadly disappointing."

"Shut up about that. You know now," said Philip.

"It took long enough. You should have said. Anyway, you've got Ivan tonight and I've got this."

"Right up your beautiful little ass," said Michael. "Ah! Ah! Oh! Any minute now. Ah! There!"

"I hope you haven't made a mess in my boat," said Ivan crossly. He didn't turn round to see.

"It'll wash off," said Tim. "Shall we stop for a meal on the way home? Nobody will feel like cooking."

That had been a good idea. The aching subsided as he ate one of 'The Cabin's' chicken pies with its 'home grown succulent beans.' The 'spring potatoes' were obviously late developers but they tasted okay. They walked back to the cottage. Ivan carried the harness that would be needed – soon he hoped. He deliberately walked behind the others, just to appraise Philip's backside. That was a mistake. By the time they reached the cottage, his cock was semi-erect and the ache had returned.

"We'll turn in straight away, eh?" he said, closing the door behind him. "You and Michael can use the bedroom. Philip and I will stay down here," he said. "At this hour? It's not eight o'clock yet," said Michael. "Yes but..."

"We'll have a mini-Bijou drinkette first," said Michael, "and then Tim can tell us more of his fascinating school experiences."

"Oh yeah! That would be great!" said Philip. Resignedly, Ivan sat down. Michael poured drinks and drew the curtains closed. "I think it might be an idea if we all got undressed first," he said.

"Ready for bed, you mean?" Ivan asked.

"Certainly not, dear! It would just make it more interesting." That didn't take long. They were only wearing jeans over their swimming trunks. Soon there was a pile of clothes in the comer and all four of them were sitting, naked in Ivan's lounge – a room that, until a few weeks previously had been his own private territory. He wouldn't have felt so embarrassed then at having an erection. Philip's cock looked as if it might come to life. Michael's and Tim's hung, shriveled and tiny – which was hardly surprising. Ivan, owner of the house and of the boat, was the only one that had missed out on all the action. He tried to suppress his anger.

"So, what do you want to hear about now? I've told you all about Mr. Powell and he's not worth talking about anyway."

"Tell us about this Rutherford character. What was his first name?" said Michael.

"Do you know, I don't remember. We never used first names at that place. Ian I think. Yes. Ian. I remember seeing a birthday card on his desk. 'To Ian with love from Mum and Dad.' Something like that."

"And he was Mr. Powell's talent scout, you said?"

"That's right. I didn't know at the time of course. There were about four classes in every year and each year had a showers monitor. Rutherford was ours. A pretty dumb sort of job. He had to report anyone that took too long, make sure the faucets were turned off and pick up anything that had been left behind. Well, of course, he had to be there the whole time we were in there and you know what kids are like: 'Mine's bigger than yours.' 'I can make spunk.' ' I'll bet you can't.' That sort of thing. What we didn't know was that all this was being reported back to Mr. Powell. Now that I come to think about it, I guess Mr. Powell got him the job."

"And was Mr. Powell having it off with him?" Philip asked. "Probably but I don't know that. They were pretty close but then most of the teachers had a crush on a boy."

"Extraordinary place!" said Michael. "I'm learning more about British education here than I've learned in all the time I've been at St. Chris's."

"It was sort of tradition," Tim continued. "They never did anything. Well... you might get a friendly pat on the backside. Even the married ones were a bit that way. 'My wife and I would love you to come to tea,' and then you got there, you found that she'd had to go to the shops or a Womens' Institute meeting. It had its good side. Extra tuition free of charge. Presents on your birthday. That sort of thing. Kids are pretty quick to know when they're onto a good thing. 'Sorry I'm a bit late, sir I forgot the time. I didn't have time to change out of my running kit. I hope it's all right.' Flash a good length of thigh when you sat down and you were all set for a nice car ride and a meal out in the coming weekend. Everybody did it."

"Including you," said Philip.

"Including me. Mr. Ormsby was my great admirer. He was the art teacher. He wanted me to pose nude for him. I got as far as taking my shirt off for one picture and then Rutherford came along. We were both much older then of course but he was still shower-monitor.

"What happened?" Despite his frustration, Ivan was getting interested.

"What do you think? There's me, happily showering and aware that Rutherford is hanging around on the bench. Then we all dried ourselves and I was just going to the door when he called me back. Said I hadn't turned the water off properly – which was his job anyway. So I went back, gave the thing another twist and just as I did that, my towel fell off. Rutherford says I've grown a lot which is hardly surprising. Most people do. 'I didn't just mean in height,' he says. 'There's this as well,' and before I can say anything he's got his hand on it and the inevitable begins to happen. Bear in mind that when you have to share a room with three other boys, wanking opportunities are not that easy to find. So... a bit of rapid thinking. He's not a bad-looking guy and because he's a monitor he has a room all to himself so, on with the towel and up the stairs to his room."

"And you lost your virginity?" said Michael whose cock was showing signs of being interested. So, for that matter, was Tim's. From happy memories Ivan supposed.

"Not that time, no. He started off about Mr. Powell and how he wasn't a bad guy really. I said I hated his guts. Rutherford said Mr. Powell really fancied me like crazy and was all set to give me a 'blow job' before he got sacked. Well, I'd never heard the term before so Rutherford kindly demonstrated and it was pretty good. Much better than a wank in the toilets. So, on the following afternoon, I went up for another, only this time Rutherford says it's my turn to give him one. I wasn't keen. I said I had had a shower before he sucked mine so it was clean. But he persuaded me and I enjoyed that even more. Just like today, I came without him having to touch it."

"Like a fountain," said Ivan. "You even hit the ceiling."

"I was kneeling on a rug Rutherford's mother had given him at that time. I made a mess on that but I noticed I wasn't the only one.

Anyway, the months went by. I suck Rutherford; Rutherford sucks me and then there was a long weekend. I couldn't go home because my folks were away. Rutherford was getting over a cold, or so he said, so we were the only two in our year to be in the school. We went for a walk. It rained. Rutherford said he was afraid his cold would come back and we both ought to have a hot shower. That sounded reasonable enough. We went into the showers. To my surprise he came into my cubicle and, to cut a long story short I ended up touching my toes with what felt like a yard of Rutherford sliding in and out of my cherry, lubricated with the shower gel marked 'Masters Only'. I guess that was all right. He was a master – at fucking ass anyway."

"After that it was a regular occurrence?" said Ivan. It was an unnecessary question. He'd known from the moment he'd first parted Tim's buttocks in the studio.

"Very regular. On Rutherford's bed on other occasions though. That was much more comfortable. Well, soon I became a sort of deputy showers monitor. It's funny. I was doing for him what he had done for Mr. Powell. When all the showers were on you could hardly hear yourself speak so we could walk up and down the line. You know the sort of thing. 'That one's got a nice ass. ' 'So he has. Nice cock too. Shall we invite him up for tea?' You've no idea how frustrated a boarding school boy can be."

Ivan was about to make a comment about frustration but suppressed it.

"It was amazing," said Tim. "I don't think we had a single failure. It was the same every time. 'No. I'm not that sort,' followed by 'Oh, all right then. Just this once.' Off with the towel and gobble the cock. Once you'd done that, they were much easier. Give them six months and they'd be on Rutherford's bed grunting like pigs and learning about the erogenous potential of their asses. How about another drink, Michael? All this talking has made my throat sore."

"I don't think it's entirely attributable to talking," said Michael, but he filled up Tim's glass all the same. Ivan declined.

Michael told a long and complex story that explained, or so he said, his bisexuality. An aunt who dressed in men's clothes, a peculiarly absent uncle and his son who found a novel use for his collection of cigar boxes when Michael went to stay with him. Ivan was beginning to tire of it all and had not the slightest intention of joining this orgy of confidential confessions.

"Nothing like that ever happened to me," said Philip. "Not

till I came to St. Chris's and met Tim."

"Think yourself lucky," said Michael. "A Panatela is manageable. A King Edward is not too bad but those big Cuban things! Wow! Feels more like a lit cigar than just the box!" Ivan stood up. The time had come to be decisive. "Bedtime, folks," he announced. "All other stories can wait till tomorrow. We all ought to have some more recent memories by that time."

"Not a bad idea," said Michael. "Come on Tim." Ivan and Philip watched as Michael, his cock already beginning to point the way eagerly, was followed by Tim Up the staircase. "Tim's got a nice ass," said Ivan. "I've never really thought about it," said Philip. "You should do. Now then. What are we going to do to you?"

"I dunno. We could just go to sleep." Ivan looked down. All that Tim had said about Philip's cock was true. During the story telling session it had been twitching into life. Now it hung limp between his legs. "Like hell," said Ivan. "What did you bring that harness thing back for?"

"I thought it might come in useful." Philip got up and retrieved the harness from under the sofa. The sight of his long legs and jutting, white butt sent a tremor through Ivan's body. Philip stood in front of him, fiddling with the buckles on the belt and twisting the cord through his fingers. "They're very strong, aren't they?" he said. His cock had withered to almost nothing again. It was only just visible against the thick mat of hair. "They have to be. The sea can be bloody strong."

"I can't get over that business of Mr. Powell. Fancy leading somebody around a classroom in one of these. It's degrading."

"You quite fancied it." For a moment, they stood there winding the cord round unwinding it again.

"Treating human beings like animals. Poor old Tim," he said at last. "There were other aspects of life there that he enjoyed," said Ivan. There was a sudden, loud noise from the bedroom above – a 'bang' and

245

then the sound of the bedsprings creaking. "And by the sound of things he's going to have another enjoyable experience," said Ivan. "Are you sure you don't mind?"

"Why should I?" said Philip.

"I know how I would feel if my boyfriend slept with somebody else."

"Have you got one?"

"No, as a matter of fact."

By this time, frustration was getting the upper hand. Ivan was faced with a remarkably good looking, well-built, naked eighteen-year-old who, by the look of him, might just as well be in line for a medical examination. There wasn't even a hint of arousal there. Just a dense mat of hair that started under his navel, thickened round Philip's tiny cock and then ran down the inside of his thighs. Ivan had to grasp the arms of the chair to prevent himself from reaching out and touching him. Somehow, he knew that to do that would be a disaster. It was a ludicrous situation. Philip knew what he wanted and Ivan was pretty sure he knew what Philip wanted. There had to be some way to break the deadlock.

"Anyway, it was all pretty unrealistic when you think about it," said Philip.

"It had the ring of truth to me. Anyway, what would be the point of making up a story like that?"

"Oh, I don't mean that Tim was telling lies. He wouldn't. It's just that ... well ... getting that Rutherford boy to feel his backside. 1 mean, a pig wouldn't be standing on two legs, would it? He should have got Tim down on all fours. That would have been a better position ... for everything."

"Like this afternoon, you mean?"

"Yes."

For a few seconds, Ivan hesitated. The bed upstairs creaked again. Michael and Tim were talking. He couldn't hear what they were saying.

"Show me," he said. Philip unwound the cord from his fingers, dropped the belt and went down on all fours. They were away at last! On the starting blocks anyway. Ivan stood up. His cock was pointing rigidly outwards and swayed slightly from side to side. He put a hand on Philip's back and ran it down the young man's vertebrae to the cleft.

"Put the belt on me." said Philip.

"As you wish." Ivan picked up the belt and passed it under Philip's waist. His skin felt cool to the touch. His fingers strayed downwards. He felt the deep-sunk navel, the slightly bristly hair and then ... there was no doubt about it. Philip's cock still had a doughy, rubbery feel but it was distinctly thicker than it had been when he was standing up. He brought the ends of the belt together on the boy's back and fastened the buckles. "There!" he said. "Feel better?"

"You're the best judge of that."

"Oh I see. Check if the pig is ready, you mean?"

"Sort of."

"Well, it looks all right to me. Bloody nice in fact." He kneaded Philip's buttocks. They would definitely appeal to Mr. Morris, he thought. That pliability was all muscle. Philip shuffled his legs farther apart – a good sign. Ivan reached down with his hand and, once again, his finger went between the soft mounds. He felt the stray, bristly hairs and the same hard, tightly closed muscle ring. There seemed absolutely no chance that it would open up for him and yet....

The bed upstairs creaked again, twice. "Aaah! Aaah!"

Then a long pause and another "Aaah!" and then "Oooh!" The unmistakable sounds of penetration seemed to fill the cottage.

Ivan wondered how many times that same voice and those sounds had echoed from various walls at Tim's school. It was a pity, he thought, that Philip hadn't received a similar education. But Michael had succeeded and that made him even more determined that Philip would yield – and Ivan wasn't prepared to wait much longer. He couldn't. The bed springs began to creak loudly and rhythmically. Every mechanical noise coincided with a human one.

247

Creak ... "Ah!" Creak ... "Ah!" Creak ... "Ah!" Lots of creaking. More creaking.

He took his hand out of the warmth of the cleft and slid it forward, under Philip's balls. He knew what he had to do. Philip had hinted at it. The problem was that Ivan had never come across anyone like that before. Unable to contain his impatience any longer, he took his hand out and slapped Philip's left buttock. "Come on! Come on!" he urged.

It worked. The effect was remarkable. "Oh yeah!" Philip gasped. "Do that again!" so Ivan did. Philip's back stiffened. He raised his head. "Yeah!" he said again. Ivan folded the cord in two so that the clip was in his hand and brought that down. Two divergent red lines appeared on the white flesh. Philip lowered his head so that his hair was almost touching the carpet. Ivan delivered another swipe – harder this time. It seemed impossible to him that any human being would accept such treatment without protest. All Philip did was to waggle his backside provocatively. It was weird.

Ivan ran a hand over the marks he had created. "Christ, you've got a lovely butt. Seems a shame to mark it," he said. "Still, as G. D. Morris said...."

"I wrote the letter," said Philip. His voice was so muffled that Ivan had to ask him to repeat it. Philip lifted his head and said it again. Whether it was excitement, remorse or just the effect of having his head lower than his trunk, Ivan didn't know. Philip's face was the color of a boiled lobster.

"What did you want to do that for?" Ivan asked. "It was stupid!"

"That's what Tim said after Michael asked him about it. I thought he sounded an interesting guy and I wondered if he had any books about – you know."

"Pain and whipping and things like that, you mean?" Philip nodded.

"Well, there's only one thing for it. You're going to have to be punished," said Ivan, and Philip nodded again. Ivan went over to the pile of clothes in the comer. His own belt was totally useless for what he had in mind, a cheap plastic thing, he'd bought it in a market stall. Michael's wasn't too much better – nor, for that matter was Philip's although it was leather. Tim provided the ideal instrument. His jeans were right at the bottom of the pile – a measure of his enthusiasm to undress. They weren't the usual white ones. Those were probably upstairs. These were blue denim and threaded through the loops was a patterned, thick leather belt. It was actually slightly too wide for the loops that contained it. Somebody, Ivan thought, was going to have the devil of a job to thread it back again but that was a problem that could wait. There was something at the other end of the room that couldn't. He glanced over. Philip's head was touching the carpet and he was watching Ivan through his outspread legs. For a moment Ivan stopped pulling the belt out of the loops. Surely, he thought, it couldn't have.... He threaded the belt out of the last loop and went back to Philip. It had. Something like seven inches of hard penis hovered almost parallel to Philip's belly. He wanted to touch it and hold it but remembered what Tim had said. It seemed unlikely that it would subside but one never knew. Everyone was different. Philip certainly was.

He said nothing but, holding the belt by the buckle and standing at what he hoped was the correct distance, he raised his arm and brought it down with all the force he could muster. The 'crack' sounded like a pistol shot. Philip moved forwards, almost as if he was about to stand on his head. "Oh yeah!" he cried. "Crack!" The next stroke was even louder. Philip dug his hands in the carpet. "Oh yeah! Yeah!" he breathed again. Like photographs in a developing tray, red blotches began to appear on his skin. Once again Ivan brought the belt down. "Crack!" His arm began to ache. How many more would it take, he wondered – and how did one know?

Once more the belt swished down. The crack that time seemed louder than ever. It didn't land as accurately as he hoped either. That mark bisected the others at an angle.

"Do it now!" Philip gasped.

"You mean ?"

"Yeah! Now. Do it now!"

Ivan dropped the belt and used his feet to push Philip's legs even farther apart and was about to get down on his knees between them when he suddenly remembered something. There was no way a cock would go into an ass like Philip's without lubrication and where was that? Up in the bedroom. It was probably lying half-empty on the floor but he couldn't retrieve it. One quick touch to the base of Philip's cock was enough to tell him that Philip was a fraction of a degree off boiling point. He had to move quickly. He did. He dashed over to the comer so fast that he almost fell over. His jacket was near the top of the pile. In seconds, the two fragments of a foil packet were on the floor and his copiously weeping cock was enveloped in latex. He went back to Philip. His mind was reeling....

Hands on his buttocks. Skin still cool. You'd think a whacking would have made it feel hot. Odd. Use both hands to part them. How did it look now? Great! That's how. How did it feel? Even greater. Soft now. Sort of flexible. Push on it. Not too hard. Just a bit of gentle pressure. Hang on. Spit. That's what they used in stories. He spat on his hand and rubbed the bubble-filled liquid up onto his finger. Try again. Not too quickly, not too violently. Just firm gentle pressure. It had to give way. Push a bit harder ... and his finger slid in.

"Jeeez!" Philip yelled.

Ivan slid his hands up and down the boy's waist. "Do nothing for a moment. Just wait till he's used to the feeling." It was like a strange inner voice, a conscience of sorts, urging restraint. "That's better. He's relaxed again. Just play around in there. Not too hard. Get the feel of it. Nice eh?"

"Yeah!" Ivan gasped.

"Beautifully relaxed. This sort are always totally submissive after a good beating. Well I never. He really is keen. Look at that!"

Philip's entire weight rested on his knees and his head. He brought his hands round and pulled his ass cheeks apart.

"Very keen. Time for two fingers," said the voice. "Don't forget the saliva."

All that was easier said than done. His finger was gripped so hard that he was beginning to lose any sense of feeling at the tip and his mouth was dry. He should have been drooling but he wasn't. Out with the ringer first. How did one do that. Twist it maybe? Yes. Twist it. Anticlockwise. Like unlocking a door. Not too hard. Philip groaned and out it came.

Spit. Got to spit. Ivan moved his tongue round his teeth. Slowly, his mouth filled with saliva. He held up the palm of his hand and let it stream down. Lots of bubbles again and one or two tiny fragments of what looked like 'The Cabin's' spring chicken. Well, that was appropriate, he thought. He rubbed it over his index and middle fingers.

"Do it! Do it!" Philip pleaded. The top of his middle finger went in easily enough but it didn't seem possible that the other one would go in as well. Surely it couldn't – not without hurting Philip badly. But did that matter? Philip was into pain. He pressed as hard as he could.

"Ow! No! Don't...." Philip dropped his hands to the floor and clutched the carpet. Soft ass cheeks closed on Ivan's fingers. "Oh! No!" Philip cried – but it was too late. Miraculously, both fingers had slid into him. "Jee ... eesus!" he gasped.

Now what? It stood to reason that any lock that hadn't had a key in it for eighteen years was going to be a bit stiff. Turn the key a few times. A bit to the left... Philip yelled. A bit to the right... he yelled again. Push it in a bit more. Philip didn't yell that time. He shuddered. Ivan saw it and felt it: a movement in Philip's shoulder blades and then a rippling feeling in his buttocks. He pushed again. That time Philip lifted his head and let out a long sighing moan. Ivan gave another couple of turns. Each one made Philip exhale loudly. Or was it Philip? They were both breathing like a couple of asthmatics on a hill climb. He put his left hand under Philip's belly and reached upwards. It was like touching a hammer handle. Tim hadn't found the key to Philip but he had! He ran his hand along the shaft until the ridge brushed against his finger. It was wet. Well – more sticky than wet. He squeezed the head and took his hand away.

"Time for something more substantial," said the inner voice. As gently as he could, Ivan twisted his fingers out and as he did so, he smeared Philip's juice onto his cock.

"Do it!" Philip groaned. Ivan shuffled forwards. He needed both hands at that moment. In fact, he could have used a third. Parting Philip's cheeks and positioning his cock on the now red and still slightly open orifice wasn't easy and Philip didn't make it any easier. His backside moved every time he panted for breath. A helper at a time like that would have been a good idea, Ivan thought. It had been stupid to banish the other two to an upper room. It would have been fun to watch Tim getting fucked and he and Michael could have held Philip still afterwards. 'Afterwards' had obviously come. There was no sound at all from the upstairs bedroom.

More by luck than careful placing, his cock touched the spot. He put both hands on Philip's waist and pushed hard. Careful oiling of a rusty lock paid off. He slid in so easily that he almost lost his balance. He was just aware of Philip's head lifting again and Ivan felt, rather than heard, his long drawn out moan. It seemed to come from somewhere much lower down in his body than his lungs.

Inch by inch, it slid in. The tightness and the warmth were unbelievable and there was a feeling of liveliness that Ivan had never experienced before. Michael was a good fuck. There was no doubt of that but he'd never experienced that strange rippling sensation with Michael. He gave a final, rather more gentle push. Something soft touched his balls – Philip's, he guessed. He'd never paid them much attention. They were pretty big. He remembered that much. He grasped Philip's waist with both hands.

"Oh!" Philip gasped. "Ah!" Ivan echoed – and they were away. How long had it taken Ivan wondered from the time Philip had, so to speak, got down on the starting blocks to that moment? Ten minutes? A quarter of an hour? He had no idea. But it had been worth it. Various images flashed through his mind. Philip standing in 'Peppercorn's' cabin, so tall that his head nearly touched the ceiling. The hair inside his thighs, above all, his beautiful virgin ass. Virgin no longer! Philip's spunk dribbling down Tim's chin – red marks on white skin...

"Aah! Yeah! Ah! Yeah! Ah!" No time for memories now. This was for real. Very real and very much alive. If only it could last for hours ... all night... all the next day...!

It didn't. It couldn't. Philip's earlier tremor was a minor affair compared to the gigantic shudder of his coming. Ivan's cock was gripped in a tight, vise-like grip. The first made him cry out with pain. The second was a bit slacker but only a bit. After that it felt as if his cock was in a milking machine – literally. He fell forward over Philip's back, smelled perspiration that was not his. He licked the place under Philip's shoulder blades as semen jetted out of him, swelling the rubber enveloping his cock. He said nothing. He couldn't. He lay there panting.

"You all right in there?" The words didn't make any sense.

"I said are you all right in there?"

Michael! What the hell? The door opened. "Oh! Sorry. I thought... We thought...."

It really was Michael. "What is it?" Ivan asked.

"Just that we heard odd sounds. Like gun shots. We wondered if you were all right."

"Yes ... thanks."

"I can see that. Sorry to have barged in."

"When was this? The gunshots, I mean."

"About five minutes ago. Not more. When you've got a boy like Tim in bed with you, it doesn't take more than five minutes for the cannon to start reloading. I couldn't even aim it at the moment."

"Now doubt you will," said Ivan. Full consciousness was gradually returning. "You bet I will."

"And so will Ivan," said Philip. "Time lapse in reverse," Ivan muttered. "What's that?" Michael asked. "Oh, nothing. Just a thought. Close the door after you."

"What people like you never seem to realize is that I am an extremely busy man. Extremely busy," said the Vice Principal. Ivan said nothing but continued to stare at the picture of a windmill on the wall.

"To come in on a Saturday morning to do some photocopying and find that you are not only not there but have taken the keys with you! It's unpardonable!"

"Mine isn't the only photocopier in the college," said Ivan. "There's one in the secretaries' office."

The V P frowned. "They've taken to hiding the key," he said. Ivan wasn't surprised. All of the academic staff seemed to have an inborn talent for jamming photo copiers.

"Where were you anyway? You always used to be in college on Saturday mornings."

"There's nothing about that in my contract. I used to come in because there was a lot to do here and nothing to do at home. Things have changed."

The Vice Principal looked up and glared at him. "There are going to be a lot more changes shortly," he said. "You've heard of Sir George Davenant, I suppose?"

"Of 'Davenant's Directions'? Of course. I have to record all the programs for the business studies people."

"Well, he'll be here on Wednesday, Thursday and Friday at my invitation and I think I can safely say, Mr. Pepper, that your services will no longer be required here. All teaching aids will be held by the appropriate department. If I were you I should spend next weekend looking for another job."

Ivan had no intention of doing so. Nonetheless, it was a hammer blow. Sir George Davenant's television series 'Davenant's Directions' was enormously popular. Sir George toured factories and businesses that were in decline, pointing out examples of inefficiency here and overspending or over staffing there. The general public loved him even if the hundreds of people that lost their jobs didn't.

He didn't get a lot of time to think on that day or on Tuesday. Practically everybody on the academic staff wanted something to impress Sir George. He issued posters and charts to people that had never been near the audio-visual block in the past. The only person who didn't appear to be panicking was Meg Burton. She took a couple of charts showing the evolution of insects. "Only to cover the graffiti on the lab wall, dear. I don't suppose it will help. I'm getting too old for this job anyway," she said.

"You're a college tradition, Meg. They'd never get rid of you," said Ivan.

"Don't you believe it, dear. It's all efficiency and cost – effectiveness these days. They'll put me out to grass. You too by all accounts. What does a businessman know about turning raw eighteen-year-olds into professional teachers? Absolutely nothing. Oh well. See you in the dole queue. Thanks for the charts."

On Tuesday evening, resigned to his fate, he went out for a drink with Michael. That didn't help much. All Michael wanted to talk about was the forthcoming weekend in Garmouth. Ivan would have liked to share his worries, and not just about his own. As far as he knew, he was the only person in the college to whom Meg Burton had confided the news that her mother was seriously ill and that almost every penny Meg earned went on nursing home fees. But Michael wouldn't have been interested. There were times when it seemed that Michael thought with his cock.

"The oddest foursome in the history of the world. That's us," said Michael, and Ivan had to agree. Weekends in Garmouth had become an established routine. The odd thing was that Tim and Philip were obviously deeply in love with each other. They held hands in the back of the car on the journey down. They spent every day in each other's company going for long walks and buying little presents for each other. And yet, when evening came, they'd kiss each other affectionately. Willingly – eagerly, in fact – one would go upstairs with Ivan. The other remained downstairs with Michael. Until the recent blow, Ivan had been contemplating building an extension bedroom. It might still be possible, he thought, as Michael jabbered on and on and on about the forthcoming weekend. Photographs of Philip after a weekend in Garmouth were a profitable spin off. They did nothing for him but a surprising number of his customers liked them. G. D. Morris was particularly pleased. He wanted as many as possible and Philip seemed to have no qualms about showing off his bruised and battered buttocks.

Ivan was still occupied with his financial position on the following Thursday afternoon. He had made very little attempt to tidy up the block for Sir George's visit. Other members of the staff ran round like headless chickens. The art lecturers even put up a 'Welcome' banner. Ivan sat at his desk with his head in his hands. 'Peppercorn' would have to go, he thought but, depending on what sort of job he got, he might be able to hold on to the cottage. On the other hand, if he was to keep his profitable sideline going, he would need a studio. He could adapt the bedroom in the cottage, but there would be no money for equipment. He pulled down a file of old invoices and was calculating the cost of cameras, lights, reflectors and lenses when the door opened and, like some sort of religious procession, they all trooped in: the Principal, the Vice Principal, the Dean of the cathedral (who was chairman of the governors), two men that Ivan didn't recognize and, finally, the great man himself.

"We have spoken at length about this particular problem," said the V P. It was left to the Principal to introduce Ivan.

"Ah, yes," said Sir George. "The audio-visual aids man. Perhaps you would care to show me round."

There wasn't, as Ivan said, a lot to see in a Visual Aids block. He showed Sir George the collections of video and audio tapes and slides. He demonstrated the data base that enabled him to find anything he needed. "Design it yourself?" Sir George barked.

"I did actually. I quite like doing jobs like that. It kept me busy at weekends. There's not a lot to do in a cathedral city on a Sunday."

The dean looked distinctly pained. Sir George made no comment but the Vice Principal said that, although satisfactory, there was a much better commercially produced program.

He led them into the studio. "What the hell is that?" asked Sir George, pointing to the three bears' bedroom set. Ivan had wondered whether to take it down and store it somewhere, but it had other uses never dreamed about by the art department that had created it.

"Last year's pantomime set! This is too much!" said the Vice Principal but Sir George was out of hearing. He had walked over to inspect it more closely. The Vice Principal hurried over to him like a small boy in danger of losing his father in a crowd. "I do apologize, Sir George," he said. "Pepper should have taken it down immediately after the pantomime. I should have known and have inspected the place before but Pepper has a habit of...."

"Is it in the way then?" asked Sir George.

"Not at all," Ivan replied. "When the stage curtains are drawn, it can't be seen."

"How many man hours would be needed to dismantle it and where would it be stored?"

"I don't know. Quite a lot of man hours and storage space is tight."

"Hm. Well, thank you Mr. Pepper. Most interesting." He turned to the Principal. "And now where?" he asked.

The Principal didn't have time to answer. The V. P. stepped in. "Our physical education department has designed a display for you, Sir George. I think you'll enjoy it," he said and they all swept out. Ivan shrugged his shoulders and went back to his invoices.

On Friday, he spotted the procession several times. They were obviously sitting in on lectures. Ivan wondered how Meg had got on but there was no way of knowing. The staff common room was off limits to people like him and she wasn't in the canteen. He'd have to wait till Monday.

At six o'clock, the other three were waiting for him in the parking lot. "Let's get away from this dump," said Michael.

Ivan said nothing. It wouldn't be long, he decided, before he'd be saying the same thing, and for the last time.

As usual, Tim and Philip sat in the back seat. Michael kept them all amused on the journey by an extremely camp account of an evening he'd spent with two second-year girl students, both of whom had been anxious to supplement their sexual education lectures with some practical experience.

"You should have told Sir George," said Tim. "He'd have been impressed. Helping the Health Education people in your spare time would have won you lots of points."

"He never came near me, ducky. Anyway, he's not my type. Can you imagine what sex with a person like him would be like? Stopwatch in one hand and a clipboard in the other. 'I've noticed that you take far too long to come. We must do something about that.' The thought makes auntie shudder!"

"He came in to our lecture," said Tim.

"With Meg Burton?" Ivan asked.

"No. Boring Dr. Evans. Photosynthesis in seaweed. Phil saved the day. He probably saved Dr. Evans too. My friend Phil is star student. Tell them, Phil."

Apparently, whereas all the other members of the party had sat on the chairs specially provided for them at the back of the lab, Sir George had sat next to Phil, and had helped him with the experiment they were doing. He'd even picked up the piece of soggy seaweed from the floor when it slipped out of Philip's forceps. He'd gone through all Philip's notes, complimented him on his neatness and, when the experiment was over, Sir George had washed out the glassware and would have stayed even longer had not other members of his party shown their impatience.

By the time they reached 'The Cabin,' Ivan felt happier. As usual, Tim and Philip left the table to play pool. Neither Ivan nor Michael minded that. Eighteen-year-olds are graceful creatures and the game of pool could have been designed to show them off to their best advantage. Crouching down to assess a shot; leaning over the table to reach the ball, or even standing with crossed legs and holding a cue – all were exciting poses. Ivan had long contemplated a series of photos of naked youths playing pool.

"I reckon Tim's got the most beautiful butt in the world," said Michael, leaning back in his chair the better to appraise it. Tim was wearing the white jeans that weekend. They really did suit him and might have been tailored to fit.

"That's what you say now," said Ivan. "Give it a couple of years and you'll find someone else. Knowing you, it'll probably be some bird. Straight up the aisle. Wedding march played on the organ and rice being slung all over the place."

"Maybe but your auntie will keep her hobby. It won't be church organs. Male ones are much more fun, and it won't be rice that gets strewn around but seed of another sort. You're right about the 'straight up' bit though. Now then, I wonder which one I ought to delight tonight."

"I'm easy either way," said Ivan, which was absolutely true – Philip's dusky, slightly hairy thighs or Tim's creamy, smooth limbs. Philip's enormous, thick cock or Tim's more modest but delightfully proportioned member. They were certainly not 'all the same' but both held promise of intense pleasure.

"Then I think I shall forego the delight of Tim's coming and work out a little aggression," said Michael.

Naturally enough, when the two lads had finished their game, they wanted to know what was in store for them.

"Chosen?"

"Yes."

"Who's having who?"

"You'll see. Drink up." Soon the big double doors closed behind them. Garmouth, as always at night, was deserted. The only sound was the crashing of the waves on the shore.

"God! I'm horny tonight. Feel this," said Tim when they had left the street lights behind. Ivan did so. Ribbed denim made a cock feel even more enticing, he thought.

By the time they reached the cottage, Ivan had already found the key. It was obviously not going to be one of those evenings of discussion or reminiscences. Even Philip had a lump, like a large and over-ripe fruit in the front of his jeans.

"Tim."

"Philip." Ivan and Michael spoke simultaneously.

"We guessed as much. Come on then," said Tim. He gave Philip a peck on the cheek and taking Ivan by the hand, led him to the foot of the stairs.

Tim was in Ivan's favorite position when they heard the lounge door open and close. Ivan didn't pay much attention. Who would with an extremely beautiful youth lying on his back, raised on a couple of pillows with his hands under his head and his legs as far apart as he can get them? He'd come once already and Ivan was happily employed licking him clean. A semen-soaked scrotum can fc« a very effective appetizer for the next main course.

"Michael's gone a-hunting," said Tim.

"Uh huh?"

259

"for some implement to use on my poor friend," Tim continued. Reluctantly, Ivan lifted his head.

"He's hardly poor. I always give him half of what I get for the photos. He's done exceptionally well in the last few weeks," he said.

"I wonder what it'll be this weekend," said Tim. "It was rope the weekend before last, wasn't it?"

"That's right. From the garden shed. He forgot to lock the door and we were kept awake all night by its banging."

"Ha! Who are you trying to kid? It wasn't door banging that kept you awake. You were doing quite a lot of banging yourself."

"True, but you never complained."

"A well – oiled door never squeaks. See if you can get your tongue in my ass again. I like that."

For a long time, Michael's quest was almost forgotten. Not entirely. He was obviously in the kitchen immediately below the bedroom and didn't seem to realize the amount of noise he was making. Doors and drawers were opened and slammed shut. Finally, the lounge door closed. He had obviously found whatever it was he was looking for and all was quiet downstairs.

That is more than could be said for the bedroom. Ivan had found what he was looking for too and Tim was making a great deal of noise. Not that Ivan heard much of it. You don't when you've got the silky thighs of an incredibly supple teen clamped against your ears. All the young man's weight was on his shoulders. Anybody entering the room at that moment would have thought he was standing on his head. His hands were under the hollow of his back pushing himself as far upwards as he could. He gasped and groaned and twisted his body from side to side, all the time gripping Ivan's head between his thighs so hard that it was difficult to get much more than the tip of a tongue into him.

Ivan slid his hands under the young man's soft and sweating buns. That helped a bit. Tim writhed and another fraction pushed past the sentinel muscle ring. Ivan stopped, just to savor the exquisite musky flavor of a horny youth. Tim wriggled a bit more. There was no time to be lost. Getting out of that soft vise was easier said than done but Tim got the message and, reluctantly, let him go. Ivan shuffled backwards. Tim's legs slipped past his ears. Tim's cock, stiff and sticky from exuded juice, slid over his chin and then down his front. He shuffled into position, grabbed the packet and slipped the rubber over the already dribbling head of his cock. His ears were still ringing from the pressure they'd been under. He was only dimly aware of Tim's entreaties. "Oh yeah! Yeah! Do it to me."

Tim's ass dealt with a cock as a baby samples a proffered finger. First there was a wet feeling, like the damp touch of tiny lips. Then came the slow sucking in – a fraction of an inch at a time. There was always the feeling in those first few seconds that it might get spat out and rejected, despite Tim's obvious enjoyment. That feeling didn't last long. There was a point of no return. After that it was just a question of patience. Ivan's cock was nothing special but it still took time to get all of it through that tight, saliva-lubricated entrance and into the warm, silky passage that welcomed and grasped it.

Finally, Ivan's balls made contact with their younger counterparts. For a moment Tim's legs pressed against his ears again. Then they relaxed their grip and he gave the first thrust; not too hard – just enough to make Tim wince slightly and bite his lip. Another. Tim opened his mouth. Another. And Tim gave a low groan.

Minutes later, Ivan was pumping away for all he was worth. Beads of sweat appeared on Tim's forehead and ran backwards, making his blond hair dank. His mouth was wide open. He groaned at every stroke. Ivan was panting. Flesh slapped against flesh. His balls began to ache. Any minute ... any minute ... Don't think of anything else! Just think of Tim. He was enjoying every moment. That was the great thing. Tim was enjoying it – and how!

He never saw Tim shoot. He never had. He felt it though. Some of it spattered on his face like warm rain. The rest landed back on Tim himself. White buttons of semen appeared on his belly, his chest and even on his face. Ivan paid them no attention. He couldn't have done. He gave one last thrust and then stopped. His head drooped from exhaustion as his spunk surged out of him.

That wasn't the only time that night. Tim dozed off from time to time. Ivan couldn't. There was always the nagging thought that this might be the last opportunity. He might easily have to sell the cottage and then where would they go? Hotels were out of the question. He played gently with Tim's cock as he pondered. That made it and its owner, wake up again and all fiscal worries were soon forgotten.

At ten o'clock the next morning, showered and refreshed to an extent, they went downstairs. There was no sign of Michael or of Philip. "They've probably gone to get the Sunday papers," said Ivan as he drew back the heavy curtains in the lounge. He rearranged the cushions on the sofa and, in so doing, found what Michael had been looking for.

"So that's it. Full marks for ingenuity," he said. Among the hundreds of kitchen utensils his aunt had left, was a wooden steak-tenderizing mallet. He'd never used it but hadn't the heart to throw it out.

"Christ! You could kill a person with a thing like that!" said Tim. "Fancy hitting a guy with that!"

"I don't but Phil does. It takes all sorts," said Ivan. He picked it up and then smiled. "I'm not at all sure that he's used the business end but I know for sure where the handle has been," he said.

In fact, the 'business end' had been used – four times. Phil wasn't in the least put out by Ivan's request for photographs and lay prone and glistening with oil on the 'Baby Bear bed' as Ivan photographed the four miniature chess boards imprinted on his butt. Ivan sent out the photos and spent the rest of that week packing his personal property and taking it home. He continued to supply the various lecturers with what they needed but, more often than not, he didn't keep a record of who had what. There seemed no point. He scanned the various educational magazines in the hope of finding a new job but everybody seemed to want university graduates. Meg Burton was in an even worse position. At her age, as she said, there was no hope at all. She came into the block to return the charts she had borrowed. There was a big, blue stain on her lab coat. In the days before Sir George's visit, that would have been unthinkable. Meg laundered her lab coats herself. They were always spotless and starched and she changed immediately if there was the slightest stain.

"We're both on the scrap heap dear. There's nothing we can do about it," she said.

"When do you think we'll know?" Ivan asked.

"Any minute now. Sir George's report is in and they had a board meeting yesterday. You haven't got any dependents, have you?"

"No. Just me."

"You're lucky. I don't know how I'm going to look after mum. I suppose one should hope for a peaceful end as soon as possible. It all seems so...." She lifted the comer of her lab coat and wiped her eye. "Come and say 'Goodbye' won't you?" she said.

"Sure," said Ivan.

Another day passed and nothing happened. Finally, unable to bear the strain much longer, Ivan made a decision. Common sense told him that finding a new job, having been sacked for inefficiency, wouldn't be easy. He typed out his resignation, printed it and set off to hand it to the Vice Principal.

For the first time since the man had been appointed the door was shut. Ivan tapped. There was no answer. He tapped again. Still no sound. Having not the slightest intention of being seen waiting like some errant schoolboy he turned the handle intending to put the letter on the man's desk. The door was locked. There was nothing for it. He'd have to bypass the V P and give it to the Principal. He didn't want to do it that way. He knew it would distress the old man but there was nothing for it. The letter had to go in before they wrote to him. Mrs. Robertson said the Principal was free. Ivan walked in. "You're quick off the mark, Ivan," said the Principal, looking up from the paper on his desk.

"I know that these things have to go through the Vice Principal but...."

"You've heard then? I thought it wouldn't take long. What we're going to do is beyond me."

"I thought audio-visual was going to be farmed out to the departments."

"Whatever gave you that idea? I was talking about our late lamented Vice Principal. He's left us, obviously in protest at Sir George's report but he wants me to put it out that he's had a heart attack. That shouldn't be difficult. Choosing to live in a windmill at his age would give anyone a heart attack."

"Can I ask why?"

"You don't know? I thought the news was out. Mrs. Robertson typed the notice for the common room this morning."

"I'm not allowed in there."

"Ah! Of course. That was unforgivable, especially as it concerns you."

"Me?"

"Sir George's report. Let me see now...." He picked up the paper. "Well, in brief, your work has so impressed him that he's recommended that you be upgraded to Lecturer Grade Two."

"But that's a senior grade. I've not got a degree."

"A degree isn't everything. I confess that one or two members of the Board quibbled but they have accepted the recommendations. Now you can read notices yourself. Take it as having immediate effect."

"Do you mind if I see the letter?" Ivan asked.

"Don't you trust me then? Of course you can. Don't get too big-headed, will you?" He handed the letter to Ivan. Ivan had handled enough sheets of that cream, handmade paper to recognize it, albeit this one had a printed address. Under the words 'From Sir George Davenant' was an address; 'Sutton Coldfield, Birmingham. ' and then the date – 18th of September 1999. He scanned down the page, 'exceptional ability' ... 'excellent rapport with staff and students'... 'devotion to his work which is rarely seen these days,' and the 'G' of the signature was the same. Ivan handed the letter back.

"He said something about inviting you and a few students to his home when I spoke to him yesterday," said the Principal. "You certainly made a good impression. Now I have to find a Vice Principal and that won't be easy."

"Can I make a suggestion?"

"Now you're officially a lecturer, of course you can."

"Dr. Burton. I know she's due to retire shortly but she's the ideal person and I think she deserves it."

"Extraordinary! That's what the Dean said. I suppose we ought really to ask for Sir George's opinion. I'd better call him."

"Oh, he'll agree. I'm quite sure he will. When you speak to him, could you pass on my regards to Mr. Morris?"

"Of course. Who's Mr. Morris?"

"Just a person he knows. And tell him I'd be glad to accept his kind invitation and bring a couple of students with me. They'll be very – impressed."

Nine days later, Ivan was sitting in the armchair he'd earmarked for himself and drinking the customary glass of sherry that preceded lunch. On the arm of the chair lay the letter that Mrs. Robertson had given him to hand over.

"She might not come in. She's got a lot of problems at home," said one of his fellow lecturers but, just as he spoke, Meg entered. Her hair was untidy and there was yet another stain on her lab coat.

"Excuse me," said Ivan, standing up. "It is college tradition for you to knock before coming in to the Lecturers' Common Room."

"Don't play silly games, Ivan dear. I'm not in the mood. Anyway, you're hardly in a position to make jokes. You've only been a lecturer for a few days," Meg replied.

Everybody had stopped talking. Some people were beginning to stand up. Out of the comer of his eye, Ivan saw Dr. Lowther pull the champagne out of its carefully concealed ice bucket.

"I was referring to the fact that Vice Principals are expected to knock," said Ivan. "Here. Read this and many, many congratulations."

265

About the Editor

JOHN PATRICK was a prolific, prize-winning author of fiction and non-fiction. One of his short stories, "The Well," was honored by PEN American Center as one of the best of 1987. His novels and anthologies, as well as his non-fiction works, including Legends and The Best of the Superstars series, continue to gain him new fans every day. One of his most famous short stories appears in the Badboy collection Southern Comfort and another appears in the collection The Mammoth Book of Gay Short Stories.

A divorced father of two, the author was a longtime member of the American Booksellers Association, the Publishing Triangle, the Florida Publishers' Association, American Civil Liberties Union, and the Adult Video Association. He lived in Florida, where he passed away on October 31, 2001.

earing any underwear. "Excuse me," I said, having a hard time loo
linded by that bulge in his crotch, "but don't I know you?" "Mayb
ind of t   bout
with Ray   God,
t loser?   in?"
aid. "Lik   s stror
ce body   e on C
lly, he l   I eve
i up to t   any id
istaking   e san
1, I coul   ery lo
ood raci   ne sw
ing with   e in s
we go c   behir
ill see u   in pu
ed?" he   vent t
rivacy.   grabl
hard. I
k, traci   t, so
ed it, ha
with m   bing
bbing, I   n coc
he sound of unzipping filled the small space. I don't know who's h
, but before I knew it, I had his rod in my hand, and mine was in h
nt to do?" he asked, his tone challenging. I knew exactly, and sank